ANTARKTOS RISING

"Jeremy Robinson is an original and exciting voice. ANTARKTOS RISING has just the right blend of menace and normality—a tale full of intrigue, treachery, and a wealth of secrets. A good old-fashioned suspense story set in one of the most desolate places of earth. It fires on all cylinders in a smart, taut thrill."

— Steve Berry, New York Times best-selling author of *The Venetian Betrayal* and *The Charlemagne Pursuit*

"Apocalypse comes to Antarctica. Jeremy Robinson balances Biblical speculation upon a dagger-edge of suspense and adventure. With ANTARKTOS RISING, Robinson opens a new dark continent of terror. Trespass at your own risk."

—James Rollins, New York Times best-selling author of *The Judas Strain* and *The Last Oracle*

"A fast paced chiller that delves into new possibilities about our future . . . and past."

— Steve Alten, best-selling author of *MEG* and *The Loch*

"An awesome journey into the beating heart of a legend. Jules Verne would be proud."

—Stel Pavlou, international best-selling author of *Decipher* and *Gene*

"How do you find an original story idea in the crowded action-thriller genre? Two words: Jeremy Robinson. ANTARKTOS combines history, science, and myth about Antarctica to create a jaw-dropping concept so real it will have you Googling like mad to learn more after the story is finished."

—Scott Sigler, best-selling author of *Ancestor* and *Infected*

RAISING THE PAST

"Jeremy Robinson's novel RAISING THE PAST is a rollicking Arctic adventure that explores the origins of the human species. Written in a solid cinematic style, it starts with the excavation of a frozen mammoth in the wilds of the Canadian tundra and ends with a pitched battle for the future of mankind. A story not to be missed!"
  —James Rollins, bestselling author of *The Judas Strain* and *The Last Oracle*

"RAISING THE PAST by Jeremy Robinson is a taut thriller that zooms. It's a wonderful mix of prehistoric intrigue, a modern-day love story, and a futuristic conspiracy bound to envelop any reader. Highly recommended."
  —Jon F. Merz, author of the Lawson novels & *Danger-Close*

THE DIDYMUS CONTINGENCY

"Jeremy Robinson's novel THE DIDYMUS CONTINGENCY blends the cutting-edge science of Crichton with the religious mystery of the LEFT BEHIND series to create his own unique and bold thriller. It is a fast-paced page-turner like no other. Not to be missed!"
  —James Rollins, international bestseller of *The Judas Strain* and *The Last Oracle*

"[A] thrilling and fast-paced "what if?" scenario."
  —MidWest Book Review

"What surprised me, with [Robinson's] take on the possibility of two 21st century men meeting Jesus, was the utter lack of predictability... He offers a new perspective on ripping apart the time-space continuum I am shocked no one has ever considered before now."
  —Round Table Reviews

KRONOS

JEREMY ROBINSON

BREAKNECK BOOKS
PUBLISHING COMPANY
AN IMPRINT OF VARIANCE
ARKANSAS

tpauschulte@variancepublishing.com

ISBN: 1-935142-00-3
ISBN-13: 978-1-935142-00-3

Published by Breakneck Books (USA) an imprint of Variance LLC.
www.breakneckbooks.com
www.variancepublishing.com

Library of Congress Control Number: 2008941632

Visit Jeremy Robinson on the World Wide Web at:
www.jeremyrobinsononline.com

Cover design © 2008 by Erik Hollander

Printed in Canada

10 9 8 7 6 5 4 3 2 1

Printed on acid-free paper.

For Spud

Acknowledgements

In the past I have thanked just about everyone I know, but I'm going to do this a little differently and focus on the folks who made Kronos a reality.

First and foremost, I must thank Tim Schulte and Jon Knecht for not just believing in my writing and business skills, but for having the guts to jump headlong into business with me. Variance is redefining the relationship between author and publisher and I'm proud to be a part of that effort.

Stan Tremblay, without you I would have never made it through the year. You have picked up the slack for me and provided a brain when mine ceased to function.

Walter Elly, you are a web genius and your guidance and advice has been invaluable. Your passion for my books and spreading the word via the web is infectious and appreciated.

Shane Thomson; I'm a sucker for red ink and you provided plenty. Your edits have made Kronos a better book and have provided insight into where I need to grow as an author.

Erik Hollander, you're a superb cover designer and a pleasure to work with. I hope to see your illustrations gracing the covers of more books in the future.

And finally, the gang without whom I'd be lost and empty: Hilaree my amazing wife, Aquila my brilliant daughter, Solomon, my endlessly fun son, and little Spud, who has yet to be born or named; you are due to be born any day now and I can't wait to meet you. I love you all.

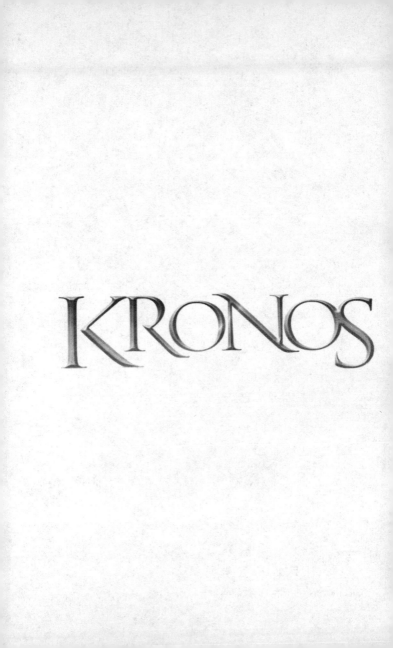

"The ocean is as vast as it is mysterious, and man's desire to venture to its depths to uncover its bounty rarely fades from the forefront of our imaginations. And it is through science and understanding that the finest results will be achieved, not through the dredging, overfishing and exploitation of the world's finest resource. These mechanisms can only lead to tragedy."

Dr. Atticus Young—*Oceans in Peril*

"When beholding the tranquil beauty and brilliancy of the ocean's skin, one forgets the tiger heart that pants beneath it; and would not willingly remember that this velvet paw but conceals a remorseless fang."

(1819–1891), *Moby Dick*

"When he raiseth up himself, the mighty are afraid: by reason of breakings they purify themselves. The sword of him that layeth at him cannot hold: the spear, the dart, nor the habergeon. He esteemeth iron as straw, and brass as rotten wood. The arrow cannot make him flee: slingstones are turned with him into stubble. Darts are counted as stubble: he laugheth at the shaking of a spear."

Job 41: 25–29 King James Translation—The Holy Bible

1

Each slice of oar through water seemed more like a guillotine splitting flesh, vertebrae, and nerve bundles over and over—unceasing agony. This was the pain the Reverend John Wheelwright felt, or a close approximation of it, when he heard the news of his banishment from the state of Massachusetts. He'd come to the New World a year previous and was well received, quickly becoming pastor of the Faxe Chapel at Mount Wollaston in Boston. He was happy for a time, leading his new flock, revealing a path to God in which free speech and opinions were welcome. The congregation blossomed, but along with his success came controversy.

Wheelwright's sister-in-law, Anne Hutchinson,

and the colony's governor, Harry Vane, clashed with local conservatives on the topic of grace versus works. Those in the grace camp, along with Vane, believed it was through God's grace and mercy that we are saved from sin and no number of good deeds can help. Those who believed that works mattered, the conservatives, felt just the opposite—good deeds earned salvation. To prove the other camp wrong was to condemn them to hell. The debate raged, and when Governor Vane lost his bid for reelection, he also lost support for his cause. Vane returned to England, leaving Hutchinson, and by familial association, Wheelwright, to handle the fallout. The conservative leadership acted swiftly and, while nonviolent, were savage in their efficiency.

Everyone associated with Vane or Hutchinson was banished from all of Massachusetts. Every friend, business associate, and, of course, the brother-in-law pastor who, without directly supporting the cause, supported the free speech that made the argument possible, were to take their leave via ocean voyage before the sun set.

This very night.

Wheelwright's muscles burned as he put the oars of the small rowboat to the water, pushing through the placid seas toward the waiting galleon anchored in the bay. After boarding the sixty-odd exiles in Boston, the ship was to head north along the coast, picking up wares and other passengers before returning to England. He looked back to the shore and saw a few lamps burning. He had pictured himself making a permanent home there. It had become his dream, but it had been taken from him. Yet having no acquaintances in the New World outside of Massachusetts, he was forced to England. There was nothing he could do but pack up his belongings and leave with his second wife, Mary, their five children, and Mary's mother in tow. They had become vagabonds in a single day, their future uncertain, and he, a man of God, humiliated.

In a burst of frustration, Wheelwright drove the oar down hard. It connected with the water at an odd angle and broke free from his grasp. He lurched out for the oar, nearly capsizing the boat before catching his thighs on the gunwale and falling back inside as the oar slipped into the darkness.

His temper mounted as he lay on his back and fought the temptation to curse God. He held his tongue, but he could not silence his thoughts:

Where art thou, God, in this, my darkest hour? Why hast thou forsaken me? Was it not thee who planted the seed of desire in my heart to come to Boston? I have always been faithful, obeyed every command, attended every whisper of guidance. But this, this is a cruel thing thou doest! I pray thee, speak Lord, even a whisper; thy servant heareth.

At that moment he longed for God to do more than whisper. The beliefs for which he had been exiled were not his own. He had surely been misjudged and mistreated by man, but would his God abandon him while on a divine errand?

Staring up at the dazzling display of stars in the

night sky, his thoughts turned to prayer. But he had no more words for his Creator.

Bile and disbelief rose within Wheelwright's breast. He sat up, leaned over the side of the boat and retched into the ocean losing his supper and easing his emotions. He gagged three more times and wiped his mouth.

"Lord," Wheelwright spoke, his voice soft and wet, "hast thou no mercy to spare thy servant?"

The boat bobbed as small waves cascaded toward shore.

"Hast thou forgotten me?"

The waves grew in size. Wheelwright held on to the side, but gave the rising waters no heed.

"No more whispers, Lord. Before I turn from thee in earnest, speak thy will to me."

The waves receded, and the sea flattened. Wheelwright sat in the boat, still clutching the side, listening...and hearing nothing.

In that moment, his mind became like stone. "Then my mind is made up. England it is and the New World be damned," he cried in false heartiness. He'd always been in good favor with the people there. His reputation was established, and any number of churches would welcome him. Wheelwright's stomach soured. Did he even want to preach again? If God could so easily desert a loyal follower, was God really worth following?

A light *clunk* sounded from the side of the boat. Wheelwright thought it might be the oar. Perhaps it was God's response? Take the oar, return to England?

He peered over the side and into the water.

No oar.

But there was something there…a reflection of something above? There were two objects, like two halves of a circle separated by several feet. A reflection of the moon? But when Wheelwright scanned the heavens, he found the full moon hung near the horizon .

Not the moon.

Nervous claws tore at Wheelwright's innards. The hair on his arms rose. His instincts screamed of a danger that his mind could not comprehend.

Then it struck him. The half circles where not reflections from above; they were physical objects from below. He looked down into the black and saw the two orbs for what they really were. Eyes. Each the size of a man's head, they looked straight up at him. "Good Lord!" His reason fought for control while his emotions swirled.

Not eyes, thought Wheelwright. *Something else. Some object loosed from a sunken vessel. Buoys perhaps? Yes, buoys.*

Then the buoys blinked.

Wheelwright rose to his feet and filled his lungs, prepared to let loose a scream he hoped would attract the galleon's attention. But his voice never escaped his open mouth. Darkness enshrouded him and closed above him. Tepid, rank air greeted him as he realized that God, angry at his disrespect had sent the devil himself to eat him alive.

A quick jolt from beneath knocked him from the

boat, and he landed on a firm, yet soft surface. The beast suddenly lifted its head and drew Wheelwright deeper into its throat. Flesh wrapped around him, and he felt himself being pushed down...down toward the creature's gullet, where a slow and torturous death awaited.

TWO DAYS later, Wheelwright woke to a blinding light. Heaven or hell? As his senses returned, he became aware of a burning sensation beneath him and sweltering hot humid air stinging his skin. Hell, he thought. But the smell was not one would expect of hell, it was more like lilacs and ocean air.

He sat up and found himself on a beach. He was still dressed in his black doublet and breeches, though the cloth looked more like rags than proper attire. His skin was sickly pale and wrinkled, but otherwise he felt fine. He didn't recognize the shoreline, but it was most definitely the New World. The maple trees lining the beach told him that much.

Looking down, Wheelwright saw a single word etched in the sand.

Exeter.

A flash of thoughts and memories came to him. His entire ordeal, the last two days and nights, crowded his mind. Had it really happened? Another look at his puffy white flesh confirmed it. But no one must know what he'd endured. It was safer that way. And he had a mission to complete. God had revealed that much to him. He had no concept of the ends, but his savings gave him the means.

Positive he was once again in God's good graces, he took a deep breath and sighed, allowing the smell of salty sand, lilac and leaf laden earth to calm his frantic mind. He smiled as the scent of his new home filled him with hope. Though he longed to see God's plans laid out before him, he felt confident that his acts, conceived of and willed by God, would have positive results for all men. God's dramatic action over the past two days could only mean that the end result would be beyond the most vivid imaginings of Wheelwright's feeble mind.

AGREEMENT OF THE SETTLERS AT EXETER, NEW HAMPSHIRE, 1639

Whereas it hath pleased the Lord to move the Heart of our dread Sovereign Charles, by the Grace of God King &c., to grant Licence and Libertye to sundry of his subjects to plant themselves in the Westerlle parts of America, we his loyal Subjects, Brethren of the Church in Exeter, situate and lying upon the River Pascataqua with other Inhabitants there, considering with ourselves the holy Will of God and our own Necessity that we should not live without wholesomne Lawes and Civil Government among us, of which we are altogether destitute, do in the name of Christ and in the sight of God combine ourselves together to erect and set up among us such Government as shall be to our best discerning agreeable to the Will of God, professing ourselves Subjects to our Sovereign Lord King Charles according to the Libertyes of our English Colony of Massachusetts, and binding of ourselves solemnly by the Grace and Help of Christ and in His Name and fear to submit ourselves to such Godly and Christian Lawes as are established in the realm of England to our best Knowledge, and to all other such Lawes which shall upon good grounds be made and enacted among us according to God that we may live quietly and peaceably together in all godliness and honesty. Mo. 8. D. 4. 1639 as attests our Hands.

Signed—John Wheelwright

DESCENT

2

The sea can do many things. It is the womb of all life on the planet. Weather patterns and natural disasters are at the mercy of the mighty blue's ebb and flow. A food chain that supplies sustenance for most life-forms on the planet begins and ends in the deep. But what Atticus Young had learned in the last two years was that the ocean, for all its might and wonder, could not heal a broken man.

Atticus stood barefoot on a barnacle-encrusted rock, one of many that formed a barrier between ocean and sand. Beyond the sand lay a man-made hump of sand and grass that guarded Route 1A and a row of homes built on the other side of the road, all facing the ocean, from storm waters. Atticus had often wondered if the homes had been erected prior to the high water-blocking sand piles—the ocean view was blocked for all but the tallest homes. But the misfortune of those few Rye residents living with obscured views was not enough to ease his distress.

The barnacles that cut into his rough feet failed to gain his attention.

A flock of frenzied seagulls pecking and squawking over the remnants of a dead skate washed in with the tide couldn't pull Atticus from his thoughts.

Even the deep blue ocean, which sparkled like the most eloquently carved sapphire, failed to pull his mind from past to present.

"SHE'S DEAD," the doctor said. "I'm sorry, but there was nothing we could do. The cancer was too much…too far…but you knew that already."

Atticus nodded and looked out the Portsmouth Regional Hospital window, glimpsing the ocean on the horizon. "Are there any papers I need to sign?" His voice was as clinical as the doctor's.

"No…no, of course not."

"I can leave then?"

"Well…yes, but…Yes, of course."

Atticus nodded and left his Maria's bedside. A single thought echoed in his mind as he walked to the staircase, mindlessly descended two flights of stairs, and entered the main lobby.

My wife is dead.

My wife is dead.

Maria is...

Atticus burst into the men's room, closed and locked the door behind him, and fell to the floor. His sobs could be heard beyond the reception desk, down the hall, and clear into the cafeteria. Even people in the rooms on the floor above could hear his anguish. That day, seventy-five people heard what it felt like to have a portion of one's soul extinguished. Few of them could stop their own tears.

As the tears subsided, replaced by a blinding headache, Atticus's awareness of his surroundings returned. The linoleum floor, pale white and sparkling clean, was cold on his palms. The air freshener, working hard to penetrate his running nose, smelled strongly of apple. The fluorescent light above buzzed gently, casting the room in dull blue. The sterility of it all helped calm his nerves and focus his mind.

Atticus stood on shaky legs, rinsed his face, and blew his nose. He knew that no amount of cold water could erase the redness and swelling his crying had brought to the flesh around his eyes, but it helped clear his mind. As Atticus left the bathroom and avoided the sympathetic eyes of the group gathered in the reception area, he put all his efforts into staying calm and reaching home safely. He couldn't lose control again, because the hardest aftershock from Maria's death was yet to come, and it would be his shoulders that carried the burden.

THE WAS two years ago, and ever since, every

morning when he woke up alone in bed, it was like being right back in that bathroom, cold and alone.

A sudden roar and a stab of frigidity on his feet finally returned him to the here and now. Atticus looked at his feet and found them covered to the ankles in water. The tide was coming in. As Atticus moved higher onto the rocky shore, he paused by a tide pool. His shadow fell over the ten-inch-deep puddle, shading it from the sun's glare and allowing him to see scads of tiny creatures—crabs, shrimp, and snails—retreat to the shadows. The empty, glassy surface of the water only left one thing to look at, and it was by far the motliest sight in the tide pool.

Atticus examined the reflection of his face. Crow's-feet had been carved into the skin around his eyes over the past ten years, but more severely in the last two. His hair, cut short, was simultaneously beginning to turn gray and recede. At only forty-one, he was beginning to look more like his father. His skin was still tanned dark brown, almost the same hue as his eyes, but the most distracting feature on his face was a long, scraggly beard that made him look more like a craggy sea captain than an oceanographer. He shook his beard and removed the few crumbs that had managed to cling since breakfast. They fell into the pool. A small, tan crab crawled out to inspect the sinking debris, snagged it, and retreated once more to the dark.

"Well," Atticus said, "*Hemigrapsus sanguineus,* fancy meeting you here."

Atticus thrust his hand into the pool like a diving

osprey and snagged the little crab. He pulled his lightly clenched fist out of the water, dripping and containing the small arthropod. Cupping his hands together, Atticus inspected the little creature to confirm its identity—the Asian shore crab—an invasive species that had made landfall in New Jersey in 1988. Now, almost twenty years later, it inhabited the coast from Maine to the Carolinas. It competed with local crab species but also threatened the famous North American lobster. Just one of many invasions most people are unaware of that threaten the ocean's ecosystem. True, the Asian shore crab might successfully replace the North American lobster in the food chain, substituting one animal for the other...but no one eats shore crab.

As Atticus looked the crab over, he knew he should crush the little thing before it could spawn and continue the invasion. But he didn't have the heart. Killing wasn't something of which he was capable, not anymore, even if it was an invasive species. He believed they should be wiped out and removed from the ecosystem, but not by his hands. He'd report the crab's presence, and a crew would be sent out to find and kill every Asian shore crab in the area. It was a noble effort, but ultimately would prove futile.

Kind of like my work, Atticus thought. Atticus was in the business of wildlife preservation, but focused on the New England's larger mammalian species, the humpback, minke, fin, and North Atlantic right whales, though he also worked with dolphins, seals, and, occasionally, sharks. He worked as an independent contractor for the New England Aquarium, the Whale Center of New England, and other independent scientific outfits, though most of his work and income went to the highest bidder, primarily the U.S. Navy, with which he still had close ties. His work could keep him at sea six months out of the year and often for weeks at a time, tracking, identifying, and tagging animals. His work for the military was often more discreet and required the signing of documents that guaranteed his silence, but it paid the bills and didn't conflict with his environmental efforts.

But none of it mattered anymore. In a week, Rye and his work on the ocean would be a memory.

After placing the crab back in the tide pool, Atticus worked his way back through the rocks, the incoming tide nipping at his heels. He trudged through the shell-filled sand and walked over the top of the water barrier. At the apex he gazed at the long strand of houses with no view, and then slid down the hill on his heels. He reached his old red Ford Explorer, climbed in, and closed the door.

Atticus turned the ignition, and the SUV started with a roar. The dashboard clock glowed blue at him, reminding him of the time. He was going to be late. With a slow sigh, Atticus pulled off the side of the road and onto Route 1A, the memories of the past fading as anxiety for the future set in. Where he was going next would be the hardest part of his day. He had to tell Giona that they were moving in a week, to

Ann Arbor. It was for the best, he knew, but he didn't look forward to breaking his daughter's heart…again.

3

PENOBSCOT BAY, MAINE—THIRTY MILES OUT

The ocean lay flat and placid, calm in a way so rarely seen in the waters off Massachusetts, New Hampshire, and Maine, collectively known as the Gulf of Maine. Jack Michaels leaned on the port rail of his fishing trawler, the *Ragnarok,* and wearily rested his chin on his hands. The herring season thus far had been abysmal, moving slower than the current four knots at which his ship was plodding along. It wasn't that the fish weren't there—other vessels were bringing in phenomenal hauls—but whether by some design of the sea or God's working against him, the herring were avoiding the *Ragnarok.*

His eyes trailed from the slowly undulating seas to the boat around him. The *Ragnarok* was ten years old, new by some standards, and carried a fresh coat of obsidian paint, giving her the look of a modern ghost ship. The look was reinforced by the myriad of dark sinew-like cables that stretched from various points on the ship to the trawler cranes, which were capable of pulling in tons of fish. The thick net dragged through the water kept the cables taut, ready to haul in the big catch.

Thus far they'd proved useless. For all the ship's modern accoutrements, including a global positioning system and hydroacoustic fishfinders, the herring had remained elusive. If things didn't pick up soon, he'd have to take out a loan to make his house payments and carry the business into the next year. If he didn't pull in a great haul next year, he'd have to declare bankruptcy and go to work for one of the other fishing ventures…maybe head down to Essex, Massachusetts, where he grew up.

Jack considered the *Ragnarok* once again. Perhaps it was the ship's gloomy visage that kept the fish at bay? He knew it wasn't true, but this prime spot on the ocean, his personal secret, was devoid of fish, when it normally teemed with little silver bodies, swimming and swirling in unison. He sighed and removed a cigar from his jacket pocket. Usually reserved for the final successful haul, he felt there would be no use for it this year. Why not enjoy it now? After clipping the cigar and lighting up, he took a long drag, tasting the flavor, but quickly realized that without the success of a big haul, the cigar tasted more like burning dirt. He pulled the smoking cylinder from his cracked lips and looked at it. Its smell was suddenly noxious, and he moved to fling the thing out to sea.

"Captain!" The voice was so shrill and sharp that he almost fell overboard. Jimmy, the excitable new kid on the boat, was prone to overreacting...though his eyes had never looked quite so wide before. Jimmy stopped, put his hands on his knees, and, in between gulps of air, said, "They're...coming!"

Jack crinkled his nose. The boredom was getting to everyone. "Who's coming?"

"The—the herring! The hydroacoustics just picked them up."

Captain Jack Michaels felt hope return. He straightened his stance and firmed his voice. "How many?"

"I have no idea..."

Jack sighed. The boy had been well trained to estimate the number of fish based on the information displayed by the fishfinder. Schools of herring often showed up as large masses of red, green, and blue speckles, and an astute mind could peg the number to within a hundred by gauging the width and length of the signature. But there was little time to scold the boy. He looked to the sky and found the telltale sign that the fish were coming. A flock of seagulls flew over the ocean, watching the waters below. Normally, the gulls would dive and pull fish from the sea, but this group looked as though they were having trouble keeping up. The herring were running. From what, Jack didn't care. They were headed straight for the *Ragnarok*.

Bounding into the bridge, Jack took a look at the hydroacoustic display screen. At the bottom were two corresponding lines, one red, and one green. They marked the ocean floor. But it was the large cloud of colored specks that sucked the air from his lungs. The school of fish stretched almost all the way across the screen, with no end in sight. "Holy…" Jack snapped to his senses, issuing loud commands before he had given them any thought. "Drop the second net! Do it now!"

Not every trawler had a second net, but Jack had designed his boat to maximize efficiency. The secondary net was smaller than the first. It would catch a great number, but those that got around it were caught by the much larger secondary net. It was a secret that only he and his crew knew about, and it had greatly increased their catches in the past. Jack's mouth spread in a wide smile. That day they would exceed the previous year's catch…in mere minutes. It might take all day to pull the enormous catch from the nets, but the work would be worth it.

Jack could hear the shouts of his crew as they frantically dropped the second net. It spread in the water not a moment too soon. The front wave of herring, the truly fast specimens, hit the net and were scooped up. Then the front end of the mass of fish entered, and Jack actually felt the impact as tons of fish filled both nets. The *Ragnarok* slowed almost to a stop. Jack slammed the throttle forward. If the boat lost momentum, the fish might escape. The engines chugged loudly in response, groaning against the extra tons of weight, but eventually the boat picked up speed. Jack watched the hydroacoustic display as the cloud of herring thinned out and ended, the majority of the fish secure in the nets.

He was about to look away, let out a whooping cheer, and slap young Jimmy on the back, when a second object entered the display, hot on the heels of the remaining herring. But this wasn't some speckled cloud of fish; it was solid. The object undulated into view, and as Jack estimated its size, he ruled out one creature after another.

Fifty feet…not the pilot, minke, or ray…

Sixty feet. He ruled out the humpbacks.

Seventy feet. Not a sperm whale, which had been his guess.

As the object continued to enter the viewfinder, he knew it was a blue whale. They grew to a maximum size of 110 feet. They were the largest living creature ever to grace the planet earth throughout its entire history. Nothing was bigger.

And yet, as this creature passed the 110-foot mark, then the 120-foot…140…150…he knew that the blue whale had been usurped as the ocean's king. Jack suddenly realized the creature was coming for the herring and wasn't slowing down. The *Ragnarok* would be obliterated. For a millisecond, Jack thought of ordering the nets cut loose, but it was too late. The behemoth had reached the nets, but at the last possible moment dived deep. It was amazingly agile for something so massive, and quicker than it had arrived, it disappeared from the hydrosonic display, as though it had never been.

Jack glanced to his side and saw Jimmy's wide eyes and slack jaw. "Hell of a thing ain't it, kid."

Jimmy nodded. "Should…shouldn't we tell someone?"

"Who would believe us?"

Cheers rose up from around the boat. Jack looked out the window and saw the ocean frothing with fish as the first net was brought up. The winches creaked under the strain, but were holding. It was the largest catch Jack had ever seen and that was only the first of two nets. Jack placed the cigar, which he'd been holding tightly the whole time, back in his mouth and took a puff. It tasted delightful.

He turned back to Jimmy. "The sea giveth and the sea taketh away. Just be thankful she was in a giving mood today and move on. Questioning things just invites trouble." Jack nodded to the hydroacoustic screen. "And that kind of trouble is something we don't want. Understand?"

Jimmy nodded.

"Good. Consider yourself promoted." Jack opened the bridge door to a blast of fresh ocean air and the hoots and hollers of his gleeful crew, who, except for young Jimmy, would never know just how close they'd all come to being Hollywood's next exploited sea tragedy. "All right," Jack shouted, "get these fish on board double time! We're heading home!"

The men cheered. They'd been at sea for weeks and missed their families. But a joyful homecoming wasn't what spurred Jack's urgency to get home. Rather, for the first time in his life, he wanted to get off the water and onto solid ground.

4

PORTSMOUTH, NEW HAMPSHIRE

She knew the men behind her had been following closely for two blocks, maybe longer, mimicking every turn, every pause. Giona could smell the tobacco from the cigarettes they lit, three each in the last ten minutes. Probably nervous. She could also hear their shuffled footfalls on the centuries-old brick sidewalks. Portsmouth was an old town, one of the original East Coast ports and home of the Portsmouth Navy Yard—also home to sound-conductive sidewalks and a few less-than-honest residents.

She wasn't sure exactly how long they'd been following her. She'd been engaged with her "inner voice," as she liked to call her. It was her private devil's advocate, conjured up by her mind when there was no one else to talk to, and had recently become a mainstay in her thought processes. Some people might call it a conscience, but it only seemed to appear with certain subjects, and none were moral questions. While she totally disagreed with the opinions of her "inner voice," it at least helped her firm up her opinions on issues she faced. She knew it was weird, but she didn't have a ton of people to talk to.

Since her mom died, she'd rarely talked to anyone, including her father. He was nice enough. A good guy. Kind. Loving. Smart. She admired him and his work. Not all girls have an ex–Navy SEAL-turned-oceanographer for a father. But the day he'd come home from the hospital, eyes burnt red from crying, and just looked at her with those sad eyes, she knew two things. Her mother was dead, and she wouldn't let herself get that close to anyone every again. Not even her father. And to let the world know to stay away, she changed everything about herself.

Her colorful wardrobe disappeared, replaced by black ill-fitting clothes purchased at the Salvation Army. She knew that might not be enough to keep everyone at bay, so she accentuated the black by dyeing her hair a variety of colors. The ridiculous number of silver bracelets on her wrists, the black-and-white-striped stockings she wore, and the piercings in her eyebrow, nose, and ears completed the look and achieved her desired goal: solitude. The only people inclined to spend any time with her were fellow recluses, who similarly had little use for close relationships.

Though she would never admit it, loneliness had become a problem; but she ignored it, fought against it, unwilling to suffer the loss that would eventually come. A few months ago, the "inner voice" had emerged. She knew the voice was slightly insane, borderline schizophrenic, but she didn't care. It didn't tell her to do things. Instead it spoke with her—argued with her, really—and oddly enough instilled a sense of peace in her; she wasn't totally alone anymore. The one drawback was that she became oblivious to the outside world when arguing internally. She'd been distracted enough that the two guys had got within twenty feet of her and, if she hadn't been snapped out of her thought processes by their overpowering odor, they could've snuck up right behind her with ease.

She had yet to look back at the two men following her. She didn't want them to realize she was aware of their presence. But she could narrow down their identities to a handful of people. She'd met many unsavory people in the last year, socializing with large groups of teens who hung around downtown. Most were rich kids playing tough, wearing ratty clothes while clutching their iPods and smoking pot. But a few were the real deal, nasty people best to be avoided—something Giona typically excelled at. But friends of friends had made introductions, and she'd found herself in the wrong place at the wrong time.

To look at her, with her purple-dyed hair, jet-black clothes, and array of ear piercings, she fit right in. But her pleasant smile and charming wit set her apart. More than that, her genius-level intelligence allowed her to talk her way out of trouble. It was her stance on drugs that really made her stand out. She was well-known for attending antidrug meetings at the high school. While many of her in-town friends were petitioning their local senators to legalize marijuana, she was testifying before a New Hampshire Senate subcommittee about how it, and even alcohol, should be banned. She wasn't a Holy Roller or ex-user, just someone who had seen too many friends' crisp minds rot and slow. Conversations that once involved quantum singularities or deep-sea creatures instead focused on Zippo lighters, Twinkies, bowl-packing procedure, and who had taken a hit from the longest bong.

Her friends had tolerated, even encouraged, Giona's antidrug crusade—drug users were easily impressed with anyone doing something more than sitting on a couch. One had even said with a slur, "You even think about…doin' drugs…and I'll kick your ass."

But not everyone within her circle appreciated her opinion, and a nickname had cropped up—nark. Everyone knew she'd never said a word to the police about who did drugs, but a few nights ago she'd found herself sitting in one of Portsmouth's alleys. Unlike many cities, Portsmouth's alleys were nicely decorated and home to frequently visited shops. But it would seem that alleys everywhere, even those with an attractive décor, invited trouble. She had been sitting on a bench, writing down the details of a strange dream from the night before. Whispered words took her attention from the page just in time to see a large cellophane-wrapped object being handed from a stranger's hand to one of the local dealers she'd done so well avoiding. The dealer went by the name Bazooka Joe, in part because of his penchant for chewing gum but also because of the large bazooka-wielding figure shooting a rocket, which trailed from his biceps to his forearm.

She instantly recognized the wrapped object as a brick of marijuana and was quick to her feet. Wrong place, wrong time. But in her haste to retreat, she tripped and fell to the sidewalk. As she quickly picked herself up, she gave a glance back, meeting the deep-set eyes of the dealer. He was rubbing his hand over his shaved head and staring at her, seeming indecisive about what to do. The man selling the brick said a few words, distracting Joe for only a moment. When he looked up, Giona was gone. But he'd already seen and recognized her face. He knew who she was…and what she believed.

The footsteps were sounding louder behind her, more frantic. Then she realized why. She was about to pass the entrance to one of Portsmouth's parking garages. Odds were that the stairwell was empty. She glanced across the street, looking for somewhere to go, but on Sunday afternoon, all of the shops were closed. Out of options, she began to run.

She'd taken three strides when two viselike arms wrapped around her waist, hoisted her into the air, and heaved her sideways into the stairwell. She caught herself just inches from cracking her skull on the concrete steps. As she turned around to face her attackers, she momentarily wondered if she'd have been better off being knocked unconscious. Having no memory of what was to come next might be a blessing.

Bazooka Joe and a man she'd never seen before were smiling widely. Their yellow tainted teeth seemed more like wolves' fangs than human teeth. As Joe leaned closer, she realized that his teeth were in fact far from normal. They'd been filed to sharp points. As he opened his mouth to talk, she felt as though she was staring into the jaws of a shark.

Joe noticed her focus on his teeth. "I won't bite if you're good."

Giona kept her mouth shut. To speak at all would only incite the man.

Joe turned to the other man, whose filthy clothes and rank odor spoke more of a quickly hired homeless man than a true compatriot. "You watch the upstairs door. No one comes through."

The man nodded nervously and ascended the stairs. Joe turned back to Giona, rubbing his hand over his shaved head. "You know why we're here, right?"

Giona nodded.

"Tell me."

"I saw your deal the other night."

Joe made a loud buzzing noise. "Wrong. Everyone knows you're not a nark. But you dropped something when you ran away."

He reached into his pocket and pulled out a four-by-six sheet of paper. Giona knew what it was before he turned it around. Taken a month before while she and her father were snorkeling...the one and only thing they'd done together all year, Giona had posed for a picture with her father. The camera, set on the captain's chair, had captured a photo that none of her punk friends would have believed. Under the dark, baggy clothes there was a bronze-skinned, fit body that could have belonged to any number of Hollywood starlets. Her body and smiling face were in stark contrast to the shaggy purple hair, but there was no denying she was a hidden beauty.

"A real diamond in the rough," Joe said, spittle flinging from his mouth. The man was all but drooling.

As Joe unbuckled his belt, she realized what was going to happen next. Her mind raced for some kind of plan, some way to escape. Joe removed his belt and looped it around the door handle and a nearby pipe, fastening it tight. Her only chance was to head up the stairs and take the other man by surprise. She began to shuffle up, ready to run, but Joe sensed the movement and lunged.

Giona struggled for a moment, but was pulled back down, landing hard on the stairs. Joe's strong right hand, which featured the projectile flung forth from the biceps bazooka, wrapped around her throat. "Make a noise, and I squeeze. Fight, and I'll gut you quick." He punctuated his last words with the flick of his left hand, revealing a switchblade.

Her body went rigid; she couldn't fight, but she

could resist. With every ounce of strength in her body, she would not allow the man to take her easily. Her only hope was that he would tire and give up, but the sculpted muscles on his exposed arms told her the effort would be futile.

Joe placed the knife under her shirt and moved it up her body, allowing his hand to graze across her flesh. He was going to cut her clothes off.

Before the blade could be pulled back, a loud *thump* sounded from above. Joe hesitated. "Zack. What's going on?"

When no response came, Joe withdrew the knife but kept his hand planted firmly on Giona's neck. "Zack, what the hell are you doing, man?"

Shuffling footsteps made their way down the stairs. A man, sniffling and wheezing, was coming down the steps. As he came into view, Giona saw a withered-looking form in disheveled clothes and sporting one of the most scraggly beards she had ever seen. Despite his scruffiness, she had to work hard to hide a smile.

"Who the hell are you?" Joe shouted. "Zack! You have about five seconds to—"

"Zack took a break man...I'm taking his place."

Joe seethed. He was clearly going to hurt Zack at some point in the future, but his options at the moment were few. "How do you know Zack?"

"Used to fish together." The words came out slurred and breathy.

Joe seemed satisfied by the answer. Apparently Zack had once been a fisherman. Joe shook his head and pointed the knife blade at the scraggly drunk. "Anyone gets by you, you're dead. Got it?"

The man nodded, then tripped, descending several stairs at once so that his feet were next to Giona's head and his face only a foot from Joe's blade. "Whoa…close one."

Joe was about to shout something when, like a blur, the drunk's hand latched on to Joe's wrist. A quick twist brought about a loud *crack*, which was followed by a ferocious scream. Joe followed the scream with, "You f—"

But before the flow of obscenities could issue forth, a rigid hand chopped through the air and caught Joe in the Adam's apple. The once-savage attacker was instantly reduced to a sad little man, writhing on the floor, gasping for breath. With Joe on the floor, clearly incapacitated, the drunk stood straighter, descended the remaining stairs, and pulled out a cell phone. After a quickly dialed call and brief discussion with a 911 operator, the man turned around, clearly relieved at the girl's safety.

"You okay?" Atticus asked.

Giona longed to run to her father's arms and be held within his safe embrace, but charade or not, the tough exterior she had built over the past two years forbade it. She wouldn't show weakness, especially not to her father. "Fine," she said, picking herself up and straightening her shirt.

It was obvious her father longed to hold her as well. He must have been petrified. The best he could muster was a pat on her shoulder. "Lucky I came by."

"You're late."

"Sorry."

"You called the cops?"

"Yes."

Giona sighed. She'd be marked as a real nark from here on.

"You won't have to worry about him anymore."

The relief Giona felt when she'd first seen her father was being consumed by years of barriers built between the two. "I can take care of myself."

"I'm sure," Atticus said, a tinge of sarcasm entering his voice as he grew impatient with his ungrateful daughter. He quickly undid the belt around the door, and with a seriousness that could not be ignored--even by an angry seventeen-year-old--said, "Wait outside."

Giona headed for the door and paused before leaving. "You're not going to…"

"In another life I would have. But not today."

Giona stepped outside, and the door clicked shut behind her. A few moments later she could hear the wheezing screams of Joe. She had no idea what her father was doing, or even what he was capable of doing (though she had her suspicions), but it was clearly something Joe would not forget. *Good*, Giona thought, *the bastard deserves whatever he gets*. But then she regretted that in some roundabout way she was responsible for bringing out demons her father had long ago buried. She crossed her arms, leaned against a mailbox, and waited for the screaming to stop.

5

The water below was whipped into a frenzy as the U.S. Coast Guard HH-60 Jayhawk helicopter's blades chopped through the ocean air. Below, Petty Officer Ryan Reilly dangled from a wire. The rescue effort was going great except for one thing—the PIW (person in the water) was unconscious. Two days of not eating and exposure to the elements had taken their toll. An hour previous, when a C-130 Hercules had spotted the woman's bright orange life jacket and deployed rescue equipment via parachute, the woman moved sluggishly.

She'd evidently been able to inflate the life raft, but she'd lacked the strength to pull herself fully in.

Her face, matted in wet blond hair, and the right side of her body were dangling inside the raft, while her left arm and leg were still submerged. She hadn't even twitched when the Jayhawk rescue team had arrived, which made the men and woman in the chopper move that much more quickly. They could see the life draining out of the woman as they hovered above her.

Little was known about her. A mayday had been sent out, in French, from a desperate-sounding man. He'd had the common sense to give coordinates in English so the Coast Guard didn't have to waste precious time translating. The search had been going on for two days, and finally, the woman, presumably the man's wife, had been found. Two C-130s were still flying patterns over the area in an attempt to locate the man, but hope was running out.

Captain Andrea Vincent looked down from the Jayhawk, toggling the winch controls that lowered Reilly toward the PIW. She'd been with the Coast Guard for six years and taken part in hundreds of rescues. Though people often doubted that the woman with wavy black hair and such a petite frame was capable of plucking waterlogged bodies from the water, it was usually her dangling from the cable. But Reilly needed the experience. He was doing a good job too.

The plan was simple. Reilly would be lowered slowly rather than jumping in. If the woman woke and was startled, she might reenter the water and take in a mouthful of water. Reilly could handle CPR in the water, but there was no reason to risk it. Vincent looked down. Reilly had entered the water. His voice came through her headset. "I'm in. Heading for the PIW."

"Copy that," Vincent said. "Go get her."

She watched as Reilly sidestroked toward the woman. All he had to do was pull her into the water slowly, wrap a second harness around her arms, connect it to his, and they'd be pulled up together.

Vincent noticed the copilot flashing her a hand signal. He pointed to his headset and flashed two fingers. He wanted her to switch to channel two. She, Reilly, and the pilot were on channel one for the rescue effort, while the copilot remained on channel two to communicate with the C-130s searching the area. It was abnormal for her to change channels during the rescue; if Reilly needed her, she'd have no way to know. But the copilot realized that, so it was probably a matter of some urgency.

"Reilly, I've got to switch over to two for a minute. You all right down there?"

"Copy that, Cap. She's out like a light. I'll have her ready to go in forty-five."

Forty-five seconds. That was all she'd give whoever was on channel two. She switched over and flinched as a chorus of shouting voices issued from the headset. The normally calm-sounding crew's of both C-130s were frantic. She couldn't make out a word of it, so she shouted, "Everyone shut the hell up, then one of you tell me what's going on!"

Her voice, though feminine, commanded attention like a Marine drill sergeant's. The line fell silent. Then the voice of Charley McCabe came back on the line. Vincent had known McCabe for the past five years. They were friends, but while on mission were all business. She knew something was wrong when McCabe spoke.

"Andrea, it's Chuck. Listen…" His voice was quivering. "We've, ah, we've picked something up, and it's coming your way."

"How far out?"

"About a mile."

"Submarine?" Vincent knew that submarines could pop out of the water suddenly, especially if something had gone wrong, but the odds were remote.

"That was our first guess. It's certainly big enough…but it's moving…look, just get out of there."

"How deep is it?"

"Will you just listen to me and get the hell out of there!" McCabe was speaking as a friend, she knew that, but it was totally unprofessional on a rescue op to break down. She wasn't leaving until the woman was secure. McCabe's forty-five seconds were up. She switched back to channel one.

"Reilly, what's your ATI?"

"Ten seconds."

"Get ready for a fast—"

Vincent's voice caught in her throat. She'd seen something moving beneath the water, about a quarter mile out and closing—a shadow of something. Moving fast. She put on UV-coated, antiglare sunglasses, and the shape became clear. It was dark beneath the blue waters, and its shape was undulating wildly, up and down. It would be on top of them in seconds.

The panic that filled the voices of her colleagues just moments before took hold of her. "Reilly, hold on to the woman! Emergency evac in two!"

She gave Reilly two seconds to do what he had to, then shoved the winch into high gear. The pilot had heard her order as well and, without any questions, pulled the Jayhawk into a vertical climb. Vincent looked out the bay door just in time to see Reilly, clinging to the woman, rise from the water. The black apparition passed right below them, leaving massive smooth footprints—typically created by the rising and descending of large whales—in its wake.

Reilly was up a few seconds later. He released the woman into Vincent's arms. "What the hell happened?"

Vincent quickly checked the woman's vitals and strapped her into a seat. When she turned to Reilly, she realized that she must have gone pale. His concerned eyes spoke volumes before he said anything. "You okay, Cap?"

She nodded. "Watson. Did you see that thing?"

"Yup," the pilot replied. "I'm on it."

Watson was a real hotdog pilot. Even a brush with a massive sea creature couldn't ruffle his feathers. The Jayhawk banked sharply and bolted south. "Almost on top of it."

The whine of the helicopter blades told Vincent

they were moving fairly fast, maybe eighty miles per hour. That'd be seventy knots in the water. Nothing natural moved that fast! She was at the window, glaring down at the water. It came into view seconds later, still moving like a missile, just beneath the surface. Reilly was next to her. "Good God…thanks for pulling me up."

She glanced at him. His face had gone as white as hers must have been.

When a face appeared next to Reilly's, they both shouted and jumped back.

The Frenchwoman was staring wide-eyed down at the ocean. She was obviously in shock, but at least part of her mind comprehended the sight below. "*Mon Dieu! Qu'est-ce que c'est? A-t-il mangé mon mari?*"

Vincent and Reilly ignored that the woman they'd rescued was out of her safety harness. They looked back out the window. The black shape suddenly sank away, going deep and leaving a massive forty-foot-wide footprint behind. Vincent looked at the Frenchwoman. "I have no idea what you said…but you said it."

Vincent glanced down. The woman was holding a digital camera—a waterproof digital camera, attached to a cord wrapped around her neck. She hadn't seen the woman take any pictures, but she hadn't been looking either. She motioned to the camera. "May I?"

The woman understood. "*Oui, oui, naturellement.*"

Vincent turned the playback screen on and scrolled

through the pictures. There were several of the Frenchwoman and her husband enjoying a cruise on their catamaran. What happened there was a mystery she'd figure out later. She kept moving until she found a blurry acrial shot of the ocean. She scrolled through three more, all blurry. Damn. The next came shockingly clear, and Vincent felt the blood leaving her face yet again. There it was. The black shape, just beneath the surface, was like…like nothing she'd ever seen. If not for this photo, she probably wouldn't have bothered even to report it. The thing was so unbelievable. The next picture was of the colossal, unbelievable footprint left behind. But the evidence she held in her hand…people would believe that.

6

PORTSMOUTH, NEW HAMPSHIRE

The man who had attacked his daughter screamed like a little girl with every slice of the blade Atticus wielded. When Atticus finished, the man and his crony were heaped on the stairs, weeping and afraid for their lives.

Good, Atticus thought. If the justice system failed, and the men walked, they wouldn't soon forget the lesson he'd just taught them. Not to mention the humiliation they were about to face.

As the sirens grew louder, Atticus closed the knife and opened the garage door. Four officers were headed his way. Giona was standing nearby. She looked petrified, probably more from hearing the men scream than from surviving her own ordeal. He gave her a wink and a smile, then greeted the police officers, handing them the knife and giving a brief explanation of what had happened. The officers gave one look at Giona, her frightened face, and peeked in at the men in the stairwell. They snickered.

"You did this?" one of the officers asked.

Atticus nodded as he wrote his contact information on the back of a business card he'd had in his wallet.

The officer had trouble hiding his smile. "You know that was probably a bad idea."

Atticus nodded again and handed the officer the business card. "They had it coming."

It was the officer's turn to nod. "Of course, now we're going to have to charge them with indecent exposure." He smiled then straightened his face. "We're going to need a statement. Down at the station."

"Absolutely," Atticus said, then thumbed toward Giona. "Mind if I take care of her first?"

"Do what you need to do. Come down today or tomorrow," the officer replied.

Atticus walked to Giona's side, her face still a mask of fear.

"What did you do to them?" Giona asked.

"Poetic justice," was Atticus's reply. "Watch."

The police exited the parking garage, moving the men in front of them. Both men had their hands cuffed behind their backs, but what was most striking about the image was that their clothes had been cut to ribbons. A group of teens burst out laughing. Others snapped pictures with their cell phones. A few older women covered their mouths and shook their heads in disgust, but watched the spectacle just the same. While Atticus had left their front sides covered, he had totally exposed their rear ends and shredded the rest of their clothing along with whatever small amount of dignity they might have had.

"I doubt they'll even set foot in Portsmouth again," Atticus said. "Not without being laughed at, anyway." He looked down at Giona. A bright smile was on her face—a rarity these days. That it had taken such a violent act to put it there disturbed him. Who had his daughter become? Would they ever be close again?

After the news he would soon deliver, he doubted it.

SITTING IN the Ford Explorer, an uncomfortable silence fell between Atticus and Giona. She had her arms crossed over her chest, where just an hour earlier a man had held a knife. He looked at her throat and saw some light bruising.

"Are you sure you're all right?"

"Fine."

"You've got some bruises forming on your neck. How hard was he squeezing?"

Giona pulled down the visor and popped on the mirror. She inspected her neck, then slumped back in her seat. Tears welled up in her eyes despite her best effort to hide them. A sob escaped her lips, followed by another and another. Atticus pulled over, slammed the car into park, and, their relationship be damned, he was going to hold his baby.

He thought he'd have to undo her seat belt and yank her over, but as soon as they were stopped, she crawled across the seat and into his lap. He wrapped his arms around her and squeezed. "I love you, baby. I love you."

Giona's sobs grew louder, and Atticus felt that she wasn't just crying because of what had just happened. She was letting out two years of pent-up grief. When he had told her about Maria, about her death, she hadn't shed a tear. A month later her hair was bright red, and a wall had been erected between them. That wall, it seemed, had just crumbled. At least Atticus hoped it had.

Ten minutes passed before either said another word. Giona's crying had subsided; she wiped her face clean, shifting back to the passenger seat. Atticus feared the wall was coming back up, but then she spoke.

"I love you too, Daddy."

Atticus's heart broke. He paused before speaking less his voice crack. "Daddy, huh?"

Giona gave him the smile he'd waited two years to see. "Thanks for saving me."

Atticus shrugged nonchalantly. "I was in the area."

She slapped his shoulder. "I mean it."

Silence filled the parked Explorer again. He desired to break the silence so badly, to continue the healing process, but what could he say to a daughter who had nearly been raped, with whom he had rarely held a conversation in two years...whose eyes looked just like Maria's and whose nose was his own. *The truth,* Atticus decided.

He opened his mouth to speak, but it was Giona's voice that broke the silence. "I know about Ann Arbor. I know we're moving."

Atticus stared are her, mouth still hanging open. She answered the next obvious question.

"I'm Generation Y, Daddy. You're generation...old. I grew up with a computer, and you don't cover your tracks well. Ever heard of deleting your history? Clearing the recently viewed documents list? I thought you Navy SEALs were supposed to be stealthy."

"There's a big difference between an M-16 and Windows XP." Atticus put the SUV in drive and pulled out onto the road. He was impressed that Giona had discovered their moving plans, but she was right. He was getting old, slow, and sloppy...not physically...but he feared the mind was dulling. He sometimes missed his exploits with the SEALs, risking his life, serving his country...firing a gun. Maria had changed all that in him, gave him something deeper to believe in—a wife, a daughter.

He'd been pacified and domesticated. He didn't resent the change, not for a moment, but he did miss the rush of an underwater insertion, how alive he felt when bullets were seeking him out but not finding their mark. It had been his life for ten years.

"Uncle Conner is excited we're moving. He—"

"You talked to my brother about it, but not to me?"

Giona's faced flush with guilt. "Well, you obviously didn't want to talk to *me* about it either. You could have asked my opinion. We could have planned it together."

"We hardly do anything together." Atticus's voice was rising. He took a breath and spoke more softly. "Look. I'm doing this for us. I have a job at the Detroit Zoo, caring for the seals. I won't be gone for months out of the year. We can spend more time together—fix what's been broken between us. Okay?"

Giona nodded quick, little agreeing nods. "Okay…When are we moving?"

"You mean you don't know?"

Giona smiled. "I can read a hard drive, but not your mind."

"Three days."

"Wow …"

"Yup."

"Nothing like waiting until the last minute, huh?"

"I didn't know how to tell you."

A pause filled Atticus with a surge of anxiety. Had he just undone the bond newly forged between them? Giona's next words erased his fears.

"You're going to miss the ocean."

Atticus nodded, relieved and surprised that her reaction to the news was concern for him. "Yup."

Giona looked out the windshield, paying attention for the first time. They'd just pulled into Rye harbor.

"We're going to say good-bye," Atticus said.

"Look in the back."

As he parked the car in the dirt parking lot and gave Pete the attendant a friendly "hello" and a five dollar bill, Giona looked in the back of the Explorer. Two sets of dive gear were there. Wet suits, oxygen tanks, everything. "We're going diving?"

"We're going on *the* dive."

Giona's eyes flashed with excitement. It had been Giona's dream to dive with whales. She'd said it would be the closest thing to a supernatural encounter a human could experience. That was a few years ago, before Maria died, but he was sure she still felt the same. The look on her face confirmed it.

"There's been a lot of humpback activity in the area. They're migrating north right now."

Giona kissed him on the cheek. "I love you, Daddy."

"Suddenly we're best friends," Atticus said with a smirk. He loved making his daughter happy. He hoped he could continue to do so in Ann Arbor. They'd be with family, and he'd be around a lot more. He would certainly miss the ocean, but he could already feel his life changing for the better.

"Listen, I know you're a good diver," he said, "but you've never dived with whales. They're gentle, but they're still wild creatures. They can be erratic at times. The ocean in general is unpredictable. We'll be using full-sized masks with headsets, so we'll be able to talk and see each other's faces. Just do exactly what I tell you, okay?"

"Your word is my command."

"Good." Atticus flashed a smile. He was as excited as she was. He'd swum with whales many times before, but the thrill was always the same. Giona was right. It was a supernatural experience. "Let's go find some whales."

7

JEFFREY'S LEDGE—GULF OF MAINE

Atticus shut down the yacht's twin diesels. He listened to the water slapping against the fiberglass hull, felt the gentle rise and fall of the ocean beneath, and breathed deeply of the salty sea air. He was home...for one more day. Leaving the sea behind pained him, but strengthening his relationship with Giona was more important, and that couldn't be done while he was away for months at a time.

The boat, on loan from a friend who owed him a favor, was sleek and fancy. It had taken Giona some time to believe that they had the seventy-foot-long, eighteen-foot-beam vessel all to themselves. Built as a ship for megasport fishermen, the *Bugaboo* also worked well as a pleasure boat, or in their case, a di-

ving platform. The white hull gleamed in the afternoon sun, a white speck on the blue ocean.

Atticus's mind turned to the ocean beneath. On
the way to Jeffrey's Ledge, they'd seen several plumes
of mist ejected from swimming whales. The temptation to give chase and jump out after them was
strong, but he knew whales in the deep water would
be moving fast, impossible to jump in with. But at
Jeffery's Ledge, a glacial deposit that created upwelling currents, the water flourished with plankton, herring, cod, and the giants of the sea that fed on them—
the whales…especially the humpbacks.

Atticus left the cushy seat of the *Bugaboo*'s air-
conditioned bridge and headed for the stern deck. He
opened the door into the eighty-five-degree air and
found Giona all geared up and eager to enter the water. She lobbed the dive buoy into the water and
turned to him, face beaming. "What are you waiting
for? Let's go!"

He wasted no time sliding into his wet suit, weight
belt, buoyancy-control vest, and air tanks. Before
donning the face mask, he double-checked Giona's
equipment, then his own. SEALs were known for entering the most dangerous environments on the planet, but they were always well prepared first. That
was why so few of them came home in body bags.
When Atticus felt they were ready for anything, he
gave Giona a thumbs-up. She was beaming.

"One last thing," he said. He opened a storage
compartment and pulled out two cameras encased in
waterproof shells. "I thought this might be a Kodak

moment. Yours is a still camera. The flash will work up to fifty feet. It's bright as hell, so don't take any pictures of yourself. Mine is a video camera. I'll get everything on tape..." He smiled. "Maybe you can show it to your kids someday."

Giona had no words. She simply accepted the camera with a wide smile.

Two minutes later, they splashed into the water. While Atticus was a master scuba diver, Giona wasn't a novice by any means. They both equalized the pressure in their ears and silently descended to fifty feet. The deep blue waters surrounded them endlessly on every side. It was as though they were floating in limbo, weightless, neither hot nor cold, where the trappings of the world, both good and evil, seemed irrelevant. Not limbo, Atticus thought, Heaven.

Then the waters spoke. A ghostly tune. The long, sad note carried through the water, passing the two small divers and continuing for thousands of miles beyond. It was answered by another. "Where are they?" Giona's voice was just a whisper in Atticus's ear.

"They're coming."

"Where?"

In fact, Atticus had no idea where they were. He could tell by the singsongy sounds that they were humpbacks, the most playful, and in his opinion, beautiful of all the whales. They were close. That was all he knew.

Atticus filled the silence with his voice. "Did you know that whale songs actually follow rules of musical composition?" His voice was filled with wonder, and he didn't wait for Giona to reply. "They learn the song from their parent…from their family, and pass it down from generation to generation, elaborating on it…improving it." He paused for a moment to listen. "I hope…I want to do that for you too, Gigi. I want to be a good dad for you, to teach you things you might find worth passing down to your kids. That's why—"

A loud, bellowing song rolled through the water all around them. The song was so loud that Atticus knew he should be able to see the creature. He spun in circles, looking everywhere. As he spun, the water below him began to lighten. He looked down and saw the belly of a massive humpback arcing below.

"Wow!" Giona had seen it too.

Then the rest of the whales came into view, one at a time, an entire pod of humpbacks, lazily swimming and spinning, enjoying the freedom of the ocean. They were moving slowly, obviously curious about the small humans keeping pace with them. Their forward movement ended, and they began circling, diving, churning, approaching, and rising to the surface for air. A curious calf approached Giona, who held her hand out to touch it.

Atticus grew nervous. If the mother sensed a threat, they'd both be in trouble. But his fear was groundless. The mother gently nudged the calf toward the surface, reminding the little one to breathe. Giona had held her breath too, and now Atticus could hear her heavy respirations over the headset.

"Steady breathing," he said. "Try to stay calm."

"Did you see that?" Giona said excitedly, ignoring her father's worried voice. "It was right there. I almost touched it."

He could see her smiling face through the mask. He couldn't resist. "Follow me," he said. "Stay close, and move slowly."

A large bull had been swimming lazily around them, clearly comfortable with the tiny creatures who, it knew, posed little threat. When Atticus and Giona swam up next to the forty-five-foot whale, it simply glanced at them and kept moving. A good sign. Atticus moved in closer so that he was swimming directly over the whale's back. He reached down and rubbed his hand against the smooth whale skin, just behind its dorsal fin. Giona followed suit. The whale let out a gentle, bass call. It apparently enjoyed the attention.

"Daddy?"

"Yeah, baby?"

"Thank you."

Before Atticus could respond, the calmness was shattered by a loud shrieking call that hadn't come from this group of whales. Atticus could tell it had come from another pod, not far off. He reacted instantly, pulling up and away from the bull. "Giona! Get away from the whale!" He knew what would happen next.

Flukes pounded water, churning the sea wildly. Atticus could feel the currents swirling all around him, spinning him like a top. The whales had bolted, all of them. The incoming call was a warning. Something had them spooked.

When a second high-pitched cry reached them, Atticus knew that their troubles had just begun. The whales were closing on their position. Something was driving them. Atticus swallowed. He and Giona were in the direct path of a runaway freight train.

8

JEFFREY'S LEDGE—ATLANTIC OCEAN

As Atticus scoured the water in search of charging humpbacks, he fought the urge to ascend with Giona at top speed. They were too deep and would risk decompression sickness, otherwise known as "the bends," if they charged to the surface. It was easily avoided. A simple slow ascent of seventeen feet per minute with a pause fifteen feet below the surface did the trick. The cause was equally simple. During a dive, large amounts of nitrogen are taken into the body because the diver is breathing air at a higher pressure than they would be at the surface. The extra nitrogen in the body poses no threat as long as the diver stays submerged. When the diver heads for the surface and the pressure decreases, the nitrogen is released from the body via the lungs. But if the diver ascends too rapidly, the nitrogen isn't released quick enough, and, like a newly opened bottle of soda, the diver's blood bubbles within the body's tissues. Headache, vertigo, and fatigue are common symptoms, but severe cases lead to unconsciousness—sometimes death.

Decompression sickness was a danger to inexperienced divers or those who panicked during a dive, but to Atticus, avoiding the bends was second nature. And at that moment, his instincts told him to stay put. First, they might not make it in time. Second, they could pass out from the bends before reaching the surface. No, they had to face whatever was coming.

Then he saw them, ten whales, surging through the water at speeds Atticus was unaware the creatures could reach. And they were headed straight for him and Giona.

"Daddy…"

Giona's voice quivered.

"Get ready to hold open your backup regulator. Blow your air tank."

"Now?"

"No. If we blow it too soon, they'll figure out its just air and keep coming. We need to surprise them."

The whales were fifty yards off and closing fast. A huge one, a bull, led the charge.

Thirty…

Twenty…

"Now!"

Twin bursts of bubbles erupted around the pair, concealing their view of the whales. Atticus's only assurance that his plan had worked was that they were still alive. The front whale must have veered off, the others following his lead. Atticus spun around, his suspicion confirmed by the flashes of white fading into the distance—the whales' flukes pounding up and down.

"Daddy!" Giona was yanking his arm, her pulling so hard it actually hurt his shoulder. He spun just in time to see a cloud of silver sparkles flooding toward them. It only took a second for Atticus to identify the small creatures as herring, but the mindless fish wouldn't be repulsed by another blast of air. They were too panicked.

The fish were on them, rushing by, slamming into their bodies like fists. Atticus hadn't felt so abused since hell weak in SEAL training. He struck out at any fish he saw coming, angry and horrified that Giona was enduring the same beating. He could hear her, shouting in pain, shouting for him. But all he could see was an undulating wall of mirrored fish.

"Giona!" He grunted as a herring struck his open gut. "Curl up into a ball! Stay tight!" Then he followed his own advice. He pulled his knees up and wrapped his arms around them, still holding the video camera. His soft spots were protected, and his body was all rounded edges. The fish were glancing off it.

He counted a full fifteen seconds more between that moment and when the last fish struck. He waited a few seconds, just in case, then unfurled like a potato bug. His body ached, but beyond a severe bruising, he would live.

He saw Giona, a hundred feet away, still curled up tight. Good girl.

"Honey…it's all right now. They're gone."

He sighed with relief as she loosened her grip on her knees and uncoiled her body. She was surprisingly unfazed by the ordeal. "Have you ever seen anything like that, Daddy?"

"Herring run all the time, we just got in their way."

"Yeah, but do herring normally chase whales?"

In that instant Atticus knew they weren't out of the woods yet. Something had spooked the whales and the herring. He hoped it was a submarine, or some other man-made disturbance, but his gut told him otherwise. Get out! His mind shouted. Get out now!

"Giona, baby, start your ascent now. Go fast, but not too fast."

"You're coming too?"

He could hear the concern in her voice. She must have realized what he had. Something else was coming. "Right behind you."

He watched as Giona headed for the surface, moving in tight circles, perhaps a little too fast, but not so fast that it would make her sick. They were still fifty feet apart when he felt a queasiness in his stomach. He could feel his hair trying to stand on end beneath the wet suit. He'd experienced a similar feeling once before, when a sniper had a bead on his head. It had saved his life then. He trusted it again.

He swung around and saw only open sea.

He turned back toward Giona and saw a nightmare unleashed upon reality. The shape slid through the water as easily as a comet through space. It looked like some kind of massive, organic roller-coaster ride, undulating up and down through the water. And Giona floated in its path.

The next five seconds were a blur, but seemed to move in agonizing slowness. He managed to shout half her name," Gio—"

A mouth opened. Teeth flashed. Then she was gone, swallowed whole by the huge...fluid...thing. It took everything in one gulp, her body, her air tank, her camera. No trace of his daughter remained.

The apparition that took her swirled deep into the darkness below.

The ocean fell silent.

Giona...his baby...his girl...had been taken from him in a surge of violence.

Alone in the depths, Atticus wailed.

Then, like a man possessed, he surged toward the surface, straight as an arrow, as fast as he could.

9

JEFFREY'S LEDGE—ATLANTIC OCEAN

Atticus exploded from the ocean and onto the stern deck of the *Bugaboo*. He was moving so fast that it appeared that the ocean, his longtime love suddenly turned enemy, had forcefully expelled him. His mask, air tanks, and weight belt fell to the deck in a clump.

His body shook with convulsions, heaving. The world spun around him. His head stabbed with intense, fiery pain. He struggled to his feet, slipping a few times, and headed for the bridge.

Before reaching the door, he vomited, covering the front of his wet suit. He entered the pristine, freezing-cold cabin, without giving any thought to the bile dripping over the shiny floor and smooth leather seats. He switched on the CB as the cabin spun around him. He'd never experienced such vertigo, such confusion.

He choked then held the CB to his mouth. "Oh God," he said, "Someone help. God, please. It took my girl! It took her! So big…Like nothing I've seen before…no record of this thing…God…please, help. Help…"

Atticus felt the cabin move around him. It was alive, closing in, consuming him. He formed the words slowly, deliberately, "Jeffery's Ledge." A moment later he was unconscious on the cabin floor. He vomited again, but was not aware of it. If he had been, he wouldn't have cared. Nothing mattered. Not anymore. Life. Death. The world.

Atticus had become a hollow man in the instant that creature had opened its powerful maw and sucked in his daughter. All that remained of the man was a void, as black and as deadly as the deep sea.

A STERILIZED odor greeted Atticus when he awoke—a hint of apple. Blue light glared from above. Maria was dead.

No.

Giona…

Atticus looked around. He was in a hospital.

After glancing out the window, he realized he was at Portsmouth Regional Hospital. The sliver of blue in the distance reminded him of his daughter's fate and confirmed his location. He had no memory of how he'd arrived or who had brought him. He couldn't remember anything after surfacing from the ocean.

He closed his eyes, not wanting to see the ocean, but even through closed eyelids he saw an open jaw, lined with teeth the size of the orange cones he'd set up for Giona's soccer games when she was little.

"You're awake."

Atticus jumped in bed, throwing off his blanket with a shout. He turned, with clenched fists toward the voice. He came face-to-face with a woman, perhaps five-five, with wavy black hair and dark chocolate brown eyes. She stood silent and still, not at all threatened by his sudden movement or clenched fists.

He breathed deep three times, looking at the woman. She wore a stiffly-pressed uniform. Not a nurse. She stood straight as an arrow, perfect posture. Her face, while soft, was firm and serious. The muscles of her arms rippled when she moved her fingers.

Through his anger he sensed familiarity. Her eyes. Looking at them again, his clouded memory opened up and transported him to a time before he became a Navy SEAL. Andrea Vincent. Every summer his family would travel to northern New Hampshire, where they owned a cabin at a privately run campground. Andrea's family did the same, and for five summers from ages twelve to seventeen, they had been an inseparable duo. They became romantic at sixteen and soon discovered they lived within a half hour drive from each other. When Atticus got his driver's license he began visiting her weekly. Despite college putting a physical distance between them, their relationship stayed strong and talk of marriage crept into their late night conversations. That is, until Atticus made the decision to join the military. It was a distance and strain that no amount of phone calls could correct. There was no dramatic break up, no "I think we should just be friends" moment. They simply lost touch and faded into each other's pasts.

But she stood before him now. A little taller. Stronger. Sporting longer hair and a more angular face. More striking than he remembered. Her uniform was what held his attention, though. She'd been opposed to his joining the Navy. Said he'd lose his soul.

"You joined the military?" he finally asked, doing his best to appear put together and in control. Too much so, he realized, in the face of an old friend he should be hugging.

"Coast Guard," she said. Her face flickered with disappointment. Had she expected a happier reunion? Or did she know about his daughter? "You must be feeling better?"

Atticus hadn't taken stock of his condition. He knew he'd been unconscious, but for how long he had no idea. Dizziness set in, and he sat down on the bed. A nurse entered the room, looking concerned. "Mr. Young, you're awake... Can I—"

"I'm fine," he said, a little too gruff. When the nurse left with a huff, he felt bad for being rude, but Andrea was with the Coast Guard. She might have answers he needed.

Andrea sat in a chair, across from the bed, in front

of the window. She looked out. "Beautiful view."

Atticus looked out the window again. The trees were bright green. A few cumulus clouds drifted past. The ocean glimmered in the distance. "Not anymore."

She turned to him, her face saddened for a moment, but not because of his rudeness. He was all business in spite of their history, and he wanted to cut through the malarkey and talk about why she was really there. "We're still looking for your daughter."

His eyes fell to the floor. "You won't find her."

"Why is that?"

"She's dead."

"It took her?"

Atticus met Andrea's eyes; his glare was full of suspicion. "That's what you're distress call said. It took her." Andrea paused. "What took her?"

"Please tell me you're not turning this into some kind of murder investigation," Atticus said, his voice becoming like stone.

"No...not a chance." She was adamant. "The police said you rescued your daughter from being raped this morning. Really put the fear of God into the men who attacked her."

He nodded.

"No one suspects you of anything. Especially not me."

"Because you know me?"

"It's been nearly twenty years. I don't know you that well." Andrea took a breath, then looked out the window, gazing at the ocean. "What took her?"

Atticus's head slowly moved from side to side as he replayed the blurry images locked forever in his memory. "I don't know."

"A great white, an eighteen-footer, was spotted off Beverly Harbor last week. Could it have been—"

"It wasn't a great white. It wasn't a shark."

"A whale then? Orca? Sperm whale? Perhaps a blue hunting krill scooped her up?"

Atticus's face flushed crimson. "Do you know who I am now? What I do? Did you do any research before coming to see me?"

"Atticus...You are an oceanographer. You do work for independent firms, sometimes for the military. You're an ex–Navy SEAL, highly decorated. You wrote *Ocean's in Peril,* which is a great book, by the way. I knew who you were when I found you choking on your own puke."

Atticus sat silently. He replayed the attack in his mind, slowed it down, took in the details. "It wasn't a shark. It wasn't a whale. I have never seen, nor has anyone else on the planet, seen anything like it."

Andrea sat down next to him. She put her hand on his shoulder, a gentle gesture from a kind woman to a hurting man. "I have," she said.

Atticus slowly craned his head around toward her. His eyebrows rose ever so slightly.

"Yesterday...we were pulling a Frenchwoman out of the water..."

Atticus nodded. He'd seen a thirty-second bit on the news about it. Her husband had been found too—drowned when the boat went down.

"But we saw something. It was huge. And I mean huge. Swam directly beneath the chopper. The Frenchwoman managed to snap a few photos."

Atticus's eyes went wide. "Where are they?"

"Taken. Some boys from the Navy took the camera and flash memory card."

Atticus's shoulders dropped.

"But not before I transferred them to my thumb drive," Andrea added with a slight smirk. She dug in her pocket and held aloft the small USB device. "Two pictures. Both from above. One shows the shadow, just beneath the surface. The other is of the footprint it caused when it dived."

"Must be one hell of a footprint," Atticus said.

"Bigger than I've ever seen."

With a shake of his head, he said, "I had a camera…Giona did too. When it…She still had her camera. Mine was video. Must have dropped it when I surfaced." Atticus cursed himself. He should have held on. He'd been recording everything. He might have got the creature on film. It could have proved useful.

"Speaking of surfacing," Andrea said. "You've got a mild case of the bends. I don't think it's what knocked you out. The doctors say that and the vomiting was shock. You might feel some nausea or headaches—"

"I know the symptoms," Atticus said. "I was trained to deal with them."

"That was a long time ago."

"A SEAL never forgets."

Andrea eyed him with suspicion for the first time. Could she tell he was already plotting?

"Just do me a favor and stay here overnight. The police have a guard outside the door."

"I thought I wasn't a suspect."

"He's not there to keep you in," Andrea said. She jerked a thumb toward the window. "It's to keep them out."

Atticus stood up and looked out the window. A crowd of reporters and news vans, even a few helicopters, all bearing news-station logos, swarmed outside the hospital.

"Your distress call was heard by everyone. You were already front-page news because of the incident this morning. Nice work, by the way. When word about who had placed the distress call spread, a fire was lit under the butts of the media machine. Some reporters actually beat us here. Got some footage of you being taken out of the Jayhawk."

Atticus sighed. He was trapped. The media had to be avoided. He didn't want anyone keeping tabs on him. No one could know what he planned to do…especially Andrea. Being with the Coast Guard, she could ruin everything.

"So you'll stay here then?"

"Looks like I don't have a choice," Atticus replied.

Her hand was on his shoulder again. Her honest eyes almost looked wet. "Atticus, I really am sorry about what happened. If you need my help, ever, for anything, please call me." She handed him a piece of paper. On it was written her address, cell-phone number, and home number. He was taken aback by the earnest tone of her voice and the friendly grip on his shoulder. Could old friends pick up where they'd left off?

"Why?" he asked.

"We share a common bond, Atticus."

"Our past."

"No. My daughter, Abigail…she was killed last year. Hit-and-run. Drunk driver. She was nine."

"I'm…sorry. And your husband?"

"Boyfriend. Left when I got pregnant." Andrea looked into his eyes, burrowing into his consciousness, or was it his conscience? "I understand how you're feeling. I *know* what you want to do. Please, just wait."

She could see right through him. Perhaps it was because she'd lived through a daughter's death herself? It didn't matter. His mind couldn't be changed. He was a missile preparing for launch. Preparing to kill.

Andrea gave his shoulder a squeeze and headed for the door. She paused, her hand on the handle. "Hang in there, Atti." With that, she left.

He stood silent and still for a moment. The only person to ever call him Atti had been Maria. He stifled his rising emotions. They would serve no purpose.

Atticus clenched his fists so tight that his palms burned with pain. The guys who'd attacked Giona that morning had got off easy. Only his responsibility to his daughter had allowed him to refrain from killing them on the spot. Maria and Giona had tempered his violent side, his training. He'd even become a pacifist. Revenge was something he'd been adept at in the past. He had gutted the sniper whose bullet had missed his skull. The drill sergeant who'd pummeled him during basic training had been found five years later, outside a bar, badly beaten, suffering from a broken nose, dislocated shoulder, and several impacted teeth. A man who'd grabbed Maria's butt and moved in for a kiss, found the four fingers on Maria's backside suddenly broken. But the woman he loved and the daughter born to him, who had turned him from a killer to a gentle man who couldn't crush an invasive species, were both gone.

The coldness and hard-heartedness of his past began creeping up on him. He felt a chill run up his back. There was a lot to do. Killing something the size of a jumbo jet was going to be a challenge. But he knew in his heart, the creature didn't stand a chance. Not against *him*.

10

The knife pierced oozing red flesh, then struck bone and fell from the wielder's hand.

"Oh, bloody hell," blurted Trevor Manfred. With stark white hair that flared out like Andy Warhol's and a lanky body clothed in black-leather pants and a dark gray turtleneck, he didn't look like a man whose every need was tended to. But when the sterling silver steak knife had finished rattling on the deck, he made no move to pick it up. Instead, he merely let out a sigh while a servant dressed in a white Armani suit accented with gold cuff links bent down, picked up the knife, and, using a fine violet-silk napkin, wiped down the deck where the knife had fallen. Only moments after the knife had fallen, the glorious sheen of the oak deck had been restored and all traces of the accident erased. Simultaneously, a similarly dressed second servant offered Trevor a new blade, sliding it handle first over his sleeve toward his employer.

Trevor looked at the half-eaten well-marbled T-bone steak, cooked rare, oozing red juices, and lined with thick strips of fat. The steak's accompaniments, deep-fried onion rings and a tall bottle of dark lager, served as a stark contrast to the otherwise opulent surroundings. "Take all but the beer. Next time make it steak tips. The only bones I want to see from now on are in the collection. Understood?"

With a nod, the silent servant made his retreat, taking the tray table, food, and utensils with him. The second servant followed, carrying only the soiled silk napkin and dropped knife. As the two men left the foremost bow deck, Trevor stood from his plush lounge chair and approached the front rail. He grasped it with one hand and downed the beer, chugging it like his chums on the college rugby team used to. The beer emptied, he wound up and sent the bottle sailing over the deck. He watched the brown missile spinning end over end, falling for a quick three seconds until it splashed into the ocean and disappeared, far, far below the forward deck of Trevor's mobile mansion on the ocean.

The *Titan,* five hundred feet long and seventy-five feet wide, was the world's largest megayacht—Trevor's megayacht. Its design was trendsetting, sporting a loggia that stretched over the whole width of the yacht, linking the fully stocked salon with the resplendent dining room. At the stern of the ship was a round room featuring a three-hundred-degree view. A garage that opened to the ocean below held a submersible at the lowest point of the ship. A black Sikorsky VH-3D helicopter (the same helicopter that transported the president of the United States) sat on the helipad at the highest point of the ship, just behind the pool.

Every piece of décor had been purchased, or otherwise obtained, by Trevor and placed specifically where he indicated. Banisters were topped with gold gargoyles or naked women...sometimes both. The pool on the *Titan*'s top deck was shaped like a Chinese dragon, undulating up and down and curving around on itself. The bow, like those of ancient ships of old, was adorned by a beautifully sculpted and scantily clad woman bearing a trident and shield, and wearing a horned helmet. Statues, pilfered from the ancient cultures of many nations, decorated everything from bathrooms to the grand library, which contained thirty thousand books. The centerpiece of the ship was *the collection*. Trevor's pride and joy. Put simply, it was a huge accumulation of art, relics, and natural phenomena over which the Museum of Natural History would salivate. The entire ship, from bow to stern, reflected the taste of a man obsessed with mythology and ancient history. But for Trevor, it wasn't enough to satiate his need to explore the unknown, to experience fresh new ideas or ancient wonders.

The bottle resurfaced and bobbed in the five-foot

swells. Trevor realized that while he was the fifth richest man on the planet, who had all the world's oceans as his playground, he had been reduced to watching a floating bottle as entertainment.

"Bored, sir?" The voice was firm yet subservient, like a pit bull barking at its master.

Trevor didn't turn around. He simply looked across the endless blue expanse stretched out before him. For a brief moment Trevor understood how humanity had once believed the world was flat. From his high perch, it certainly looked as though one could simply fall off the edge of the world. He shrugged and spun to meet Remus, his head of security, who was dressed as though he were on a pleasure cruise—khaki shorts and a Hawaiian shirt. "Bored doesn't begin to do justice to the drudgery that has become my existence…nor to the lack of imagination implicit in your outfit. Good God, man."

Remus smiled, ignoring the jab. "There is always Shanghai, sir."

The thought brought a smile to Trevor's face. The pleasures of Shanghai were always enticing, but Trevor was not in the mood for wine and women. "I crave an adventure, Remus."

"A whale hunt perhaps?"

Trevor looked down to the deck, at a three-foot-wide, six-foot-long rectangular seam. Hidden below the two men was a powerful harpoon gun, containing a razor-sharp, titanium-tipped projectile capable of piercing solid steel. "The end is predictable. No creature in the ocean can outrun the *Titan*."

"Perhaps violence is not the way to satiate your earthly hungers?" A third, more melancholic voice added. The man approached, wearing a broad grin on his young face. He wore the garments of a priest, but walked with the cocksure gait of a movie star. His worldly gray eyes revealed he had been party to more sin than the average priest, and his wrinkled brow showed that he had yet to pass the burden on to God or anyone else.

"Ah, Father O'Shea, to what do we owe the pleasure? Mass isn't until Saturday, and alas, today is but Monday. You absolved me of my past trespasses only two days ago," Trevor said.

Remus snorted. "Come to thump your Bible early, O'Shea?"

"Hardly," he replied.

"You going to reveal the answers to all of life's problems?"

"That would take a long time for you, wouldn't it?" Ignoring Remus's glare, O'Shea approached Trevor. He held aloft a computer printout as though it was a long-sought-after prize. "The answer to your dilemma, Trevor."

Father O'Shea was the only member of the *Titan*'s crew who dared to call Trevor by his first name; and, for reasons unknown to the rest of the crew, he was the only man Trevor would allow to do so.

"The Pope is dead?" Remus quipped with a chuckle.

"Remus…" Trevor's voice contained just a hint of rebuke, causing Remus to clamp his lips shut tight.

"His Holiness is to be respected. He has the ability to clear the taint from a man's soul, a service which you and I benefit from more than most."

"Yes, sir," Remus said.

Trevor took the paper from O'Shea. Placing his black-rimmed oval reading glasses on the tip of his nose, he scanned what appeared to be an article from that morning's online edition of a small newspaper: *The Portsmouth Herald.* He read the headline with widening eyes, then virtually devoured the entire article.

RYE MAN'S DAUGHTER EATEN BY SEA MONSTER

Scuba diving at Jeffrey's Ledge yesterday, Atticus Young and his daughter, Giona Young, both Rye residents, are believed to have been in search of whales. They found tragedy instead. Young's daughter disappeared after what is being called an "animal attack" and is believed to be dead.

Young, 41, ex–Navy SEAL, prominent oceanographer, and author of *Oceans in Peril,* had first been seen earlier in the day after roughing up two men who had attacked his daughter. The men's clothing had been cut to ribbons in an apparent attempt by Young to teach the two a lesson in humiliation. But it was later in the day when horror struck the man who had so well protected his daughter that morning.

At 3:45, a distress call was placed from a boat anchored at Jeffery's Ledge, a shallow portion of the

Gulf of Maine in which whales congregate to feed in the nutrient-rich waters, where Young and his daughter were diving. Here is the transcript of that distress call:

"Oh God. Someone help. God, please. It took my girl! It took her! So big…Like nothing I've seen before…no record of this thing…Someone…please, help. Help…"

The distress call, which was heard by more than one hundred individuals, including the Coast Guard, who later pulled Young from his boat, has set off rumors of a giant sea creature roaming the waters of the Gulf of Maine. Local fishermen…

The article continued for another page, but Trevor knew it was all speculation from that point on. He looked up, his green eyes wide above his low-perched glasses. "Remus, instruct the bridge to take us to New Hampshire. I want to be there before the night is through."

Remus nodded.

"And get me every bit of information available on this Atticus Young of Rye, New Hampshire. I want to know the most intimate details, including his record with the Navy."

A nervous twitch appeared at the corner of Remus's lips. Then, with assurance, he said, "Consider it done," and walked briskly toward the bridge.

Trevor turned to O'Shea and stuck out his hand. O'Shea took his hand and shook it. "You may be a man of God," Trevor said, "and money may be of little use to you, but consider your bonus this year doubled. Even if this turns out to be a hoax, you have cured my sad reverie, if only for a few days, something the rest of this motley crew has rarely done without having to spend my money. How is that possible? Hmm?"

O'Shea smiled and answered the rhetorical question. "God works in mysterious ways."

"Ha!" Trevor belched a laugh and slapped O'Shea hard on the back. "Indeed he does!"

11

PORTSMOUTH HOSPITAL

With the night came a quiet stillness that made it difficult for Atticus to ignore his surroundings. The slight apple scent in the air assaulted his memory. Maria lying in bed. Her last breath. The feeling of his insides shaking with fear as her body convulsed, then lay still. Her room had been nearby…perhaps on the floor above. He wasn't sure, but this was where she had died; this was the last place on earth he wanted to be. In fact, there was only one place he wanted to be at all, and that was on the ocean, hunting that thing down.

He stuck his head out the window and took in the side of the hospital. The brick building rose straight and flat, but around the windows, grooved designs had been created with the brickwork. They'd make nice hand and footholds. Then there was the brick windowsills—only about five inches deep, but wide enough to stand on. Fifteen feet to his left, the hospital wall jutted out to the right for five feet and continued beyond his field of vision. His eyes scanned the outer corner, where a pattern of bricks, protruding two inches each in a staggered formation, ran toward the ground—a sorry excuse for architectural aesthetics but useful for scaling the side of the building. The brick pattern ended five feet above the bushes that rimmed the parking lot.

Atticus figured the bricks didn't run all the way to the ground because some kid might get the idea to climb up the side of the building after seeing *Spiderman*. But the hospital's architect hadn't considered anyone's climbing out a window.

After climbing onto the sill, Atticus crouched in the window, judging the distance to the next sill over. There was one window between him and the brick ladder. He'd have to jump. His heart began to beat faster, his muscles burning with adrenaline. He looked down again at the five-story drop then back to the windowsill. It was a two-foot jump, not very far, but the narrow sill didn't give him a margin for error. If he missed, he'd join his family in death. What that would look or feel like, he had no idea. He'd never considered it, not even after Maria died. But now…where were they? Atticus clenched his jaw, pushing such thoughts out of his mind. He could wrestle with death after he finished with the creature.

With that, he leapt.

He crossed the two-foot divide with ease, planting his left foot, then his right, onto the adjacent sill. He flattened his body against the window glass and caught his breath…then saw his reflection in the window and smiled.

Spiderman indeed.

The room on the other side of the window suddenly filled with light. He saw a shadow moving on the other side. He quickly gazed back and judged the distance to the corner. He could make it. His legs tensed for the jump.

The shades were flung open.

Atticus found himself staring into the eyes of the last person he expected to be in the next room over—Andrea Vincent. Her eyes were wide. At first she appeared terrified, but after gazing into his eyes for a moment, mouthed, "Atticus?"

He'd been caught.

It was during that moment of distraction that Atticus failed to notice the sound of grinding mortar. The brick beneath his right foot gave way and tilted at an angle. The sudden jolt caused Atticus to lose his footing. He fell straight down.

His hands slapped hard against the sill, tingling with pain, but held firm. Atticus was dangling five stories up from a windowsill with a penchant for falling apart. He heard the window above slide open and the sound of a knife tearing through the metal screen but focused on his footing. Using his strong abdominal muscles, Atticus pulled his legs up so that his toes pressed flat against the wall. His fingers strained, digging down into the small space between the sill and the bricks, struggling for purchase.

"Atticus?" The voice was shaky, tinged with fear. "What the hell are you doing?"

He looked up and found Andrea's eyes burrowing into his. Her face was twisted with concern. He just stared up at her, silent.

She must have sensed his legs tensing. "Don't."

Atticus looked back to the corner. It was six feet away, but in his current position, all squished like a spring, the leap shouldn't be a challenge for a six-foot-two man.

"I can help you," Andrea said, sounding desperate.

"The best thing you can do," Atticus said, "is stay out of my way."

Andrea pursed her lips tightly. "Please…"

Then he was airborne, sailing out over the five-story drop like a fearless flying squirrel. And just as a squirrel clings to a tree, Atticus found himself clutching the corner of the hospital. His left hand and foot found holds; then, he swung his body around the corner and found a brick for his other hand and foot. He gave one last look to Andrea, her black hair blowing in the wind, dancing around her worried face.

Then it hit him.

"Why are you here?" he asked, forgetting for the moment that he was hugging the side of a building.

"The room was empty."

"What?"

Andrea paused, her face flushing. She wanted tell

him the truth—that she'd always regretted losing him and that she had never stopped wondering about him, how his life had turned out, if they would ever see each other again. She stared into his eyes, unable to find any words.

Atticus smiled. Andrea had never been short on words, yet here she was, mute. At first he thought she had changed dramatically, become mousey for some reason, but the redness in her cheeks betrayed embarrassment over the unspoken answer, which suddenly struck him as obvious. There she was, hanging out of a window, looking like some damsel in distress, and she was worried for his well-being—a man she hadn't seen in twenty years. Or was it more? Perhaps the Coast Guard simply assigned her to keep an eye on him?

Her eyes continued staring into his, conveying the message her mouth could not form.

This had nothing to do with the Coast Guard.

A gust of wind caused Atticus to tighten his grip. A brief fear of falling took his eyes away from hers, but his grip remained secure. He looked at her again, this time allowing his frown to convey a silent message of his own. *Sorry.*

His hands and feet burst into action, and he began a rapid descent. He glanced up one last time. Andrea was no longer in the window.

He doubled his pace.

Andrea hadn't waited for the elevator, hadn't even pushed the button. She barreled down the staircase, taking two stairs at a time. *What is he thinking? Does he want to get himself killed?*

She entered the lobby in just under forty seconds, a much faster time, she believed, than Atticus could have made his way safely down the side of the building. Of course, she realized the he could have fallen the rest of the way and beat her by a long shot. He could already be dead.

She blew past the bewildered receptionist and burst out of the air-conditioned hospital and into the summer humidity that smelled of seawater and roses. She turned left and kept running without missing a beat. She looked up, spotted the two open windows, and headed toward them.

Her eyes followed her room to the small corner down which Atticus had climbed. She searched the corner up and down, but the silhouette of a climbing man eluded her. Before she reached the bottom, her view was blocked by a tall line of lilac bushes. She continued forward, but moved out and away from the hospital, increasing her angle of sight.

For the briefest moment she thought she saw a shape clinging to the lowest portion of the corner, but then it was gone. She nearly shouted his name, but, knowing she'd alert the media, held her tongue and quickened her pace.

She reached the corner, panting. No one was there.

A black cargo van sat five feet away. The lights were off, the engine silent. Most likely a news van, but she saw nowhere else he could have hidden. She

doubted he could have arranged a pickup…they'd
have sped away if that were the case. But still…

Approaching the van slowly, she reached out and
took hold of the back-door handle. She depressed the
button and gave it a yank. Locked. She made her way
around and checked the other handles. All locked. She
rested her hand on the hood of the van. The night air
was warmer. The van had been there for some time.

She gave one last look around. He'd vanished like
an apparition.

No, she thought, *like a SEAL.*

12

PORTSMOUTH HOSPITAL

Atticus watched Andrea approach the van.

Just moments before, he'd fallen the remaining ten feet to the ground, rolled, and listened. He immediately heard her running feet and heavy breathing. He was in no mood for an argument but also saw there was nowhere to go. Then he felt a hand wrap around his mouth and an arm around his waist. They were strong, and he found himself pulled up and into a cargo van. The well-oiled door slid shut without a noise.

He heard Andrea check the back door and move around to check the others.

If it hadn't been for Andrea's approach, he would have quickly broken the hand of his captor, but he couldn't afford to involve her. Whoever was in the van with him obviously had no interest in Andrea. They could have easily taken her as well. As Andrea began walking away, still searching the parking lot with her eyes, Atticus felt the hand around his mouth loosen its formidable grip.

"If you're reporters," Atticus said seriously, "this is going to hurt."

Before Atticus could let loose, the interior light flicked on.

"Now, now, Dr. Young, you wouldn't hit a priest, would you?" said a smiling man dressed as a Catholic priest. He was young, in his twenties, and appeared to be as friendly as possible under the circumstances.

The man next to him looked like a giant with bad taste—his Hawaiian shirt as ugly as his face. The man's ears were misshapen, probably from years of brawling, as was his nose, bent slightly to one side. But the sight of the man didn't intimidate Atticus. He'd been in many fights with men determined to kill him, and *his* face remained untouched. No one had ever made contact. Being in a tightly enclosed van gave the larger man the advantage, but Atticus needed only one shot to take down most men. Still, better to take no chances.

He readied himself for a fight, but it never came. The priest moved forward, still smiling, hand extended.

Atticus didn't take it. "You've got thirty seconds." He didn't have to add a threat. His eyes did that for him.

The man in the awful shirt snickered. Atticus shot

him a look that said, "You'll get yours."

The man's smirk faded ever so slightly.

"Dr. Young," the priest said, "I am Father O'Shea." He motioned to the other man. "This is my associate, Remus. We've been sent to retrieve you by our employer."

Atticus didn't say a word. He didn't even acknowledge that he'd heard anything.

"He's very eager to meet you." The priest grew nervous. "He wants to help you."

"Help with what?" Atticus's voice boomed like lion's bellow. "Bury my daughter? Psychoanalyze me? Put me on *The Today Show* and get my teary story?"

O'Shea backed off a little, "No, nothing like that. He wants to help you kill it. He wants to find the beast…and he wants you to kill it."

Atticus sized the men up. They were clearly not military. The Remus character might have been at one time, but it must have been a while. He couldn't conceive of a reason they might be lying, but he wondered how anyone could possibly help him kill such a thing. "What's his name?"

"He would prefer to remain anonymous."

"His name or I walk." Atticus moved toward the door.

"Trevor Manfred."

The odd name struck Atticus as familiar. Where had he heard it before?

"He's the fifth richest man in the world," Remus added proudly.

Then Atticus remembered. He'd read an article in

Time a few years back. The man was a recluse, living on the ocean in some kind of super-yacht. While being well-known for funding scientific expeditions as well, Manfred's track record for success was sketchy. Few artifacts were ever recovered and very few scientific discoveries had been made. Most believed that the man kept most of the finds to himself and, as a result, he was unwelcome on the shores of many nations. But, if he could help...

"You know where I live?"

The men nodded. He knew they would.

"Take me home."

13

Leaving the van and two strangers at the street, Atticus moved, like the living dead, toward his home. Every step Atticus took felt like a conglomeration of old and new wounds, opening and festering together, making him ill. He hadn't made it past the slate walkway, when he felt he couldn't continue. Just the sight of the white Victorian home with its navy blue shutters had knocked the wind out of him. What would he be able to endure once inside? The photos. The smells. The memories would assault him worse than any weapon mankind had yet to devise. Standing before his house, Atticus knew that a torture worse than any faced on the battlefield awaited him inside.

Then he stepped forward. He'd been trained to

enter hell and come back out.

The front steps creaked underfoot as they always did.

The first memory hit. Giona had learned to read on those steps when she was three, long before her classmates. She had astounded them as she suddenly read *Goodnight Moon* to them on the steps. She was reading *James and the Giant Peach* by five and never slowed down.

It had only been a day since he'd been home, but after opening the front door and entering, he felt he'd walked into an alien world. Nothing seemed right: the arrangement of shoes and sneakers, two different sizes lining the front hall; the dirty pans in the kitchen; the Sudoku puzzles spread out on the coffee table. He and Giona might not have had the best relationship over the last two years, but they worked on the Sudoku puzzles separately, trying to outdo each other. It was a silent game, a competition between father and daughter that bridged the gap.

And then there were the pictures.

He'd grown used to seeing pictures of Maria around the house. He'd never taken them down, feeling it was totally inappropriate to try to forget her. Love was love. You couldn't erase it, mask it, or forget it. So why try?

You could, Atticus thought, *avenge love lost...love stolen.*

He paused at the pictures; each one brought with it an emotional rush that felt like an extreme allergic reaction, building pressure deep in his skull, between his eyes. He scanned each memory, each adventure, traveling back in time to Giona's birth, his wedding to Maria. Last on the wall was a photo of his entire family, including his parents and his brother.

Oddly enough, it was those pictures, images of the still living that hit him the hardest. He hadn't called them yet. It crossed his mind that they had no idea Giona was gone; they would still be planning to see him and Giona in two days.

He dialed the number slowly, his hand shaking.

"Hello?" It was a slight voice with a kind tone.

"M-om?" Atticus's voice cracked, and it's all he needed to say.

"Oh, baby. I'm so sorry." She was crying on the other end. "We saw it on the news; I can't imagine. Oh, baby…"

Atticus looked at his answering machine. Sixteen messages. They'd been trying to reach him. "Sorry I didn't call sooner."

"Sweetie, don't you worry about that." She had begun sniffing, obviously congested from crying. "Conner is on his way there; should be there any time."

Atticus took a deep breath and held it. He would have liked nothing more than to see his brother. Few people on the planet understood him, thought like him, but there wasn't time to waste, and the two people waiting for him outside didn't want to draw too much attention to themselves, or their employer. "I won't be here," he said.

"Why…why not?"

"I have…things to do." He couldn't think of any other way to say it. He certainly couldn't tell his mother that he was going to risk his life—risk putting her through more of what she was already experiencing. "I'll leave the door unlocked. He can hold down the fort while I'm gone." His mind raced to change the subject. "Is Dad there?"

There was a pause on the other end. He held his breath.

"When the news came on…and we heard your name…and we saw you on the stretcher…he was near hysterical, shouting and ranting. Then they said Giona was… he passed out. He's at the hospital now for observation. They're worried about his heart. But he's fine. Made me come home in case you called, and it's a good thing he did."

Atticus's mind swirled with emotion. Concern for his father and mother and the desire to see them waged war with his thirst for vengeance. In the end, it was the image of Giona's being swallowed that forced his hand. "I have to go, Mom."

She sighed. "All right…and, baby?"

"Yeah, Mom…"

"When you find the thing, put an extra bullet in it for me."

Atticus couldn't help but smile. His mother was a fighter. She'd always been, and most people who knew the family well believed that if women could have been Navy SEALs, she'd have been Atticus's drill commander. "You know me too well."

"Don't tell your father I said that."

"Do me a favor and call for me. I'm out of time."

"Of course. I love you."

"You too."

Atticus hung up the phone, feeling some of his burden lifted. Having his actions supported, especially by a person he cared about, made all of the indecisiveness wracking his mind, disappear. His resolve returned, and with it, action.

He made his way up the stairs, heading straight for his bedroom. He entered the room and felt nothing. It was the one room he'd redone after Maria died. Her picture was still there, but the décor was much more masculine, and the hints of Maria, her perfumes, her clothes, her jewelry, had all been removed. He hadn't slept until they were.

He quickly dressed in blue jeans and a formfitting navy blue T-shirt. He pocketed his reflective sunglasses and keys and slipped on his sneakers.

He moved to the closet next. It was filled entirely with men's clothing. There wasn't a hint of the fact that he'd shared the closet with a woman just two years ago. He reached up for a duffel bag on the top shelf and pulled it down. He opened the bag and double-checked the equipment he knew was there. Black Special Ops uniforms, a grappling hook and rope, night-vision goggles, flares, SEAL Pup dive knife, black concealment makeup and a high-tech diving suit that put his everyday one to shame. He didn't know what he'd need, so he left everything as it was and took it all.

Next, he knelt inside the closet and slid the hanging clothes aside. He punched the wall in two spots, loosening a panel. He pulled it free and moved it aside. Inside the alcove were two padlocked cases. He pulled both out and unlocked them with a key on his key chain. He opened the smaller of the two and pulled out a Smith & Wesson Model 60 .357 Magnum. Its rust-resistant stainless-steel body made it perfect for water-bound missions.

Otherwise known as pocket artillery, the six-round revolver would drop an assailant with a single shot to any part of the body—guaranteed. While many younger SEALs were adopting the SIG SAUER 9226, a fifteen-round, compact handgun, as their weapon of choice, SEALs with experience knew a .357 could not be beat. After attaching the .357's holster to his belt, he loaded six rounds and slid the weapon home. Its weight on his hip made him feel a little more secure. He tossed a box of rounds in the open duffel bag.

He opened the second case to reveal a Heckler & Koch MP5, a sinister-looking compact submachine gun capable of firing 9mm projectiles at eight hundred rounds per minute. It could fire single shots; three-shot bursts, or unleash hell on full automatic. It was light, easy to conceal, and ideal for close quarters combat. He checked the six magazines, making sure they were full, and closed the case, putting the whole thing in the bag.

After adding a few changes of clothing, Atticus had everything he could think to take. He had no idea if the weapons would do any good against the creature

he'd seen; 9mm rounds might simply feel like pin-
pricks to the beast. But he was heading into unknown
waters with men he didn't trust. It never hurt to have
backup...just in case. He slung the bag over his
shoulder and left the room—ready for war.

But he was not prepared for her room. He glanced
into Giona's room, papered from floor to ceiling with
posters of bands and a large periodic table. She had
been a melding of two worlds, so opposite; but in her,
they merged in perfect harmony. He missed her purple hair...or blue...or whatever color it might have
been next week. He dropped the bag and entered the
room.

The smell of orange and patchouli was
strong...her favorite scent. Her black clothes were
draped over the bed, the dresser, still a mess, but not
chaotic. Her desk was covered in summer reading:
textbooks and scientific journals. At the top of the pile
he saw a familiar cover and title: *Oceans in Peril* by
Dr. Atticus Young. He didn't remember giving her a
copy. It had been published five years ago, long before
her interest in science emerged. He opened the book
and was surprised to see it highlighted throughout
with little notes gracing the margins, including one
that said, "Dad is so smart!"

Atticus could feel the emotions swelling. If he
broke down it would be permanent. He could feel it.
He was about to crack. He took a deep breath, held it
and let it out slowly, remembering how he would
calm his mind before a firefight.

As his body relaxed, the rising sun streaming

through the bedroom window drew his eyes. But it was the aberration approaching beneath the sun that held his attention. His ride was coming. Chopping through the air toward the house was a massive black helicopter. O'Shea and Remus hadn't said anything about a helicopter, but he knew it was for them. Only a very rich man could afford such a thing.

Two minutes later, Atticus left the ground in the helicopter, looking down at his house, wondering if he'd ever see it again. Then he saw her, standing in his driveway. Andrea was there, hands on hips, watching him fly away. She'd just missed him again. He wondered why she still cared at all, after so much time, but for a moment he was just glad that she did.

ANDREA CURSED so loudly she was sure that the noise would have rattled Atticus's neighbors had the sound of the helicopter not done so already. She had missed him by seconds, pulling her blue Volvo into his driveway as the unmarked, spectacularly large helicopter lifted off from his near-acre-sized backyard.

If she hadn't had to stop five times to ask directions after getting his address out of the phone book, she would have arrived in time. She would have tried to stop him, of course, but if she couldn't have, she would have gone with him.

She couldn't forget the eight years they spent together. She'd always wondered what life would have been like if they hadn't grown apart. Marriage seemed likely. Kids, too. She'd never really stopped loving him, just held different values, different goals. They both did, and being stubborn, neither had given them up for the other. When she'd looked into his eyes at the hospital, the long-buried feelings reemerged and twisted her stomach into knots. Could feelings that old be rekindled? She had no idea. What she did know was that Atticus had been her friend once. One of her closest. The bond forged from childhood to young adult still remained.

And, serendipity, or fate, had brought them back together. She wouldn't abandon him again, not when he needed help the most. She wanted to give him that much, even if it meant setting aside her personal goals for a time. She realized now, far too late, that it's what one of them should have done so long ago.

She watched the helicopter fly out to sea and knew she'd find him. The ocean was her territory, and she had resources to track him down. For starters, anyone out there with a ship big enough to accommodate such a gigantic chopper wouldn't be too hard to locate.

When she could no longer see the helicopter, she headed to the front door and found it unlocked. If she was going to understand who Atticus had become and what he might be thinking, she had to do some digging first. They'd been comfortable entering each other's homes before, even shared keys with each other, but she couldn't help wondering what might happen if someone found her in his house. Breaking and entering wouldn't look good for a Coast Guard captain. But it was a risk she was willing to take.

She entered the house and closed the door behind her, not fully prepared for what she'd find.

14

Atticus looked down at the ocean, seventy-five feet below. The shadow of the Sikorsky VH-3D helicopter rose and fell with the waves…waves that concealed a great creature, which he was sure could pluck them out of the air even then. He'd been part of several airborne insertions in his SEAL days, but none felt nearly as dangerous as the particular mission he found himself on the verge of undertaking. None had held as much personal meaning either.

The two men seated across from him, O'Shea the priest and Remus the thug, did little to ease his nerves. They were a dichotomy. The priest clearly had brains, but lacked any kind of physical prowess that might suggest he was accustomed to action. He was a priest, after all…but not every priest was a stick-in-the-mud. Then there was Remus. He was a brooding man, whose chiseled smile appeared more like a jackal's snarl than an honest man's grin. His pockmarked face didn't help his grim appearance, and the jagged scar across his forehead was simply a nightcap after drinking in his ugly mug. The bright-colored Hawaiian shirt he wore seemed like a pitiful attempt to pull attention away from his face, but his nonstop chatter about the fiftieth state to join the union revealed a true passion for the culture there.

"Why the obsession with Hawaii?" O'Shea asked, interrupting Remus's mini-lecture about how slow-moving lava fields destroy houses, roads, and crops. "Isn't it just becoming a tourist trap? I read that the scads of new million-dollar homes were raising taxes and that the high-paying jobs were being given to mainland Americans, pushing native Hawaiians and their culture to the mainland. It won't be a paradise much longer."

Remus glared at O'Shea. *These two are not friends,* Atticus thought. He tucked the observation into a pocket of his mind and listened as Remus gave the answer. "*Ua mau ke ea o ka aina i ka pono.*"

Both O'Shea and Atticus looked at him queerly. He heaved a sigh that was supposed to demean the other two men and make them feel like fools for not knowing what the saying meant.

"The life of the land is perpetuated in righteousness," Remus said. "When land is holy, its essence cannot be destroyed."

Obviously, the man had not been to Jerusalem, Atticus thought. While it was still an impressive place, the city's holy sites were a far cry from what they had once been. He and Maria had gone on a tour of the Holy Land before Giona had been born. It was Maria's idea, and was fascinating, but the state of the region's holy sites had made Atticus realize that history had taken its toll on the land. But he felt that the people there, both Jew and Muslim, had deep convictions that found meaning in the very soil of the place. Thoughts of the night he and Maria had spent in Jerusalem began creeping into his mind. Giona had been conceived there.

"Sounds like a state motto," O'Shea said with a smirk.

Remus didn't hear the sarcasm and smiled proudly. "It is!"

Atticus clung to the conversation, joining it to avoid fond memories. They'd do him no good under the circumstances. "I did some work in Hawaii once," Atticus said, the first words he'd spoken since the helicopter had left his home… "Tagging humpbacks. To track their migration and numbers."

Remus nodded, smiling. "The state animal."

Atticus wondered if Remus had simply memorized the encyclopedia entry for Hawaii, just to make people believe he knew what he was talking about.

"What did you think?" Remus asked.

Atticus knew to the core of his being that he should befriend the man. Remus was dangerous and untrustworthy. Getting on his good side could only help. There were a number of answers to the question, any of which would have done the trick. Atticus was surprised by his quick answer. "Overrated."

It was an honest answer, but the effect was profound. Remus frowned, squinted his eyes the way seventh-grade girls do when they are teased.

The priest was smiling ear to ear. "A man of few words speaks the truth powerfully."

At least he'd made one friend, though he doubted a priest would be useful...unless he could pull him back out of hell...because that's where they were headed—and a confrontation with the devil. Only hell wasn't beneath the earth, brewing with boiling magma. It was found beneath the seas, cold and remorseless.

The helicopter fell silent again, except for the *whup whup whup* of its long rotor blades. After ten blessedly quiet minutes, Remus ended the reprieve with a strained, "We're here."

Atticus looked out the window and took in a ship the likes of which he had never seen in all his years at sea or in the Navy. It was massive, the size of a U.S. destroyer, and gleamed bright white in the morning sun. The pool on the top deck appeared to be shaped like a Chinese dragon. A hardwood carved masthead of a beautiful, but thoroughly dangerous-looking Viking woman graced the bow. The decks were staggered up from the main deck, each oval and lined with tinted glass. Atop the bridge, a mass of antennae and satellite dishes rose toward the sky. It was a ship obviously designed to stay at sea for long stretches...if not indefinitely.

The helicopter set down gently. "Follow me," Remus said as he opened the side door.

To Atticus's surprise, no one asked him to relinquish the sidearm still hanging on his hip, though two servants, dressed to the nines, asked to carry his duffel bag to his room for him. He declined the offer, preferring to keep his belongings, not to mention his arsenal, close by. Once on board, O'Shea went his separate way, while Remus took the lead, taking him through one hallway after the next. But they weren't headed to the upper decks, where he'd assumed most billionaires would prefer to be; instead they were headed down. They descended three flights of stairs, all carpeted in maroon and lined with ivory supporting posts and gold banisters. The smell of the boat was pleasant, clean but not sanitized like the hospital. At the base flight were long hallways, all decorated with expertly carved statues of marble, rough stone, and wood--all originating from a variety of cultures. The fourth floor down brought with it an extended staircase that revealed the floor's cathedral ceilings...on a boat. Atticus was impressed by the engineering and beauty of it all, though it did little to calm his nerves. His reason for being there was still ominous.

At the base of the stairs, where they flared out onto a marble floor, Atticus was greeted by an amazing sight. Positioned at the center of a large atrium was a full-size rendition of a statue on Easter Island. He had never been to the island, but there were few people in the modern world that wouldn't recognize the megaliths. "That's an amazing replica," Atticus said, more to himself than to Remus.

But the man snickered anyway. "It's real."

Atticus placed his hand against the statue and felt its cold surface, as bleak as the once-lush island that had been its home. To obtain such a magnificent artifact meant that Trevor Manfred was either extremely well connected or extremely cunning. Either way, he'd soon find out.

Remus opened a door engraved with the words, sitting room. It sounded innocent enough, but when Atticus stepped through, he entered another world.

"You're on your own now," Remus said. "Try not to say anything stupid. *Aloha.*"

With that, Remus closed the door, leaving Atticus alone in the room. Atticus knew Remus's final word was a warning. *Aloha. Don't mock Trevor Manfred like you did me.*

Atticus took in the fifty-foot, rounded room. An amazingly realistic underwater mural covered the vaulted ceiling; the realism of the artwork was astounding. The walls were similarly painted, featuring whales, sharks, seals, and assorted other creatures. Atticus felt at home in the room, though unnerved to be standing, rather than swimming. The floor was an illusion as well, painted dark blue, just as the depths looked from above. The only break to the illusion was the presence of two elegant chairs—thrones really—rimmed with gold and cushioned by red velvet, and a gold-legged, glass-topped coffee table.

"Come in," came a loud, cheerful voice from across the room. "You're just in time for tea."

Atticus could see a hand waggling him over to the chairs. After placing his duffel bag on the floor, Atticus made his way over. The man sitting there was not what he'd expected. His eyes gleamed with excitement. His hair sprang up, white and wild in a way that Giona would have loved. His clothing was all black, his skin nearly as white as his hair, though clearly not albino. His eyes shown bright green and alive. "Dr. Young, welcome to the *Titan*."

Atticus decided in that moment that he liked the eccentric man who sat in the deep-sea illusion, surrounded by ancient artifacts and mysteries from around the world. *A riddle wrapped in a mystery inside an enigma*, Atticus thought, remembering Churchill's description of World War II's Russia. He was instantly as interested in this man as Churchill had been with Russia's role in the war. But Atticus felt that the diminutive man posed far less threat than Stalin's gulags and certainly much less than Remus would have had him believe.

As Atticus opened his mouth to speak, the corner of his eye caught movement. The wall…the outer hull to his left, was not a painting at all! And something very large was swimming just outside, watching them.

15

RYE, NEW HAMPSHIRE

The photo held memories of a happier time for a now-broken family. Atticus sat in the sand, building a sand castle with a little girl Andrea could only assume was his dead daughter, Giona. His hands intertwined with those of the girl, who looked to be about seven, drizzled wet sand on the castle walls. The dripping sand created small structures that looked more like miniature versions of the stone spires that decorate the desert of Moab. But beyond the obvious sand-castling skills, it was the woman to Atticus's side who held Andrea's attention.

Her hair had been caught by the wind and partially covered her and Atticus's faces. Her eyes were bright, full of life, and her full, puckered lips were kissing Atticus on the cheek. The photo embodied everything Andrea always felt a family should be. In the moment the camera's iris opened, collected, and recorded the light, it captured an image that Norman Rockwell would have been proud to produce. There was one large discrepancy between Rockwell's paintings and the photo—the latter pictured reality. A family in love, once hale, but since wrecked by time.

Andrea had never met his wife or daughter, but knowing that everything in this image had been taken from Atticus struck a chord in her heart. To love so deeply and have it taken away in two devastating instants could destroy a man...or woman. She knew that from experience.

Giving little thought to the act, Andrea removed the framed photo from the hallway wall and took it to the kitchen. She opened the frame and removed the four-by-six picture. She flipped it over and read the back.

2001, old orchard beach, Atti, Maria, and Gi Gi.

The handwriting was beautiful and feminine—a reminder of the woman whose loving face graced the front of the picture. She looked at the photo again, and rather than feeling envious or even jealous of the woman whose lips were pressed against the cheek of the man who'd been her first real love, she was filled with a sense of kinship...of responsibility.

She imagined Maria's voice, urging her, *Take care of him*. But would she mind? Had he ever told Maria about their young love? About his broken heart...if that was what he'd experienced at all? There was no way to be sure, but the woman in the photo would most certainly appreciate *someone* looking out for her husband. "I'll take care of him."

"Funny," a friendly yet masculine voice said, "I thought that would be my job."

Andrea turned quickly to the voice. A man whose eyes were Atticus's yet whose pudgy body revealed a life more adapted to sitting behind a computer rather than that of a former Navy SEAL, stood in the doorway. His brother, older and rounder perhaps, but she still recognized him.

"Been a long time, Andrea," he said.

"Hello, Conner."

He smiled, stepping into the kitchen, and shook her hand. "So, Coast Guard, huh? Isn't this a little out of your jurisdiction?" He motioned to the empty frame on the table but didn't let her respond.

"He never did stop pining for you, you know." He sat down next to her and pointed at the photo still in her hand. "Not until he met her, anyway. And that was after he left the Navy. I always wondered if he'd try to find you again after Maria passed; looks like he did. How long has he been keeping you a secret from us?"

Andrea's stare was a mix of confusion and guilt.

Conner's eyebrows rose high. "You're not together, are you?"

"No," she replied. "Is he with...someone?"

"No, no. Not that I know of anyway. I thought he

might be holding out on me, but if you're not his girlfriend, then he's been telling the truth. Not that he doesn't need one; mind you…the job's open if you want it."

Andrea smiled.

Conner's eyes returned to the photo in her hands. His lips suddenly turned down, his voice grew cold. "I was behind the camera in that picture. I'm no photographer, but that's the best shot I ever took. I have the same one hanging on my wall at home. There's just something about it. He had everything, you know?" Conner sighed. "I have a family. I love my wife. My kids are great. But that"—he pointed at the photo—"is something I've never experienced."

Andrea felt a twinge of guilt take root in her gut. She handed the picture to Conner. "I was going to give it to him when I found him."

In that instant, Conner seemed to forget about the photo. "He's not here?"

"No."

"Where is he?"

Andrea wasn't sure how to respond. She had just returned to Atticus's life and wasn't even sure if she was welcome. She didn't know how he'd feel about her divulging what she knew—what she suspected, but this *was* his brother. Her memories of Conner included a lot of teasing and arguing. But they were brothers…and Conner had come to Atticus's aid. Before she could utter a syllable, Conner spoke up.

"He went after it," Conner said. "Damn it."

It wasn't a question. He simply knew, just like

that, just as she had.

"How did you know?"

He shook his head. "It's always been a weird thing with Atticus. People who love him can read him like a book."

Andrea remembered the hospital. She'd had the same feeling. She had known he intended to go after the creature.

"I don't know the details yet," she added, "but I'm going to try tracking him down. He was picked up this morning by a helicopter. They headed out to sea."

"The man moves fast. Was it Navy?"

Andrea shook her head. "No, but I'll find out who owns it."

"You'll bring him back?"

"If I can."

Conner handed the picture back. "Give this to him when you find him."

"I will," she said as she stood, suddenly more resolute about finding him right away. "Will you be here?"

Conner smiled again, forcing back his good nature. "I've nowhere else to go."

Andrea smiled and headed for the door. Conner stopped her with his voice.

"You know...it's a rare woman who will drop everything and search the high seas for an old friend. Even if it is her job."

Andrea's face heated as her embarrassment grew.

"Your picture was in the paper and on the news,"

he said, with a knowing smile. "Thanks for going to his rescue. Thanks for going now. "

Andrea nodded, surprised by the kindness in Conner's voice. He knew who she was—an old friend, almost something more, but really just a woman who by chance was on the job when his brother needed help. Any number of people could have got to him first. She might have had a cold, and it would have been someone else giving him mouth to mouth after he'd thrown up while unconscious and choked on his own bile. She knew Atticus had no idea she'd resuscitated him, that he'd been dead, if only for a moment. She wondered if he might even resent being brought back. His brother had no idea either, yet there he was, acting as though she were…

"Andrea," he added, interrupting her thoughts, "welcome back to the family."

With those few words, Andrea's thoughts cleared. For eight years she'd spent every waking moment with Atticus, and many of them with his family as well. They'd eaten, played, laughed, and adventured together. Inseparable. Kindred. Family. Those memories formed the bond that motivated her now, regardless of their broken past or feelings about what might have been. They were family. And that was enough.

16

GULF OF MAINE—ABOARD THE TITAN

Serrated teeth tore through flesh, rending sinew and vessel, crushing bones and doing a precise job at what they were designed to do—kill.

Atticus watched in amazement as white membranes slid over the obsidian eyes of the great white shark tearing into a tuna. He'd seen great whites feeding, as well as many other sharks, but never…*never* in the Gulf of Maine, nor a shark so enormous.

"It's at least thirty feet long!" Atticus stood at what he now knew was a pane of glass looking out at the undersea world below the waterline.

"Twenty-eight, actually," replied Trevor, who was now standing beside Atticus, watching the shark.

"You're feeding it?" Atticus had seen the live tuna

fall into the water, dazed and tired. It hadn't stood a chance against the ocean's greatest predator. *Second greatest predator*, Atticus reminded himself.

"Indeed. The little beastie is something of a pet, really." Trevor placed his hand against the glass as the great white tore the fish in half and gulped it down. "Good girl, Laurel."

"Laurel?"

Trevor smiled. "Named after a flower actually. Sheep laurel, a nasty little flower also known as Lambkill. It's extremely poisonous and kills scores of sheep to be sure, and should a human ingest the flower, or worse, honey made from the flower, it is quite deadly. We're lambs to the slaughter when it comes to Laurel," he finished with a snicker.

Atticus watched as the massive shark polished off the tuna. He nodded. "A fitting name. But how is this possible…and why?"

"We spotted Laurel five years ago, in deep Pacific waters. She was quite big, even then, and for our amusement, we fed her. Her appetite was, as you've seen, voracious, and she followed us. We've been feeding her ever since."

"But why would you want…"

"Protection, good doctor. This boat contains a wealth greater than that of many nations, and there are many who would love nothing more than to pilfer what is mine. Laurel does a nice job of stopping anyone who might attempt an underwater insertion."

"I would imagine so," Atticus said, picturing how he would feel encountering this giant underwater.

"Does it work?"

Trevor smiled wide. "There have been a few times when she refused her breakfast. I can only assume she had her fill the night before. I cannot say whether she ate some poor fellow or not, but she has grown accustomed to her slow-moving meals. She never gives chase to healthy fish. If it moves fast, she won't bother."

Atticus made a mental note to not fall overboard, then turned his attention to Trevor. "What interest does the fifth richest man in the world have with a marine biologist?"

"I thought that would be very clear, Dr. Young."

"Atticus will do."

"Very well," Trevor motioned to the chairs. "Please, sit." They sat in the chairs, which were very comfortable. Atticus felt his body sink in, and, for the first time in days, his muscles relaxed. There was something about the room, being underwater yet not, that filled him with wonder while allowing him to lower his defenses.

On the coffee table, Atticus smiled upon finding two Sam Adams resting in a silver wine cooler, packed in ice. Based on Trevor's invitation to tea, his thick British accent, and his almost feminine hand gestures, he expected to see a set of bone china with Earl Grey and crumpets.

Trevor read his expression. "I may be a Brit, but American cuisine tickles my fancy. Please, help yourself."

Atticus pulled a bottle from the ice and popped

the top with his teeth.

"Oh ho!" Trevor clapped. "A real man's man!" He then produced a bottle opener from his pocket. "A much more civilized approach, don't you think?" Trevor took the second beer, popped the top with a grunt, and drank greedily from the bottle.

Atticus wondered how such a diminutive man could drink like a college frat boy. Trevor was a living monochrome, black and white, day and night. Further study of the man would have to wait. There were more important issues at hand. "You were about to tell me why I'm here?"

Trevor placed the now-empty beer on the coffee table and sighed. "Ah yes." He crossed his legs and placed his hands delicately on his knee. "Well, quite frankly, I'm bored."

Atticus raised an eyebrow.

"Not right now, mind you. I meant to say I *was* bored, until I heard about your predicament. ...In no way do I mean to overlook your tragic loss, but this creature has stirred feelings in me I have not felt since I first laid eyes on the ocean as a child. I want to find the creature, Dr. Young. I want to find it and kill it."

"Why kill it?"

"Well, you obviously have your reasons...but mine, I'm afraid, are much more selfish. Please, come with me." Trevor stood with a grin. "To fully appreciate my goals, it would be best for you to see the collection."

Atticus polished off the beer, retrieved his duffel bag, and followed Trevor to the door. He was led past the Easter Island sculpture and down a long hallway. The hallway, which wound in a wide arc, had doors along the right side, but the left was blank. Trevor led the way, humming joyfully to himself. Then the hall widened and opened into a grand foyer. Double staircases led down from the deck above and ended at three sculptures of hauntingly beautiful women. In every way the women were perfect, clothed only in formfitting robes. Their upper torsos displayed firm-looking breasts. Their slightly agape mouths showed full lips and supported high cheekbones. But their hair...snakes, coiled and twisting. And below the waist, where there should have been long, sumptuous legs, tightly coiled serpentine bodies reached the floor. "Medusa," Atticus whispered.

"Only one of them," Trevor said as he unlocked a pair of double doors with a skeleton key. *Another oddity,* Atticus noted. Most of the security on the ship thus far had been top-of-the-line stuff—voice, retina, and fingerprint-activated. Yet here, in the man's most prized room, the contents were protected by a simple skeleton key. "The other two are named Stheno and Euryale; quite attractive really. They guard the collection."

With fervor, Trevor pushed the two doors open, revealing a massive room beyond. It stretched for one hundred feet in either direction and stood four stories tall. But it wasn't the size of the room that was most impressive. It was the absolute beauty of what it contained.

Atticus entered with wide eyes, taking in every

morsel. Hanging on the walls were paintings he recognized from Monet, van Gogh, Rembrandt, da Vinci, and Picasso—famous paintings—the sort that hung in the Louvre, yet there they were, displayed as though they were the real thing. Again, Trevor seemed to read his thoughts, though Atticus imagined that everyone who saw the collection thought the same thing.

"They're all real, I assure you," Trevor said.

Atticus stood in front of da Vinci's *The Last Supper,* beautiful in every way, even more impressive than the version the world adored. Atticus felt dwarfed by the fifteen-by-twenty-nine-foot painting. "The other is a fake?"

"Oh no," Trevor said, clearly tickled to be able to explain, "They're both quite real. But the one displayed at convent of Santa Maria delle Grazie is merely a practice run for the real thing…a very detailed practice run, mind you, but not the final product. Da Vinci would have known that tempera on gesso, pitch, and mastic wouldn't last. This final version is oil on canvas, a much more durable…and vibrant medium. Don't you think?"

Atticus nodded, his jaw slightly slack. He'd seen photos of *The Last Supper* and had never been that impressed, but this…this was a true masterpiece. He turned his attention toward the rest of the room. There were statues—Roman and Greek gods. A miniature version of the Sphinx, yet more complete than its famous companion in the Egyptian desert and sporting a lion's head, stood alongside an ornately engraved obelisk. A variety of smaller artifacts from all over the world, the greatest treasures of mankind, lined the insides of several long glass cases. An entire portion of cave wall, covered in primitive pictographs, stood mounted, dark and brooding. Atticus stood before it, trying to decipher the meaning, but the images jumbled in his mind, impossible to glean any meaning at all.

"It's quite possibly one of the earliest pictographs in the world." Trevor stood next to Atticus.

"What does it mean?"

"Not a clue." Trevor smiled. "Everyone who looks at it regardless of education and experience, is immediately confounded. O'Shea believes it was written when the Tower of Babel was built. God jumbled the world's languages at the time and apparently its artwork as well. Can you imagine if everyone you spoke to was as confusing to hear as this wall is to gaze at?"

Atticus had seen more amazing things in the room than most men would in a lifetime, and yet Trevor had said he was bored. Could the man really have exhausted his interest in what he'd already collected? Rather than ask, Atticus moved to the center of the room, where the oldest, most unusual figure, the centerpiece of the space stood. A skeletal Tyrannosaurus Rex and a triceratops locked in battle. The scene looked like something straight out of a children's dinosaur book, except that the animals were real.

"There are two distinctions to be made between what you see here and what you find at your local museum," Trevor announced. "First, these are very real. Both are full skeletons, complete in every way."

Atticus's mind whirled. He knew there were several *T. rex* specimens in the world, but he hadn't heard of any complete specimens though he'd always assumed they existed.

"Most skeletons seen in museums are reproductions of the few complete samples, which are kept safe in climate-controlled warehouses and laboratories. Second…" Trevor moved in close and rested his hand on one of the Tyrannosaur's tibia. "Here, Atticus, you can touch!"

Atticus moved in close, past Trevor's gleaming smile, and rested his hand on a cool fibula of the world's most fearsome land predator. A chill ran through his body. This creature had once lived, once breathed and eventually died on the planet earth. Looking up into its open jaw, seeing its large, pointed teeth, only reassured him that what he'd seen in the ocean, what he'd watched devour his daughter, was real. He removed his hand from the bone and locked eyes with Trevor. "You want to add it to your collection?"

"Precisely."

"Dead?"

Trevor nodded.

"And what makes you think you can?"

Trevor smiled. "Because of this ship. While in appearance it is but a pleasure boat, I assure you, the *Titan* packs more than enough firepower to bring down a U.S. battle group, let alone a single flesh-and-blood creature. You'll have considerably more at your disposal than that small arsenal you have packed in your bag there."

It was Atticus's turn to smile. He liked Trevor Manfred, despite what the media said about him, and the man was the best chance he had for exacting his revenge. There was only one question that remained unanswered. "Why me? If you have everything you need to find and kill the creature, you don't need me."

"That is where you are wrong, Atticus. Every great sea hunt needs its Ahab."

"Then I'm here to entertain you, is that it?"

"'Entertain' is a harsh word." Trevor pursed his lips for a moment. "You raise the stakes. For you this is personal. The emotions are real. I'm afraid that I've become too distant from the rest of the world to have any real human connections. It's so rare that I experience emotions such as loss, despair, or rage. Consider it a moral lesson for me, an experience by proxy through a man with deeper convictions than mine.

"Plus there is the added bonus that you are an expert oceanographer, you've encountered the beast and lived…and you're past…well; *you* know how deadly a man you are. To be honest, I'm not sure that we could accomplish our goal without you, even with the amount of technology at our disposal. One man possessed, as Ahab was, can do more to turn the tide against the wild than a cruise missile, though we will do our best to help you avoid Ahab's fate."

17

OVER THE GULF OF MAINE

"Nothing yet," Andrea shouted into her headset.

"Same here," Reilly said.

"*Nada* upfront," came Watson's cool voice.

Earlier, Andrea had approached her commanding officer at the Coast Guard, Gordon Schrumzen. Though a stickler for protocol, she had expected the man, who was a father figure to most in the Guard, to cut her some slack. But he had flat out denied her request to mount a search for a friend at sea. Even if she believed the man was in danger, there was no proof, no distress call. They weren't the police, and it sounded like the man had gone of his own volition.

When she explained that the man was Dr. Atticus Young, whose daughter had been eaten by whatever sea creature the Jayhawk crew had seen, Gordon's eyes looked to the floor. He explained that the Navy had confiscated the images, that they were not to contact the press, and that "the event had never happened." But then he smiled and said they were all due for a training mission. He told her to organize it under whatever scenario she chose.

When she'd told her crew, every one of them was on board, raring to go. It would not only give them a chance to try finding the monster, but they'd also help Andrea find the man whose personal goal was to find, and most likely kill, the creature. They had mixed feelings about that, as did she, but no one wanted to be left out of the "training" mission.

"I've got something," a kind voice said over the headset. Even old Chuck McCabe and his C-130 were in the air. "It's big…really big; about ten miles north of your position.

"Copy that," Watson replied. "Cap, you want to check it out?"

"Affirmative," Andrea said. "But don't get too close. Just move parallel to them so they don't get spooked if they spot us."

"You got it."

For the next ten minutes, Andrea kept watch. She had no idea what to expect or what she might find. While the rest of her crew kept their eyes on the sea, searching for the creature, Andrea looked inward. While everyone else was searching for a monster, she was searching for a man…a friend…maybe more.

The Jayhawk suddenly banked to the right, pulling Andrea from her thoughts.

"Sorry about that," Watson said. "We came up on them pretty quick. It looks like they're just sitting there."

Andrea looked out the side window and saw a white ship in the distance, perhaps a mile away. Placing binoculars against her eyes, she took in the ship. "What the hell…"

"I hear that," Reilly said, peering through his own set of binoculars. "That's the biggest, weirdest yacht I've ever seen."

"Yeah," said Watson, "and it's the weirdest, biggest yacht you'll ever see. It's the biggest yacht in the world; belongs to Trevor Manfred."

Andrea knew the name, as she was sure most people in the world did. It was as common as "Bill Gates" or "Steve Jobs" or "Walt Disney." The man was a legend. An eccentric, rich business mogul whose collecting habits made him a man to watch by the U.S. Coast Guard. While there was no concrete evidence against him, there were indications that he'd been the recipient of several priceless artifacts taken from the U.S. over the past twenty years, including a complete *Tyrannosaurus rex* skeleton. While her team had never encountered him, they were all well aware that he was to be monitored.

As Andrea scanned the top decks, she came to rest on a large black helicopter, perched silently on a landing pad. Her heart skipped a beat. The last time she'd seen it, Atticus was watching her from inside. "I want a boat out here, ASAP."

"Umm, this is still just a 'training exercise,' Cap,"

Watson said, his voice cool. "And a boat wasn't part of the plan."

"Training's over, boys," Andrea said. "Trevor Manfred is in the Gulf of Maine, and it's our business to know why. Now call in a damn cutter."

Andrea could hear Watson chuckling. The man knew she could call in a ship to watch Trevor; he just liked getting her worked up. It was known she had something of a fiery temper, and many of her crew got a kick out of seeing her in action. *They haven't seen anything yet,* Andrea thought.

Andrea caught Reilly chuckling. "What's so funny?" she asked.

"First a sea monster, not some giant squid or sperm whale, the real thing." Reilly's eyes were beaming with excitement. "And now Trevor Manfred himself is in our territory. I'm not sure I can handle much more excitement!"

He was joking, of course, but Andrea took him seriously. "Me too, kid. Me too."

As the sun set, casting an orange glow over the ocean, the Jayhawk rendezvoused with a 270-foot Coast Guard cutter out of Kittery, Maine. They were en route to the *Titan,* Trevor Manfred's castle on the high seas, for a confrontation with one of the most powerful men on the planet. Andrea felt sick to her stomach with worry, but not over an encounter with Manfred; rich, spoiled men she could handle. As for Atticus Young, well, she had no idea what to say to him. The truth, she told herself. She was there for him. Simple as that.

Her eyes returned to the ocean as she stood at the port rail, watching the cutter plow a swath through the sea, toward her unknown destiny. She clenched her jaw, resolute in what she had to do: protect Atticus Young, not from Trevor Manfred, but from himself.

18

ABOARD THE TITAN

The night came quick and brought a cool breeze from the gulf waters. Atticus fought back a shiver, but his body shook regardless. His muscles tensed. His hands gripped the guardrail at the bow of the *Titan*. He couldn't see the black water beneath, but he could hear it lapping against the giant hull.

Unable to sleep, Atticus had left his quarters, which were more lush and extravagant than any in the finest hotel. He'd been waited on, consoled, and taken care of by Trevor's top-notch crew. But the attention did nothing to mend his broken heart. He felt crushed on the inside, even as he willed himself to continue forward, at least long enough to exact his revenge. He just wanted to be alone and, rather than join the crew for dinner, had retired early, hoping to drown the pain in deep sleep.

But his eyes never closed. When the digital clock next to his bed read 3:00 a.m., he'd climbed out of the feather bed, slipped on some clothes, and stolen to the main deck for a look at the stars.

They glowed down at him as they had before during countless nights at sea. Being so familiar to him, the celestial lights typically comforted him in times of distress, filling the void with a sense of wonder, but not that night. He watched the sky in silence, unmoved by their beauty. He stood that way, like a stoic statue, for a half hour before a voice, kind and gentle, glided to him on the night air. "I cannot begin to imagine the utter misery you must be experiencing. I have never had an emotional attachment to another living thing…let alone a daughter…or a wife. Perhaps I am not even capable. I do not know. But I do know this, when a man is hurting, friend or not, a smooth brandy and a warm blanket can dull the pain, if only for a short time."

Trevor.

Atticus felt embarrassed for a moment at being caught in such a moment of weakness … not weakness … despair. But Trevor's words revealed a kindness and understanding he hadn't realized the man possessed. He'd offered help the only way he knew how. And as a matter of fact, brandy sounded good.

Atticus turned and faced the silhouette of Trevor Manfred. "I'll take you up on the brandy," Atticus said, "but I've got plenty of blankets in my room."

"That you do," Trevor said, his voice still gentle. "Come; let me fix you that drink."

Ten minutes later, Atticus was admiring the golden hue of his third shot of brandy. His mood lightened as the spirits chased away his demons. "This is…I think, the best brandy I've ever had."

Trevor raised his glass and downed the blond liquid. "It's Courvoisier from France; the favored drink of Napoleon." He stood from his barstool and poured himself another glass. "'Claret is the liquor for boys; port for men; but he who aspires to be a hero must drink brandy.' Samuel Johnson said that, and I happen to agree with him."

Atticus finished his glass and placed it upside down on the rich mahogany bar that was the centerpiece of a fully stocked, and what appeared to be old-fashioned, American bar. It produced a strange sensation. On one hand, Atticus knew he was at sea—the gentle rise and fall of the ocean reminded him of that every few seconds. But the décor and feel of the place told him that if he exited the room, he'd step out into the hot Texas desert. If he'd still been wearing his .357 magnum on his hip, he'd have fit right in too.

"I'm no hero," Atticus said.

"You served your country. Truth, justice, the American way, and all that."

"It was my job."

"And now? You're still fighting. You're still doing what's right in the eyes of men, facing insurmountable odds—a modern-day Hercules."

"It's still my job."

Trevor opened his mouth to ask, but no words formed. His thoughts were plain enough.

"I'm a father," Atticus added.

Trevor nodded slowly, as though attempting to translate a foreign language. "I see."

With a clear mind, despite the brandy, he took in Trevor; dressed in black-silk pajamas, his stark white hair tousled about and milking yet another brandy, the man was a caricature of himself. He'd always thought the rich tycoon would be unapproachable, cold or so strange that a normal conversation would be impossible. Yet he'd offered exactly what Atticus needed to bring himself back under control. For that he was grateful. Perhaps the man would become a friend.

"Do you really think we can catch the beast?" Trevor asked, leaning both elbows against the bar.

"Can and will," Atticus said, leaving no doubt.

"I like that about you, Atticus. You've a strong will. And I, for one, don't doubt your resolve." Trevor smiled. "But you won't be doing much of anything if you don't sleep, right?"

Trevor walked behind the bar, opened a drawer, and took out a bottle. He shook a single blue pill into his hand and offered it to Atticus. "This will knock you out. You'll wake feeling refreshed. There are no adverse side effects, I assure you."

Atticus took the pill and downed it dry without question. "Thanks."

Trevor shrugged, "I own the company that makes them. They're no cost to me."

Atticus smiled. He wasn't thanking him for the money spent on a single pill. He knew that was inconsequential. "Not for the pill," he said, "for your kindness."

His words brought a smile to Trevor's face. "You may be the first person to thank me for that…and my motives are actually quite selfish. I can't have my Ahab checking out before our first chase, can I?"

Trevor almost seemed nervous about being called kind…or was it that the gesture was so foreign to him that he really didn't know how to respond? Regardless of his motive, Trevor had been kind to him. Atticus made a note not to forget, even with the alcohol clouding his mind … and the sleeping pill quickly pulling on his eyelids. Atticus slouched. "That sleeping pill is working fast."

"Right then," Trevor said. "Off to bed with you."

Trevor helped Atticus to his room and laid the groggy man in bed. Atticus looked up, his body fully relaxed, the anguish of his life diffused by a drug-induced haze. "Trevor," he said, as the rich man stole for the exit. "You're a good friend."

"We'll see about that," Trevor replied before stepping out of the room. "We'll see…"

Atticus's eyes closed before the door, and he was blissfully asleep within seconds, unaware that his new "friend" had never left the room.

19

The rising sun cut through the cobwebs in Andrea's mind. She'd slept fitfully the night before, not because of the swelling seas or rocking boat, but because of the nightmares that wracked her slumbering mind. She'd seen her own version, conjured up by her darkest imaginations, of what had happened to Atticus the day he'd lost his daughter. But with each waking and returning to sleep, the dream steadily changed until she was Atticus, and he was Giona.

Then she watched as a dark form rose from the depths, its teeth impossibly long and sharp, its size without equal. A massive jaw opened and sucked Atticus inside. She could still see his body as he slid, kicking and fighting, down the creature's throat.

She had wakened with a start, crying. That was at

5:00 a.m. She'd stayed up since, hoping a sunrise would calm her spirit. With the sun on her face and the darkness of night washed away, she felt herself returning to normal—or some semblance thereof. She still had to face Manfred and talk sense into Atticus, but the dreams of the previous night had planted a seed of doubt. She wondered if Atticus would listen to her at all, or the strange request she'd make if he didn't.

As the sun cleared the horizon and became too bright to look at, she turned around and realized just how soon the confrontation would take place. The massive yacht known as the *Titan* sat less than a mile away, gleaming in the morning sunlight. It looked like a marine home for a god or a phantom ship from some other time—mysterious and imposing.

"Well, they know we're here, and they're not running," said Reilly as he approached from a staircase that led belowdecks. "That's a good sign, right?"

"Not with a man like Trevor Manfred," Andrea replied, glad for the distraction. "He's so confident in his own power that he could have that ship filled with cocaine and not flinch at our presence."

Reilly looked surprised. "You think he does?"

Andrea chuckled. Her muscles relaxing a bit. "No. Of course not. Trevor Manfred may be many things, but a drug smuggler he is not. People as rich as he is have plenty of other ways to make more money."

"Then he's legit?" Reilly looked confused.

"It's not Manfred's wealth or how he's acquired it that's been in question. It's what he does with it. His hobbies, his collections. Much of what we believe is either speculation or based on secondhand information, but there is enough to make his ship an unwelcome sight in most ports."

"Huh?" Reilly rubbed his face with his hands, waking himself up and clearly not impressed with Manfred or his reputation. "Captain says he's ready to move when you are. Just give the say-so."

Andrea met Reilly's eyes. "Tell him to take us in, but slow and casual. Let's not spook them. That ship is huge, but I have a feeling it could outrun us if need be."

Reilly nodded after stifling a yawn. "You got it, Cap." He headed for the bridge, leaving Andrea alone with the rising sun and her returning doubts. She had to do everything right or she might lose Atticus again. Only this time, he might end up in the gullet of an honest-to-God sea monster.

"THEY'RE CRAZY," Remus said as he peered through a pair of binoculars, watching the Coast Guard cutter bearing down on their position. It wasn't moving fast enough to be perceived as a boarding attempt, but it was by no means a casual visit. "They have no good reason…"

Trevor relaxed in a floating lounge chair at the center of the dragon-shaped pool. The heated water steamed into the cool morning air, masking his features and any trepidation his facial expression might have revealed. "The U.S. Coast Guard is paying us a visit, I presume?"

"We've got about ten minutes."

"And our guest?"

"Still out cold."

"Good, good. This will be easier without him, and we need him focused on his task. His loyalties to his daughter are without bounds. There is no doubt about that. But as a former Navy man, we can't discount that he might fall into line with the military when the U.S. government shows up to inspect us. You did well in locating them last night."

"Thank you, sir."

"It was rather fortunate that our friend had trouble sleeping. Injecting a trained killer with a sleep aid would not have been the wisest course of action."

"I could've done it," Remus said, his voice filled with confidence.

"Yes, of course you could." Trevor's tone was that of a man speaking to a dog. "But he is our guest and our best chance of finding and killing the creature, so I'd prefer to treat him with respect."

Remus nodded. "Understood."

"Good, now fetch my towel and prep the loudspeaker. I want to give them a reason to maintain a healthy distance."

Trevor heaved his small frame from the pool and took the towel extended by Remus. He wrapped himself tightly, his muscles beginning to shiver. "Good God, it's chilly!"

Remus smiled. One of the most powerful men in the world was also one of the most frail. Trevor headed into a warmer hallway, followed by Remus, who closed the door behind them.

"Did you find anything in his bag?" Remus asked.

Trevor stopped in the hallway and faced Remus. "Nothing that would indicate that he was anything but honestly out for revenge. His weapons are quite formidable though, and it makes me wonder why he'd bring them to use against a sea serpent; but I doubt that Young was thinking much when he prepared for this little jaunt."

The seriousness in Trevor's eyes caught him off guard, and he came to an abrupt stop. "I can say this for the man. He is broken. I tell you that I've never seen a man in such a sorry state. I doubt if he'll ever recover. Once we have the beast and his vengeance is complete, I wouldn't be surprised if the man took his own life. He literally has nothing left to live for."

"Then you don't foresee him becoming a problem?"

"Not at all. I'm beginning to think he might be a worthy asset to have on board." Trevor smiled at Remus's furrowed brow. "All the king's horses and all the king's men didn't have Trevor Manfred as a friend."

"Cute."

"Not to fear, good Remus. There isn't a man alive I trust more than you. Your station is secure." Trevor gave him a reassuring pat on the shoulder. "But if we can shape Dr. Young into a real monster hunter, a man willing to track down...items of interest, well then, he might just be worth keeping around."

Remus visibly relaxed.

"Come, the Coast Guard is nearly upon us. To arms! To arms!" Trevor was having fun. He lived for such situations. The conflict. The intrigue. The heartbreak. So far, the adventure had been exactly what he'd hoped for. Even a possible run-in with the Coast Guard, raising the stakes, increased his pleasure.

But there was little time to spare. After the Coast Guard was sent packing, Atticus would have to be roused and prepared for his first confrontation with the beast the *Titan* had been tracking for the past three hours.

ONLY AS the cutter approached Manfred's ship did Andrea feel intimidated by the vast size of the *Titan*. The Coast Guard craft was dwarfed by it. As they cut a path around the ship, the sun disappeared behind it. As a child she'd visited New York, and was dizzied as she stared up at the towering skyscrapers. The same feeling struck her now, staring up at a wonder of modern engineering and science, and it left her mouth hanging open.

"You said it." Reilly said as he noticed her open jaw. "I doubt we could board that thing if we wanted."

While his presence wasn't required, Reilly had joined her on deck. He said it was for more moral support, but he was eager to know how she would handle the situation. What he didn't understand was that the deck of a ship usually wasn't her place. She spent more time in the air pulling people from the water than anything else. When she'd pursued this matter, turning the training into a mission and boarding the cutter in pursuit of Manfred, she had assumed she would be a bystander in the process.

She'd been wrong.

Her "training exercise" had led them there, and she had chosen to summon the cutter for assistance. The captain, a kind and fair man, requested that since Andrea was so eager to pursue Manfred, she be the one to experience his charms firsthand. Apparently the man had dealt with the rich tycoon before, and neither he nor his crew felt like matching wits with the "little white devil" again. Andrea had reluctantly agreed. She would see it through.

As she stood on the bow of the boat with only Reilly for support, she raised a megaphone to her lips and prepared to begin the conversation. The *Titan* had been informed of their approach by radio, and she could see a few crewmen and a white-haired man, who she could only assume was Manfred himself, dressed in black, standing on the main deck three decks above where she stood. She could even see the smug smile on his face. But, before a single word left her mouth; a voice as loud as the sound barrier being broken boomed through the air.

"Beautiful sunrise this morning, don't you think?" The voice rang like that of a British sixteen-year-old, not quite a child, but not yet a man. It held a taunting undercurrent that instantly irritated Andrea.

"Could you turn down your speaker?" Andrea said, her voice, magnified by her megaphone, a mere buzzing of a mosquito in comparison to whatever sound system Trevor utilized.

"What was that, my dear?" Trevor's voice pounded into her skull. "I couldn't quite make it out."

Andrea set her teeth grinding and turned the megaphone volume all the way up. "Could you turn down your speaker?" Andrea paused for a moment and when no reply was forthcoming added, "Now."

"Why of course, my dear." There was a pause. "Is that better?" The voice was still unnecessarily loud, but it was bearable and as good as she was likely to get. She knew two things about Manfred already. First, he liked toying with people. The volume wouldn't have been so loud without his instruction. Second, he wasn't fond of women in positions of authority. His use of, "my dear," twice, wasn't meant to be kind; it was a jab at her gender.

Neither bothered her beyond annoyance. It was just the kind of spoiled behavior she had expected. She often felt that money made people not only reclusive, but also monumentally immature. Money bought freedom, and in most people, no longer being bound by the restrictions of law or society meant a return to the baser qualities of mankind, or in Trevor Manfred's case, back to puberty.

"Why are you in the Gulf of Maine?" she asked.

"Right to business then? Are you sure you wouldn't want to pop over for a spot of tea?" She could see Trevor's face gleaming down at her, his smile ridiculous. She just stared back at him.

"Some other time then? Well, my dear, we are here for sport."

"Please clarify."

"Fishing, my dear. What else?"

Andrea knew his response was a load of bull, but there was no way to argue the point. And she had no grounds to assert otherwise. He'd pushed her into a corner. But she had one hand left to play, and not even Reilly knew it was coming.

"May I speak to Dr. Atticus Young, then?" Andrea paused after speaking, watching the smile on Trevor's face fade slightly. Atticus was on board. "We know he's on board and would like to consult with him."

In an instant, Trevor's smile returned. "I'm sorry, my dear, but I'm afraid I don't know who you are talking about. No man by that name is on my crew."

Andrea persisted. "He is not on your crew. He is a guest."

"My dear, please do not insult me by telling me who is on my ship and who is not." Trevor's irritation sounded loud and clear.

Good, Andrea thought. Trevor might keep her from speaking to Atticus, but she was winning the psychological battle. She knew the man was rattled, and without giving him a chance to recover, she motioned to the bridge. It was time to move off.

"Your actions will be monitored as long as you stay off the coast of the United States," Andrea said, filling her voice with authority, willing it to sound deeper, and more assertive, than Trevor's. "Please let Dr. Young know the Coast Guard is watching."

The engines of the cutter roared to life, drowning out the beginning of Trevor's response. They'd cut the man off. It was her turn to smile.

Reilly turned to her. "That was great, but who is Atticus Young?

Andrea smiled, an image of Atticus entering her mind. "A friend."

"He's the real reason we're here." It wasn't a question.

Baffled by the young man's intuitiveness, Andrea stammered over a few words, searching for an appropriate answer, but then gave up. "Yes."

"Not to fear, *my dear*." Reilly smiled wide. "Your secret's safe with me."

She knew he wouldn't tell a soul, but she'd have to live with every bit of guff Reilly decided to give her. Her only consolation was that Reilly didn't know the half of it.

20

THE TITAN—GULF OF MAINE

In an instant, Atticus woke and hopped to his feet. Whatever Trevor had given him the night before delivered as promised. He hadn't felt so rested in years and experienced no residual grogginess. He took in the VIP guest suite around him and sighed. Maria would have loved the place. He had two rooms to himself and an Incan-themed bathroom the likes of which he'd never seen. The bedroom held a forty-inch flat-screen TV mounted on the wall opposite the bed, a fully stocked minibar, and a superb view of the ocean. The living room held a second TV, also mounted on the wall, a forty-gallon tank filled with exotic fish, and furniture that was not only exquisitely comfortable, but also hand-crafted from what appeared to be single pieces of redwood trees.

If not for the twisting knot of despair and loneliness coiling in his gut, Atticus might have enjoyed himself. He entered the bathroom and shook his head at the décor. The mirror was framed by small skulls—monkeys, Atticus believed. Below the mirror, a sink carved into the top of a large boulder looked like a natural water basin formed from millennia of erosion. But the showpiece of the bathroom was the shower itself. The walls of the shower enclosure were formed from stones, set together neatly. But on the stonework grew moss and vines—real moss and vines. The shower itself was a waterfall that dropped from the mouth of a large statue of the serpentine Incan god, Quetzalcoatl. Atticus ran his hand along the curves and details of the statue. Cold and heavy, he had no doubt that the showerhead, like everything else on the *Titan,* was the genuine article.

Atticus turned on the shower, shed his clothes, and let the warm water cascade over his body. He was instantly transported to another world. The moss and vines filled the shower with an earthy odor. The sound of the falling water was accompanied by the chirping of birds and distant monkey calls from a sound system that had been triggered the moment the shower door closed. Atticus felt his mind wander and relax. He appreciated the *Titan*'s otherworldly feel. And he enjoyed the oddity known as Trevor Manfred. Perhaps, when his quest was complete, he would find some way to remain on board…perhaps.

After finishing his shower, he dressed in casual clothes rather than the military garb he'd brought. He was still serious about his intentions—to kill the beast—but he felt silly for bringing along equipment that would serve no purpose on a sea hunt. Dressed in khaki cargo shorts and a gray T-shirt with navy across the front, he exited his room into a long hallway.

The dim light of the hall revealed three doors on either side. He looked into all of them and each led to another VIP suite. Atticus headed down the hallway, not exactly sure where he was going, but he felt no apprehension about moving about the ship on his own. He passed a door and heard a loud beat from behind it…repetitious…catchy…familiar.

He pressed his ear against the door and was instantly transported back to his teenage years. He was eighteen and at a Rolling Stones concert with Andrea. One of their songs captured his imagination, and it had become his theme song while in the SEALs—the song he imagined that his enemies heard before he paid them a visit. It seemed strangely appropriate to hear the song again; after so long, he still remembered every word to "Sympathy for the Devil." In his mind, the song was about him, and he was the Devil. But he didn't want sympathy…only vengeance.

Atticus knocked on the door. For some reason he felt compelled to know who was listening to the music. The beat shut off in an instant and the door opened a crack. Atticus was surprised to see the priest, O'Shea, peeking out. Atticus couldn't help but smile.

"I never thought I'd meet a priest who was a fan of the Stones," Atticus said.

O'Shea smiled. "We all have our vices." He

opened the door, motioning for Atticus to enter. "You are actually just the man I wanted to see."

O'Shea led Atticus into the suite, which looked to be a cross between what a priest's chambers would look like: a crucifix (though it was large enough to have come from a church...and probably had), a small desk sporting a Bible and pages of notes, and a minimum of décor. On the other hand, the three laptop computer stations situated on a U-shaped desk in the center of the living room spoke of a man possibly more in touch with modern technology than with God.

O'Shea saw Atticus's eyes lingering on the laptops. "Knowledge is power, my friend, and saving the few souls on this ship that care to listen will take a lot of knowledge. I can't count on one hand the number of people here willing to hear the good word."

Atticus smiled. "Well, don't add me to the handful either."

"No? I took you for a God-fearing man."

Atticus suddenly grew uncomfortable with the topic. Discussing God with a priest could only lead to argument, and if Atticus were to consider God at that moment, after what he'd been through (and where he was going), he knew that belief would cause him to curse God rather than praise him. That road was better left not traveled.

"You said you wanted to talk to me?"

O'Shea picked up on the hint easily enough and let the subject drop. "Ah, yes. I've been doing some research on your little beastie."

"First of all, it wasn't little. Second, how can you do research on something no one has ever seen before?"

"That's where you're wrong. There have, in fact, been more than two hundred sightings of the creature since the United States was first colonized in the 1600s." O'Shea sat in a black-leather, swiveling, computer chair and rolled a second one toward Atticus. He used the touch pads on all three laptops to, bring their screens to life. On each was displayed several Firefox Internet browser windows containing various articles.

Atticus caught one of the headlines, obviously from an old newspaper.

A Monstrous Sea Serpent
The largest seen in America
Has just made its appearance in
Gloucester Harbor,
Cape Ann, on August 14, 1817, and
has been seen by hundreds of Respectable Citizens.

The next one that caught his eye was much the same.

THE REAL SEA SERPENT
THAT CAME ASHORE AT OLD ORCHARD,
MAINE, IN JUNE 1905
~ THE MOST MARVELOUS MAMMAL IN
CREATION. ~

In fact, all of the articles were very similar, each telling of a massive creature spotted in the waters of the Gulf of Maine. Atticus went numb as his mind soaked up the possibilities. The creature had been around for untold generations. It had been seen by hundreds of witnesses, yet had never been confirmed to exist by science—let alone discussed by anyone in his profession. He'd spent his life at sea, primarily in the Gulf of Maine, and he had never even heard of it.

He spotted a book on the desk next to one of the laptops. Its cover featured a picture of a sea serpent, obviously an old print. It was eerily familiar in some ways, but so wrong in others. He picked it up and read the title: *The Great New England Sea Serpent,* by J.P. O'Neill.

Atticus must not have heard O'Shea talking because he was repeating his name over and over. "Atticus. Hello. Atticus?" "Yeah, sorry," Atticus said. "This is just a little unexpected."

"You're telling me." O'Shea took the book from him and flipped through the pages. "Look at this," he said, holding the open book up for Atticus to see. "This thing, which can only be your creature, has been spotted hundreds of times all over the Gulf of Maine." The pages O'Shea flipped through contained dates, places, and names for all of the sightings. "And these are just the reported sightings!"

Atticus recognized most of the hundred-odd cities named: Gloucester, Lynn, Penobscot Bay, Nahant, Salem, Portland, Kennebunk, Boston Harbor, Rockport, and Portsmouth. All were cities strung along the coasts of Massachusetts, New Hampshire, and Maine that gilded the entire Gulf of Maine. Next, the numbers and professions of the witnesses struck him. In some instances the creature had been seen by more than two hundred people at a time. Other sightings had been reported by fishermen, lobstermen, ship captains—even the Coast Guard. All were people accustomed to life at sea. If the creature struck them as unusual, as it had Atticus, who better to judge between shark, whale, or something else entirely?

"Why don't more people know about this? Why didn't I?" Atticus asked, his voice nearly a whisper.

O'Shea shrugged. "The Loch Ness Monster became a tourist attraction. It was good for the community. But this just didn't catch on. Perhaps the no-nonsense New England atmosphere was simply too much for the creature to pierce? The world knows how strong-willed and stuck in your ways you New Englanders can be."

Atticus smiled. He knew O'Shea was trying to lighten the mood. He flipped through the pages of the book one more time, stopping at drawings of the serpent and descriptions given by witnesses. As before, he noted that several details were accurate, while others fell short. It was at least 150 feet long and showed a black coloration on top and white beneath. Its double-decker-bus-sized head looked like a horse's. It undulated up and down as it swam, like a mythical marine serpent, but it had large fins like a whale's, two in front and two in back. And its eyes were lemon yellow and split by dark serpentine pupils. Atticus jolted from the memory. He suddenly recalled more details, and it jarred him to the core. For a moment he felt terrified of the water, thinking twice about facing that thing again.

Then the door burst open.

"Don't you ever knock?" O'Shea blurted out at the brightly Hawaiian-clad Remus.

"Trevor wanted me to get you," Remus said to Atticus, totally ignoring O'Shea. "We're tracking the creature and will be on top of it within the hour."

As Remus delivered his last bit of shocking news, Atticus felt the *Titan* lurch into motion, making his feet unsteady and his stomach constrict uncomfortably. But rather than give in to his fear and misstep, he righted himself, followed Remus, and set his mind to the task; it was time to face his fears.

Time to kill the beast.

21

THE *TITAN*—GULF OF MAINE

"How are you tracking it?" Atticus sounded unbelieving and indignant as he entered the bridge of the *Titan*, followed closely by Remus and O'Shea.

Trevor turned to him with a gleaming smile. "Good morning, Atticus. I trust you slept well?"

Oblivious to Trevor's polite conversation, Atticus took in the bridge. A technological wonder, the bridge had more screens and buttons than the space shuttle. In fact, it looked like something straight out of a science-fiction film. A crew of five, including a captain, who never spoke, sat around the oval room, working at computer consoles and wearing headsets. At the center of the oval bridge, which had a 360-degree view of the ocean, sat an oval table that displayed maps and charts digitally, a massive touch screen.

Trevor's words intruded again, but this time captured his attention. "The beast hasn't traveled far since your initial encounter."

"Where are we?"

"Where we have been since you boarded…Jeffery's Ledge."

Atticus met his eyes. "How are you tracking it?" he asked a second time, adding resolve to his voice.

"Ahh, yes," Trevor said. "While you slept I had crews deploying sonar buoys throughout the Gulf of Maine."

Atticus squinted. It was a ridiculous notion. The Gulf of Maine was simply too big to cover with radar buoys.

Trevor picked up on Atticus's disbelief and added, "Not the entire gulf, mind you, just the spots that most resembled the location in which we knew it had been sighted. We knew from your account that it had been pursuing a school of herring, so we buoyed all known herring hot spots, which was no small task, mind you.

"But it seems the creature is in no hurry to leave. It has been slowly following a school of herring, I assume keeping its prey close by."

Atticus nodded. That was certainly an odd behavior, but the creature was completely unknown and unrelated to anything Atticus had ever studied. Predicting its hunting habits would be impossible. But if it shadowed a school of herring, he had no doubt it would eventually feed on them. "It will surface when it feeds on the herring."

"My thoughts exactly," Trevor added with a glimmer of excitement. "And we'll be waiting for it when it does. But I must ask a favor of you before such an encounter occurs."

Atticus waited, neither nodding nor speaking.

"I need to know everything you do about this creature. Anything you can recall about the beast will help us immeasurably. To kill it, we must first know it."

Atticus pictured the attack—his memory still fractured. He thought about drawing the beast, but he was no artist and didn't want to misrepresent its size, abilities, or speed. "I'm not sure how much help I could be…I don't remember…"

"Don't remember or don't want to remember?" Trevor asked, his voice gentle and soothing, just as it had been the previous night. He topped the sentence off with a firm grip on Atticus's shoulder.

Remus and O'Shea shared a glance. It seemed everyone found the gentle touch and calm voice to be strange.

"Either way," Atticus said, "any information I provide would be suspect."

Trevor sighed and relented. "Understood, but we still must—"

"Wait." Atticus's eyes were wide. "Where are we?"

"The man already told you," Remus chimed in, "Jeffery's Ledge."

Atticus glowered at the man. "Jeffery's Ledge isn't a small place. Where are we, exactly?"

Trevor looked at the floor for a moment. "I hope it won't ruffle your feathers too much, my friend. We are at the coordinates you broadcast in your distress call. We have been here since your boat was taken away."

Atticus smiled, which in turn caused Trevor to relax. "Perfect."

Confusion washed over Trevor's face. "Why is that, precisely?"

"Giona…my daughter…and I were carrying cameras that day," Atticus said, feeling cold as he spoke. The day she was taken seemed like a lifetime ago, yet was only two days previous. So much had changed. Would Giona understand what he was doing? Would Maria? Before the guilt found purchase, he pushed it away. "I was carrying a video camera. I dropped it when I surfaced, but there's a chance I got it on tape."

Trevor's eyes lit up. "Where is the creature now?"

The captain, who was most likely not even needed, as the ship that could pilot itself if need be, looked at a circular screen displaying several green blobs of varying sizes. Atticus approached the screen and instantly understood what he was looking at. Schools of fish, whales, and other assorted sea creatures made their appearances on the screen, but most obvious was an ominous object moving slowly behind a smaller hazy one.

"It's three miles out, still following the fish," the captain said. "Still moving slowly."

Trevor looked at Atticus.

"I'm going in," said Atticus.

Trevor thought for a moment, chewing his pale lower lip. "We'll go together." Trevor suddenly stood tall, smiling and filled with energy. "Prepare the sub! Ready the harpoon! Hoist the mainsails! Batten the hatches! Et cetera! Et cetera!"

When Trevor was finished, the captain and three other crew members scuttled from the room, intent on fulfilling Trevor's requests.

Remus stepped forward. "You're not actually planning on going down in the sub with that thing down there?"

"Try not to fret, Remus. We will be perfectly safe, and I will hear no more arguments about it."

The tone in Trevor's voice silenced any further argument. "At least let me drive." Remus said.

"I would rather you man the harpoon gun. If we run into trouble, we will surface, and you may defend us as gallantly as you wish."

"And who pilots the submersible?"

"Why, Atticus, of course."

Atticus seemed taken unawares by that pronouncement. He had not expected to pilot the sub. His experience with submersibles was not a matter of public record. He was about to inquire about the assignment when Trevor explained.

"Atticus took part in a top-secret one-man attack-sub program. NAVY SEALs could use the subs to approach enemy ships, submarines, oil platforms, what have you. And no one would be the wiser. The subs moved quickly and quietly, but in every way they appeared to be denizens of the deep—shaped as mantas, sharks, even turtles. PUSS (Personal Underwater Stealth Submersible). I won't repeat what they called the pilots, but several SEALs, who were not submersible pilots, were used in testing the devices. Since they were to be used by your average SEAL, they had to be tested by average SEALs. Not that Atticus here was anything but stellar, but his previous experience at the helm of a submersible was nonexistent."

Atticus stared at Trevor unblinking, astounded by the man's in-depth knowledge of a project few even in the Navy knew about. Trevor turned from Remus and looked at Atticus. "I do believe you will find our submersible not too dissimilar from the ones you piloted during your days with the PUSS program, except, of course, for its size."

Atticus smiled. He didn't care how Trevor had come upon the information, and he knew Trevor could sense as much. The two men were united in a common cause. Rules and morality would be set aside until their quest concluded. Maybe Trevor had an informant. Maybe he'd had the priest hack into a Navy database. Atticus didn't care. Getting that tape off the bottom of the ocean and using the information it contained to hunt down and kill the creature was all that mattered. Nothing else did.

Not anymore.

ANDREA PACED the deck of the Coast Guard cutter, watching the gleaming *Titan* just sitting in the distance.

What were they up to?

Where was Atticus?

Why weren't they moving?

She couldn't stop running through the questions that wracked her mind over and over. With so little information, the number of unknowns was driving her crazy. Worse, she couldn't tell her commanding officers of her concerns about Atticus. It would be clear to all that she wasn't out there to watch Manfred; she was there for something—someone—far less official.

But she also sure as hell couldn't justify keeping a Coast Guard cutter in pursuit of Trevor Manfred if he was simply sitting still! To make matters worse, Trevor had done exactly what she thought he would. Ever since the confrontation in the morning, several men could be seen fishing off the back of the *Titan*. They'd been monitored closely, but what was discovered only backed up Trevor's fishing trip claim. The men were occasionally catching fish, and one man was nearly pulled in by something before his line snapped.

She'd seen the men hauling in large fish, easily a hundred pounds, some maybe more. Their lines had to be tough. What could have snapped the line? *Something huge,* Andrea thought.

Something huge. The torrent of thoughts in her mind came to a screeching halt. She knew why Trevor was there. She knew why Atticus had joined him.

They were working together to find and kill the creature. How Atticus had contacted the mogul so quickly was beyond her, but he obviously had. Atticus and Trevor Manfred were in league with each other.

Atticus, you have no idea what you're in for, Andrea thought, shaking her head. In that moment, Andrea determined she would get in contact with Atticus one way or another, even if she had to swim to the *Titan*.

22

THE TITAN—GULF OF MAINE

If not for the unholy goal of the mission, Atticus might have felt excited. But the footage they were going to retrieve at the bottom of Jeffery's Ledge filled Atticus with dread. His memory, fragmented and blurred as it was, would be brought into crystal clarity as the 3CCD video camera and its slow-motion capabilities would cause him to relive the violent end of his daughter's life…again…and again.

Atticus followed Trevor deeper into the belly of the *Titan* than he had yet been. The air grew cool and moist. The extravagant décor faded, leaving only pale gray metal and a rubber-grip-coated floor. Trevor had explained that he'd been prone to slipping when his feet got wet, and the rubber grips kept him from floundering like a fish.

They approached a large metal hatch labeled: ray's bay.

"Ray's Bay?" Atticus asked.

"*Ray* is our submersible," Trevor said proudly. "I realize it's not the most formidable name. Nonetheless, I believe you'll find it appropriate."

Trevor twisted the hatch's lever and it opened with a dull *clunk*. It swung open noiselessly, revealing a large docking bay with a hatch, currently closed, that opened to the ocean. But the most startling feature in the room was what hung above the floor, supported by four thick metal cables.

The submersible was jet-black and shaped like a stealth fighter. *No*, Atticus thought, *like a manta ray.* "*Ray…*"

Atticus walked around the suspended sub and took in the details. The craft was fifteen feet long and twenty at its beam. He slid his finger across the gently sloping tail end—smooth, almost soft to the touch. Two large pump-jet vents protruded from the back, an impressive feature. He moved around to the front. In place of a real ray's eyes, two glass bubbles, for pilot and copilot, rose out of the smooth surface, providing a 360-degree view from the top of the craft. Each side of the submersible had three small windows. The thing was so aerodynamic it looked like it could fly. "Are there no manipulator arms?"

Trevor met Atticus at the front of the submersible. Suspended above them, they stood at eye level with its underbelly, which like a real manta ray's, gleamed white. "The arms are recessed until needed," Trevor said, pointing out four small hatches, two on each side. "The hatches in the middle house the manipulator arms. The two on the outer extremities hold mini-torpedoes."

Atticus couldn't hide his surprise. Trevor spoke before he could ask. "You never know what you'll run into while traversing the deep, wouldn't you agree? Though I doubt the punch these torpedoes carry would be enough to kill our creature."

Atticus was impressed. The Navy versions of the submersible were half the size and not nearly as well designed, or armed. What was still in the design and testing phase with the Navy had been perfected by Trevor Manfred for his own personal use.

"What's the maximum depth?"

"Three thousand feet." Trevor rocked on his feet, with his hands clutched behind his back. Atticus thought he looked like an excited child showing off a new toy. But he had a right to gloat. Three thousand feet was extremely deep, and with the top of Jeffery's Ledge ranging between one hundred and two hundred feet, depth would not be an issue.

The captain from the bridge approached Trevor. "*Ray* is powered up and ready to go."

Trevor waved the man away with a swoosh of his hand. "Flood the chamber and open the hatch."

"Yes, sir." The captain gave a curt nod and headed for the hatch. As he was leaving, O'Shea squeezed past the man and entered the room.

Trevor's eyes rose to his forehead. "And what, dear

Father, do you want?"

"I was hoping to come with you," O'Shea explained in a voice that Atticus realized was more relaxed than those of the rest of the crew. "I've never been down and thought this might be the perfect opportunity."

"I never knew you were interested in the depths," Trevor said.

"It is one of God's creations I have not yet seen firsthand."

"Ah yes," Trevor said with a smile, then gesticulating as though he were reciting Shakespeare, added, "And God said, 'Let the water teem with living creatures, and let birds fly above the earth across the expanse of the sky.' So God created the great creatures of the sea and every living and moving thing with which the water teems, according to their kinds, and every winged bird according to its kind." Trevor raised both hands in the air. "And God saw that it was good."

He bowed, as though taking praise for being able to quote the Bible so fluently. When he stood straight again, his white hair was raised madly, and his eyes were twinkling. Atticus had never met a man so capable of amusing himself.

"And I assure you, Father, it is good. However, this trip is exclusive I'm afraid." Trevor squinted and scrunched his nose. "Though now I feel I'm forgetting something. Is there another reason for your joining us?"

O'Shea smiled and nodded. "I didn't want to

mention it, but you missed your confession this morning. If something should happen to…go wrong. You will need me to—"

"Yes, yes. Quite right."

Loud *clanks* sounded out around the room. Trevor's orders were always followed and rarely delayed. The grinding of gears and whirring of unseen motors revealed that the hatch would soon be open and the room flooded with water. "Quickly, chop-chop."

Trevor moved beneath the submersible and pushed a series of buttons. The code was simple, only four buttons. Atticus made a note of them: 2009. It first struck Atticus as a date, the year 2009, but he decided it was coincidence, though it made the number easy to remember. A hatch slid open, and a ladder descended. The three men quickly climbed the ladder and entered the submersible, just as the chamber began flooding with cold ocean water.

The submersible's interior looked like the bridge of the Starship *Enterprise*—plush, comfortable, and ultramodern. Like the *Titan,* Atticus assumed that the sub could pilot itself if need be. Even the manual controls looked ridiculously simple. There was a control stick, like that in a jet fighter, but there were few buttons to worry about and almost no gauges. The screens in front of each chair led him to believe that all the systems were monitored and adjusted by computer. The cabin smelled of leather and warm electronics. The air felt cool and breathable, and, while small, the sub was far from cramped. Trevor directed Atticus to the right-hand chair, which sat beneath one of the glass eyes. Trevor sat beneath the left eye, and O'Shea took one of the two rear seats, which had a view through the side windows.

After Atticus adjusted to the seat, he looked up and found the glass viewing port to be a foot above his head. "Was this thing designed for giants?" he asked.

Trevor smiled and reached his hand over the side. As in a car, each seat had a small control panel. Trevor depressed a button, and his seat rose into the air, bringing his shaggy-haired head within the confines of the glass bubble. Atticus did the same and was happy to see the control stick rise with him.

"I wanted to be able to stand up inside," Trevor said without offering any other explanation. "If you tire of looking at the ocean from the eye of a manta, there is a concealed front viewing port."

Atticus twisted from side to side. The mobility and field of view were far beyond those of any submersible he'd ever been in. "No. This is great." As he spoke, water rose to the lower edge of the window and quickly covered it. He hadn't even been aware that it was rising.

"When the cables let go," Trevor said, "don't touch the controls until we're in the open ocean. The computer will guide us out."

A moment later a slight drop signified that they were no longer attached to the support cables. True to Trevor's word, the submersible came to life and descended through the open floor, into the ocean.

They were immediately greeted by a pair of massive jaws bearing rows of razor-sharp teeth. For a moment, Atticus thought he must be having some kind of hallucination brought on by a subconscious fear of entering the ocean again. But as the bubbles and froth cleared, he could make out the distinct triangular teeth of a shark, a very large great white shark—Laurel.

"Is she a danger to the sub?" Atticus asked.

"Not at all." Trevor said with a chuckle. "She comes to say hello every time we descend in *Ray*. I'll tell you, she's given many a guest quite the start!"

Laurel circled *Ray* twice before swimming lazily away. "You see," Trevor said, "she's a friendly girl when she wants to be." Atticus looked at Trevor, whose face was distorted by the two glass bubbles separating them. The way the glass bent and stretched his image made the man look more like a Troll doll than a multibillionaire. When Trevor flashed a wide smile at him, Atticus couldn't help but laugh.

Trevor's next words immediately erased his smile. "Take us down, good Ahab! Down, down into the depths to recover the record of the beast that we might glimpse what makes it tick and discover a chink in its armor."

The jovial tone of Trevor's theatrics had no effect on Atticus. He was not looking forward to recovering the tape, or seeing the creature again. He would move toward it regardless. Like a meteorite through the galaxy, propelled by forces out of his control, he would not stop until he met an unmovable force and collided with it. Atticus gripped the control stick and thrust it forward, sending *Ray* into a fast dive through the azure depths.

23

ABOARD RAY—BENEATH THE GULF OF MAINE

Though his sorrow fought against it, a smile grew on Atticus's face. He twisted the control stick and took the sleek submersible into a spin. He followed the spin with a twist in the other direction and a loop that brought them toward the ocean's bright blue surface, then back to the depths.

Atticus hadn't planned on the joyride, but after feeling the speeds the sub could reach and how easily it handled, he'd started testing its limits. He had yet to find them. It handled like a jet fighter—an amazing jet fighter—underwater.

Trevor bellowed a laugh. He was enjoying himself as well. It wasn't until O'Shea groaned loudly from the back that Atticus eased up on the controls and slowed. He ducked down out of the bubble and looked back at O'Shea. "You all right back there?"

"Peachy..." O'Shea looked green. "Just, slow down, will you? I've never been fond of amusement parks for a reason."

Trevor was peeking out of his side. "Oh, Father. You can't tell me that didn't make you feel alive."

"God makes me feel alive," O'Shea said with just a hint of a smile.

"Oh, phooey on you," Trevor said with a wave of his hand. He looked at Atticus. "And you! When this business is finished, you have a spot on my crew if you'd like it."

Atticus wasn't sure what to think of the offer. It was a temptation filled with the prospect of money and adventure, but those things seemed so hollow in the wake of all that had happened and might happen. He'd already considered the idea and imagined he would accept. He liked Trevor, and if he survived the confrontation with the creature, he'd need to do something with his life, no matter how shallow. He nodded his response and returned to the confines of his glass bubble.

The rest of the descent was made in silence and without reaching breakneck speeds. As they neared the seafloor some two hundred feet below, the light from the sun filtered away to a blue so dark that they couldn't see more than a few feet.

"Trevor," Atticus said, "this thing has lights, correct? And can you work the manipulator arms once we find the camera?"

Atticus saw Trevor look at him, his troll-shaped

face deep in thought through the two glass bubbles. He seemed to be seriously considering something. Then he smiled and saluted. "Aye aye, *mon capitaine.*"

The ocean became a globe of bright blue as two exterior five-hundred-watt metal halide lights blazed to life, lighting the surrounding area to near-daylight conditions. The seafloor came into view, glowing golden brown under the light. The sandy bottom was pocked with orange cerianthids, burrowing anemones, their jellylike limbs swaying with the ocean currents. Skittering across the sand were several small crabs, fleeing from *Ray*'s bright lights. Tiny specks of life, known as zooplankton, flittered all around the sub, not even aware of it.

Atticus ignored the life that normally would have enthralled him and set about the task at hand. "I'm going to run a search grid. It will be tedious, but we should find it."

Trevor nodded his agreement and Atticus pushed the sub forward.

Forty-five minutes later they were rewarded for their efforts. A flicker of reflected light in the distance revealed something on the sandy surface. Atticus wasted no time in approaching the object. He caught his breath, instantly recognizing the camera resting in its protective casing.

As they approached the case, Trevor spoke up. "We're approaching the edge of the ledge, Atticus. Watch out for upwelling currents."

Atticus nodded. He'd already noticed the building currents and was working hard to compensate for them. "Just grab the camera."

Atticus couldn't see Trevor's hands working, but he could hear small motors moving within the submersible. Then two mechanical arms gradually reached out from *Ray,* stretching toward the sunken camera. As Trevor latched both manipulator arms tightly to the camera case handholds, a hiding flounder panicked and burst from the sand, swimming quickly away over the sandy seafloor. The movement brought Trevor's eyes up from the camera.

He screamed.

A massive shadow rose from the depths beyond the ledge. A creature of undetermined length ascended, its massive mouth held agape.

"Get us out of here!" Trevor shouted, his voice squeaking in fear. "The beast is upon us!"

Atticus laughed hard, grateful for the distraction from the lump that had been forming in his throat since he first laid eyes on the camera. "It's just a basking shark."

As the forty-foot shark continued to rise, sucking down and filtering out a cloud of helpless copepods, Trevor slowed his anxious breathing and took in the creature. "A shark. A damn shark! That thing is huge!"

"Basking sharks are the second largest fish in the ocean. The first is the whale shark."

"But, it's so big."

"Trust me," Atticus said, "when you get your first

look at what we're after, this toothless giant will seem small and gentle. In fact, it makes Laurel look like a sweet little puppy."

A voice echoed through the cabin, transmitted from the *Titan* above. "Mr. Manfred! We just picked up something huge on—"

Trevor slid on a headset, flicked it on, and cut the panic-filled voice off. "It's a shark, you nervous twit. And the next time you let something this big get this close to me without warning; I'll have your head. Understood?"

"Yes. Yes, sir. Sorry, sir."

"Where is the creature now?"

"Umm, the shark is moving away."

"Not the shark!" Trevor shouted. "The…the creature. The monster!"

"Oh, it's ahh…it's still following the herring. It's about three miles east of your current position, moving north."

Trevor switched off the headset and put it down. "Imbeciles."

Atticus gave one last look at the basking shark as it swam gently away, gobbling up more copepods. Not everything in the ocean is an evil monster, Atticus thought, as a shred of his old self surfaced for a moment. He worked the controls and rather than head directly for the surface, he gave chase to the basking shark. He pulled up next to its head as it lazily swam through the water. As it was illuminated by the bright lights, Atticus could clearly see its brownish coloration, conical snout, and large gill slits. While being far from attractive, a basking shark's size and smooth glide made it a wonder to behold.

Suddenly its massive jaw snapped shut. The shark hovered for a moment, then, with a speed Atticus thought impossible for one of its kind, turned tail and fled back into the depths beyond the ledge.

Atticus's body went rigid. "Oh hell."

Trevor's eyes were wide. "What?"

Atticus put the submersible at a steep angle and accelerated as fast as he could. A voice, yelling this time, came over the intercom. "It's coming your way. It just changed course. Holy…It's fast!"

Trevor switched off the intercom and shouted to Atticus. "Hit the yellow button on the control stick, aim for the *Titan*'s underside. When we get within twenty feet let go, and the computer will take over."

Atticus didn't bother to ask why. He simply flipped up the button's protective covering and pushed it with his thumb. In the split second before anything happened, he wondered what the green, red, and blue buttons were for. Then they were off. It felt like the beginning of a terrible roller coaster. Atticus felt himself pinned to his seat as the craft reached fifty knots in just a few seconds. He heard O'Shea groan, but he didn't sound sick.

"Oh, Dear Lord, there it is," O'Shea said.

Atticus knew O'Shea's view was out the port side and looked in that direction. He looked past Trevor's glass bubble and saw a huge shape shifting through the water. At that distance he could only see its dark silhouette, but the up-and-down undulation was unmistakable. If the creature hadn't been moving past them, in the direction of the basking shark, Atticus might not have looked forward. But he did, and in that instant realized they were going to crash head-long into the hull of the *Titan*.

He let go of the controls and felt the craft shift as the computer immediately took over. Huge jets of bubbles exploded from *Ray*'s roof. The jets served to correct their angle of approach and slow them down. In seconds, what surely would have been a quick and violent death morphed into a smooth, gliding ascent. They rose smoothly into the confines of *Ray*'s bay.

With their safety assured, Trevor lowered his seat. Atticus followed suit and met his eyes. Trevor was near tears and his skin paler than usual. "It was beau-tiful," he said, wiping wetness away from his eyes with his black sleeve. "I simply must have it."

O'Shea spoke from the back. His voice was quiver-ing with fear, not holding an iota of Trevor's excite-ment. "Are you sure that is wise? This...this creature might be out of even your league."

"Yea, though I walk through the valley of the sha-dow of death..." Trevor started.

"I shall fear no evil," Atticus finished.

O'Shea gave a nervous smile. "Except for that thing."

24

COAST GUARD CUTTER—GULF OF MAINE

Andrea stood on Coast Guard cutter's deck feeling more alone than ever. Most of the crew had lost interest in the *Titan* and the men still fishing—incessantly fishing—off the back of the giant ship. But she found herself locked to the top deck of the cutter, unable to leave. She knew the crew suspected there was more to her obsession with Trevor Manfred than she'd explained, but short of lying to them, she couldn't change that perception. It was the truth.

She raised the binoculars to her eyes and scanned the *Titan* again. Except for the men fishing off the stern, there was no movement. Nothing at all. She scanned the men at the back of the boat, watching them cast their lines into the ocean, searching for a fuzzy white-mopped head of hair. Nothing. Trevor had been missing in action all day.

He'd claimed the fishermen were his guests. *If they're guests, why isn't he with them?* Andrea thought. Just then, one of the men yanked hard on his rod. The pole bent sharply into an upside-down U. The man had hooked something big, but as he locked himself into the seat and began pulling and reeling, Andrea could see it wasn't too big to handle. *Just another small tuna,* she thought. They'd pulled in two already.

She watched the man battling with the fish, his face not more than a millimeter in size, but she could see the flash of his teeth when he smiled. She could see the other men cheering around him, whooping it up, and having fun. Maybe they were guests? Maybe Trevor was sick, or just a rude host?

Then the men froze. They seemed to be listening to something. The man holding the fishing rod suddenly let go. The rod flew through the air and into the water. The stern deck cleared as the men rushed inside.

What the hell?

The sound of a metal door clanging against the side of the bridge startled Andrea away from her spying. She turned around to see the captain rushing out of the bridge, heading her way with a scowl on his face. She'd been caught. Maybe Reilly had spilled his guts? She stood tall, ready for a verbal barrage, still confident in the choices she'd made and the secrets she'd kept.

She remained silent until the captain was upon

her. "Sir, I can explain," she blurted.

"I seriously doubt that," the captain said as her stood before her, glancing at the *Titan*.

Andrea was confused. Up close, he didn't seem angry, not at her anyway. His eyes were more interested in the *Titan* than in her. She decided to keep her explanations to herself and let the man speak.

The captain sighed. He removed his captain's hat and rubbed his temples. "Look, we all know about what you and your crew saw. We all heard about the rescue, the creature. Rumor spreads quickly. You know that. To be honest, not many of us took it seriously. We figured that was why you were really out here; we figured that was why Manfred was here too. But, none of us really believed it. We were going to turn back today. Some of the crew wasn't all that happy about being on a wild-goose chase."

Where was he going with this? She opened her mouth to ask, but decided silence would be better for now.

"Look," he said. "We just intercepted a transmission."

Andrea's forehead wrinkled with her rising interest. "From the *Titan*?"

"Yes, but the response came from"—the captain pointed a finger over the side of the cutter, straight toward the ocean—"down there."

Andrea looked to the waves, trying to see through, imagining what could be down there.

"It's seems they've had an encounter with your creature. Some men must have gone down in a submersible launched from the *Titan*. Honest to God, I didn't think it was real, but the fear in those men's voices…" The captain trailed off and looked over to the *Titan*. He squinted and crunched his forehead. "What happened to the men fishing?"

Andrea returned her gaze to the *Titan*, remembering the rush of the men on deck. Coupled with the information she now had, she could picture the crew hurrying throughout the ship, preparing, recovering the submersible, destroying their cover story.

Why?

Andrea gasped. "They're going after it!"

TREVOR BURST onto the bridge of the *Titan* and began shouting orders. Atticus and O'Shea stood behind him. The cabin became a flurry of motion as the captain and crew rushed about, preparing for a rapid pursuit. Remus greeted them on the bridge, his colorful shirt nearly washing out the pitiful look in his eyes.

"I should have been with you," Remus said to Trevor, with a look of genuine concern.

"Fret not, Remus. Atticus handled the sub like a pro." Trevor gave the man a pat on the shoulder and moved to the front window.

Remus gave Atticus a scowl and stood next to Trevor, waiting for his command.

O'Shea slid up next to Atticus and whispered, "You better watch out for that one." He motioned to

Remus. "He doesn't like it when other people get close to Trevor."

"He's worried about nothing," Atticus said. "I've only just met the man."

"You called him by his first name," O'Shea said.

Atticus shrugged. "So?"

"Only those who criticize Trevor on TV or in the papers, or those in his extreme favor, can call him by his first name. On the *Titan,* only I get away with calling him by his first name, and that's simply because he fears the power I represent."

"I doubt Trevor fears God," Atticus said.

"No, but he fears eternity. He believes, for some reason, in the power of priests to erase sins and save souls. I am his ticket to a blessed eternal life."

"That's not really how it works, is it?"

O'Shea smiled. "Not at all, but he believes it."

"Then why are you here? I doubt it's common for a priest to be paid to hear confession."

"That," said O'Shea, "is a story for another day."

Trevor's voice pierced the cabin again. "Where is the creature now?"

"It's returned to the school of herring," the captain said, leaning over the sonar screen, still being fed multiple signals from the array of sonar buoys.

"Must have seen the basking shark as a competitor and driven it out of the area," Atticus said, unable to stop himself from analyzing the creature's actions from the standpoint of an oceanographer.

"It's...it's rising," the captain said, his voice tight with tension. "It's going after the herring."

Atticus felt a surge of adrenaline. He knew what was coming next.

"Full steam ahead!" Trevor shouted. "I want us on top of it in ten minutes or heads will roll!" He turned to Remus and spoke in a calmer voice. "Prepare the harpoon, will you?"

Remus nodded. "Yes, sir." Then he was gone in a flash.

Trevor turned to Atticus, a gleam in his eye. "Are you ready, Atticus? The game is afoot. I believe Melville called this portion of the hunt, 'The Chase'"

"That was at the end of the book," O'Shea said.

Trevor smiled. "I'm an impatient man."

WHITE FOAM burst from the back of the *Titan*. It lurched forward and churned through the water. "There they go!" Andrea shouted.

Standing in the bridge of the cutter alongside the captain, her shout was unnecessary but understandable. From the moment they'd realized what was happening, the crew had been on alert and ready to move.

"Set a course to follow," the captain said. "Bring us alongside, but keep a safe distance."

Andrea braced for sudden movement as the cutter's engines roared to life. The propellers dug into the water and pushed them forward in pursuit of the *Titan*. While the captain and crew had their minds set on the chase and the possibility that the sea monster they'd all been joking about was real, Andrea's thoughts were on the man she'd been pursuing from the moment she'd brought him back to life. She knew Atticus was on the *Titan*. But as she watched the megayacht pounding through the water, a glint of metal rising from its bow, she realized it might be too late to save him.

While his life might not be at risk while aboard the *Titan,* he was going to lose himself in the fight. She feared he'd become as much a monster as the creature he sought to kill.

A reassuring hand gripped her shoulder. She turned and found the captain looking at the photo. "He's why we're really here, right? He's the man you pulled from the water, the one who lost his daughter?"

She nodded.

"He's on the *Titan*?"

She nodded again.

He squeezed her shoulder. "We'll get him back."

"How long have you known?"

"I've been a sailor long enough to know what a woman looks like when she's waiting for a man to return from sea." The captain smiled. "You've been standing on that deck watching that ship with the same look in your eyes I see in my wife's every time she greets me at the dock."

Andrea smiled. She'd been found out after all, but, amazingly, it didn't seem to matter. The captain was a good man. Only then did she realize she had yet to learn his name. "Captain, what's your name?"

"Jon Knecht," he said.

"Well Captain Knecht," she said, "thank you."

25

THE TITAN—GULF OF MAINE

As the *Titan* began its charge through the ocean, its girth surged up and down as it cut through eight-foot swells. At full speed, the ship simply bored a path through the water. Atticus found himself enjoying the slight undulation of the deck beneath him. He felt more at home at sea than on land.

As he headed for the foredeck, following Trevor, with O'Shea close behind, he saw something large rising out of the deck where just the night before he'd been weeping for his daughter. Its polished surface glowed in the sunlight. He recognized it instantly—a harpoon gun.

Remus greeted them as they approached. "Almost ready, sir."

Trevor nodded and looked to Atticus. "Impressive,

is it not?"

Atticus loathed the killing of whales. It drove him nuts that several Japanese fleets still slaughtered the beautiful creatures. "For scientific research," they said. Only fools believed that as the meat, oil, and fins found their way to Japanese markets. And he knew the only reason anyone would have a harpoon gun strapped to the front of a ship was to hunt whales. He wanted to ask if the harpoon gun had been used on a whale, but the answer was clear. Of course it had. Atticus felt a twist of revulsion inside him. *What am I becoming, that a man like Trevor Manfred could become such a close friend so quickly? Are we really that much alike? Could I join this crew and watch as this harpoon gun kills a defenseless whale? How different is what I intend to do now?*

Atticus shoved the questions from his mind. The plan wasn't about sport. He took no pleasure in the act. If an alligator in Florida ate a child, it would be killed. If a bear savaged a family, it would be hunted down. *This is no different*, Atticus told himself. *This is nature.*

No, a voice shouted from deep within. *When a lion takes a calf from a herd of buffalo, they don't seek revenge; they don't hunt down the lion. They mew for the baby animal, mourn its loss, and move on.* That's *nature!*

Fine, Atticus thought, *this is* humanity. He could live with that. He'd killed for his country in the past. He could kill for his daughter. With his resolve rein

forced, Atticus focused on the harpoon gun with renewed interest. Remus carefully looped a thick rope
onto the deck, which was attached to the sinister-
looking four-pronged harpoon jutting from the front
of a cannon that looked like an oversized, futuristic
laser gun.

"Beautiful, isn't it?" Trevor said. "Every part is titanium. Overkill, I know, but it will never fail me and
never dull. Cost a fortune, but it serves me well. The
four flukes are razor-sharp on the outside and barbed
on the inside, so the harpoon grips after it pierces.
Once inside the beast, the flukes will extend and hold
tight, while this…" Trevor waved his hand over the
tip of the harpoon, which had an opening between
each of the flukes. Inside the opening was an unla-
beled cylinder. "…explosive charge finishes the job.
Most people don't know this, but harpoons carry explosive heads that explode after impaling the target,
inflicting a mortal wound that slowly kills the animal."

"And makes one hell of a mess," Remus chimed in.

"I know," Atticus said through gritted teeth.

"Of course you do," Trevor said, "And regardless
of your past persuasions about the use of a weapon
such as this, I think you'll agree that in this case, the
slow death brought on by Excalibur here is well deserved."

Atticus nodded, centering his mind on the task as
hand, trying not to think about the whales killed by
the device he would soon wield. "I'm not sure this

will be enough. This thing is bigger than any whale."

"Indeed," Trevor said. "But we've doubled the explosive charge. The beast may take some time bleeding to death, but no amount of white blood cells will be able to plug the hole this creates."

"Off the port bow!" The voice from the bridge was ragged. Atticus followed the captain's pointing finger out to sea, where he saw a cloud of shimmering silver, just beneath the surface, and below that, an ominous shape rising from the depths.

He turned to Trevor. "Is it ready?"

"Have at it!"

Atticus stood behind the large harpoon gun, taking its handle with both hands. He swiveled it quickly from side to side and up and down, getting a feel for how quickly it could be maneuvered. It handled like a charm. "Get us on top of that thing." Atticus's voice rang with rage as his thirst for vengeance reached a crescendo. "I will not miss."

"You heard the man," Trevor said to Remus. "Take the helm and show those lollygaggers how to pilot this ship!"

"Yes, sir!" Remus beamed with pride at being given the station normally occupied by the captain. He stormed off to the bridge, shouting orders the entire way.

Atticus gripped the harpoon gun tightly; bringing it around toward the cloud of herring, now thrashing at the ocean's surface, panicked and mindless, just as they had been…that day. The boat turned to port and thundered toward the herring. Atticus roared like a man possessed, feeling the thrill of the hunt, the moment of revenge at hand.

Trevor stood beside him, his eyes wide, his lips spread thin in a smile. He was clearly eager, brimming with excitement. And beside him stood O'Shea, taking everything in and doing little to hide his nervousness. While his eyes moved from the ocean to Atticus, his hands clasped together tightly in anticipation.

The herring lay dead ahead. In an explosion of movement, they launched from the water, trying to swim into the sky. This was it. The beast rose. Its prey fled.

You should have killed me too, Atticus thought as he readied a hand on the trigger.

The water beneath the herring bulged then exploded outward. Herring flew through the air while others fell into a massive open mouth. All three men gasped. The beast rose and fell in a fluid motion, like a whale coming up for a breath, but before the first hump had come and gone, the head was up again, taking in more fish. The head rose and fell again, and still the first hump had not submerged. A trail of humps formed behind the head as it moved forward through the water.

"My God," Trevor said. "It's a sea serpent. An honest-to-God sea serpent."

Ten humps in all rolled through the water before the creature's stubby tail appeared. It pushed forward, scooping up herring and swallowing them whole. Atticus knew that wasn't how the creature moved underwater. It moved much more fluidly there, but still…

"Fire the damn harpoon!" Trevor shouted. "It's descending."

Atticus focused on the creature, whose head had gone down but not returned. One by one, the humps were following the head, disappearing into the depths. Atticus took aim at the largest hump using the harpoon gun's sight board and held his breath before pulling the trigger. He doubted whether holding his breath would make a difference with the aim of this particular weapon, but it was a habit instilled in him after his training behind a sniper rifle.

The harpoon exploded from the cannon, soaring through the air and trailing a long line of cable. Atticus smiled as he looked over the harpoon gun. He could see that his aim was true.

"There she goes!" Trevor said as he leaned against the bow rail, watching the harpoon fly through the air.

Atticus felt his whole body go rigid with anticipation. As the harpoon closed in on the creature, the world slowed down. Everything became vivid and clear. The nightmare would soon end. With a resounding *clang*, the harpoon struck the creature's back…and glanced off. It bounded forward, hit a second hump, and again, with a sound resembling metal on metal, bounced up into the air out over the open ocean—where it exploded.

Atticus grasped O'Shea and Trevor more out of instinct than a belief that they'd be peppered by shrapnel, and tackled them to the deck.

Smoke from the explosion quickly wafted over the deck as the *Titan* pushed forward. Trevor was laughing beneath Atticus. "Well played! Well played!"

Atticus rolled off Trevor, who sat up and clapped his hands. "Bravo!"

"You're happy?" Atticus said with a growl as he stood, looked to the ocean, and saw nothing but blue seas ahead. "It got away."

"And we will give chase again." Trevor said with a grin. "This is better than I had hoped. The beast is more formidable than I thought. What an adventure! Though I must say, I'm not fond of being tackled."

O'Shea helped Trevor stand. Before they left, Trevor added, "Fear not, brave Atticus. Your vengeance will be completed. I promise you that."

Atticus felt little comfort as the men left. He was alone on the deck, alone in the world, and in that instant he realized how empty the world appeared. The ocean had lost its magic. His family was gone. He'd betrayed his ethics.

The crashing of water that was not caused by the *Titan* immediately told Atticus that a second ship cruised the water next to the yacht. He turned and looked over the port bow. Pounding the waves next to the *Titan* was a gleaming white, red-striped Coast Guard cutter. While the cutter was dwarfed by the *Titan,* Atticus still found himself impressed by the power of the ship and the audacity of its captain, bringing it so close to the megayacht.

An oddity at the cutter's bow caught his attention.

As the ships pounded up and down through the waves, Atticus saw a woman, whose black hair caught in the wind, obscuring her face. His heart lurched with familiarity.

Maria.

But when the wind shifted, and her hair blew away, he came eye to eye with a woman of equal beauty but whose scowl spoke volumes.

Andrea.

Her arms were crossed, her shoulders high and rigid. She'd obviously seen his attack on the creature and was not impressed. Maria wouldn't have been either.

26

THE TITAN—GULF OF MAINE

Atticus didn't bother asking why the Coast Guard was tailing them. He didn't much care. He'd come so close to killing the beast and providing some closure to his grief that little else mattered. As for Andrea, he'd come to the decision that she had, from the beginning, taken an interest for personal gain.

Forget our past, he thought. *She can't be the same person she was then. It's more likely that she sees my high-profile tragedy as a way to make a quick buck. That's what motivates most people. By becoming part of the action, maybe she'll score a memoir or film deal.*

But if that's true, he thought, *then why am I still thinking about her?*

Sporting a scowl any football player intimidating a

rival would be proud of, Atticus propped his feet up on the theater chair in front of him, crossed his arms, and waited for the film to roll. He already had his movie deal. It was the sickest, most vile footage ever captured, and it featured his daughter's death.

"Don't look so foul," Trevor said as he leaned over the arm of a chaise lounge and looked at Atticus from across the aisle of his personal movie theater. The front wall held a fifteen-foot screen, while the sloping floor contained eight leather lounge chairs, split by an aisle running down the center. The room was dimly lit by sconces on the walls and a strip of tiny lights running up the sides of the central aisle, adding an authentic atmosphere to the place. "It was only our first attempt at conquering the mightiest beast on this planet. We'll not cease until we've accomplished our noble goal."

Trevor's pep talk, while well-intentioned, did little to calm Atticus's nerves—a man who would soon watch his daughter die—for the second time in four days. Before the following silence became uncomfortable, they were joined by Remus, who held a remote, a bottle of Coke, and a bucket of well-buttered popcorn. Atticus was instantly offended.

"You fucking prick," Atticus said, jumping to his feet. He stood inches from Remus, crushing the popcorn between them. "Is this some kind of treat for you? Do you plan on being entertained?" The sudden rage-filled outburst shocked Remus into silence, but anger quickly followed. He tried to stare Atticus down, but once their eyes met, he knew in an instant that if they were to come to blows, it would only end with one of their deaths, and he was not prepared to find out whose death that would be. "Do you?" Atticus shouted again.

Remus grunted, which was as close to an apology he could muster, placing the popcorn and soda on the floor. He sat down without saying a word.

Atticus glanced at Trevor, whose eyes were wide. He looked at Atticus and raised his eyebrows, silently communicating that he was shocked that Remus had backed down. The door at the back of the room opened, and a seemingly emotionless O'Shea entered. He was wearing blue jeans and a T-shirt. In casual clothes, he looked more like a grad student than a priest. He slid past Atticus and took the seat next to him. No one questioned his presence or attire.

"Start it up," Trevor instructed.

Remus pointed the remote over his shoulder, toward the back of the room, and pushed a button. The camera recorded video straight to DVD and was able to be played immediately. Atticus hadn't been thrilled about the idea of viewing such a large image of the tape, but Trevor insisted the finer details might be worth noticing, and Atticus couldn't argue with that. Whatever chink this creature might have, Atticus felt certain it would be infinitesimal.

The large screen lit up blue, then turned black as the footage started to roll. Atticus grew rigid as the voice of his daughter bellowed from the powerful surround-sound speakers that encircled the room. "Daddy, c'mon, let's go." The image of Giona, wrapped

tight in her wet suit, with her wild purple hair blowing in the wind, almost caused him to retch.

"Cute kid," Remus said.

"I like the hair," Trevor added.

"Fast forward," Atticus said, his voice barely more
than a whisper.

Remus let the video continue for a moment, long
enough for it to be apparent he was either trying to
torture Atticus or was too busy checking out the
man's now-dead sixteen-year-old daughter.

Trevor slapped the back of Remus's head. "Do it."

The video became a blur. Atticus watched as footage of Giona swimming passed by, flashes of his past
that seemed like faded nightmare made real. The
peaceful pod of whales appeared on the screen.

The video moved forward, and they all watched in
silence as Atticus and Giona swam with the whales,
touched the bull, and shared their last moments together. The first warning call sounded loud over the
speakers. Atticus broke out into a sweat.

Here it comes...

The image spun as the whales' mighty flukes
churned the water. Then the second pod of whales
emerged from the depths. Atticus listened as he instructed Giona to blow her air tank. Seeing the video,
he could make out how close the lead bull had actually come to plowing through them.

Atticus saw Remus nodding. Apparently, even the
thug was impressed.

A silver cloud burst onto the screen. Thumps
sounded out as the fish careened into Atticus and the

camera. At one point a single herring became lodged between the camera lens and Atticus's body.

The image stabilized again, and the ocean returned to its calm blue glow. But what Atticus couldn't see at the time had been picked up clearly by the sensitive video camera. The dark silhouette of the creature could be seen in the distance. It wasn't moving toward them at all. But then the front end, the creature's head, turned toward them as if sensing their presence. Its body suddenly undulated even faster and headed straight for Giona, as though it were seeking her out.

The creature emerged from the darkness, jaws open, teeth gleaming, then, it froze. Before them was a crystal-clear image of the front half of the creature, its mouth open wide. Giona, arms outstretched in fear, floated just inside the giant's maw.

"Oh God…" O'Shea whispered.

Trevor got to his feet, mouth open wide. "Kronos."

Remus munched quietly on his popcorn.

And Atticus…laughed.

What started as a light chuckle became a grotesque snicker and finally emerged as a sinister bellow mixed with tears and a white-hot glare. He shook his head back and forth, "I'm going to kill it. I'm going to kill it."

Atticus turned to Trevor, who jumped back. Atticus had not realized the three men had been staring at him in silence, afraid he had become a madman. He kept his voice low, but the savagery behind his words was plain. "What else does the submersible have for armament?"

Trevor opened his mouth to reply.

"Be honest," Atticus said. It was clearly a warning that only the truth would be tolerated.

"Electric-shock cables, high-yield torpedoes, and a micro nuclear dart capable of sinking an aircraft carrier…"

"I'm going to need it."

Trevor nodded. "In the morning. When we fully understand what it is you are facing, then you can face the beast. Then you can kill Kronos."

Atticus knew he was right, but the rage inside him needed an outlet. He could bury it for the time needed to learn about the creature, but his control wouldn't last long. The rage boiling inside him would spew out at some point, and waiting until morning would be a challenge.

"Why? Why Kronos?" O'Shea asked, his voice quivering. "Wasn't he the king of the Greek gods?"

"Indeed," Trevor replied. "While the name is fitting from a power perspective, the most powerful of the gods and the most powerful of living things, but I named it for its appearance."

"A Kronosaurus," Atticus said.

"Precisely."

"That's not a Kronosaurus," Atticus added.

"Undoubtedly. While the Kronosaurus was the world's largest marine reptile, its maximum size was closer to forty-five feet. Our beast would have made a meal of the dinosaur. But the head shape and lower fins smack of the Kronosaurus. Perhaps they're related; or this is simply an evolved specimen whose species survived the mass extinction and flourished in the depths?"

"Look," Atticus said, "while speculating about its origins might be interesting to you, it won't help how to kill it; where it's vital organs are; how it breathes. This is what needs to be learned. The key to its death lies in what keeps it alive."

27

COAST GUARD CUTTER—GULF OF MAINE

As the sun set and darkness spread over the easterly
sky, Andrea basked in the last rays of sunlight cast in
hues of orange, pink, and yellow as it mingled with
the clouds and humid atmosphere; a beautiful sky.
One that would make couples swoon, cause photo-
graphers to snap pictures, and the religious to think
about God. But the vivid colors did little to ease her
tension or erase her fear.

Her plan of action was risky. When darkness finally settled she would slip into the ebony abyss and
board the *Titan* under the cover of night. Her swim
from the cutter to the *Titan* would be aided by high-
tech fins designed to maximize water displacement
and minimize resistance, but that was little consolation as the two boats were a half mile apart. If the

Titan made a run for it, she'd be stuck in the water and the cutter couldn't pursue until she was hauled back in.

Andrea shuddered. She couldn't imagine how someone like Atticus used to do things like this for a living. The idea of sneaking onto a boat and searching for someone without being found out made her queasy. She wasn't even sure that Atticus wouldn't hand her over if she did manage to find him without being detected. While Conner had kindly welcomed her back, and her impression of Atticus was that despite his military training, he had become a loving man, that didn't change the fact that she really didn't know him very well anymore.

"Are you sure you want to do this?" came the voice of Captain Knecht.

Andrea was surprised to find herself standing in the dark. She'd been so wrapped up in her thoughts that she hadn't noticed the remaining light of day slip away. She faced Knecht and nodded. "I have to."

"You realize that if something goes wrong—if you get caught—we have to deny we sent you." Knecht sighed. "As soon as you're off this ship, you're on your own."

Andrea swallowed hard. "I know."

"We'll move off, give them some breathing room. If they head for international waters…"

"It'd be a long swim back."

Knecht smiled. "A very long swim."

He started for the bridge. "Gear up and get in the water. We'll pull out at 0200 hours. Make them think we headed back to port." He paused and glanced back, meeting her eyes with a serious stare. "I hope he's worth it."

With that, Knecht walked away, leaving her to her preparations and doubt. "So do I."

THE ABSOLUTE void experienced during a night dive always made Andrea think it's what being in space would feel like, except for the external pressure. The cold and the emptiness, devoid of any visible light, caused eyes to strain and colors to emerge. The depths of the ocean seemed much more ominous at night, though what she'd seen that day, in crystal clarity, chilled her more than the dark water. The lonely expanse hiding dangers below tempted her to reconsider, to give credence to her fears, but she pushed them out of her mind and kicked harder. She imagined herself as a torpedo, mindlessly seeking its target. She pushed forward, not keeping track of time. It wasn't until her mind registered the slap of waves upon a hull that she realized she'd bridged the gap between the two ships.

She'd made it.

Finding the hull with her hand, she kept one hand against the smooth exterior while kicking her way toward the back of the boat. She'd board where the crew had staged the great fishing excursion. She kept her ears keenly aware to the sounds of the sea, listening for the roar of engines. As she took action, her fears and doubts faded, to be replaced by an adrena-

line rush that gave her strength and an unwavering
determination. She felt she could swim throughout
the night if need be.

Suddenly the hull next to her lit up like a UFO's
teleporter beam. She scurried from the light like a
frightened cockroach, sure she'd been discovered. After taking several deep breaths from her regulator, she
calmed herself enough to realize the light was coming
from a window on the side of the hull—an underwater viewing port. Slowly, Andrea swam a few feet
away from the hull, so she'd be less illuminated, and
peered into the room.

The massive chamber on the other side of the glass
was like none she'd seen before. It almost appeared to
be an aquarium, but the stillness of the creatures
painted on the curved walls spoke otherwise. There,
at the center of the room were two extravagant-
looking chairs, a small table holding a bottle of brandy, and two glasses. A burst of bubbles shot from her
mouth as she saw Atticus and Trevor Manfred heading for the chairs.

They sat together and were speaking calmly. She
tried to read their lips but could only make out a few
words…"tomorrow"…"torpedo"…"nuke"? Andrea
was sure she'd misread the last word as it was so ridiculous and had come from Atticus's mouth. Moving
closer, yet careful to stay out of direct view, Andrea
attempted to see their lips more clearly. If she could
find out where Atticus would be, she'd have a much
easier time locating him on this behemoth of a ship.
She knew she was too close when her reflection came

into view. She slowly moved sideways, careful not to move too quickly. As she moved, another reflection filled the void where hers had been.

The sight of it made her scream, expelling her regulator, and flail madly.

THE BRANDY slid down Atticus's throat, warming his insides and calming his nerves. He smiled as Trevor poured him a second glass. "You know you're going to get me addicted to this stuff." Atticus downed the second shot. The alcohol and pleasant atmosphere of the underwater sitting room were having the intended effect of soothing the raging soul of a man who just watched his daughter get eaten alive. They'd watched the video over and over, yet found nothing, aside from fueling Atticus's rage, that would offer them any aid in killing the sea serpent.

"Every good man has a flaw," Trevor said with a smile and drinking his second shot as well. "Tell me, then, what does my intrepid hero have planned for the morrow? Hmm?"

"I'll need the sub."

Trevor crossed his legs and perched his hands daintily on his knees. "Yes, you mentioned that earlier."

"Alone."

A single eyebrow arched high on Trevor's head. "While I share your desire to see Kronos dead, I would very much like to see the event take place."

"I'll drive it to the surface in the sub, where you

can hit it with whatever big guns you've got hidden on board."

Trevor grinned. "And if the weapons on the sub fail to push the creature onward and upward?"

"Then it will chase me to the surface."

"Sounds like a fool's errand."

"It will work."

"And if it doesn't?"

"You mean if it eats me?"

Trevor offered a feeble nod.

"Then I'll use the mininuke and send us both to hell."

"Ahh yes. You know that was designed to be a long-range weapon; but I suppose it would function well as a self-destruct mechanism." Trevor sighed long and deep. "You will, of course, do me the common courtesy of warning us before detonating a nuclear device? Will you not? We would need time to steer clear. It may be a small charge, but it will create a sizeable splash."

"I'll wait until my last breath."

After chewing on his lower lips, Trevor let out a chuckle and slapped his knee. "You do know how to raise the stakes don't you! Very well then—"

An enormous collision reverberated through the room, sending Atticus and Trevor immediately to their feet.

"Are we under attack?" Trevor asked eyes wide.

When Atticus saw it, he knew they had nothing to fear. He pointed to the window with a view of the dark undersea kingdom. There, chomping his jaws on something indeterminable was Laurel, the twenty-eight-foot great white shark.

"Ahh," Trevor said as he straightened his rumpled black turtleneck. "Laurel, you naughty fish. You nearly caused me to soil myself."

Atticus moved closer to the window, watching Laurel devour whatever was in her mouth. "What's she eating?"

"Late-night snack I suppose. One never knows."

28

UNDER THE TITAN—GULF OF MAINE

Pain wracked Andrea's body as her insides tore. She'd moved so frantically to avoid the freight train of a shark that she'd pulled several muscles in her legs, arms, and chest. But the most painful of pulls came when the great white locked its jaws upon her fin, nearly taking her toes off, and yanking it from her foot. With the giant's jerk, the muscles of her right leg stretched like the strings of an over-tightened harp.

If not for the shark's total dedication to devouring the rubber fin, breaking away would not have been possible. Even then, her chances of escape remained slim as she feebly kicked her way toward the back of the *Titan,* relying on one bare foot and one finned foot to propel her forward and outrun the ocean's top predator.

As she kicked, a burn filled her chest. She'd been holding her breath. Worse than that, she had yet to replace the regulator that she'd spat out when she screamed. Reaching back for the regulator caused multiple fresh muscle pulls to protest painfully, but she pushed past the pain and found the regulator hose dangling from her air tank. As the regulator met her lips and she took a deep breath, her strength returned. But she was nowhere near the stern of the *Titan*. If the shark gave chase, she'd never make it, injuries or not.

She dove under the *Titan* in an attempt to remove herself from the shark's field of view. In the end it wouldn't help much, but she refused to make an easy meal of herself. Sharks had evolved to sense their prey using more than eyesight. They could smell a drop of blood a quarter mile away. More than that, the shark's ampullae of Lorenzini, jelly-filled canals in its head and snout, could detect the electrical fields emitted by all living things, especially panicking, thrashing prey trying to escape.

Andrea doubted the shark had ever lost track of her, but she had no other recourse.

Upon reaching the bottommost portion of the hull, Andrea discovered something that lent her hope. A second portal, extremely large, glowed at the center of the lower hull. If it turned out to be another viewing port she'd be eaten for all to see, but if it was an open bay.

She kicked hard and yanked at the water with her hands. As the bright light from the portal illuminated the water, she could clearly make out small waves rippling in the open space.

Even as a massive, dark silhouette circled the light, once, then twice, she kept moving forward. The shark was taking its time, unaware of the escape route.

As Andrea angled up toward the open hatch, she sensed the water behind her shifting, driving forward. The shark charged from behind. Andrea clawed toward the hatch, only five feet ahead.

Overcome by fear and instinct, Andrea pulled herself upright and turned around, arms outstretched, facing her attacker. A moment later and she would have lost her legs in the shark's jaws. And though her action saved her legs by pulling them away from the shark's jaws, she faced the open maw of a twenty-eight-foot super-predator head-on. She kicked up, grasped the shark's head, and took the impact in the gut. The force drew all of her breath from her and knocked the regulator from her mouth.

With her body wrapped around the snout of the shark, her limbs were safe from being snapped up by the shark's mouth, but she could feel the lower jaw opening and closing, snapping at her legs and scraping against her wet suit. She was about to become a frog in a blender.

Andrea screamed, expelling the last bit of air in her lungs, filling the water with a bubbly howl before jabbing a thumb into the shark's eye.

With a sudden jolt, her backward motion stopped, and the shark vanished into the gloom. She saw it circling again, moving fast, agitated. It would be back...and soon. Andrea looked up and found herself directly beneath the open hatch. But unless she could fly, it did her no good. She surfaced, took a desperate drag of air, quickly shed her air tank, weight belt, and regulator, and pounded toward the edge of the thirty-foot pool.

She swore she could feel the shark behind her again, but had no energy to turn around and face the monster. She knew it would only end in her demise, and this time she had no desire to look death in the face.

Andrea winced as her hand struck metal. She reached the edge. She threw an arm up over the edge and found the floor surface wet and slippery. She dug in, feeling her nails scratch against the cold floor. She began pulling herself out, grunting with exertion. But her tortured muscles, burning lungs, and bruised ribs fought against her, pushing her back into the drink. As she gripped the edge of the hatch again she glanced back and saw the shark shrinking the distance between them, its jaws open wide and its white, nictitating membrane covering its black eyes, protecting them from the struggles of its prey.

Her spirit broken, Andrea let go of the floor, prepared to meet her maker, whoever that might be. But before her hand slid beneath the water and her body into the jaws of the shark, a crushing pressure took hold of her wrist and yanked her up out of the water.

She became airborne and collapsed onto the bay's metal floor.

Exhaustion quickly set in along with a kind of numbness that came softly over her. Her field of vision dwindled to that of a peephole, and her body fell limp. She looked toward the pool, where her rescuer stood. A tall, beefy man, whose attire suggested a jovial or comical personality.

As her vision faded to black, she heard the man's dull footsteps clang against the metal floor, growing closer. As he spoke, his hot breath, which smelled of popcorn, seemed oddly close to her face. "Well, well. Look at what the fish dragged in."

If Andrea had been conscious enough to see the man's lust-filled eyes, the bent smile, and rough beefy hands advancing toward her hips, she would have known how wrong her assumptions about the man had been. If she'd known he had a history of violence against women, she would have been thankful for being unconscious.

Remus slung Andrea over his shoulder and exited Ray's Bay, whistling a happy Hawaiian tune. He knew he couldn't do anything to the woman until Trevor questioned her, but then he'd have his way with her. The fact that she'd survived an encounter with Laurel meant she was a fighter; and he liked a woman who fought back. They reminded him of his wife.

May she rest in peace.

29

THE TITAN—GULF OF MAINE

Atticus woke as the foot-long teeth pierced his belly and ran him through, severing his body in two. He'd had the same dream three times since retiring to bed that night. The first two times he hadn't wakened until after he'd looked down and found his entrails unraveling into the water. Mercifully, this time he awoke just as vertebrae separated from disk.

The nightmare left him covered in sweat and tense. He sat up in bed, controlling his breathing, attempting to move his thoughts away from the dream, away from Kronos or the impending encounter. His mind wandered to Giona, but the wound of her death was too fresh, and he felt his emotions swelling. He pushed his thoughts to Maria and found himself consumed with guilt for his actions, then sadness for having to face the loss of Giona alone. Unsure of what to focus on—it seemed every good thing had been taken from him—Atticus suddenly pictured the angry face staring at him from the Coast Guard cutter. Andrea.

His thoughts turned to their first kiss. The gazebo. Still sixteen, they stood beneath a gazebo as a torrential downpour pelted its roof and provided them with a rare moment of privacy. They'd stood in silence, awkward at first, then comfortable. The kiss came a moment later. Mutual. Soft. It ended when the rain faded moments later and neither spoke of it for weeks after. But it had been the beginning of their romance.

He smiled, picturing her scowling at him from the Coast Guard cutter. Why were they there? He imagined that the Coast Guard would take an interest in Trevor's presence, but why watch him so closely? Before waking the previous morning he'd thought he heard her voice calling for him.

No, Atticus thought, *it's just a coincidence. She's in the Coast Guard. It's her job.* Still, he knew that she deserved an explanation, and he resigned himself to contacting her in the morning.

Dully distracted from the nightmare, Atticus felt his eyes grow weary again, and he lay back down. Though his eyes were closed, Atticus suddenly sensed a shift in the moonlight sneaking past the shades. He listened. Feet shuffled over the floor.

Someone was in his room.

He could hear the person breathing, quick and labored. Nervous, Atticus thought.

Possibilities flooded his mind. It couldn't be Remus. The man might be excited about killing him, but he was a professional. He wouldn't be so sloppy. Trevor would have simply turned on the lights and announced his presence. Besides, the silhouette of the man moving toward him lacked the explosion of hair atop top his head. With a smile, he realized who it was, but the cause of his late-night visit remained a mystery.

"Atticus," the man said. "Atticus, are you here?"

Atticus shot up and whispered, "Boo."

Father O'Shea stumbled back against the wall with a thud. "Dear Lord!"

Atticus turned on the bedside light, smiling at the panicked priest. "I thought priests didn't take the Lord's name in vain?" Then, before O'Shea could speak added, "Another vice perhaps?"

O'Shea wore only loose-fitting sweatpants, revealing a cut, fit upper torso. The priest's athletic build struck Atticus as odd. What kind of priest cursed, listened to the Stones and had a body like Bruce Lee? He thought to ask, but kept his thoughts to himself. Everything on the ship held secrets, and the good Father was only one of them.

"Sorry for sneaking up on you," O'Shea said. "Though I suppose it was you who got the best of it"

Atticus looked O'Shea over. The man was wiggling his fingers about and glancing around the room, clearly nervous about something more than being caught sneaking into his room.

"Why are you here?" Atticus asked.

"You must swear to tell no one how you found out."

Atticus nodded and crossed his arms over his equally bare, yet more muscular chest.

"I saw a woman today; Remus caught her trying to board the ship." O'Shea sighed. "I just thought you would want to know." He drew a deep breath and cracked his knuckles. It was clear he was about to share something he believed he shouldn't.

Atticus stood straighter. "What? Who?"

"I don't know who, but that woman from the cutter. Earlier in the day, when you were still sleeping, she confronted Trevor and asked to speak with you specifically."

He *had* heard her voice. Atticus squinted. "Why didn't Trevor tell me?"

"Why the man does anything at all is a mystery to me."

"And yet here you are."

"Here *we* are."

Atticus stood in silent thought for a moment. O'Shea continued.

"I went for a walk to clear my head. That damned beast of yours is giving me nightmares."

You're not the only one, Atticus thought.

"I overheard Remus telling some crew members that a woman had been caught. His description of the woman matched the one I saw on the cutter. She'd almost been eaten by Laurel, but survived."

Images of Laurel smashing against the viewing port in the sitting room flashed through Atticus's mind. The chomping jaws smashing an object to bits. In his mind's eye Atticus could now see the object for what it was—a swim fin. Why hadn't he seen it before? Was he so blinded by his own need for revenge that his senses were dulling?

"Where's Trevor?"

O'Shea stepped up quickly. "Why?"

"He's a reasonable man. If he knows Remus is holding a member of the Coast Guard—my friend—he will let her go."

O'Shea headed for the door, his desire to not be found out moving him forward. "Obviously, you don't know Trevor very well. Look, Trevor may not know about her yet. But if your friend has been captured, it is in her interest to leave the ship *tonight*. Under the circumstances, I thought you would be the right man for the job."

"Why tell me this? You're obviously risking a lot by coming to me."

O'Shea smiled. "I may be a bad priest, but I'm still a good person." With that, he exited, closing the door silently behind him as he entered the hallway.

Atticus looked to his duffel bag of armaments, yet to be unpacked. He opened the bag and smiled. *It's been a long time,* he thought.

Ten minutes later he was fully clothed and armed. If the woman caught on board was indeed Andrea, he would heed O'Shea's warning and get her off the *Titan* before she was in any danger. If the woman was a stranger and had no business being on board, he'd make damn sure Remus wasn't mistreating her. After the treatment he'd administered to the thugs who attacked Giona, his patience for deviant men threatened to boil over.

Atticus slid into the dark hallway, cloaked by his ebony Special Ops uniform. The only indication that he hid among the shadows came from a sparkle of light glinting off the .357 strapped to his hip. Unnecessary, perhaps, but Atticus had no doubt that Remus was a killer. Better safe than sorry.

30

THE TITAN—GULF OF MAINE

It had been a month since the *Titan* had visited any
port of call; hence a month since Remus had experienced the pleasures of a woman. But the skip in his
step as he made his way through the underbelly of the
ship revealed that his need for physical gratification
would soon be satisfied.

Trevor had not been overly surprised by the woman's appearance and, while he suspected there might
be a connection between her and Atticus, she could
not be allowed to remain. Even more, because of her
status as a member of the U.S. Coast Guard, and a
feisty one at that, she would have to be dealt with delicately. Why she had attempted to board the ship and
what she knew wasn't clear, but Trevor couldn't risk
exposing himself to the U.S. government.

Trevor's anchoring off the coast of the United States, while not welcome, was tolerated simply because the accusations against him could never be proved. If any evidence of the artifacts contained on board were to be discovered, even Trevor Manfred couldn't escape the clutches of U.S. law. It would undo him.

"Have you searched the rest of the ship?"

Remus nodded. "I saw nothing on the monitors. The crew checked every cabin, hold and closet. She came alone."

Trevor grunted and twitched his mouth to the side. "Keep a close eye on her. Make certain she sees nothing, and keep her from contacting anyone."

"And if she tries anything?"

"Just keep her occupied. I'm sure you can handle that, hmm?"

Remus nodded.

With that, their conversation ended, and Remus headed for the medical quarters. After snatching a needle and a syringe of epinephrine, or liquid adrenaline, he set out for the brig. While the woman might be exhausted and injured from her encounter with Laurel, after a shot of adrenaline, she'd be wide-awake and fighting like a champ—just the way he liked it. *Keep her occupied…hell, I could do that all night.*

As Remus descended onto the lower deck and stepped onto the black-rubber-matted floor, he thought he heard a noise behind him. He spun and prepared to strangle the intruder with his beefy hands. But no one was there, and after a minute of waiting and watching the dark stairwell, he continued on.

The idea of breaking a woman who had been so impertinent earlier in the day was arousing him even as he walked through the slate gray, moist-smelling hallway. He reached the brig door and looked through the round glass window. She was still unconscious, still dressed in her skintight wet suit, and still roasting hot. *This is going to be fun.*

Remus depressed his thumb on a small LCD screen connected to the locking mechanism. After a moment, the door unlocked and swung open. Remus stepped inside, ignoring the still-open door. The room was a fifteen-foot cube— large enough to hold a small band of mutineers—with flat wooden slats attached to three of the four walls. Stark white light flooded the space, shining from eight halogen bulbs recessed into the ceiling. The ultrabright lighting made those unfortunate enough to be in the brig extremely uncomfortable, not only from the light, but also from the heat they generated.

Wiping his forehead, Remus smiled. *Time to work up a real sweat.*

He crouched next to Andrea, who was still unconscious on the back wall wooden slat. He ran a hand up her leg and over her hip, then lingered for a moment on the deep curve where her hip tapered to her slim belly. His eyes advanced and found her breasts. He imagined they would be much larger once freed from the constricting wet suit. Full of fiendish thoughts, Remus removed the shot of adrenaline from the front pocket on his Hawaiian shirt and, without a moment's hesitation, plunged the needle into Andrea's butt, where his hand had just lingered a moment before.

He could have taken her clothes off while she was unconscious. It would have been amusing to see her confusion upon waking naked, but he would enjoy tearing her clothes off her struggling body even more. Still, in the moments before the drug took effect, his hand crept toward her breasts.

As his fingers moved to cup and fondle, a flash of black moved past his eyes, to his hand. Before he could react to the sudden movement, a sharp pain burst in his pinky accompanied by a dull *crack*. As his broken finger was pulled up, his body reacted instantly and stood instinctively, hoping to lessen the pain. A tightness clenched around his throat. Then a sudden pressure and push from behind. He found himself careening forward and smashing headlong into the white-metal wall. The flash of white turned black.

WITH A gasp Andrea awoke and launched into a sitting position, her eyes wide, and her chest heaving with each adrenaline-filled breath. The bright white light assaulted her first, then an overwhelming sense of moist constriction. She blinked rapidly as she tried to make sense of the stark white surroundings. Her mind spun furiously as thoughts came and went before she could process them.

Then something moving toward her caught her attention. A slice of black on white. A figure hovering. A man bending down. A face etched with concern.

"Are you all right?" Atticus asked.

Andrea's vision cleared, and she saw Atticus. His forehead was wrinkled with concern and covered in sweat. The oppressive heat of the room felt like a heavy electric blanket.

"I'm hot," she said as she sat up straighter. A stab of pain in her ribs caused her to wince. "Think I bruised my ribs."

As Atticus took her by the hand and began pulling her to her feet, her thoughts slowed enough for her memory to return. She had questions that needed to be answered before she went anywhere with him. She yanked her hand away. "Why have you been avoiding me?"

"Now's not the time."

"Now or never. I'll take my chances with the Hawaiian."

Atticus sighed. "I guess...I thought you might talk me out of it."

That wasn't the answer she was expecting. How could she talk a man bent on avenging his daughter's death out of what he believed needed to be done? Her face softened as she realized he was being truthful. "How is that even possible?"

"Remember the wallets?"

History slammed into Andrea's mind, replaying in flashes. During their first summer together, Atticus had stolen a case of wallets from the local church basement. They were ugly and plastic, colored maroon and blue, featuring a flowered design surely created by a ninety-year-old woman. Atticus took the wallets door to door, selling them for a dollar each, far more than the hideous wallets were worth, but doing a good job of peddling them nonetheless. At the end of the day, he had made fourteen dollars, from selling wallets he had stolen from a church.

The culmination of his plan had been to buy toys with his illicit money, but Andrea had laid into him, pouring on guilt, exposing him to higher morals. In the end, she talked him into giving the money back to the church, but in a way that would not get him in trouble. That night, they attended the nighttime summer church service and sat through an awful concert. When the offering came around, he placed the fourteen dollars in the offering plate. No one missed the wallets and the church had made more money from them than they would have trying to sell them in the church bookstore.

Andrea smiled. "I still have one of those wallets."

"Me too," Atticus said. In fact, several still hid around the family cabin. "You always knew how to make me see things from a different perspective. I was afraid you still could."

"And this time I'm not alone. I have something for you." She unzipped the front of her wet suit, reached in, and pulled out a small Ziploc bag. It held a single photo; the one from the beach. Atticus took the photo, his hand immediately trembling. "Thank you— oof!"

A blur of bright colors flashed by Andrea's vision,

erasing Atticus from her view.

"I'll kill you!"

Andrea looked down and found her Hawaiian-clad rescuer pummeling Atticus. He took the first two blows, one to the head and one on his shoulder, but quickly managed to block the next few. Frozen by the sudden violence, she watched as Atticus's face changed from that of a kind man missing his family to a trained killer's.

Then it happened. Atticus caught both of Remus's hands, pulled himself farther down through his straddled legs, brought his own legs up behind the man, and looped them around his throat. With a sudden jerk, Remus gagged and was flung backwards.

As Atticus and Remus regained their feet, Remus produced a five-inch blade and grinned fiendishly. Atticus moved his hand to his waist and found the .357 holster empty.

"Looking for that?" Remus said, pointing behind him, where the revolver rested on the floor. There was no way Atticus could reach the weapon without receiving a five-inch puncture wound in his back.

Remus moved in, whipping the knife back and forth so haphazardly that Atticus couldn't block or predict where the next attack would come from. Each slice cut air as Atticus dodged backwards. The backs of his legs bumped into the slat of wood jutting from the wall. He fell back onto the seat just as the knife swept across his eyes, missing by inches.

"Stop!" Andrea yelled, but neither man heard her. "Stop or I'll shoot" She accented the statement by pulling back the hammer of her Coast-Guard-issue SIG P229R-DAK .40 caliber handgun.

Remus froze.

Atticus moved.

With amazing speed, Atticus twisted Remus's wrist, dislodging the knife. As Remus was just beginning to register the pain, Atticus caught the knife and brought it up to Remus's throat.

With a growl, he said, "Try to kill me again and I'll return the favor."

Remus trembled as he glared at Atticus with liquid hatred, tempted to act even with a knife to his throat and a gun to his head. He looked like an animal, barely contained in the shell of a man.

"Oh dear, oh dear. I do believe that will be quite enough of that." Trevor Manfred slid into the room with a grin on his face. "Now that you've all had your fun, why don't you explain to me what the devil is going on?"

Remus replied, "He tried to—"

"I would prefer to receive an answer from someone with more brains," Trevor said. "It's clear you have, yet again, offended our guest."

"He wasn't that much trouble. Like a fly, easily swatted." Atticus removed the knife from Remus's throat and shoved him away. Remus caught himself against the wall, clearly enraged and ready to continue the fight.

A strong slap on his ear shocked him out of his rage.

"Switch off, you oaf!" Trevor shouted. "You are to

stay away from both Atticus and his guest. I'm docking you one month's pay. Don't fail me again."

He bowed his head.

"Now sod off."

Remus exited, his head turned down, afraid to look Trevor in the eyes.

Trevor turned his attention to Andrea. His eyes burned with anger. "You have no business being on this vessel, and if I didn't think your government would give me the runaround, I'd press charges. In the meantime, I leave you in Atticus's hands. However, you must first sign a nondisclosure form."

With that, Trevor removed a folded piece of paper and a pen. "It's fortunate I was on my way down here with this."

Andrea was incredulous. "What!"

"Make no mistake; you are trespassing on this ship. If you do not sign a nondisclosure form, stating that everything you see, hear, and smell on this ship will be kept confidential, you will be thrown overboard."

"This is ridiculous."

"There are a number of technologies on the *Titan*, the nations of the world would love to get their hands on. I can't have you leaking information."

"More like national treasures."

Trevor smiled. "You say tomatoes…Now sign it."

Andrea looked up at Atticus. With a sour face, he nodded his agreement. "Any testimony you could give about what you see on board would be disallowed anyway because you broke into the ship."

"The voice of reason!" Trevor slapped Atticus playfully on the back. "I like this man more and more every day."

Andrea took the pen and paper and quickly signed. Trevor took the paper and pocketed it. "There now, that wasn't so hard, was it, *my dear*?" Before Andrea could object to being called "my dear" one more time, Trevor headed for the door. "Welcome to the *Titan*. Do try to get some sleep tonight; for in the morn, we hunt!"

"Wait," Andrea said. "Do I have a room?"

Trevor smiled wide. "You can stay where you undoubtedly want to stay, with Atticus. After all, every hero needs a woman to couple with before the final battle." With a "ta ta," Trevor left the room.

Atticus bent down and picked up the photo of his family and his .357, placing the gun back in its holster. "C'mon," he said. "Let's get out of here. It's hot as hell." He looked back at her and reached out his hand, causing a nervous twang to move up through her body. The idea of spending the night with Atticus was tantalizing, yet wrong. Too soon. When Atticus spoke, she realized there was nothing to worry about, or look forward to.

"Tomorrow's going to be a hard day, and I need to sleep."

Andrea left the room with him, glad to be out of the glowing white inferno but terrified by what the next day might bring. She'd seen the look of a killer in Atticus's eyes twice—first, when he was launching the harpoon at the creature, then again, when he fought with Remus. When he transformed into that killer, when hatred clouded his soul, she feared him. But now, calm as he was, leading her to his room, she felt at ease and safe. She wasn't sure she could handle seeing his dark side again, but knew she would.

31

THE TITAN—GULF OF MAINE

The heavy double doors opened automatically, allowing Remus access to his opulent bedroom. He silently stole through the room, avoiding the plush king-size bed set atop a frame of ivory tusks. He moved through the dimly lit space without incident, having memorized the room's unchanging layout years ago. From the bedroom he entered a small library full of several aging first editions, then on to a living room, the modern accoutrements of which spoke in marked contrast to the ancient relics found around the ship.

In addition to the pixel-perfect, fifty-inch flat-screen TV, superbly concealed surround-sound system, dark-wood executive desk, and plush leather seating found in the living rooms of the rich and famous, this room had an entire wall covered in security monitors through which every room on the *Titan* could be viewed in full color. The wall shone brightly with streaming video from every lounge, bedroom, and bathroom.

As Remus entered the room, Trevor acknowledged his presence by leaning forward and tapping on one of the screens with a letter opener fashioned like a scimitar. The brig, currently empty, filled the screen in all its stark white glory.

"You're lucky I was watching," Trevor said. "I do believe you would have met your demise had I not arrived when I did. Do you know how hard it is for this frail body to move that quickly down so many flights of stairs? I expressed nearly a day's worth of water through my armpits at the effort."

Remus huffed. "I could've taken him."

Trevor spun around in his jet-black swivel chair, his black-clothed body seemingly melting into it so that his face and Muppet-like burst of white hair hovered in space like a fuzzy planet. His crooked posture added to the odd look. "That' I'm afraid, is still up for debate. It was the woman that would have done you in."

"Stupid bitch. I'll—"

Trevor waggled his finger in Remus's face. "You are to treat the woman with respect for as long as she and Atticus are aboard the *Titan*. When she leaves, I will grant you shore leave so you can finish what you started in the brig." Trevor sighed and looked back to the empty security screen. "It's a pity, though; I was looking forward to the entertainment."

Trevor stood and moved to the room's single window. The black sky outside shimmered with radiant stars and the white glow of the Milky Way. "Tell me, Remus, what were your mistakes tonight?"

Remus stood suddenly rigid. He knew the answers to the questions would result in either a reward or punishment. He mentally replayed the night's events and everything that went wrong. "I should have locked the brig behind me."

"Correct. You're extracurricular activities will have to be conducted in a more clandestine manner while Atticus is on board. He may be a killer, but he's got the moral fortitude of a saint. If he chooses to remain on board," Trevor set his eyes to burrowing in Remus's. "I expect this to be a permanent change."

"Yes, sir."

"Now then, what else?"

"I should have known I was being followed."

"Correct again. While having your fun, do be more aware of your surroundings. I'm sure Atticus is stealthier than most, but you know this ship. Stay off the beaten path from now on. What else?"

"I...Damn. I didn't check her for a weapon."

"Indeed. While you're foolish mistake almost made your life forfeit, next time it could very well be mine. Do *not* make that mistake again, or it will cost you more than one month's pay. Understood?"

Remus began sweating beneath his Hawaiian shirt. Trevor's calm exterior and half smile were no consolation because Remus knew better than to truly anger him.

"Now, then, a final question." Trevor clasped his hands behind his back and strode over to Remus so that they were face-to-face. "What two valuable bits of information did we learn tonight?"

The first answer came in a flash. Remus gripped his fists tight. "Someone tipped him off about the woman."

Trevor nodded. "We'll need to find out whom, of course, but I suspect any number of our crew might be cursed with consciences, so that will prove futile until the hunt is over. And, the second?"

Remus grew nervous as nothing came to mind. Unable to concentrate he glanced away from Trevor's piercing, light blue eyes. His vision landed on one of the security screens, and he smiled. He met Trevor's eyes. "Atticus has a weakness. He cares for the woman."

Trevor smiled. "You just earned back your lost pay and saved your testicles."

Remus paled and looked down to find a silenced pistol aimed at his crotch. He let out a long sigh as Trevor moved away and placed the pistol on the desk. He turned to the security monitors. "Now then, let's see what you were looking at."

An image of Andrea filled a security screen. She stood in Atticus's Incan bathroom, removing first her wet suit, then a formfitting blue T-shirt, revealing her ample breasts concealed only by a sports bra. A moment later, Atticus entered the bathroom and crouched in front of her.

"Oh, ho, ho! Our man moves fast!" Trevor said as he threw himself back into his swivel chair and propped his feet up on an end table topped in petrified wood. "It appears I will find entertainment tonight after all!"

Remus pulled up a chair and settled in. He looked at the monitor, and growled, "Shoulda been me."

"Someday," Trevor said, patting the hulking man's arm. "You still have your manhood intact. Be happy for that. Now shush and watch."

Remus crossed his arms and focused on the screen. Atticus had his hands on her stomach and was moving up. Remus made a silent pledge to himself. No matter how much Trevor liked Atticus, he'd make him pay for what had happened. If Atticus left the *Titan,* Remus would hunt him down. If he stayed on board, Remus would bide his time and arrange an accident. And when Atticus was dead, the Coast Guard chick would be his. He'd keep her on board and alive until he got bored with her. Then Laurel could have his way with her.

32

THE TITAN—GULF OF MAINE

A groan escaped Andrea's lips as Atticus probed her body with his fingers. She'd involuntary convulsed when he'd first touched her, and she found herself growing more nervous with every passing moment. Very few men had seen her in just a bra. Even fewer had touched her so gently.

"Ouch!" Andrea winced, as Atticus pressed on her ribs with his fingers. "That hurt like hell."

Atticus smiled and stood. "It'd hurt a lot more if it were broken. You've got some good bruises though. You're lucky to be alive."

"Tell me about it."

"Anywhere else hurt?"

Andrea thought about telling him that all sorts of body parts hurt, just to see if he'd give them the same kind attention as her ribs, but decided against it. Though they'd once been close, there was a lot he still didn't know about her, and she didn't want him to get the wrong impression. But what was the right impression? Every minute she spent with him, she was less and less sure. "No. Aside from being exhausted, just my ribs hurt."

Andrea moved to put her blue T-shirt back on, but he stopped her by taking hold of her wrist. "Not so fast. Hold on." He moved back into the bedroom. What he was doing, she had no idea, and she did her best not to imagine.

He returned a moment later holding three ice cubes. He opened up the bathroom closet and took out a thin washcloth, which he used to wrap up the ice. "Hold this against your ribs for about fifteen minutes. It will help with—"

"I know what it's for," Andrea said. She looked out after him as he snatched a blanket off the bed and moved to the couch in the living room. *I guess that settles that question,* Andrea thought.

Andrea sighed and returned her attention to the amazing bathroom surrounding her. It was otherworldly, and most likely belonged to a nation that didn't know it was missing. She glanced back into the living room one more time and found Atticus's eyes closed. Asleep already.

Without bothering to shut the bathroom door, Andrea removed the rest of her clothes and turned on the Incan shower, which cascaded like a mountain waterfall. As soon as the water fell, gentle jungle sounds filled the air from a speaker in the ceiling. She felt her muscles relax and the tension that had build up over the past few days ebb slightly. As she stepped under the warm water, her eyes returned to the open door. It was a sophomoric invitation, leaving the door open like that, and she knew she'd chastise herself for it in the morning, but she couldn't help but wish Atticus would join her, if only to hold her.

As the room filled with steam, Andrea turned away from the door and let the water pour over her face, ignorant of the mechanical eye focusing in on her body from the ceiling above.

THE CUSHY sofa did little to ease Atticus's chaotic emotional state. His body grew heavy and tense as it came down from the adrenaline rush brought on by his encounter with Remus. Memories of happier times resurfaced from the photo Andrea had given him and shouted to be recognized. Plans for the confrontation with the creature dubbed Kronos scratched at his mind's eye, eager to be seen. The death of Giona, still fresh, festered in his soul like an open wound. On top of all that, Andrea's presence in the next room fought for his attention.

Somehow her presence cast a shadow over the dueling thoughts and emotions, and as he lay on the sofa, pretending to be asleep, his mind fixed most keenly on his old friend, now a woman. He could still feel her soft skin under his fingers as he felt first her ribs for signs of fracture, then her belly and sides for signs of hemorrhage. Finding none, he let his hands linger on her body for a few moments' longer, gaining renewed energy and hope from her warmth.

Sensing motion, Atticus opened his eyes. He looked to the bed. Andrea had yet to return. The bathroom door remained wide open, and the sound of the waterfall shower falling onto the stone floor echoed out. She was in the shower. She'd left the door open.

He knew Andrea was naked in the shower, but he couldn't see her. He knew he had feelings for her, resurfacing with her return to his life, and had no doubt she returned…something for him. She was there, after all. But was the open door merely carelessness after the trials of the night or was it truly what it appeared to be: an invitation?

Atticus sat up on the couch and rubbed his eyes with the palms of his hands. He stood and paced. He walked toward the open bathroom door, but stopped at the mini-fridge. He popped an ice cube in his mouth, and returned to the sofa.

As the plush cushion absorbed him, he noticed the photo of himself, Maria, and Giona at the beach, still resting on the coffee table. He picked it up and allowed his eyes to trace the lines of his dead girls.

God, I miss them.

Andrea had risked her life to deliver the photo, somehow knowing that the sight of it might return some of his sanity. The woman was obviously insane.

TREVOR GROANED as the bathroom's view clouded with steam, blocking his view of Andrea's stellar body. He looked at Remus, whose smile had turned to a grimace. "You know, we're really going to have to turn the water temperature down at some point. This is bloody ridiculous."

Pursing his lips, Trevor sat up and leaned forward, never taking his eyes off the screen displaying an image of the steamy bathroom. "I think, perhaps, we misjudged Atticus's attachment to the woman."

"I bet he's gay," Remus said with a snort.

"Mmm. At any rate, it's quite possible his rescue of her was merely an act of conscience. I swear to you, morality boggles my mind."

Remus turned to him. "But you believe in God."

"Indeed, I do. I just happen to disagree with Him. Besides, I've got O'Shea to wipe my slate clean. You know, you should really think about going to confession."

Remus laughed. "No thanks. I'm looking forward to hell."

"A prince among devils, is that it?" Trevor stood and stretched. "Ahh, well. Off to bed with you then. Tomorrow's going to be quite the day. No use in spending the night trying to see through steam." With that, he flicked a switch on the desk, and the wall of monitors went black.

Remus stood, scowling at the now-blank monitor where Andrea had only moments ago stood naked before their eyes.

"Having seen the fruit, you long to eat it that

much more, eh?" Trevor asked with a smile, reading Remus's one-track mind with ease.

Remus just nodded.

Trevor rubbed his back like a consoling father. "All in good time, dear Remus. All in good time."

ANDREA HAD just finished rinsing an exotic shampoo from her hair when a cool draft snapped her out of the South American jungle and back onto Trevor Manfred's ship. She spun around and found a figure, concealed by steam, standing at the shower's entrance.

"Who's there?"

Andrea sighed with relief. It was Atticus.

It was Atticus!

A quiver filled her voice as she replied, unsure of whether or not she should cover her nakedness. "I...I don't—"

"Did the Coast Guard send you? Are you here about the creature? To stop me?"

"No, Atti. I'm here for you."

"Why did you bring the photo?"

"I promised your wife...Maria...in the photo. It's stupid, but I promised her I'd take care of you."

"You broke into my house?"

"You left it unlocked. Your brother—"

"You saw Conner? What...what did he say?"

"He knew you would go after it." Andrea's heart beat like a double bass in a heavy-metal anthem. She was shocked as the next words escaped her mouth.

"He said it's a rare woman who will drop everything and search the high seas for an old friend."

Andrea felt a wave of heat rush through her body as a shadow moved toward her through the steam. She sighed with relief and a little bit of disappointment when she saw only Atticus's hand, holding a towel. She took it, and stepped out of the water, wrapping herself up.

"Is that all?" he asked.

"No." Andrea could feel her emotions rising as Atticus grew closer. "He said, 'welcome back to the family.'"

With that, Atticus was through the steam, standing in a pair of boxers and a T-shirt. She felt oddly comfortable in his presence.

"It's been so long," he said.

"I know."

"How is it possible, then?"

"It's not just me?"

Atticus slipped his hands around her waist and let them linger on the small of her back. She pulled him closer, and they stumbled back into the water, soaking both towel and clothes. Their bodies meshed together as rivulets of water cascaded down the valley where their bodies met. He pressed his lips against hers, letting them linger, his top lip on her lower. He pulled back and looked her in the eyes.

"I have to finish what I started here."

"I know."

"Then you won't try to stop me?"

"No. I'll help."

Andrea fell into Atticus's embrace, lost in her emotions, swept up in the moment, and for the first time in a long time, felt loved and alive. *This was worth the risk*, she thought. In that moment, she realized how empty her life had become since losing her Abigail. But somehow through chance of fate—or the will of God—they'd found each other; or rather, she'd found him—dead—and brought him back. Now he was returning the favor, bringing her back to life.

33

THE TITAN—GULF OF MAINE

A loud, angry thumping pulled Atticus from his sleep. He sat up quickly and found the bed empty. Andrea was gone. The banging continued, and flashes of Remus pummeling Andrea sprang into his mind. He leapt from the bed and vaulted into the living room where he found Andrea reaching for the door.

"Hold your horses," Andrea said as she opened the suite door.

Atticus slid to a stop behind Andrea as the door opened to reveal O'Shea, dressed in his black priest's clothing. His eyes opened wide as he took in Andrea's form, standing in one of Atticus's Navy T-shirts. It fit her loosely, but it was clear she wore nothing but panties underneath.

"Holy..." O'Shea whispered before Andrea's voice

diced his unpriestly fantasies to ribbons.

"And what kind of priest are you supposed to be?" Andrea grumbled, before moving to close the door on O'Shea.

"Hold on," Atticus said as he approached, wearing only his boxers. "He's not exactly a normal priest, and you're not exactly dressed like a nun. Besides, he saved your life."

Andrea shot Atticus a confused look.

"He tipped me off that you had been captured," Atticus said.

Andrea offered O'Shea a half smile. "Then I owe you my thanks."

"Think nothing of it," O'Shea said, "Just do me a favor and put on some clothes. I may be a priest, but I've yet to be castrated."

Andrea smiled and left for the bedroom.

As soon as she was gone, O'Shea punched Atticus lightly on the shoulder. "You devil. A regular action hero, saving the day and getting the girl."

"Nothing happened," Atticus said.

"Sure," O'Shea said with a lopsided grin that told Atticus he'd never believe anything other than the two had been up all night having sinful sex.

Only then did Atticus notice that O'Shea was slightly out of breath and sweating. "Did you come by for a reason?"

"Oh! Right." O'Shea said. "It seems we've located Kronos again. Same pattern as yesterday, following the fish. Trevor thinks it's a feeding pattern and that it will rise again today around the same time as yesterday."

Atticus squinted in thought. "It's possible. Daily routine isn't uncommon in many animals, but ocean predators are typically opportunistic feeders because it's not always certain when the next meal will be found. Then again, I doubt this thing has any trouble finding something to eat, so a routine of feeding might make sense."

When Atticus finished speaking, O'Shea's face turned curious—squinted eyes, pursed lips.

"What?" Atticus said.

"I was expecting a mad dash to the bridge, followed by a quick dive in *Ray* to face and kill the beast, not hypotheses from an oceanographer. Beauty, it seems, truly can kill the beast."

Andrea was suddenly at Atticus's side, fully dressed in her shorts and blue T-shirt. Her feet were bare, as she'd worn no shoes, only her flippers. "If you're going to do this, get dressed, and let's get it over with." She shoved Atticus's clothes into his arms and moved past O'Shea into the hallway.

O'Shea smiled. "Or not."

"Which way to the bridge?" Andrea asked.

"I'm not sure Trevor—"

Andrea blew past him.

O'Shea looked at Atticus questioningly. Atticus shrugged. "She signed a waiver."

Andrea never slowed. Atticus fumbled with his pants as he pulled them up. "Better follow her," he said to O'Shea. "Keep her out of trouble."

O'Shea moved to follow Andrea, then paused. "Where are you going?"

The lightness that had been in Atticus's voice disappeared. "I'm going to kill it."

"Heading straight for *Ray*?"

Atticus nodded, as Andrea's thumping footfalls on the stairs reverberated down the hallway. "Keep her out of trouble while I'm gone."

O'Shea nodded, then ran after Andrea. "Godspeed, Atticus" he shouted back before heading up the stairs.

As Atticus, fully dressed in jeans, a T-shirt, and sneakers, tore off down the hall in the opposite direction, he doubted even God could help him. He would become the devil himself, death and destruction incarnate. As he ran toward the stairwell that would take him into the depths of the *Titan*, each step quickened his pulse and charged his rage. He would soon be a perpetual-motion machine of pure hatred, and it would fuel his mad quest to kill a creature that shrugged off a titanium harpoon as though it had been a flicked toothpick. Had anyone been in the stairwell as Atticus descended, they would have mistaken for a wild creature, grunting savagely, on the hunt.

It wasn't far from the truth.

O'SHEA BURST onto the bridge to find Trevor and Andrea laughing over a cup of coffee. Trevor noted the concern on O'Shea's face. "Come to keep me in line, Father?"

"I just…"

"Fear not, good man, I am not immune to the charms of a woman whilst she is a guest aboard the *Titan*. Freed of her burden to the U.S. government, she's rather a delight." He clinked his mug with Andrea's and took a sip.

Andrea met O'Shea's eyes briefly and rolled her own, silently letting him know the feeling of kinship was far from mutual. In fact, O'Shea knew from experience that Trevor's own benign assertions were simply a ruse meant to befriend an adversary before he moved in for the kill…sometimes literally. He'd heard enough confessions to have no doubts about that.

"Sir!" the captain shouted. "We're tracking the creature, but now there's something else, something smaller, but—"

"Yes, yes," Trevor said. "Our hero has taken the call as we knew he would."

Andrea straightened. "What?" She looked at O'Shea. "Where's Atticus?"

He pointed to the green screen the captain stood over. It displayed several small dots representing fish or other small sea creatures. A hazy large blob could be seen, followed by an immense mass. Moving toward the larger of the two readings was a small oval. Trevor stood next to Andrea and pointed at the fast-moving oval.

"You see? Atticus has decided to meet his fate head-on." He traced the direction the oval was heading straight out. It met with the larger blob. Trevor tapped it. "He who fights with monsters might take care lest he thereby become a monster. And if you gaze for long into an abyss, the abyss gazes also into you." Trevor smiled wide and gazed at Andrea through crazed blue eyes. "Beware Kronos. For the monster is now hunting you!"

Andrea stood silently, her feelings of safety now far removed.

"You'll be happy to know," Trevor said to Andrea, "that we planned ahead for Atticus's lone assault." He flicked a switch, activating a panel of five monitors at the back of the bridge. Four showed a view from each side of the submersible, providing a 360-degree view. The fifth showed the sub's interior, where Atticus sat, wearing a scowl and a sinister gaze.

"Can we speak to him?" Andrea asked, attempting not to sound overly eager.

"Indeed, but we won't, lest we cause the locomotive to falter in its course." Trevor said. "Atticus will meet his destiny as he wished—on his own."

Remus entered the bridge through one of the outer doors, wearing a bright orange Hawaiian shirt and a grin. He glowered at Andrea for a moment, then took the captain's position behind the helm.

"As we all do," Trevor finished, fixing Andrea with a suddenly serious gaze. "Remus, commence the chase."

O'Shea fought the urge to retch. He knew Trevor well enough to realize that Andrea wouldn't survive the day if Atticus didn't. If Atticus didn't survive, he needed to find a way to get Andrea off the *Titan*. He had no idea how he'd accomplish such a task. And so, for the first time in his life, he prayed—not offering the sort of prayer he'd concocted over the years for Trevor's benefit, but an honest-to-goodness prayer to the God of the universe, whoever that might be.

34

THE TITAN—GULF OF MAINE

As *Ray* rocketed forward twenty feet below the ocean's surface, Atticus kept his eyes locked forward. Some might call his current state of mind a throwback to earlier times, when men hunted and killed prey with their bare hands, as that had required such a fixated concentration. But most would believe those days, when men had savagely killed for food, were long past. But Atticus knew otherwise. He'd seen the savagery of man, and at times, had become its embodiment.

As now.

The recent emotional wounds buried so desperately over the past few days were allowed to reopen and fester. The enmity built within him, surging and billowing out like a mushroom cloud, eradicating his sensibilities and absorbing his hesitation. The rage channeled his core to a laser focus, beaming through the ocean, boiling it away.

As he closed the distance to his target, his adrenaline pumped with anticipation of a life-or-death struggle. He ground his teeth and focused his eyes on the distant blue. Then he saw it.

A wave of shadow moving through the water below.

He was already above it!

Without thought to the possible consequences of his actions, Atticus spun *Ray* upside down and plunged, nose first into the depths like a diving fighter jet. His thumbs jittered over the torpedo-launch button. He knew a single torpedo might have little effect, but *Ray* carried ten, and the cumulative effect might be enough.

The shadow emerged from the depths at two hundred feet down, just fifteen feet shy of the ocean shelf's floor. Atticus caught his breath, and the sight of the thing nearly sapped his determination. The shadow he'd seen from a distance with Trevor and O'Shea appeared inconsequential compared to this. He was a crab attacking a great white, and just as the great white would ignore a crab, Kronos paid little attention to the approaching submersible.

Atticus continued his dive, intent on each torpedo hitting its mark. He cruised in toward the massive horse-shaped head, and was momentarily struck by the peaceful movement of the beast. Its rhythmic up and down undulations propelled it through the water, guided by long pectoral fins and very small lateral fins. Atticus realized Trevor's comparison to the Kronosaurus wasn't too far off. If only the creature's torso were about one hundred feet shorter. Its mouth lolled slightly agape, revealing devilish teeth. And its eyes…Atticus stared at its eyes, haunted by the memories that returned with its gaze.

With a rage-filled scream, Atticus hit the yellow button, powering *Ray* toward Kronos at speeds that almost guaranteed a collision. Then, with quick flicks of his thumbs he launched all ten torpedoes, aiming straight for Kronos's head. After launching the torpedoes, Atticus quickly realized that *Ray* was still accelerating and *gaining* on the torpedoes, just seconds away from detonation. He swung *Ray* low, beneath the torpedoes, and as Kronos's body arced, he spun *Ray* between its body and the seafloor, zipping through the momentary arch just before it closed.

A second later, the ocean convulsed as ten explosions pulsed through it, each one sending a shock wave rolling out from the point of impact. Caught from behind, *Ray* flipped end over end. Atticus cut the engines and side-slipped to the bottom like a coin tossed in a wishing well. *Ray* landed on the seafloor with a jolt that sent up a plume of sand.

As the sand settled on top of *Ray*, Atticus heard a deep bellow reverberate through the waters. A death wallow? Had he succeeded?

The wail turned into a roar, angry and energetic.

Kronos had taken ten torpedoes at close range and the only thing Atticus had achieved was to enrage the beast. He took some consolation in the fact that he was, like a real ray, concealed beneath the sand. But the fight was far from over. He thumbed the trigger for the electric-shock cables. They worked like stun guns, each locking onto the target by piercing or suction, then unleashing an electric current through insulated cables that kept the charge from being dissipated into the water. Unlike a stun gun, the charge unleashed was enough to kill a whale ten times over...or the entire crew of a U.S. Coast Guard cutter.

As the remaining cloud of silt settled, and the view cleared, Atticus found himself in a dire situation. No longer undulating, the whole mass of Kronos's body slowly glided in a circle around *Ray,* propelled only by its four fins. It had located him instantly, and was apparently making up its mind as how best to kill him. He watched as the head moved past, following just behind the tail, its body forming a massive ring. One great eye glanced at Atticus. He was sure it could see him inside *Ray.*

Perhaps that's why it had yet to attack? If the creature held any intelligence, like that of a whale or a dolphin, it might be curious as to how a creature could survive in the gut of another. As the body passed by again, its long front flippers pushed it forward and grazed the seafloor with every beat, casting sand into the waters around its sleek, black-topped, white-bellied body.

For an instant, Atticus saw the creature for what it was—not a freak of nature or killing machine, but a miraculous creation, unique in every way.

Then he thumbed the shock-cable trigger and waited for the head to pass again. A shot to the open eye should do the trick. The snout appeared from the right, then the eye again, still watching him. He waited as the head came into range, preparing to surge out of the sand and fire. He'd have a front row seat to watch the thing boil in its own skin.

Atticus held his breath. He could feel his heart beat behind his eyes.

With each beat he imagined faces of the living and the dead.

Giona.

Maria.

Andrea…

He blinked and realized the time had come. He accelerated out of the sand, exploding a cloud of silt from around *Ray* as he rose. Most denizens of the sea would have turned tail and fled at the sight of *Ray* rising off the seafloor, but Kronos turned toward the submersible and opened its maw, ready to snatch its prey.

Atticus fired the shock cables and rocketed forward. Their aim was true; each headed for Kronos's eyes. It would be a fatal shot. Even a beast that large couldn't survive a jolt straight to its brain.

But at the last possible moment, Kronos twisted its head and clamped its jaws shut on the cables, quickly severing them. The electric current meant for the target alone burst into the open ocean and hit *Ray* and Kronos alike.

The jolt coursed through the sub, striking Atticus and nearly knocking him unconscious. But just as soon as it had come, the shock was exhausted. *Ray*'s internal electronics shorted and again the sub began fluttering back toward the seafloor.

As Atticus regained his wits and realized what had happened, he screamed as the sight that had been Giona's last enveloped him. The dark, gaping mouth of Kronos opened wide and sucked *Ray* in. *Ray*'s size kept Atticus from being swallowed whole, but he had no doubt the creature's powerful jaws could crush *Ray* with ease. High-pitched squeaks tore through the cabin as Kronos's teeth etched the glass above Atticus's head. *Ray*'s systems reset, and its external lights blinked back on, illuminating Kronos's jaws. Atticus gazed at the spear-like teeth and wondered what kept them from piercing the glass and finishing the job.

Whatever the reason, he wouldn't waste this last opportunity. Atticus prepped the small nuclear device, doing his best to not look up; any distraction might cost him the time he needed to type in the activation code Trevor had given him. His finger worked the number pad recessed in the armrest, ticking out the fifteen-digit code. Once complete, Atticus's index finger hovered over the final key.

Then he looked up and paused.

He hadn't noticed the slight motion of the submersible or the gentle shake as it was set down gently into the sand. But now, as the gaping jaws loosened around the sub's hull and dim sunlight filtering down from above filled the cabin, Atticus realized what Kronos had done.

"What the hell?" Atticus moved his hand away from the activation keypad and gazed at Kronos as the creature backed away, its eyes locked onto his. Reaching a distance of twenty feet, it resumed its circular course around *Ray*. It was waiting for something, but what?

Atticus knew this behavior was completely unheard of in the animal kingdom. Its life had been threatened. It had been under attack, yet it didn't fight or flee. It had defended itself, to be sure, but then it showed restraint. Perhaps even mercy.

Atticus shook his head at the last thought. He remembered Giona and the way she'd been so quickly eaten. If this creature was intelligent, it had eaten her on purpose, and toyed with him now. He reached over for the activation keypad, but froze before reaching the halfway point. The creature's body, or something inside the creature, caught his attention.

Atticus focused on the anomaly.

A flashing from inside its body. Perhaps it was building up its own electric charge, like an electric eel? If that were true, the herring wouldn't have been able to flee, and he and Giona would have been shocked. Then what the hell was it?

As though in answer to his unspoken question, Kronos brought his body closer, a mere ten feet from *Ray*. Its body filled the view. Moving out of instinct more than anything else, Atticus switched off the exterior lights, turning Kronos's side into a dark canvas.

Then he saw it—a flash from inside the creature, emanating from a precise source. Then with a sudden brilliance, the flash repeated like a strobe light, and an image coalesced at the center of the light.

A silhouette of something at its source.

A form.

A body.

A shape that Atticus immediately recognized.

"Oh, God no…" Atticus leaned so far forward that he hit his head on the lexan glass bubble of *Ray*'s eye socket viewing port, which separated him from the ocean. He didn't even register the impact.

He knew the shape, however impossible. Sadness, then rage, took hold of him, shaking his body. The beast tormented him!

Before Atticus could act and destroy them both with a small thermonuclear device, the impossible happened. The silhouette moved amid the continuing flashes. He could see her arms. He watched her knees rise up to her chest.

Still alive.

Giona was alive—inside Kronos.

Hot tears came with a torrent of emotion. Atticus pushed against the glass bubble, willing himself to burst forth into the ocean, tear Kronos apart, and extract his still-living daughter from its gullet.

"Oh, baby, I'm here ." Atticus filled his lungs and screamed. "Giona! I'm here! I'm going to get you out! I won't leave you! Giona!"

He was pounding on the glass now, beating his

fists as his heart broke for the second time in five days. Then the flashing stopped, and she disappeared, hidden behind Kronos's black skin. Kronos slowly backed away, his body sliding backwards as his massive face turned toward *Ray*. Atticus felt the intelligence behind the massive beast's eyes once again, yet more clearly. It was conveying a message with its eyes—a look of consternation, of disapproval.

Atticus slumped in his chair. How was this possible? It wasn't! His mind kept shouting it at him.

She's dead!

Giona is dead!

No, damn it, she's alive!

Atticus could sense the message coming from the beast. Its eyes, once frightening, now tranquil. It bore him no ill will. And then it let out a cry, a sound so peaceful that Atticus, despite the dire situation, felt comforted. In that moment, he realized that the creature had no intention of truly devouring Giona. She lay inside the creature, yet even after days inside, was still alive and undigested.

A single thought burrowed into Atticus's mind. What kind of creature is this?

ASCENT

35

The flesh supporting her body felt like a waterbed, comfortable and cozy, yet visions of monsters played behind Giona's eyes as she slept. Her hair lay damp and matted to her face and the slick tissue beneath her body. Her wetsuit, still secure, kept the majority of her body free from moisture, but her face, long exposed to the humid air, had paled and wrinkled.

Her breaths, previously even with deep sleep, came ragged and quick. When her eyes finally opened, it seemed that the nightmare she'd just been having continued on into reality.

An all-consuming blackness surrounded her. Light did not exist. Her body didn't exist. As Giona tried to comprehend the absolute darkness, a violation of her senses assailed her nose. The smell of rotting fish, fat, and bloated, thickened the air. She gagged and dry heaved, her stomach lacking substance to issue forth. She breathed through her mouth, which turned out to be a mistake; she could taste the odor. As her body built toward a second dry heave, she became aware of a noise, deep and repeating. It pulled her attention away from the smells.

A deep *whump-whump* came again and again, double beating like a distant machine, working without tire. A momentary hope tugged at her thoughts as she imagined she'd somehow been transported to a fish factory. That would account for the smell and the sound, but...

Giona rested her hands on her bed. It rolled beneath her like the massaging chairs she was fond of trying out at the mall. The surface beneath her suddenly shifted. She tumbled and fell against a wall. It, too, felt soft and smooth, like silk. She stood for a moment, bumping her head on the low ceiling. But the ceiling flexed as her head connected. She'd been trapped inside a giant balloon, or some kind of cocoon.

Panic rising, Giona shuffled around her enclosure, probing the soft walls with her hands. Since she found no method of egress, sobs wracked her body.

Trapped.

"Daddy?" Giona said between vaults of emotion. "Daddy!"

But the darkness around her absorbed her voice. No echo returned. No sound escaped. The fleshy walls held in everything.

Fleshy…

Giona's thoughts lost focus on reality as a flood of memories washed through her mind, overloading her synapses and quickening her breath. She no longer noticed the smell. A single image emerged from the deep, consumed her mind, opening its dagger-filled mouth and sucking her down. Giona opened her mouth to scream as the full realization of her situation struck her, but before the sound could escape, her body left the floor and smashed into the ceiling above.

Then she hit the floor again. Each wall greeted her in rapid succession, pummeling her body. As consciousness slipped away, Giona found breathing nearly impossible. Her body, while being twisted and jounced violently, was ultimately protected by the soft walls that formed her meaty prison. A searing pain turned the darkness all white as something solid struck her head. She blinked back to consciousness seconds later, not knowing how long she'd been out because the murk of unconsciousness was no darker than that of her current waking world. But the pain in her skull told her the impact had been real.

All that mattered was that it had stopped. She held a hand to her throbbing head and felt a warm, sticky wetness beneath her hair. A cut caused by the projectile that had struck her head had swollen and gushed, but the blood had clumped and coagulated in her hair. She imagined the sight of it would send most kids running in fear, but at least the bleeding had stopped. Then she remembered her watch. Her father

had given it to her on her last birthday—a Luminox
Navy SEAL dive watch, the same as her father's. She
pressed a button on the watch and its yellow face
glowed to life. The little light seemed like a spotlight
in her eyes, and she squinted against it as her eyes adjusted.

While the watch did the job of illuminating the
time, it did little to reveal her surroundings. She
checked the time—9:30 a.m. Then she saw the date
and gasped. It'd been four days...four days since her
dive with her father! As her eyes began to water again,
she noted a slight glint of light reflecting from the
floor. She reached her glowing watch out toward it
and saw her camera, now freed from its waterproof
casing.

Her dank cubby had stopped moving almost completely, just rising and falling gently. She slid over to
the camera and snatched it up. After finding the power button, she turned it on. The view screen blazed to
life, causing her to squint again; but while the screen
glowed brighter than the pitch-darkness surrounding
her; it could only project the light it took in through
its lens, which, at the time, was none.

Giona pushed the button on her watch again and
held it down, moving the watch face in front of the
camera's lens. The light of the watch magnified
through the camera and bloomed from the view
screen. For the first time, Giona saw her own body.
Then the watch was extinguished, and the light disappeared. She needed more light. Feeling the camera's
solid frame in the dark, Giona realized she held a

bright light source in her hands. Snapping a few pictures would reveal everything.

Not bothering to aim, Giona held up the camera
and took a photo. The flash exploded into the small
dark chamber like an atom bomb. The brightness shot
stabs of pain through Giona's fully dilated eyes. She
groaned, and in the resuming dark, now colored by
shades of purple dancing in her vision, she lowered
the brightness and set the camera to take multiple
photos. She hoped the lower light level but would
allow her eyes to adjust.

With three quick bursts, she held the button
down, unleashing a strobe of light on the small chamber. With each successive barrage, her eyes adjusted.
Then she held the button down. The flash burst bril-
liantly, twice a second for thirty seconds.

Giona took in the space around her. Blue veins
pulsed just beneath the pink flesh above, below, and
all around her. At one end of the cavity, a large swirl
of taut flesh, like a giant, muscled sphincter, emerged
from the darkness. She realized that was how she'd
entered the chamber.

The full weight of her situation fell on her as she
saw the small chamber for the first time, realizing she
was trapped in some godforsaken portion of s sea
monster's gullet. She'd either die of starvation or be
digested alive. A chill enveloped her body. She pulled
her knees to her chest while leaning against one of the
soft walls. Having seen enough of her situation, she
dropped the camera and longed for the blessed escape
of unconsciousness to return.

She didn't want to be awake when the beast began to digest her.

36

THE TITAN—GULF OF MAINE

"Bloody hell!" Trevor shouted as he stared at the video feed transmitting to the bridge of the *Titan* from *Ray* below.

He saw it. He saw her as clearly as every other living soul standing on the bridge. In a brilliant display of light, the silhouette of a young woman pierced the skin of the leviathan just as it seemed Atticus would finish it off. The girl still lived. Atticus's daughter was still alive, in the belly of the beast. "This can't be happening."

Andrea placed her hand on the screen display of Atticus placing his hand against the lexan bubble of the submersible. "She's alive." Tears rolled down her cheeks, tracing the wrinkles formed by her wide smile.

O'Shea was equally taken aback. He moved away from the screens, deep in thought, his forehead a crossroads of creases. "A miracle."

Trevor focused on Atticus's face, watching his expression morph from despair to hope. Of all the accursed things that could have happened, this was not only the most unlikely, but also the worst. His warrior, his brave hero, had been reduced to a blathering father in the thirty seconds that it took him to register the form of his living daughter inside Kronos.

"Do it, Atticus," Trevor shouted. "Finish the beast! Finish the activation code! Do it, man!" Trevor shook the screen.

"No!" Trevor bleated as he shoved away from the offensive screen. Atticus wouldn't act. He had the creature safely at the bottom of the sea. He could finish it without posing a danger to the *Titan*.

If only his daughter were still dead.

Trevor turned his eyes back to the scene going on below and felt a chill ripple through him. Staring through the central screen and burrowing into his soul were two yellow eyes.

Kronos.

The beast mocked him. Taunted him.

Damn the beast, and damn Atticus!

Trevor slipped back to Remus while the others stared silently at the screen, watching Atticus and Kronos simply sit and gawk at each other. "Are we directly above them?"

Remus pealed his eyes away from the screens. He shook his head slightly, snapped out of his daze, and nodded. Then a smile spread on his face as he read Trevor's mind.

"Drop a spread of depth charges. Force the beast to the surface. Have a crew take the heli up with a full load of torpedoes, high-yield. Ready the antisub rockets with mortars...and load the 356mm." Trevor glared at the screens. Atticus had yet to move. "We're doing this my way now."

Remus grabbed the captain and two more of the crew, quietly delivering his orders. All three nodded rapidly, mentally preparing for the tasks at hand. As Trevor watched, he couldn't help but smile. The crew had been trained in the fine art of war as much as how to polish brass. They'd prepared for a moment like this for years. He could see by the sparkle in each man's eyes that they were ready and eager.

Still, Trevor wished it weren't necessary, but his hero had betrayed them all. Of course, he blamed himself for the snafu. While there was no way he could have foreseen Giona's still being alive, it wasn't wise to allow Atticus access to *Ray* alone. But the man had seemed such a competent and determined killer, Trevor hadn't considered the idea that there might be a reason to change his mind.

But there it was.

No matter, Trevor thought. His prize was within reach, and no man, no matter how liked, had ever stood between Trevor Manfred and his goal. If the depth charges didn't succeed in killing the beast, they would force it to the surface. Trevor would then unleash a barrage of torpedoes from air and from sea, followed by missiles packed with antisubmarine mortars, and if they were really lucky, they'd get off a clean shot with the big gun and fourteen-inch cannon salvaged from a World War II battleship that Trevor had refitted for the *Titan*. Hidden below decks, the gun had only one barrel instead of three, but it could still sink, and kill, most anything in the ocean.

Remus slid back to Trevor. "The chopper will be in the air in five minutes. The torpedoes are being loaded. The missiles are warming up and the cannon…" Remus smiled. "We'll take care of that from here."

ANDREA GASPED and spun around to find Remus and Trevor speaking in hushed voices, but she had heard them. A single word had trickled through her preoccupied mind and had shaken her out of her emotional stupor. "Did you say cannon?"

Her eyebrows furrowed angrily. She knew they had. As she stalked toward the two men, the rest of the conversation, which she'd heard but not registered, began to penetrate her consciousness.

"Atticus is still down there. His—his daughter is still alive."

Trevor grinned. "I'm afraid—" Trevor scratched his head through his fluffy white hair, "how can I put this—not for long."

Andrea couldn't believe what she was hearing. She knew Trevor was evil. The man reeked of darkness, but she wouldn't have guessed him capable of this;

nor had she ever imagined that the *Titan* was much more than the world's largest pleasure yacht. It was, in fact, the world's most luxurious battleship! "You son of a—"

Remus's backhand caught her across the cheek, nearly breaking her jaw. She spilled across the bridge, falling into a chair and slumping to the floor. She'd never been hit like that in her life, and while it didn't hurt as much as she would have expected, it left her dazed.

Andrea stood as blood trickled from her mouth. Remus chuckled, enraging her.

But before she could launch herself into action, a pair of strong arms reached under hers and then up and around the back of her head. The hands locked tight and held firm. She grunted and tried to free herself, but it was no use. When the man spoke, she was shocked to hear the voice of O'Shea. "I've got her."

"I don't need your help," Remus growled as he took a step forward.

"There isn't time!" O'Shea shouted. "I've seen the eyes of the devil, and it must be destroyed!"

Remus apparently didn't hear and continued forward, determined to finish her off. But Trevor's light grip on his arm stopped him cold. "The good Father is right, Remus. There isn't time."

Remus snarled at Andrea. "Later..."

"To arms! To arms!" Trevor shouted, his excitement for the hunt returning.

As Trevor and Remus returned to the controls, Andrea whispered to O'Shea, "You bastard."

"I had no choice," O'Shea whispered back as he dragged her toward the door.

"Liar."

"They would have killed you."

"You could have helped."

O'Shea sighed. "I promised Atticus I would get you off the *Titan* if things went wrong. And things are going very wrong."

Andrea's insides twisted at the thought of Atticus. "What about Atticus?"

"He strikes me as a man who can take care of himself."

Andrea knew he was right. There was nothing they could do to help Atticus. They were outnumbered and outgunned. Just getting off the *Titan* would be tricky.

O'Shea's hands slipped away from around her neck. A moment later she felt a hard object pressed against her back. A gun.

"Get moving," O'Shea said with authority, jabbing the gun into her back.

"Hey," she shouted angrily, then moved forward to the door. Her head suddenly yanked back, pulled by her hair. She shouted in pain.

O'Shea filled his voice with anger. "Don't try anything or—"

"And where might you be off to?" Trevor asked, spinning around slowly with a smile.

"The brig. She shouldn't be here," O'Shea said.

"On the contrary," Trevor said. "Her presence here serves to raise the emotional stakes. She must stay and watch. It will be a much more...well-rounded experience." Trevor fixed his eyes on Andrea. "Don't you think, my dear?"

"Go to hell!" she shouted.

"Ha!" Trevor threw his head back with the laugh. "I'm afraid the good priest has cleared me of that fate. Though I imagine after this day's exploits, I may have need of his services in the morning." Trevor moved his gaze to O'Shea. "Bring her to the window, where she has a good view."

After a quickly whispered "sorry," O'Shea led Andrea to the bridge's front window. Two decks below, she could see a large, gray gun rising out of the deck, its ominous fourteen-inch barrel at the ready.

She looked back at the video display. Atticus and Kronos still sat silently, staring at each other. *Move, Atti, move*, Andrea willed him, but he remained fixated on Kronos. Whether it was the beast's stare or shock over his daughter's being alive that held him so still, Atticus failed to budge, locked in the path of a madman's destructive fantasy.

"The chopper is in the air," Remus said. "The hedgehog is ready to deploy the depth charges."

"You're going to get us all killed," Andrea spat.

Trevor smiled widely. "A coward turns away, but a brave man's choice is danger."

37

RAY—JEFFERY'S LEDGE

Gloom fell over the seafloor below Atticus and Kronos. Two hundred feet above, the *Titan* blocked out the midmorning sun. Kronos swirled into motion. It rose from the seafloor in a flurry, building speed, preparing to flee. But why? The *Titan* posed no threat to it.

Then he saw them, caught in *Ray's* lights. Yellow cylinders like oversized coffee cans tumbling toward the seafloor. Atticus spun in his seat. They were everywhere. "What…"

Recognition slammed into Atticus a second before the first shock wave.

Ray shook as the first depth charge exploded fifty feet to the rear. The metal shell of the submersible groaned as it pitched forward, burying its nose in the sand. The second explosion, ten feet closer, but to port, almost knocked Atticus from his seat. His mind whirled as he fought with the control stick, urging the sub to free itself from the sand.

"What the hell are you doing, Trevor?" Atticus's eyes settled on the radiant, yet determined, face of his patron. Had Trevor gone insane?

Atticus realized the truth. He had become expendable, a mere obstacle standing in the way of Trevor's goal.

Atticus pushed the throttle full ahead and pulled back on the control stick. *Ray*'s nose lifted out of the sand, pulling up a mound of the terrain with it. The extra weight made *Ray* unstable and sluggish. Two more explosions rocked the sub. A second to port and another dead ahead. The shock wave from the second, much closer explosion, lifted *Ray*'s nose toward the surface. The sand slid down the surface of the sleek, black sub, covering the lexan bubble. Visibility became totally obscured, but with the throttle still at full, *Ray* broke free from the seafloor and shot up toward the surface, shedding the sandy covering.

Atticus looked up and saw the hull of the *Titan* high above—a black swath surrounded by sparkling blue sea. Motion to his right caught his attention. He caught his breath when he saw Kronos rising alongside him. The explosions that continued to pound the seafloor had startled the beast.

Kronos's movement through the water became erratic, undulating left and right as well as up and down. Atticus realized it was trying to bunch up, away from the explosions below. While he was 100 feet above the explosions and still rising, a large portion of Kronos's 150-foot body still remained near the seafloor. The creature moved faster than anything Atticus had ever seen in the ocean, but its massive size made attaining that speed a lengthy process.

As a large portion of Kronos's body moved his way, Atticus rolled *Ray* over and around the bending body. For a few moments their movements were entwined, each rising and falling, moving in and around, like two synchronous fighter jets. A shallow explosion rocked Atticus to the side. *Ray* spun away from Kronos, and they ascended on two different paths— Kronos up and away from the *Titan,* and Atticus up and directly toward the *Titan*'s bow.

The bursting depth charges shook the *Ray* as they detonated closer and closer to the surface. It was dumb luck that Atticus hadn't been struck by one yet. He guessed the charges had been dropped in a radius, designed to force Kronos to the surface. Trevor knew the charges couldn't kill it. But what did he have planned for it at the surface? What kind of weapons did the *Titan* have on board?

A projectile shot across Atticus's field of view in answer to that question; then four more. Atticus recognized them as MK-54 lightweight, high-yield torpedoes. But they moved like nothing Atticus had seen before. As they shot through the water, he could see a pocket of air blasting bubbles away from the nose of each projectile.

They're cavitating! Atticus thought.

He'd seen failed tests of cavitating torpedoes on one of his post-SEAL, top-secret Navy projects. His job had been to assess the lethality of the weapons and gauge any environmental impacts the warheads might have. A cavitating torpedo pushes water away from the projectile, allowing it to move through a pocket of air, reducing friction and allowing it to move at incredibly fast speeds. An underwater missile. The ones Atticus had seen worked, but the high speeds made the trajectories erratic, sometimes veering off target. Until guidance technology caught up with the speed, they were unpredictable at best. But the consistency of these torpedoes made it clear that Trevor had overcome the technological hang-up.

Kronos neared the surface and picked up speed, but the torpedoes closed the distance with ease. A wail tore through the ocean following the first explosion. Each torpedo found its target, and they were hurting the creature.

Giona…

Atticus focused his vision on the bow of the *Titan*. He had to put a stop to this. He had to save his girl. By the time he parked the sub and sprinted up countless decks, he'd be too tired to stop anyone, and the hunt would most likely have come to a conclusion by then. He knew Trevor was driven, but he'd also proven himself to be sensitive, or a very good actor. Still, he might negotiate.

With the surface fifty feet above, Atticus saw only one chance to reach Trevor in time. He positioned

Ray at a forty-five-degree angle, heading straight for the *Titan*'s bow. Then he crammed his thumb down on the yellow button, activating the sub's auxiliary thrusters. If *Ray* was as aerodynamic as he thought, his plan might work. If not, he'd give the *Titan*'s side its first blemish on the otherwise pristine hull. As the sub's speed built far beyond the rate at which it had gone the first time Atticus had pushed the button… for just a moment, he saw an explosion of bubbles burst from the sub's nose.

Ray could cavitate!

Before Atticus checked the sub's speed, the air bubble at the sub's nose, burped into the open air. As the ship rose higher and higher through the air, the white hull of the *Titan* loomed. Rising quickly, the airborne *Ray* shot toward the figurehead, a shouting Viking woman brandishing sword and shield. She threatened to put a quick end to Ray's first flight, but merely managed to scratch the sub's white underbelly.

As the sub leveled out, Atticus got a clear view of the *Titan*. The first thing he saw was a massive cannon aiming out to sea. *Where did that thing come from?* He thought. Then his eyes widened as he saw the bridge come into view. *Ray* plummeted straight for it. Atticus quickly located his seat belt, yanked it tight, and waited for the head-on collision that would end his life and save his daughter's.

38

THE TITAN

After the depth-charge-spewing machine known as a hedgehog spat out its barrage of the underwater incendiaries, the group on the *Titan*'s bridge had turned their attention back to the viewscreens. The pictures provided by *Ray*'s several cameras provided a perfect view for what was about to transpire.

Atticus and the beast had both become aware of the falling depth charges, but neither had reacted quickly enough to escape the thunder that followed. The water around *Ray* had become a cauldron of bubbles, pushed and shoved by the tumultuous force of the explosions. The group watched in rapt attention as Atticus steadied himself in his seat and managed to lift off the seafloor with the help of a nearby explosion that almost knocked the submersible on its back.

Trevor clapped gleefully. "That's it, Atticus old boy! Make a run for it! Show us what you've got!"

And Atticus did.

Trevor's eyes remained fixed and unblinking, absorbing every detail of Atticus's ascent, commingling with that of the beast. Mortal enemies locked in combat only moments before, now fled together, moving about each other like participants in a well-choreographed dance.

Trevor realized that they were two of a kind. Top predators each. For a moment he felt sick to his stomach, wondering if attacking so abruptly had been prudent. Atticus remained a dangerous man, and it became quite evident he might survive the depth-charge assault. Would he understand the decision to attack? Perhaps from a military point of view. But with his daughter alive inside Kronos, Trevor doubted it. Then he remembered who he was and that it was his God-given right to do whatever the hell he pleased.

His fear turned to excitement when he realized that for the first time in ages, he actually felt fear. A smile spread across his face, and he laughed as Atticus neared the surface and parted ways with the creature.

Turning to Remus, he said, "Launch four torpedoes from the *Titan* at once and take aim with the cannon. I want you to take the first possible shot when Kronos breaches the surface.

Remus relayed the command to fire torpedoes one

through four, then sat behind a console featuring a
targeting screen with a crosshair at its center. Gone
were the days of entering coordinates to aim the cannon. Using the *Sat-Optics Hawkeye* system procured
by Trevor, Remus could aim using the screen, zooming in up to 100x optically on a target to ensure accu-
racy. Or he could uplink to a satellite and select the
target with the click of a mouse; like a video game if
the target was in range, the cannon would adjust and
fire. He was using the optic option at the moment,
watching for some sign of Kronos's body to swell out
of the ocean.

"Torpedoes away." Trevor stood over Remus's
shoulder, watching the screen, waiting for the torpedoes to finish Kronos off. A rising mountain of water
told him the first torpedo had found its target.

Having heard the explosion near the surface, Andrea began struggling and shouting obscenities. But
nothing could pull Trevor's attention away from the
task at hand.

"Almost, my good Remus," Trevor encouraged
with a whisper. "The time to act will soon be at
hand."

A second plume of water burst to the surface as
another torpedo exploded. It was followed by a swell
of water, forced up by a massive body rising from beneath. Remus steadied himself for the kill.

"Holy shit! Is he insane?" O'Shea's voice instantly
caught Trevor's attention and threw off Remus's aim.
He whirled around, found O'Shea's eyes upon the
video screens, and looked to them. Three of the four

screens showed nothing but blue sky. The fourth revealed an image of the ocean, shrinking away. And the fifth showed Atticus, face set with a solid gaze, finger still gripping *Ray*'s booster trigger. The man had flown *Ray* right out of the ocean!

Remus turned and looked at the screen. "What the hell?"

As all eyes were locked on the strange spectacle of Atticus flying through the air, each pair widened as the front view from *Ray* leveled out, and they saw the bridge of the *Titan*. Trevor whirled around and saw for himself that it was true. Atticus had not only taken *Ray* airborne, but he'd also aimed it straight for the bridge. It seemed the man was so angry about Trevor's disregard for his and his daughter's lives, that Atticus embraced the way of the kamikaze.

As Trevor shifted his weight, about to break for the exit, he noticed the targeting screen for the cannon. Rising out of the water was a large hump of sleek, dark flesh. Kronos had risen. "Fire, Remus! Fire!" he screamed.

It only took a fraction of a second for Remus to look at the screen, see that his aim was true, and fire the big gun. The shock wave of the cannon rocked the bridge and sent hands to ears. The projectile exploded faster than the eye could follow, passing just beneath the flying submersible's belly. The only evidence Trevor had that something had issued from the cannon was a brilliant splash of red in the distance.

Blood.

Success!

Remembering his own dire predicament, Trevor moved his eyes from the screen to the view outside the bridge window. Expecting a sudden death, he was pleased to see the curvature of *Ray*'s design and the wind pushing against it, direct the sub in a downward motion. With a thunderous boom that shook the bridge, *Ray* careened into the deck below the bridge and behind the cannon.

Trevor returned his eyes to the cannon's viewscreen. He saw a pool of red where Kronos's body had once been. They'd hit the creature and pierced its armor. Twin explosions sent water skyward as the second and third torpedoes found their mark. Trevor waited with great anticipation for Kronos to rise again. He longed to take a second chunk of flesh from the beast's hide.

But the beast remained below the surface.

"It's moving away," Remus said as he watched the sonar screen displaying the creature as it was tracked by the network of sonar buoys they'd laid down. "But not fast." He met Trevor's eyes. "It's hurt"

Trevor was about to order the helicopter in pursuit, four more torpedoes fired, and the hedgehog reloaded with a fresh volley of depth charges, but a series of small explosions gave him pause.

Someone was firing a gun.

Atticus.

THE EXPLOSION from the cannon as *Ray* soared

above it snapped Atticus's jaw shut so fast that one of his molars cracked and fell apart into his mouth. But there wasn't time to give the shattered tooth a second thought as the sub's nose pitched forward, partly in response to the shock wave emitted from the cannon, and dived toward the deck just below the bridge.

Atticus braced himself just before the submersible made contact with the *Titan*'s hull. The impact wasn't what Atticus thought it would be, and though the jolt was severe, he managed to stay conscious. As *Ray* slid across the deck, he realized that the sub's forward momentum was much greater than its downward, so when it hit the deck, the energy was expelled through a grinding, screeching halt that was sure to sully Trevor's immaculate deck permanently.

With a final jerk, the sub lurched to a stop. Wasting no time, Atticus jumped down from the chair and unlatched the lower hatch. He shoved down, but it was stuck tight, wedged by the weight of *Ray* upon the deck.

He was trapped.

Atticus growled in frustration and began pacing the small craft like a desperate lion in a cage. His eyes fell on the lexan bubbles that provided Ray's eyes and pilot viewing ports. Simultaneously, his hand fell to his hip, clutching the .357 magnum.

Drawing the weapon, Atticus moved beneath one of the windows. He knew the polycarbonate resin used to make the windows would withstand the bullets, even those sent screaming from the magnum. His hope was that the braces used to attach the window were more suited to withstand the massive pressures of the ocean out than the striking force of a hand cannon's projectiles trying to get out.

The true danger lay in one of the bullets ricocheting off the window and striking Atticus, but the only other choice he had was to wait for Trevor to free him. That wouldn't be until after Kronos had been killed, which was precisely the enterprise Atticus intended to disrupt.

Atticus hid behind a seat, reached around with the .357, and took aim. He pulled the trigger six times in rapid succession. When he was done, his ears rang from the booming reports. Shaking his head free of the disorienting effects, he stood and looked to see the lexan window still in place.

About to curse the God of all living things, Atticus paused when he saw a sliver of blue sky forming a crescent where the glass met the hull. He jumped into the chair and pushed up on the glass bubble. It gave way slowly, then, all at once, burst away from the sub's hull and rattled to the *Titan*'s deck.

After hoisting himself out of the sub and sliding down to the wooden deck, Atticus freed his SEAL dive knife from its sheath and ran toward the bridge. He knew he wouldn't be able to accomplish much with the knife, especially if he found the bridge well guarded, but he'd dispatched enough enemies using a blade during his time with the SEALs to know he wouldn't die alone.

Images of Giona's darkened form moving inside the belly of the beast flashed through Atticus's mind, lending him strength, purpose, and determination. As he found his feet striding up the stairs that led to the bridge, Atticus offered a small prayer to the God he was about to curse just moments before. "Give me strength."

With that, Atticus burst through the door and with a snap of the wrist, sent the knife soaring.

39

THE TITAN

After the burst of gunfire from the submersible sitting on the *Titan*'s front deck, Trevor realized two things: Atticus was coming…and he was pissed. He leaned forward and peered out the bridge's front window, taking in a view of *Ray* resting below. He could see Atticus pulling himself through one of the lexan viewing ports. Atticus slid onto the deck, reached down, and pulled a long knife from a sheath attached to his belt.

"Oh hell," Trevor whispered to himself.

He had no illusions about what Atticus could accomplish with the single blade. And he felt sure that the instrument of death would find him first if the attack on Kronos persisted. He was, of course, the man who had given the order to attack while Atticus was in the danger zone and his daughter…

Yes, he's coming for me, Trevor thought.

Remus took a look through the bridge window as well and immediately took action. He drew a 9mm Beretta and snatched Andrea by the hair, pulling her roughly into the center of the bridge. Andrea let out a squeal of pain, but she was manhandled so roughly that the words she tried to form were knocked out of her along with her breath.

In that moment, as Remus began raising his weapon toward Andrea's head, and Atticus's footsteps clanged on the stairs to the bridge, Trevor became inspired. He imagined that Mozart or van Gogh must have felt something akin to this at times. When time either slows or the mind speeds up and all things become clear. The bridge door opened and for a fraction of a second his eyes looked into Atticus's. It was like staring into a tiger's eyes before being eaten. In that infinitesimal moment, Trevor felt he might die, but then set his visionary plan into action.

Nothing on Trevor's face revealed he had seen Atticus. Rather, it exploded with surprise as he twisted toward Remus, raising his hands and shouted, "Remus, no!"

With those words, a quick facial expression and a flail of the hands, Trevor transferred Atticus's attention to Remus. He didn't even see the knife leave the former SEAL's hand but he heard the clang of metal on metal as the knife struck the gun from Remus's hand.

Remus cursed and screamed, loosening his grip on Andrea, who ducked to the floor. Before Remus could recover from the attack—before the dropped gun landed on the floor—Atticus took to the air and extended his leg like a piston. Atticus's foot slammed into Remus's sternum with a *crack* that sent the brightly clad behemoth soaring back into the control console.

Trevor blanched as Remus slumped over unconscious. The ease with which Atticus had knocked the giant unconscious disturbed him. Trevor raised both his hands over his head, yet remained cool and collected. "I pose no threat to a man like you, good sir."

Atticus whipped around toward Trevor and stalked him like a silverback gorilla bent on destruction. Their faces were inches apart.

"You ordered the attack. Why?"

Trevor nodded, knowing a lie would be seen through and result in a painful experience of some sort.

"To kill the beast. That is what we're here to do, is it not? You had obviously given up on the task." Trevor took a breath and when he didn't get strangled or punched in the gut, continued. "You knew the risks. When you descended into the deep, you were quite prepared to die if I recall corr—"

Atticus's hand rocketed out, took Trevor's black-silk shirt in tight, and yanked him even closer. Trevor could feel his hot breath washing over his face. "My daughter is alive."

A quiver entered Trevor's voice as he spoke, and

this time it was genuine. "Atticus, please…think logically for a moment. Your daughter is in the belly of a sea creature…a predator of enormous proportions. She has been there for days. It is simply not possible that she is still alive."

"But I saw—"

"What you wanted to see. It was a shape. A silhouette. The odds of the shape being your daughter's *dead* body shifting inside the creature's gullet is beyond remote, but I would more quickly believe that than the ludicrous idea of your daughter still living…still *breathing* inside Kronos. Please believe that I was acting on what I thought your desires were—to kill the beast or die trying. I—"

A squawking voice from the radio interrupted. "Target is in range. Permission to fire?"

Trevor froze as the helicopter's pilot spoke the words. Kronos was injured, bleeding in the water. The torpedoes would find their mark and could quite possibly exploit the newly formed chink in the beast's armor. If he gave the order, the fight could be won. The prize claimed!

But the tightening fist on his shirt told him that Atticus had yet to give up hope. How could he? Trevor had merely planted a seed of doubt, but he'd seen the images himself. Even he knew that somehow, for some reason, Atticus's daughter still lived. Atticus would not give up, and if Trevor gave the order to fire, the words he spoke might be his last.

Atticus stole a glance at the big gun's target screen, where the bloodied body of Kronos rose and fell through the waves. A pool of red had formed around the creature's body, but it moved steadily away. Then the screen shifted, moving through the sky until it landed on the helicopter, fitted with four torpedoes. Trevor looked to see who was controlling the gun. Andrea sat behind the controls, her finger on the trigger. "Tell them to stand down, or I'll do it for you."

While Trevor would feel no remorse over the death of the men on board the chopper and cared little for the vehicle's worth, he knew to do anything but issue a stand-down order would end in disaster.

Trevor nodded.

Atticus let go of Trevor, picked up a headset, and handed it to Trevor. "Stand down." Trevor said into the mike. "Do not fire. I repeat, do not fire. Return to the *Titan*. The fight is over."

Trevor put the headset down as the pilot replied without question, "Yes, sir."

"Now then," Trevor said as he turned to face Atticus again, "I will cease my assault on the beast if you truly believe there is merit to the images we saw. If your daughter is still alive, we will find a way to get her back. If not...I will have my prize."

Trevor wasn't sure if speaking with such confidence would go over well, but he *was* Trevor Manfred, and this *was* his ship. While he might compromise for the moment in order to save his life, he would not be given another order. He knew what Atticus wanted and would grant it to him for the time being. But he would not suffer the indignity of being told what to do.

"Giona *is* alive. I'm sure of it. If you help me get her back, I swear to you, I'll kill Kronos for you after she's safe."

Trevor chewed on the proposal. Atticus, it seemed, could think clearly regardless of the adrenaline no doubt pumping through his veins. The offer was reasonable, but would Atticus hold to his end of the bargain once his daughter was freed? Better yet, how would they retrieve the girl from the belly of the beast without first killing it or themselves in the process? *Questions for another time,* Trevor thought. He would truly make up his mind about what to do later. First, Atticus needed to be placated. "Agreed," Trevor said with a smile. "You've managed to raise the stakes yet again. Well done!"

Atticus stepped back, satisfied. "Are you okay?" he asked Andrea.

"Peachy," she said, rubbing her head where Remus had yanked her hair. "Just your average day on the Love Boat."

Remus stirred and Trevor saw his opportunity to bring things to a close. "I believe it best if we all retire to our quarters for the remainder of the day. Some time apart will allow heads to clear and plans of action to be formulated. We will talk again in the morning."

Trevor could see that Atticus was about to protest, but a gentle hand on his shoulder and a calm voice put an end to it. "I think he's right, Atticus. Nothing productive can be done today. We're all too…shook-up. Especially you." O'Shea pointed to the sonar screen. The large green mass that represented Kronos had gone deep—out of their range. "And Kronos is out of our reach."

Trevor had never been happier to have O'Shea on board. The man had become indispensable at disarming confrontations. While Remus's techniques proved entertaining, O'Shea's gentle touch had a far more profound effect in volatile situations. The priest deserved another bonus.

Atticus relented with a nod and moved toward Remus, who was rubbing his head and looking around in a daze. Atticus bent down, picking up his knife and the Beretta. He held the gun up in front of Remus's eyes. "Thanks for the gift."

"Go to hell," Remus grunted with a cough that caused him to wince and clutch his ribs.

With that, Atticus turned to Trevor, and said, "In the morning we'll talk. If I don't like what you have to say, you're packing it up and leaving."

And there it was. Another order. It was said so coolly and confidently that a lesser man would have simply agreed and left it at that. But Trevor was not a lesser man. His insides became a roiling caldron of fury. Atticus transformed from an admired warrior to insolent whelp in Trevor's eyes. A very dangerous whelp, Trevor reminded himself.

"Enjoy the night…" Trevor said through a tight smile as O'Shea led Atticus and Andrea off the bridge.

It will be your last.

40

THE TITAN

Atticus paced in front of the long window that stretched along the outside wall of his cabin's living room, agitated eager for action. With every glimmer of light reflecting off the ocean outside, he would glance up, hoping to catch sight of Kronos rising and falling—alive. The creature he'd fought so passionately to kill could live without fear of death at Atticus's hands. In fact, he would do everything he could to make sure Kronos survived. He'd promised Trevor he would kill Kronos once Giona's safety had been ensured, but he knew he couldn't do it. His thirst for revenge, now squelched, had been replaced by concern for his daughter and a renewed interest in preserving the ocean's life, of which Kronos represented the pinnacle.

A modern mystery. An unknown species. Primal yet intelligent. What did it want? Why would it swallow Giona if it had no intention of digesting her? And why did it let him live?

Answers to his questions did not exist, so he buried them, ignoring their repetitious chant. But in the absence of questions came a torrent of emotions. Self-loathing over wrecking the submersible, preventing him or anyone else from returning to the deep, pummeled his nerves. Relief that Kronos and Giona had survived the battle gave him hope but twisted a knot in his gut. Giona sat alone, *inside* a giant sea creature. She needed him more than ever, and he couldn't get to her. And fear, the most powerful of the emotions torturing him, fueled his doubts. Giona might have been alive earlier, but she could already be dead. The shell fired from the big cannon could have hit her. Kronos could have spat her out, deep underwater. Stomach juices could have finally done her in. A lack of oxygen…The many ways Giona could die inside the belly of the beast numbered so high they overwhelmed Atticus.

He pictured his girl, terrified, sitting in Kronos's belly, knowing she would eventually die there, alone. Images of her crying throughout her life filled his mind's eye. Age three after a toy had been stolen. Age six after stubbing a toe. Age ten when she fell off her bike. He'd always had trouble seeing her cry. Her face had a way of looking so sad and desperate for comfort. The memory of her face haunted his imagination and distracted him from the question at hand.

What do I do now?

A hopeful glance at a distant wave found nothing but the setting sun. Night would soon arrive, then the morning. By that time he'd need a course of action that would allow him not only to retrieve Giona, but also convince Trevor that Kronos would die soon after. With the return of his daughter's life also came his previous values. But with this renewed moral compass came guilt. He'd betrayed all that he held dear for an act of vengeance. Killing had once been a part of his life, but Maria had changed that. He couldn't shake the feeling that she would have been ashamed of him.

One look at Andrea as she entered the living room from the bedroom told him he was wrong. Andrea had forgiven him, and Maria would have as well. As Atticus continued his internal monologue, he failed to notice Andrea toss a water bottle to him and shout, "Catch!"

The bottle caught him in the side of the head and bounced to the floor. Atticus, caught off guard, staggered backward and nearly fell over. Once stable, he looked to the floor to see what hit him and turned to Andrea, who had her hands clasped over her mouth. Atticus couldn't tell if she was afraid she'd hurt him or if she was hiding a smile.

Atticus chuckled. "You trying to finish me off?"

"I said, 'catch,'" Andrea pointed out, allowing her own infectious giggle to escape. She moved over to him and examined the mark left by the bottle. "You'll be fine." She stood on her toes and kissed his forehead. "See? All better."

"Gee, thanks. You'd make a great mom"

Andrea's smile faded, and Atticus cursed himself as he realized what he'd said. "Sorry."

"It's not your fault," Andrea said. A slight smile returned to her lips. "And for the record, I *was* a great mom."

Atticus looked into Andrea's eyes as their bodies moved closer. Like a ship caught in a whirlpool, he slid toward her, unable to stop. In that moment, all his concerns, worries, and self-torture disappeared. "Maybe you will be again?"

Andrea's smile grew, and she was about to respond when a quick knock came at the door. Atticus's hand went to his side and rested on the reloaded .357. He and Trevor might have an understanding, but Remus would be trouble again. His ego had been bruised too many times to see clearly and was too stupid to know when to quit.

Moving silently over the smooth, hardwood floor, Atticus reached the door and peered through the peephole. His hand came away from the magnum when he saw O'Shea standing outside the door looking about nervously.

Atticus opened the door and greeted the black-clad priest with a half smile. "Come on in, Father."

When O'Shea didn't move forward, Atticus frowned. "What?

"All of the rooms have hidden cameras," O'Shea said softly. "Trevor is on the bridge right now, so no one is watching, but I guarantee he's recording your room."

Atticus squinted. He wasn't surprised Trevor had surveillance, but he was a little taken aback that O'Shea didn't want to be seen. "What's wrong?"

"I'll explain in my quarters," O'Shea said, taking a step back.

Atticus knew when to shut up and follow someone. He stepped out into the hall, followed by Andrea.

"You're not under surveillance?" Atticus asked as they moved down the hall.

"Trevor trusts me more than most, but that's like saying you'd prefer baby poop on a blanket over dog crap on the rug. Either way, it's still a pile of shit." O'Shea glanced over his shoulder with a smile. "Something my father used to say."

"A wise man," Andrea said, her voice laced with sarcasm.

"What I mean," O'Shea said, "is that while Trevor trusts me, he really trusts no one. He's had my quarters under surveillance since I came on board."

"Then why—"

"Are we going to my quarters over yours?" O'Shea finished. "I rerouted the video feed from my room so it plays back old loops of my quarters at the same time of day. When I'm not doing something…fishy, I let the cameras watch. But when I need to, I can sync a loop in and do as I please without Trevor or the Hawaiian gorilla knowing what I'm doing."

"And what would a priest being doing that

shouldn't be seen?" Atticus asked, his interest growing.

"Honestly, at first I was just looking at pornography, but lately I've been selling corporate secrets."

O'Shea paused as Atticus and Andrea froze, their faces flat. "Well, c'mon," he said. "We don't want to be found out."

O'Shea unlocked the door to his quarters and swung it open. He motioned them within. Sensing O'Shea's urgency, they moved inside without another word. But once the door closed behind them, Andrea spoke as she looked up at the massive crucifix hanging on the wall. It hung above a U-shaped desk with three laptops, which filled the darkened room with an electric glow. "So you're a computer-savvy, porno-loving, corporate-secrets-selling priest?"

"Not all men of the cloth are pure, Ms. Vincent." O'Shea laughed. "Of course, to be a man of the cloth, I'd have to be a priest. And that, good lady, I am not.

41

THE TITAN

"That's a real shocker," Andrea said with a snort. "You're no more a priest than I'm Mother Teresa."

O'Shea smiled as he sat in the black-leather swivel chair. He put his hands behind his head and leaned back. "And yet here I am, taking confession from one of the world's most sinful men."

Though impressed with O'Shea's subterfuge, Atticus masked his face to show no surprise. He'd bought O'Shea's priest routine hook, line, and sinker, believing him to be an eccentric priest rather than a phony. He just didn't want anyone else to know he'd been so gullible. What other lies had he believed while blinded by his thirst for vengeance? "Why tell us?"

"Two reasons," O'Shea said. "First, I need your help getting off the *Titan*. It's becoming too dangerous. Trevor's at a dangerous level of Cold War paranoia, and it's only a matter of time before I'm found out. I may be in Trevor's good graces now, but if that were to change, Remus would most likely have his way with me, and I'd just become another afternoon snack for Laurel."

O'Shea sat back again, his smile fading. After chewing on his lip for a moment, he said, "You may find this hard to believe. Hell, I find it hard to believe. I'm a con man...was a con man. I've taken Trevor for millions of dollars while pretending to save his soul from damnation. And while most people would congratulate me for stealing from a man like Trevor..."

Andrea raised her hand and nodded.

"I can't do it anymore. I'd like to say that after all this time pretending to be a priest that I've developed an inconvenient sense of morality. Hell, I've studied the Bible enough. It seems to have rubbed off, and besides...I just don't feel safe here anymore. Sooner or later, whether or not he believes I'm helping save his eternal soul, he's going to see me as a liability. I do not want to be on board when that happens."

Atticus smiled. He was sure that it had taken equal parts brains and guts to pull off what O'Shea had. Trevor had the best security his money could buy, and yet a single man masquerading as a priest had taken him for millions. He wouldn't have cared if O'Shea had stolen a billion dollars from Trevor. The *Titan* was a treasure trove of stolen artifacts. *What comes around goes around.*

"I'll get you off the *Titan,*" Atticus said.

O'Shea's smile returned.

"But I'm going to need your help first."

O'Shea nodded as though he knew an exchange would be necessary. "I've already started."

Atticus furrowed his brow. He wasn't sure what O'Shea could do to help, even though he had proved himself cunning and was still in Trevor's good graces. But O'Shea seemed to have his own ideas.

The erstwhile "priest" swiveled around in his chair and rolled up to the desk. He used all three touch pads and the seventeen-inch screens came to life. On them, Atticus saw many of the same articles about the "New England Sea Serpent" that he had already read. Andrea leaned in close, looking at one particularly detailed sketch. "Oh my…That's it."

O'Shea nodded.

"How many people have seen this thing?" Andrea asked.

"Over two hundred reported sightings in the Gulf of Maine sine the 1600s," O'Shea answered. "Most sightings have the general description correct. The way it swims with a vertical undulation. The shape of its head. The dark top and light underbelly. But details around the finer points, like the eyes, fins, and teeth have varied some. I would imagine anyone sighting it would have a hard time recollecting the details because adrenaline can affect the memory."

"You got that right," Atticus said, recalling his blurred memories of his first encounter with Kronos.

"The size has also come into question, with reports ranging from 50 to 150 feet in length. This is most likely because Kronos keeps a large portion of his body submerged while moving across the surface. In fact, given the way he swims, it's impossible to see him all at once from the surface. At first I thought it was a new species—"

"There's no way Kronos is the first of his kind, and I doubt he's the last," Atticus said. "The Gulf of Maine is probably the species' spawning ground. That would account for the high frequency of sightings, especially if the species reproduces on a multiple-year cycle, rather than yearly."

"That's what I thought at first, too," O'Shea said. "But if there were a population of these things, let's say one thousand of them—enough to keep the species alive—we'd be seeing them all the time. Creatures as big as Kronos, especially those that breathe air, are impossible to hide."

Atticus was about to ask O'Shea how he knew Kronos breathed air, but stopped when he realized that the con man was right. Kronos didn't have gills. Unless the creature had some other way of extracting oxygen from the water, it breathed air like a whale. He kicked himself for not thinking of that before. There he was, an oceanographer, yet distracted enough to miss the obvious.

"But I have a new theory," O'Shea said. "What if Kronos were one of a kind?"

"Impossible," Atticus said. "Complex creatures don't simply form out of nothing, and Kronos is more complex than most."

"I'll grant you that," O'Shea said, "but I'd have to disagree on the point of forming something out of nothing. The whole universe, whether you believe in God or the Big Bang, is something from nothing. At one point before there was time, there was nothing—then poof, there was everything."

"And then, poof, there was a 150-foot sea serpent," Andrea said with a laugh. "I'm no oceanographer or quantum physicist, but I know that's not possible. Didn't it take millions of years for the first single-celled organisms to appear on earth?"

"Hundreds of millions," Atticus added.

"I'm not suggesting that Kronos emerged out of some primordial ooze at the bottom of the ocean. But I think nature can play the genetic scientist when it wants to…when a niche needs to be filled."

Atticus raised a single disbelieving eyebrow.

O'Shea held up his hands. "I know. I know. This is your area of expertise. Just hear me out." O'Shea pulled up a picture of a platypus on one of the laptops. "Take the platypus. It's a mammal that lays eggs. It has an elongated snout that looks like a duck's bill. It uses electroreception to track its prey. It's venomous like a snake, though it uses a spur to deliver its venom, not fangs. And you don't even want to hear what the thing has for sex chromosomes. It's related to only one other creature on earth, the echidna, but only the platypus feeds underwater, has webbed feet and a bill. The point is, the platypus is one of a kind in the animal kingdom. Even its closest relative looks, feeds, and behaves nothing like it. While it has a population that sustains it from generation to generation, it is certainly a genetic aberration."

Atticus crossed his arms. "And this unique species, this one-of-a-kind mutation of something previous, say an actual Kronosaurus, has lived for how long?"

Though O'Shea could clearly see Atticus wasn't buying a word of it, he took the question seriously and ran with it. "Let's assume you're right, that Kronos started as a Kronosaurus...but lived long enough to adapt and mutate to a new world. Kronosaurus was supposed to have gone extinct during the Cretaceous period, which ended 65 million years ago. But we already know that several species thought to have gone extinct, like the coelacanth, which we believed went extinct 60 million years ago, still thrive today. I'm not saying Kronos is 65 million years old, but it's not unreasonable to say the Kronosaurus went extinct as little as, say, four thousand years ago.

"Before you state the obvious—that no creature could live the four thousand years between then and now, let's first keep in mind that we're talking about a total genetic aberration. I won't pretend to be a geneticist, so forgive the simple explanation. All living things have these things called telomeres. Their length determines the length of a life, barring any kind of accident or terminal disease. It's been shown that lengthening telomeres can prolong life. The pharmaceutical company Gernetrix is developing two drugs that trigger telomere lengthening even now."

"Where have I heard of that company before?" Andrea asked.

"It's one of Trevor's. And let me tell you, he puts a lot of stock in the technology. The man plans on becoming as immortal as the ancient gods he admires so much. My point is, if something radical happened to Kronos's genes, right down to the DNA, there is no reason he couldn't have either extremely long telomeres…or they simply aren't shortening with age as they do with every other living creature on the planet. It's not completely impossible that Kronos is a one-of-a-kind creature with an incredibly long life span. In fact, I'm positive he's at least thirty-five-hundred years old."

Atticus squinted. "What are you getting at?"

O'Shea sighed. He was just a con man after all. Though Atticus had to admit, he was the smartest con man he'd ever met—not that he'd met many— but he imagined most didn't have minds like O'Shea's. "Sightings of Kronos were passed down in oral tradition through generations. The first recorded sighting was put to page in 1400 B.C."

O'Shea turned to his desk and reached beyond one of the laptops. He picked up an old leather Bible.

"You think Kronos is in the Bible?" Atticus asked.

O'Shea nodded and flipped through the pages. "At first I thought Kronos might be the creature, Leviathan, which in Hebrew means, 'twisted' or 'coiled.'" O'Shea stopped turning pages, worked the laptop's touch pad for a moment, and brought up an image of Leviathan.

A dark, brooding engraving filled the screen. Atop peaks of black waves sat a twisting serpentine creature that looked to be a cross between a snake and a dragon. In the sky above the creature flew a sword-wielding angel. Atticus read the title: *Destruction of Leviathan* by Gustave Doré. The similarities between the creature in the engraving and Kronos were striking, but not quite right.

O'Shea resumed turning pages. "If Kronos had been Leviathan, we'd all be in a heap of trouble. Some rabbinical writings say that God destroyed the female Leviathan shortly after creating it, so that the species could not multiply. If the Leviathans had been allowed to procreate the world could not have stood before them. And the Bible is very detailed about how impervious to attack Leviathan is. It all lines up with my theories on Kronos."

"But, Kronos isn't Leviathan?" Atticus asked.

O'Shea stopped turning pages. "I didn't start figuring things out until the moment you, and the rest of us, saw your daughter alive in the belly of that thing." O'Shea placed his finger on a verse in the bible. "Listen…'Now the Lord had prepared a great fish to swallow up Jonah. And Jonah was in the belly of the fish three days and three nights.'"

Atticus's eyes grew wide. "Jonah? You think that thing out there was created by God, somehow survived all this time, and swallowed my daughter?"

"I'm not saying I believe any of this. I'm just asking, 'What if?' and keeping an open mind. If I'm going to consider that Kronos is a genetic aberration in the extreme, it seems only fair to consider the idea that God created Kronos. The majority of people on this planet believe that God created everything there is. What's one more creature?"

"But wasn't Jonah swallowed by a whale or a fish or something?" Andrea asked. Her demeanor didn't strike him as being incredulous, but more interested. Atticus realized he still knew so little about who she had become. He had no idea what her religious beliefs were and decided to tone his reactions down...just in case.

"Most people think so," O'Shea said with a nod. "But if Jonah's 'whale' already existed, then it's something that went extinct in the last few thousand years and has yet to be uncovered. Studies have been done on great whites, whale sharks, and every species of whale large enough to swallow someone whole, which is very few, mind you. It's simply impossible that someone could sit inside the belly of say, a blue whale, and survive.

"But the verse mentioning the creature reveals more than is normally considered. Read the verse slowly. What stands out?"

Atticus barely contained his urge to fling the Bible out the window and curse O'Shea's absurd theories, but when Andrea stood next to him and began reading, he calmed down. She seemed to take O'Shea seriously. He read the verse. Then again. On the third pass, a single word struck him.

"Prepared," Andrea said. She'd seen it too. "The Lord *prepared* a great fish."

"Exactly!" O'Shea said, thrusting a victorious finger in the air. "God created something specifically for the task of swallowing a human being whole and keeping the person alive for days on end. Now we know from the rest of the passage that Jonah was in no way comfortable inside the belly of the beast, but we do know he survived. I can't explain how Kronos is able to sustain a human inside him as he does, but what if God designed him that way?

"Look, at the very least, I'm saying that Kronos has been around for thousands of years, and whether he is the inspiration for a Jonah myth or was in fact created by God, the beast has an M.O."

Andrea smiled. "He spits people back out."

"Precisely," O'Shea said with a smile.

"Kronos eating and spitting out one person thousands of years ago doesn't mean he'll do it again." Atticus felt ready to explode.

O'Shea held up his hands defensively. "I don't think Giona's the first since Jonah. I think Kronos has repeated this behavior several times over the past several thousand years, and acting as a bastion of God or not, has altered people's lives, redirecting them on new paths.

"Throughout history, but not widely reported, there are stories of people disappearing at sea only to be found washed up on a beach, days later. What isn't noticed at the time, but can be seen in hindsight, is that the direction of each of these people's lives is dramatically altered by the event, usually in some spiritual way. Some people would write the whole thing off as stress-induced hallucinations, but I think most would see it as a type of miraculous event that, for most people, could only originate from God.

"For example…" O'Shea worked two different laptops, one with each hand—a regular ambidextrous computer geek. "In 1638, a preacher by the name of John Wheelwright went missing as he rowed a boat to an awaiting galleon. He was believed to be drowned. But two days later he washed up on a beach in New Hampshire. Shortly after, rather than returning to England, as he had planned, he founded the town of Exeter."

Atticus glanced at Andrea and noticed her face had paled. "You okay?" he whispered.

"Huh? Yeah, fine." Andrea offered a feeble smile, then looked back to the computer screen. On the first screen there was a text document titled, "Agreement of the Settlers at Exeter, New Hampshire, 1639." One year after he'd gone missing at sea.

O'Shea brought up a separate image on the second laptop. The screen displayed a photo of an old, handwritten journal page. It was nearly illegible, but O'Shea already knew what it said. "This is the account of John Josselyn. He recorded the first modern sighting of Kronos. The sighting took place in Cape Ann, which you probably know as Gloucester and Rockport, Massachusetts, just north of Boston. What's most important is that this sighting took place in 1638, the same year Wheelwright went missing, and to reach the coast of New Hampshire from Boston Harbor, you have to pass right by Cape Ann."

Atticus shook his head. He couldn't believe what he was hearing. He wanted to, but it defied logic.

O'Shea beamed. "Atticus, listen. Don't you see what this means? I don't think your daughter is going to die, not from Kronos anyway. This creature, for whatever reason, maybe some kind of temporary symbiotic need, eats people, keeps them alive, and spits them back out like a hairball."

Atticus's defenses crumbled, and he began to feel hopeful. The fact was, Giona still lived inside Kronos, and that alone gave him reason to consider the impossible. Relief assaulted his anxiety and fear, threatening to overtake his rational mind, but then he recalled O'Shea's final words. "What do you mean, 'not from Kronos anyway.' You're implying she's still going to die."

O'Shea's smile disappeared. "I suppose that depends on us." O'Shea met Atticus's eyes. "Please understand, I know nothing except the ways of Trevor Manfred. There is *no way* he will stop in his quest to kill Kronos. When the man starts something, he finishes it. He *will* kill Kronos, and I doubt he has any intention of first trying to retrieve your daughter."

"We'll explain this to him," Andrea said. "He'll listen to us. He has to."

O'Shea shrugged. "Have it your way."

Atticus fixed his eyes on the digital image of the Leviathan, his mind focused on how to save Giona. He'd been an unstoppable force when seeking vengeance, but not even God could stop him from saving her. And if O'Shea's Jonah theory held true, then God would be on his side.

42

THE TITAN

With Atticus's mind made up, he and Andrea snuck back to their room and, upon O'Shea's suggestion, made small talk about how beautiful the night sky at sea looked, providing an excuse for why they'd left the room. They also talked about Giona and how they hoped Trevor would aid them. No malice toward Trevor was mentioned, and their conversation was lighthearted, hopeful…and phony—designed to convince Trevor that they had no mutinous intentions.

As darkness descended over the Gulf of Maine, Atticus dimmed the lights in the room so that only the faintest glow emanated. The low light allowed them to relax. Not even the best camera could see them in the near-pitch-dark conditions. According to O'Shea, the cameras did not have night-vision or infrared capabilities, so they could move about without being watched. But to not be heard required whispering…or background noise.

A saxophone ballad, compliments of Kenny G, blared from the bedside CD player. They'd checked for radio stations, but nothing came in so far out to sea, and Kenny G was the very best CD they found in the dreadful collection stored in the bedside cabinet. Atticus had thought about asking O'Shea for his Stones CD, but figured the techno-geek faux-priest was more likely to have a hard drive full of downloaded MP3s rather than actual CDs. A tumultuous cascade of saxified jazz ripped through the air before settling down to a calmer tune.

"Please, God, kill me now," Atticus said, sure his head would burst from the agony.

"It's not that bad," Andrea said as she stretched her weary body under the sheets of the bed they occupied. During the night of phony conversation, they'd also tended to each other's wounds, applying ice, gauze, and gentle gestures, but nothing beyond normal doctor-patient behavior. They were most likely being watched, and certainly recorded.

But when Atticus extinguished all the lights except for the bathroom, its dull glow barely reaching the edge of the bedroom, they settled into bed, expecting sleep to come fast. But they talked instead, first about Giona, then about Abigail. When Andrea began crying, Atticus turned on the music. While Kenny G wasn't exactly appropriate for the moment, neither was letting some peeping Tom get a kick out of her pain.

As Atticus held her, Andrea told him all about Abigail, how well she played the piano, how funny she was when she danced, and how much she loved playing basketball. They'd been close. A single mom and her daughter forging their way through life together—a team. But a year ago, some jerk drank too much and decided to go for a joyride. He ran a stop sign, sideswiped three cars, then plowed up onto the sidewalk, where he ran over Abigail and continued on without tapping the brakes. The car turned out to be stolen, and the man was never found.

Beyond feeling sorrow for her loss, Atticus felt a deep, welling shame. She'd borne a burden as heavy as his and had continued on with her life. While he was prepared to die for his vengeance, she'd mourned the loss and kept jumping out of helicopters to save other people's lives.

As Andrea calmed under the soothing effects of Atticus's fingertips through her hair, she snuggled up against him. They shared the embrace for several minutes without speaking, listening to Kenny's sax ballads, until Atticus couldn't stand it any longer.

Having broken the silence, Atticus felt Andrea's spirit lifting. She'd revealed the darkest moment in her life, and the confessions of her tortured soul further strengthened the old bond between them. At first, Atticus found it hard to believe that his love for Andrea could have returned so quickly. He worried that his feelings resulted from the desperation and sense of loss he felt; but now Giona was alive, and with that hope came a fervent desire to be with Andrea.

"You know," Andrea said. "When I first found you…"

"On the *Titan*."

Andrea sighed. "When you were…when I rescued you on the yacht."

"Oh, that boat." Atticus wasn't sure where she was going, but hoisted his head up from the pillow and rested it on his propped up hand to let her know he was listening. He continued to stroke her arm as she spoke.

"When I found you, you were dead."

Atticus felt a lump, like a cancerous tumor, suddenly grow in his throat.

"When I flipped you over and saw your face again, I felt something in me change. Whatever walls I'd put up after Abigail died came crumbling down. I worked on you for a minute straight before you came back. At first, I honestly thought you might hate me for saving you. I heard the anguish in your voice. The pain. Bringing you back meant you'd have to live with that pain for the rest of your life. That's why I didn't tell you before. But now— I just thought you should know. I don't want to los—"

Atticus leaned forward and kissed her hard on the lips. As he leaned over her, embracing her, his back wrenched with pain, and he grunted.

"You okay?" she asked, ready to pull him down but sensing his pain was genuine.

"Just my back," Atticus said.

"Roll over, let me take a whack at it."

Atticus rolled onto his stomach. Just as the bed finished absorbing his pressure points, Andrea had mounted his backside. "Where does it hurt?"

"Pretty much everywhere," Atticus said with a smile.

Andrea dug into his back, working the muscles up and down, locating knots and easing them out. Atticus felt his tension forced away, in part because of the physical attention, but also from the love he felt pouring into him with every squeeze. After several minutes, Atticus flexed and stretched his back.

Andrea's noted his movement. "Did I get all the kinks worked out?"

Atticus rolled over beneath Andrea so that she sat just below his waist, which was exactly where he wanted her. He smiled craftily in the dark, and though he doubted she could see him, he knew she heard the intention in his voice. "All but one."

She leaned down and kissed him, giving his chest the same treatment his back had just received. As she sat up, tugging her shirt up, Atticus caught movement out of the corner of his eye. He immediately tensed and stopped moving. Andrea followed suit.

"What is it?" she whispered.

Three silhouettes suddenly blotted out the light from the bathroom.

"No!" Atticus spat as he spun beneath Andrea's body, reaching for the .357 on the nightstand. But a sharp sting in his shoulder and a gasp from Andrea told him he'd never make it. His hand slid away from the nightstand and fell limp to the side of the bed. As consciousness faded away, Atticus heard a single word that would fuel each and every nightmare he'd have while unconscious.

"*Aloha!*"

ATTICUS WOKE to a blaring headache and a light so bright he could barely open his eyes. Each pump of his heart brought a throb of blinding pain. He opened his eyes again, but the light assaulted his visual senses and caused him to double over. He fell to the hard floor, eyelids clenched. The pain in his head was coupled with dizziness and nausea. He worked on his breathing first, calming himself, using his other senses to probe the room. He smelled metal and paint. He body felt hot and sticky with sweat.

With his head still bowed to the floor, Atticus opened his eyes again. When he saw the stark white floor below him, he clenched them shut again. The brig. The white-hot, no-way-out brig of the *Titan*. He cursed himself for letting his guard down. He shouldn't have trusted Trevor.

Andrea.

Atticus opened his eyes again, fighting against the pain, and scanned the room. He found Andrea slumped atop one of the wooden benches. She looked unharmed and unmolested. He crawled to her and placed two fingers against her wrist. Her blood pulsed strong beneath her skin. Remus could have easily killed them both but didn't. He couldn't be sure, but he imagined the man wanted them awake when he finished them off. And after a few more hours of roasting, Atticus wouldn't have much fight left in him.

43

KRONOS

The impenetrable darkness that enveloped Giona consumed her senses. The smell of rancid fish and the
reverberation of the giant's beating heart clouded her
mind, keeping her thoughts from solidifying into anything useful.

The realization that she would sooner or later be
digested had defeated the best mental defenses she
possessed. She sat cross-legged on the undulating
floor of the chamber, rocking back and forth like a
forgotten child. No one would be coming for her.

Hours earlier she'd experienced the most grueling
experience of her life, topping the previous, which had
involved being eaten alive. The…*thing* she would
soon provide nourishment for had become a volcano
of movement, just minutes after she'd fired off her

camera and gotten her first glimpse of her sickening surroundings.

At first she'd thought the camera's flash had somehow disturbed it, but when thunderous explosions began echoing through the chamber, muffled by the beast's flesh, yet still ear-shatteringly loud, she had realized the creature was under attack. For a moment she had felt a surge of hope. But after a near miss sent a shock wave of pain through her body, she realized that if the creature died underwater, she'd go down with the ship like an ill-fated captain.

The creature's movements became so quick and violent that Giona knew a mortal wound had been delivered, causing the creature to thrash in its death throes. As she slammed into the fleshy walls, her hand clung to the camera. If she let go, it could have struck her again, but she also didn't want to part with her only source of light. As the thrashing intensified, Giona felt sure her neck would be broken, but giant muscles, hidden beneath the vein-filled flesh, contracted and squeezed the chamber. If the walls had moved any quicker, she'd have been folded in half. But she had time to adjust her body so that the walls squeezed in around her. She felt like Luke Skywalker in the Death Star trash compacter, but since R2-D2 wouldn't be stopping the encroaching walls, she took a deep breath and waited to be crushed.

As soon as her capacity to move was completely eliminated, the inward clutch stopped—locked in place—surrounding her on all sides by tight walls of flesh. Her breathing quickened as her lungs failed to fill to full capacity. Her eyes widened as thoughts of asphyxiation surged through her wearying mind. As her panicked breaths quickened, glowing orbs filled her vision and her fingertips tingled. An agonizing roar slammed through the tight chamber, so loud that her teeth vibrated within her clenched jaw. The beast was hurt. For a moment Giona had felt sad for the creature, but then the tingling in her hands moved to her head.

It seemed only a moment had passed, but the next sensation Giona had was of being free from the crushing grasp. She'd passed out again. Upon waking, she sat on the floor, shivering not with cold, for the innards of the monster were quite warm, but with absolute dread. She'd unwittingly entered an alien world where logic and human senses became useless.

Exhaustion took over Giona's cross-legged form, and her rocking slowed. She slipped back and leaned against the soft chamber wall. The flesh that met her body gave some and gathered around her back like a cushioned chaise. She closed her eyes—they were no good to her anyway—and tried to think about something happy.

But she became distracted by a sensation on the back of her head. The cushion of flesh behind her head pulsed up and down. The movement wasn't violent, merely a repeated rising and falling. With each pulse, she felt more energized.

As though waking from a dream, Giona found her thoughts coming more easily. She realized that the palpitating behind her head came from a massive artery, pulsing blood from the creature's heart to some other organ. Giona's mind fought to gain some understanding of her new environment. Her fear ebbed slightly as reason began to take over. She'd been smart—scratch that—brilliant, before being consumed by this beast, but had since been reduced to a mindless prey animal. She longed for a return of her old self.

As Giona's curiosity climbed to the surface of her consciousness, she turned and placed a hand on the artery. It was ten inches from top to bottom and, she imagined, stretched the length of her prison. She pondered the meaning of her mental revival and remembered that some blood vessels, the arteries, weren't merely the mass transit system for white and red blood cells, they also transported oxygen. She leaned in close to the throbbing vessel, which she could feel pulse with every thud of the beast's heart, and took a deep breath. The air smelled and tasted of coppery fish, but the surge of energy she received confirmed that oxygen was entering into the chamber by osmosis through the giant artery. Her life-support system. Without it, she would have died long ago.

But how long could she survive? She had no water, no food, and her body suffered for that absence already. Between the constant hammering pain in her skull and the agonizing knot in her gut, death couldn't be far off. All the oxygen in the world couldn't keep her from starving.

An odd thought struck Giona. What if the creature wanted her to live? It certainly seemed that way.

That the chamber existed at all was strange in the extreme, but she'd also been physically protected during the attack. It might have been uncomfortable to the point of her losing consciousness, but Giona knew that without the firm grip of those walls, she would have been beaten to a pulp. And now she'd discovered an oxygen supply.

Giona lit her watch, feeling emboldened, and found her way to the oversized sphincter. Her nose crinkled with disgust at what she was about to do. She extinguished the watch light and pounded on the coiled muscle. "Let me out!"

Emotions Giona thought she'd buried beyond reach resurfaced. She pounded with both fists, screaming. "Let me out! Let me out!"

Tears broke free.

"Please, God, let me out!"

Giona sobbed and unclenched her fists to cover her face with her palms. When her sobs died to a whimper, she sighed. "At least give me something to eat."

A subtle change in direction caused Giona to slip back away from the fleshy spiral of muscle. The beast was rising. She could also tell by the rapidity of the chamber's undulation that it was speeding up.

Before Giona could wonder what would happen next, the sphincter burst open. A blast of cool, salty sweet air burst into the chamber, knocking Giona farther back. When she regained her balance, she realized she could see. A cool white glow lit the chamber from above. She looked past the opening, past the silhouettes of dagger teeth, and saw something she believed her eyes would never gaze upon again—the moon.

An instant later, the moon and its light were gone. A roar like thunder filled the void and rushed toward her. A torrent of water surged into the chamber and slammed her against the doughy back wall. As the space filled with water, covering her head, Giona found herself thinking about the cool air and glowing moon. If they were the last things she experienced before drowning, at least the creature had given her that final joy.

Water suddenly cleared from her face. She took a gulp of air. In moments her whole head emerged from the water, then her torso, thighs, and knees. As the water continued to course out through some unseen drain, Giona lit her watch. The water-covered floor shivered, alive with movement. She could feel tiny bodies flicking against her feet. Thrashing water echoed through the small chamber, filling Giona's ears with an unceasing static hiss. Needing to know whether or not she should be petrified, Giona aimed her camera down, closed her eyes, and snapped a picture. Even with her eyes clenched shut; she saw the bright flash through her eyelids as a pink glow. She blinked her eyes open and looked at the camera's viewscreen. Then gasped. The reflection was brilliant, but the image revealed a mass of silver-bodied herring.

Fish!

Food! Giona's mind shouted.

Giona dropped the camera and fell to her knees. She completely forgot that she didn't like sushi and began grasping the small fish in her hands. With a savagery long tamed by civilization but unleashed through starvation, Giona ripped into the fish, swallowing chunks of flesh, not knowing or caring whether the juices running down her chin were blood or bile. She ate for minutes, until sated, then slumped against the oxygen-supplying artery.

She was breathing.

She was sustained.

She was alive.

"Thank you," she muttered, but to whom she was talking, she had no idea.

44

THE TITAN

Atticus slapped Andrea gently on the cheek. She roused from unconsciousness with a grunt and blinked at the brightness assaulting her unadjusted eyes. She immediately recognized where they were. "Not again."

"Welcome back sleepyhead," Atticus forced a smile, knowing it would do little to keep Andrea from quickly realizing their predicament. Atticus had been awake for an hour. He'd tried to rouse Andrea three times, but the drugs she'd been given had had a stronger effect on her smaller body.

As he'd sat in the room, guarding Andrea's inanimate form, he'd tried to distract himself with thoughts of his family: Mom, Dad and, Conner. Was Dad still in the hospital? Was Conner still waiting for him at home? But the thoughts came and went in a haze. He struggled to come up with some kind of escape plan, but his mind had been unable to concentrate.

With Andrea awake, he felt a part of his mind refocus, but he was no closer to coming up with a useful strategy. He stood on wobbly legs and sat next to her on the wooden bench. His body sagged. "Hell of a first date."

"Second date," Andrea said. "Our first included you jumping from a hospital window and scaling down the side of the building like Spider-Man."

A slight smile crept onto Atticus's face. He couldn't imagine ever having the energy to pull off a stunt like that. "I'm far from a superhero."

Andrea rested her head on his shoulder while rubbing one of her temples with her fingers, fighting off the same blazing headache still hammering Atticus. "Well, you're *my* hero."

"You won't think so when that door opens and the only thing I can do to defend you is shout obscenities."

She slid an arm up around his back and patted gently. "They've got bigger fish to fry...much bigger fish. I'm sure they've forgotten about us for now."

A resounding *clunk* signified that the brig door was being unlocked.

"Or not..." Andrea said as she did her best to stand. Atticus could see she wouldn't go down without a fight, and he'd be damned if she would have to fight alone. He stood and nearly collapsed as the world momentarily fizzled to black. His vision returned just as the white door swung open to reveal a black specter.

"O'Shea?" Atticus said, not trusting his eyes.

O'Shea bowed. "At your service." He quickly handed them bottles of water. They twisted off the caps in an instant and chugged down the cool liquid.

After finishing their drinks, O'Shea handed Atticus his dive knife and .357. "I was able to get these, but I'm afraid your other weapons have been impounded, or in some cases, dispersed among the crew."

Atticus checked the .357. It held six rounds. Not exactly enough to combat the entire crew of the *Titan* if it came to that, but if his aim was true, six shots would be enough to incapacitate six people—permanently—and do a fairly good job of intimidating the rest of the crew. The knife, on the other hand, would never run dry. And in his previous experience with the SEALs, it had ended the lives of more enemies than any other weapon he'd used. SEALs often relied on stealth, and nothing attracted less attention than a blade. Atticus slid the .357 into his belt and was about pocket the knife when O'Shea suddenly turned pale.

"What are you doing here, Father?" The voice wasn't familiar to Atticus. It must be one of the many crew members Atticus had yet to meet.

"Just making sure our prisoners are well cared for," O'Shea said, doing his best to sound cool and collected.

"Is that so?" O'Shea tumbled into the brig, shoved from behind. A tall man carrying an H&K UMP submachine gun followed him in. The man's lanky body showed a dark tan. Patchy stubble coated his face, giving him the look of a sixteen-year-old trying to grow his first beard. But the ferocious gleam in his deep-set, hazel eyes told Atticus the man's innocence had died a long time ago. He suspected that most every man on the *Titan*'s crew had either been a criminal before being hired, or at the very least, had become one since.

The man positioned himself behind O'Shea and kept the UMP against his back. At that range, the .45mm rounds would blast straight through O'Shea and pepper the brig. The man was taking precautions. *Smart man,* Atticus thought. Some of his strength had returned since drinking the water. Atticus stood sideways to hide his right hand and hip. He let the dive knife slip down so that he was holding the razor-sharp blade between his fingers, which he suddenly realized, still shook from the effects of dehydration.

"Let me see what's in your hands," the guard said. Atticus and Andrea held up their emptied water bottles.

"They would have died in here without a drink," O'Shea said, sounding as humanitarian as possible.

"Maybe that was the point," the guard said.

"I do believe Remus wants them alive when he returns," O'Shea said matter-of-factly.

The man considered this, and, while he did, O'Shea took the opportunity to roll his neck, stretching the muscles that were becoming tight with anxiety. In that moment, time slowed for Atticus. It'd been a lifetime since he had taken another man's life, but he didn't see how he could disarm the man without O'Shea's being shot in the process. He also knew that the guard would soon discover that O'Shea had betrayed Trevor, and the brig would become a shooting gallery with no place to hide. Atticus's vision narrowed. He saw nothing but the guard and O'Shea.

O'Shea's head stretched one way, then the other. The guard spoke the words Atticus had been hoping for. "I want to see both hands."

Atticus raised his knife hand so that the back side faced the guard, hiding the blade behind his palm and wrist. As he turned his palm toward the guard, Atticus gave his wrist a quick snap. No one saw the knife fly through the air, but a sickening sound like scissors cutting through thick fabric followed by a wet *pop* confirmed its passage to the man's brain. His body fell in a slump behind O'Shea, who'd gone rigid, in mid-stretch as the reality of what had just happened dawned on him.

O'Shea spun quickly, looked down, and jumped back. "Wow!" he whispered.

"Sorry," Atticus said to O'Shea. "I didn't have a choice."

O'Shea snapped out of his daze and looked to Atticus. He smiled. "You forget, I'm not a priest. And that man was a killer. He would have killed us all."

Atticus felt relieved by O'Shea's assessment. He took no pleasure in taking another man's life. That there had been no other recourse eased his guilt. But he doubted the man's death would be the last one on his hands before they escaped the *Titan*. The stakes had been raised again, but he doubted Trevor would enjoy these as much as those he set himself.

Atticus bent down to the dead guard, searching his body. He picked up the UMP and found two spare magazines. With twenty-five rounds each, the weapon improved their odds.

With a quick yank, Atticus extracted the dive knife from the man's eye socket. After wiping the blade clean on the dead man's pant leg, Atticus pocketed it and turned to Andrea.

Although she was a member of the U.S. military, she fought to save lives, not take them. She might have pulled a corpse or two from the water during her career, but she'd obviously never seen a man slain. Her eyes focused on the man's head, where a pool of blood had collected in his deep-set eye socket.

Atticus gripped her shoulder. "Hey."

She met his eyes.

"Don't look at him," Atticus said. "The night-mares will fade faster if you don't look at his face." He'd learned that from personal experience. While taking the UMP and retrieving his knife, Atticus hadn't once looked at the man's face.

Andrea gave a faint nod. Atticus handed the .357 Magnum to Andrea. The weight of it in her hand brought her fully back to reality. "It's got a pretty severe kick to it, so take time to aim between shots. You've got six rounds. Make them count."

He felt no fear of being judged by Andrea for what he'd done. While the shock of seeing a man violently killed had taken her by surprise, she was still a member of the United States Coast Guard and no doubt recognized the need to fight and kill when necessary. She took the gun and held it firm. "I'm ready," she said.

"We need to get out of here," O'Shea said. "Trevor has the *Titan* on high alert. Every crew member is armed, and it won't be long before someone comes looking for him." O'Shea nodded toward the dead man. "I rigged the security system. All the cameras are running on fifteen-minute loops, and I've disabled the lock systems so they work for anyone. They won't care whose thumbprint or retina they scan. If the system is reset, everything goes back to normal; so, once they notice, we're stuck. We're dead."

Atticus moved to the door and checked both directions, leading with the UMP. The hall was empty. "We need someplace to hide. Someplace no one would ever go without Trevor."

A crafty grin spread as O'Shea began to speak. "I know just the place."

45

THE TITAN

With a watchful eye, Atticus guarded the opulent staircase that led to the collection room's double doors. After gaping in awe at the three Gorgon statues standing guard, Andrea monitored the hallway in both directions. So far they hadn't run into any other guards, and no alarms had been sounded. Atticus knew that Trevor was most likely concentrating his crew's efforts on finding and killing Kronos, believing his captives were secure in the blazing hot brig. They needed time to form some kind of plan. Whether it would be an escape plan, or attack plan, Atticus had yet to decide.

O'Shea knelt by the collection-room doors, working on the skeleton-key lock with some small metal tools. He'd come prepared.

"You sure you know what you're doing?" Andrea asked.

"Before I was a con artist, I stole my money through more conventional means." The lock clicked and unlocked. But the small click was followed by a second and a third. "Duck!"

O'Shea hit the floor, and Andrea followed suit. Atticus learned long ago that when someone shouted, "duck!" certain death greeted those that didn't heed the warning. As a result he reacted first and hit the floor before O'Shea. Had any of them hesitated, the spread of darts sprayed from the mouths of the Gorgon women would have cut them down. Darts coated the walls, staircase, and doors to the collection.

Atticus stood, holding the UMP ready, wary of a follow-up assault. Their freedom might have gone unnoticed, but the killer crew of the *Titan* would eventually stumble upon them. "Collect the darts," he said, "but don't prick yourself. They're probably laced with poison."

Atticus moved to the open doors of the collection room. "Is there another way out of here?"

O'Shea's eyes widened. "Uh, no."

Not good, Atticus thought. A dead end in a firefight was usually just that, a *dead* end.

"But," O'Shea said hopefully, "the men wouldn't dare fire a shot in the collection room. Trevor would have them beheaded."

Good enough.

"C'mon," Atticus said as he followed Andrea into the expansive chamber. "Lock the door behind you."

Atticus entered the large room and deposited the darts on the floor.

Darkness fell around them as O'Shea closed the door to the unlit collection room.

"What is this place?" Andrea asked, her echoing voice betraying the room's size. With a blazing fury, the lights snapped on. Atticus, expecting an ambush, took aim and panned the room with the UMP, looking for targets.

"At ease, soldier," O'Shea joked as he moved away from the light switch.

Atticus shot O'Shea an annoyed glance.

"Sorry," O'Shea said. "I joke when I'm nervous."

Andrea missed the exchange entirely as she scoured the room with wide eyes, her mouth slowly falling open. "Okay, that's it. I don't care what piece of paper I signed, this guy is going down."

"Those waivers of his will stand up in any court," O'Shea said. "I signed the same one a long time ago."

"Be quiet. Both of you. And kill the lights," Atticus said. It was an order not to be discussed.

As O'Shea immediately went for the lights, Andrea spun on Atticus. "You can't just let this go. We have to find some way to...to protect all this!" Andrea waved her arms wildly in the air, gesticulating to the collection of treasures from around the world.

"First," Atticus said seriously, but keeping his voice down, "I never signed a waiver. And second, your nose flares when you're angry. It's kind of cute."

"Oh, dear Lord." With that, O'Shea switched off

the lights.

"You didn't sign a waiver?" Andrea whispered.

"No," Atticus said. "He never asked. Probably too distracted by the hunt."

"I feel like such a fool."

Atticus found her hand in the dark and gave it a squeeze. "You had no choice. I would have signed it too if he'd asked." A *clunk* on the other side of the room perked his ears. "O'Shea," he whispered. "Where are you?"

The lack of reply made Atticus nervous, but O'Shea obviously knew his way around. A gentle glow from the far side of the exhibition space revealed as much. "Over here," O'Shea said in a carrying whisper.

Using the small amount of light provided by O'Shea, they made their way past an Egyptian obelisk, the *T. rex* skeleton, and an array of glass cases housing several smaller artifacts hidden in shadow. When they reached O'Shea, they found him sitting on the floor by a small bar, an open minifridge providing the light. Inside were four bottled waters and a six-pack of Sam Adams. O'Shea had already started in on one of the beers.

"The man really does want to be American," Andrea said, with a shake of her head.

"I wouldn't say he wants to be American," O'Shea countered. "Not many people outside America *want* to be Americans anymore. He just appreciates American cuisine."

Atticus took two waters from the fridge and

handed one to Andrea. The water O'Shea had given them earlier had helped, but in no way replenished the amount of fluids they'd lost in the brig. They both drank greedily, then moved on to the two remaining bottles.

"You two better watch it, or you're going to have to pee while you're running for your lives later," O'Shea said with a smile.

"Just drink a few more beers," Atticus said, "and I'll refill them for Trevor before we leave."

O'Shea had to work hard to stifle his laughter.

Andrea slapped Atticus on the shoulder. "Oh, that's nasty."

After a moment, the laughter settled, and as though sharing a single mind, the three grew serious. "The way I see it," Atticus started, "we have three goals."

"Get off the *Titan*," O'Shea said anxiously.

Atticus nodded and held up a finger, counting them down.

"Save Giona," Andrea said.

Atticus held up a second finger. "And stop Trevor from killing Kronos." He raised his third finger. "We're going to need help. I assume the only mode of contacting the outside world is on the bridge."

"We'd never make it," O'Shea said. "But, I've got satellite Internet access in my room. I can send e-mails and instant messages."

"Can I access my Coast Guard account?"

"Sure."

"If I send an e-mail, it should get a response."

O'Shea shook his head. "We'd never make it together. I should go alone. They don't know I'm helping you yet."

"Not a chance," Andrea said. "You may have saved our lives, but I don't trust you yet. My account would give you access to sensitive materials."

"Well, I wouldn't have known that if you hadn't told me," O'Shea said, exasperated.

"Andrea's right. You two head for the room. Get a message out to the Coast Guard and anyone else who might pay attention and find a way to get us off the *Titan.*" Atticus didn't want either of them with him, because no matter what course of action they decided on, he would head for the bridge and a direct confrontation. O'Shea would most likely just get in the way, and he wanted Andrea nowhere near when things got hot.

"But, what if we run into trouble?" O'Shea asked.

"I think the crew will be...preoccupied," Atticus replied.

Andrea gave him a nervous glance. She didn't have to say anything for him to know what she was thinking.

"I know," he said. "But Giona is still alive. I have to stop them. I have to try."

Andrea nodded. There was nothing else she could do.

Muffled voices at the door caught Atticus's attention. He spun to the closed double doors, which could be seen between the legs of the *T. rex.* Shadows shifted across the line of light tracing the outside edge of the doors. He couldn't tell how many men were there, but it didn't matter. They'd been found out and the rest of the crew wouldn't be far behind.

Atticus readied his UMP and took aim between the *T. rex*'s legs. Andrea caught his shoulder. "You can't fire in here. The artifacts…"

Atticus gritted his teeth. His mind spun for solutions, then his eyes went wide. "Where are your darts?"

"Mine are by the door, with yours" Andrea said.

Atticus's hope dwindled. He'd left his by the door as well.

"Mine are on the bar," O'Shea said.

Yes! Atticus stood and searched the dimly lit bar. Atticus stifled a groan. "Two darts? You only picked up two darts?"

"Hey, I'm just a phony priest, not G.I. Joe."

Atticus sighed. They would have to do. But if the darts weren't poisoned, he'd only manage to make the men angry before they shot him full of holes. "Shut the fridge," he said, before handing Andrea his UMP and heading off into the darkness. "Stay down and be ready to run when I signal."

Atticus moved like a wraith through the gloom that fell over the room as the fridge door closed. His feet, still bare since being interrupted in bed the night before, aided his silent advance across the cool, solid-wood floor.

As the doors opened, a wide beam of light cut through the middle of the vast space, illuminating the battling *T. rex* and triceratops as though they were actors on a grand stage. Atticus flattened himself against the smooth, obsidian obelisk and peeked quickly around the corner.

The silhouettes of three guards filled the doorway. Two were armed with UMPs, the third had a radio to his lips. "I think they're in the collection."

Atticus could just make out the static-filled response from the radio. "You have permission to engage."

Remus.

But why would he give permission for the men to fire in the collection? Were these men that good, or was something else, something more important happening? Atticus knew the answer when he trained his senses on the movements of the massive yacht. He'd grown so accustomed the motion of boats upon the ocean that he didn't always notice changes in speed, pitch, or yaw. His body simply adjusted to the movements of the ship without conscious thought. It'd become as natural as breathing.

But now that he was paying attention, he could feel the rumble of the engines and the rapid rise and fall as the *Titan* burrowed through the ocean. They were moving fast. The chase had begun anew.

With little time to spare, Atticus spun from around the obelisk and flung the two darts, one after the other. The first was a perfect strike, hitting the man in the neck. He dropped in a heap as though he'd been shot.

Definitely poison-tipped.

The second dart struck the other guard in the

thigh, but the poison didn't take immediate effect. The man grunted and searched for a target, as Atticus charged him from the side. He had charged just after throwing the darts and he approached from the side of the radioman.

The man saw him coming and ducked as Atticus launched into the air, delivering a savage kick to the side of his head. Atticus wasn't sure if it was his heel striking the man's temple, the crack of the man's neck, or the dart's poison that killed the man, but there was no question the man was dead when he hit the floor.

Before the radioman could bring a pistol to bear, Atticus flew at him, shooting his legs around his neck, and twisted his body hard in the air to bring the man down on his head. Atticus felt the man's neck pop between his knees as they hit the ground together. The entire battle began and ended in less than fifteen seconds.

Atticus moved quickly, relieving the guards of their weapons, ammo, and the radio. All in all, he collected two more UMPs with four spare magazines and a fully loaded 9mm Glock. Now, they might just be enough to cause some damage. Bearing his new arms, he entered the hallway, checked every avenue of approach, and reentered the collection.

He flicked on the lights, knowing there was no need to conceal their position, and waved Andrea and O'Shea over. When they reached him, he handed each an UMP and traded the Glock for his .357. They weren't exactly ready to wage war, but it was a start.

"How many crew members on board?" Atticus asked.

"Fifty," O'Shea answered. "Forty-six, if you subtract the four you've killed forty-eight, if you include Remus and Trevor."

Forty-eight to one...They were the most abysmal odds he'd ever faced in a firefight. As a SEAL he had the support of his squad, intel, satellite surveillance, and often air assaults if necessary. Here he had a con man and a Coast Guard rescue worker against forty-six armed killers, one maniac, and one rich eccentric, who might just be the most dangerous of them all. Still, for his daughter, he'd kill each and every one of them if he had to.

"You ready?" he asked.

Andrea and O'Shea nodded. Atticus kissed Andrea, and said, "Get the word out, then find a way off the *Titan*. I'll catch up." He could sense Andrea was about to argue, but there wasn't time to stand around. He looked at O'Shea. "Take the road less traveled. Avoid confrontation."

With that, Atticus bounded up the stairs, taking three at a time. When he reached the first landing, he paused, scanned with the UMP, then continued up— a soldier on a mission with more at stake than ever before.

46

KRONOS

The rapid undulations of the soft floor beneath her told Giona that the creature had accelerated, perhaps running from another attack. She cringed with each jolt, expecting the walls to close in on her, snuffing her out again. Since eating and learning to keep her head near the large, oxygen-providing artery, Giona's thoughts had cleared. But with the clarity came desperation and depression over what seemed to be her fate—to die slowly inside a sea monster.

And she'd realized that was what the creature was—an honest-to-God sea monster. She had no real idea of its size. Her only view of it had been its open jaws before being sucked in, and an opposite view from the inside out just hours ago. All she could recall of those jaws, other than their grand scale, was the teeth, prodigious and needle tipped.

Sea monster or not, the creature wasn't impervious. It had been injured in the previous attack. Giona still couldn't fathom who could assault the creature in the open ocean or how they'd find it. But someone had tried to kill the creature, and whoever it was had yet to give up the chase. The monster's nonstop movement told her that much. But sooner or later, the creature would slow, and the battle would commence again; she felt sure of it. No matter what happened, death seemed to be following her like a Hollywood stalker, just waiting for the perfect moment to strike. If the beast died, she'd die with it. If the creature lived, she'd either be digested at some point, or she'd live for a while in this pocket, but she couldn't live like this forever.

Better to be dead than go insane living inside this thing, she thought.

With a sigh, Giona leaned her head back on the large, pulsing artery. The slight give in the tissue, gentle pulse of the vessel and the extra oxygen relaxed her. She closed her eyes, did her best to block out the smell, and let the booming bass heartbeat calm her mind and body. Her imagination found a toehold and climbed into the forefront of her mind.

Setting her thoughts free to wander where they might was a technique she often used to find creative solutions to challenges she faced. Whether academic, artistic, or emotional, the clearing of her mind and subsequent freeing of her imagination often provided more ingenious answers to questions than her intellect could achieve. As her mind became more agile, images appeared in place of the darkness, so much so that she could see a three-dimensional world around her. First she was home, in her room. Then at the beach, building a sand castle with her parents. Then she was diving with her father.

With a quickening pulse, Giona focused on the attack. First the whales, then the herring, and then *it*, emerging from the gloom. She slowed the images in her mind and repeated them again and again, each time seeing it more clearly. The body was massive and moved up and down. That made sense now. It looked reptilian—like a marine reptile—but had fins and smooth, dark skin like a killer whale. She held her breath as she focused on the eyes. In contrast to the violent attack, sharp teeth, and otherworldly appearance, the eyes struck her as somehow different from those of any creature she'd ever seen. They looked like a snake's, but there was something more... Intelligence. Then she saw the oddity. It wasn't in the eyes themselves, but in the forehead above the eyes. Unlike any whale, shark, or reptile she'd ever seen, this monster had an expressive face. Nothing like a human or even a dog or seal for that matter, but she could see it. The expression in its eyes, the moment before it sucked her down, weren't those of a hungry predator. They almost seemed gentle.

The images shattered and fled as Giona's logic exploded in denial. It was ridiculous to think that this predator— this apex predator— saw her as anything but food. Yet here she was, still alive after five days, contemplating her fate. But what other purpose could there have been in eating her? Could she have simply been in the way as the creature pursued the herring? Or was there something more she had overlooked?

It struck her as a one-of-a-kind creature. Nothing like this had ever been seen before, or if it had been seen, had never been caught and authenticated. If it had, people would know about it; her father would know about it. She'd heard of oarfish growing to enormous lengths and being reported as sea serpents, but there was no way an oarfish could grow to this size without being noticed. Besides, oarfish were silver.

She knew that it couldn't truly be one of a kind, though. It just wasn't possible. It could be old, for sure, but not unique. There had to be a whole slew of these creatures so that they could reproduce without genetic defects; but then why hadn't they been seen before? If even a handful of these giants roamed the oceans, people would see them all the time.

But how could something be unique? How could a creature simply just form in the ocean?

Maybe it's the mutated spawn of some whale, she thought.

But that seemed just as ridiculous as the other possibility, which harassed her thoughts, vying to be given credence. She'd ignored it long enough, and while she completely disagreed with the notion, it was time to consider whether or not the creature had been created unique. But by whom? A scientist? Not likely. Who else could create a living creature? God?

Giona shook her head. Nothing else made sense.

The problem with this theory is that Giona didn't believe in God. She didn't have a problem with people who did, and she didn't embrace atheism. Nor was she agnostic. She simply hadn't given the subject much attention. Her mind had been on other things and, admittedly, slightly distracted since her mother's death. She simply didn't have time to consider God.

Well I do now, Giona thought.

Not really knowing where to begin in forming her thoughts, Giona spoke aloud, addressing God as though he would respond, though she knew he wouldn't. "So, if you made this...*thing*, why? Why create something unique? Why create a creature that can't reproduce?

"Let's just assume for a second that you did create it—that all the weirdness about this thing serves some kind of purpose. What is it? It seems to me that the only thing a creature like this would be good for, aside from eating lots of fish like any other predator would be to eat...and keep alive..."

Giona's voice trailed off as she realized the truth. This chamber she was in. It was perfectly situated to keep a human being alive. The oxygen supply from the artery. The food supplied by the fish. Even the constricting walls that had kept her from being thrashed to death. But why keep her alive inside the beast? What possible reason could there be?

Continuing her dialogue with God, Giona raised her arms in frustration. "At least give me some kind of hint!"

Giona.

She froze.

Was that a voice?

She craned her neck, straining to listen. Perhaps her father had been eaten too and caged in another chamber like this one, shouting her name? She knew it wasn't true. Her name sounded no more loudly than a whisper, but she'd felt nothing through her ears. The voice had come from within. It was like a thought, but crystal clear.

Yet, even with the clarity, she'd heard it wrong, twisted it so that it made sense, hearing it as her name. But the name didn't belong to her...it belonged to someone else.

Jonah.

47

THE TITAN

Atticus hadn't seen enough of the *Titan* to really know his way around, but his keen sense of direction and knowledge of which end was the bow allowed him to move inexorably toward the bridge. He moved forward and up at every opportunity, vaulting stairs and stalking through hallways until he found himself at a dead end.

Two heavy, oak doors blocked his path. They looked hand-carved, featuring designs of naked women and scenes from mythology. The door struck Atticus as new, probably commissioned to fit that very spot. Most of the treasures on the *Titan* had been taken from other cultures, but the image on the doors revealed the mind of the man behind it—Trevor. The lust-filled minotaur, scorpion men, and cyclopses chased down and captured nude woman who ran in fear. It reminded Atticus of a painting he'd once seen, *Rape of the Sabine Women,* but this was much more grotesque.

The room clearly served some personal function for Trevor and might be useful to scout for weapons and information. But the retinal scanner and handprint analyzer to the side of the door kept him at bay for a moment. Atticus smiled as he remembered that O'Shea had disabled the *Titan*'s locking systems. Small holes in the ceiling made him wary of more poisoned darts, but he couldn't stop. Not now. As Atticus moved toward the retinal scanner, he hoped whatever trap had been set there, wouldn't be activated after a failed attempt. For all he knew, O'Shea's handiwork might have already been undone.

Atticus placed his eye against the scanner. A line of red light slid across his eye and back again. The device beeped and displayed a green light, which promptly turned red. A slight buzz emanated from the system. Atticus jumped back, expecting to be struck down by any number of potential booby traps. When nothing happened, he relaxed slightly and noticed that a light over the handprint analyzer was also glowing red.

Biting his lip, Atticus approached the locking system again, but rather than try the retinal scanner again, he tried both at once. The system activated once more and as the red light scanned his eyes, a green one pulsed at his palm. The lights on both turned green and the doors slid open automatically.

Walking slowly, UMP at the ready, Atticus en-

tered the room. It wasn't any more extravagant than
the rest of the rooms on the ship, which wasn't much
of a comparison—they were all extravagant in the
extreme. The wall opposite the door curved around in
a smooth arc and consisted of a single pane of glass,
running from one side of the wedge-shaped room to
the other, and framing the rising sun. Its vaulted ceilings held two skylights, one casting a square of light
onto the hardwood floor, the other illuminating the
king-size bed, framed by ivory tusks. The room was
devoid of other furnishings. Atticus imagined that
either drawers were cleverly concealed in the walls or
that servants brought Trevor fresh clothing every day,
which, knowing Trevor, seemed to be the more likely
scenario.

As Atticus moved through the bedroom and into a
small library, he realized he'd been wrong about Trevor's quarters. They were *very* different from the other suites. While other rooms' décors were spectacles of
grandeur, his quarters reflected a more personal side
of Trevor Manfred. The books that lined the shelves
ranged in subject matter from history and mythology
to science and technology. A dog-eared copy of *Moby
Dick*, which appeared to be a first printing, lay on an
end table next to a plush lounge chair. Reading glasses
rested atop the book. Finding nothing of real interest,
Atticus crept forward through the undistinguished,
though pricey, living room and into a room that gave
him pause.

It was an office of sorts, featuring normal office
furniture—a desk, chairs, lamps, and small tables

formed from petrified wood—but full-color security monitors coated the entire back wall. It was like being in some kind of freakish electronics store with an overzealous sales team. But these screens didn't feature the same movie in slightly varying color tones; they displayed views of every room on the *Titan*. Atticus grew tense when he saw his own bedroom, and next to it, his bathroom.

"Pervert," Atticus muttered.

An almost imperceptible flicker hit all the screens at once, then they continued on as before. Atticus realized that the blip was O'Shea's fifteen-minute loop starting again. If anyone stood there long enough, or simply came by at the right moment as Atticus had, he'd know to restart the system. As Atticus began considering how best to destroy all the screens without alerting anyone, a nagging question took hold. Why, with the crew having full knowledge of their escape, was no one there to monitor the screens?

Before he could fully comprehend his mistake, a force struck him from behind. The solid blow sent him sprawling to the floor. The UMP fell from his hands and skittered across the smooth floor, coming to a stop underneath the heavy executive desk, which sat directly in front of the viewscreen-covered wall.

Atticus's head cleared a moment before his forward momentum stopped. He turned the slide into a roll and ended in a crouch, ready to pounce or dive away. He did neither. Standing before him were three gargantuan men. They wore all black and sported military crew cuts. Their black T-shirts displayed a logo that read, Cerberus Security. *Great*, Atticus thought, *security specialists*. But while they were probably very good at their job, they'd already made two mistakes.

Their hands were free of any weapons. Instead, they were clenched at their sides. It was obvious the men had either seen him in action or had at least heard of the Navy SEAL on board. The ferocity in their eyes made it clear they intended to pummel him to death: mistake number one. Mistake number two was their assumption that Atticus would consent to fighting all three of them in hand-to-hand combat. He had no intention of doing such a thing. If the throbbing pain at the back of his skull was any indication of what was to come, he'd prefer to avoid a fist-fight at all costs, even if he had to fight dirty, which a fight to the death often required.

The men stood their ground, waiting for Atticus to attack first, putting himself at a disadvantage. He decided to see if they would respond to a verbal attack. Thick-bodied men like them were often thick-skulled as well. "Cerberus Security, huh?" Atticus showed a lopsided grin. "Cerberus is the three-headed guardian dog of the underworld, right?" He didn't wait for a reply. "You must have borrowed the shirts because all I see are three cute puppies."

That did it. All three men lost their tempers, and, feeling supremely confident that their three-on-one bulk would win the day, charged. Only two steps into his charge the first man fell. The second jumped over him just as Atticus rolled over the broad desk. When he came out of his roll, his hand came up with a snap.

The second man fell as well, hitting his head on the desk in the process.

The third man ignored his clumsy partners and leapt like a linebacker about to sack the quarterback. The man's forward momentum was impressive, but as a massive explosion rang out, the man snapped back in midflight, almost as if his foot had been tied to a rope. What had actually happened was much more messy.

Atticus stood, breathing hard, knowing that if anyone of the three had got in a good shot, he'd have been finished. As he scanned the floor where the men lay in a bloody line, he knew none of them would threaten anyone ever again. The first to fall had Atticus's dive knife lodged in his throat. The second had a scimitar-shaped letter opener in his heart. And the third had a fist-sized hole in his back, where Atticus's .357 magnum had punched through.

Ignoring the gore and the men's faces, Atticus looked for some way to shut off the wall of surveillance monitors. The monitors behind him suddenly exploded as thunder rumbled through the office. A burning pain ripped through his body as a bullet pierced his flesh. Atticus doubled over in pain, but the motion spared him from being cut in half by the ensuing barrage.

As bullets wrecked the back side of the hardwood desk and punched holes through the monitors, Atticus took a moment to inspect his body. He found his left shoulder soaked with blood. The pain had dulled as endorphins kicked in, but he knew it would hurt like hell once his body's natural painkillers wore off. He still had full movement of the arm, though not without pain; but at least that meant the bullet hadn't severed too much muscle or hit the bone. While his fresh wound wouldn't kill him, it made him realize just how out of practice he'd become. When the bullets stopped flying, the wall of security monitors smoked and smoldered, devoid of images and pocked with holes.

Well, he thought, *took care of that.*

The sound of clacking metal sounded as whoever had fired at him struggled to reload. The sounds revealed that his attacker lacked experience in conflict situations and didn't truly understand the weapon—possibly a waiter or cook who'd been armed. And while Atticus might be out of practice, he'd be damned before letting a submachine-gun-toting maitre d' get the best of him twice.

Grabbing his UMP from under the desk, Atticus stood and let loose a three-round burst toward the office door. His attacker dropped from sight, his weapon clattering to the floor. Atticus rose and contemplated his most recent kill, still twitching, before heading for the door.

But the sight that greeted him sent him running. Five men, all packing UMPs, took aim and unleashed hell. The floor at Atticus's feet exploded as the five opened fire. The walls burst apart as bullets pushed through, searching for Atticus.

Knowing there was little chance of surviving a close-quarters gun battle with five men, Atticus fired his UMP at the long window. As it lost its structural integrity, the window disintegrated and fell to pieces. But before the shards of glass could fall away, Atticus threw himself through the wall of descending daggers.

48

The Titan

Taking the opposite approach to Atticus's bold charge toward the bridge, O'Shea and Andrea, hoping to avoid any kind of confrontation, snuck along carefully. They entered a long hallway leading to a staircase that would take them to the priority guest deck, where O'Shea's and Atticus's quarters were located. Several hand-carved, wooden statues lined both sides of the hall.

Andrea couldn't help but stare at the frightening, yet ornately carved statues, many of which were brightly painted. She recognized several as totem poles, but others were bears standing upright, stylized mountain lions, wolves, and birds. All had been carved by Native Americans, but only the totems looked familiar to her.

O'Shea noticed her attention on the statues. "They're Native American," he said.

"Obviously, but they're unlike anything I've ever seen."

"That's because no one has seen them in many centuries," O'Shea said, a hint of guilt in his voice. "They came from an excavation…I don't know where exactly, but they were found inside a cave. The archaeologist said he believed they were the work of the first recorded Native American master artist."

Andrea looked into the dark eyes of a supremely carved Kodiak bear, whose bared teeth looked real enough to sever a man's head from his shoulders. "What happened to the archaeologist? How come no one knows about this?"

O'Shea looked back with a frown. "Sometimes people working in remote areas…get lost." His eyes focused forward, as he knew that even a momentary glance might cause him to crash into one of the sculptures that made the hallway more of a slalom course than a walkway. "But more often than not, if archaeologists find something unique, somehow they meet Trevor. And if his offer of money in exchange for silence isn't accepted, he can—"

"Father."

The voice was a simple greeting, yet it threw O'Shea into a panic. He looked up with a gasp. Two men who he knew were kitchen workers, Reggie and James, walked toward him, each carrying a Glock 18C machine pistol. O'Shea held his breath as he was sure the guns would soon be raised and fired.

But nothing happened. When O'Shea failed to return the greeting, the men stopped. "You okay, Father?"

How were they not seeing Andrea? he wondered. But they hadn't, and he didn't want to risk looking back for her. He clutched his chest and let out a deep breath, adding a little drama to the motion. "Good Lord, Reggie, you scared the dickens out of me. I thought for sure you were the escaped prisoners." O'Shea widened his eyes, stretching them in mock relief. "That will teach me to pray while walking the ship."

"You need an escort back to your quarters, or can you handle that?" Reggie asked, pointing to the UMP O'Shea had forgotten he was carrying.

"I'd be damned to hell for firing this at a human being, but it does provide some measure of comfort, doesn't it? I'm sure I can make it to my quarters without incident though, thank you." O'Shea smiled and stepped aside, allowing the men to walk past. "Keep safe."

O'Shea let out a silent sigh of relief as the two continued on their way. His eyes began searching the hallway for some sign of Andrea. He found her as she stood up, moving silently, from behind the great bear carving. The men had walked right past her.

As O'Shea motioned for Andrea to hurry up, Reggie turned around. "Oh, Father, I meant to ask y—"

In that moment, that small slice of time, Reggie could plainly see Andrea and his mind made the quick mental connection that she and O'Shea were in league. He raised his Glock, but he was too slow. O'Shea had already taken aim with his UMP. The stream of bullets that issued from the UMP shot wildly through the hall. He'd never fired a handgun, let alone a submachine gun, and his aim was dismal. Of course, with a submachine gun pumping out seven hundred rounds per minute, perfect aim wasn't a requirement. In seconds, the weapon jettisoned all twenty-five rounds. Of the twenty-five, four connected.

Reggie took three in his torso as the bullets strafed diagonally upward. The fourth hit, following the same diagonal path, struck the other man in the side of the head as he spun to bring his own weapon to bear. In the silence that followed, O'Shea could hear a distinct ringing in his ears, coupled with his heartbeat. Then the sound of distant gunfire caught his attention. Atticus was somewhere else on the ship, waging his own personal war.

Andrea grasped his shoulders. He spun to her, his eyes wide, his breathing quick and shallow.

"You did the right thing," she said.

"How can killing be the right thing?" O'Shea asked.

"Because," Andrea took O'Shea's UMP, ejected the spent magazine, and slammed a fresh one home, "we're the good guys."

With that, Andrea ran down the hallway, making for the stairway. Andrea's support did little to assuage O'Shea's guilt, but it did feel good to be on the side of right for the first time in his life. He followed her

down the hallway, hoping that, somehow, the gunfire
had gone unnoticed.

WITHOUT MEETING further resistance, Andrea
and O'Shea reached his quarters. They entered quickly, locked the door, and headed for the laptops. They
each took one, connected to the Internet, and accessed
their individual e-mail accounts. Andrea wasn't sure
her message would be seen in time. While e-mail was
certainly convenient, there was no guarantee that the
addressee would see it soon enough to be of any assistance. As she typed her message, she hoped her commanding officer checked his e-mail like an addict.

O'Shea typed furiously, catching Andrea's attention. "Who are you sending to?" she asked.

"I'm transferring my funds into a secure bank account."

Andrea paused, incredulous. "What?"

"Just kidding," he said. "I'm e-mailing *everyone*."

Andrea signed her name, rank, and serial number
to the e-mail, so there would be no doubt about its
authenticity, and moved the cursor to the send button. As she depressed the button, the screen exploded.
O'Shea's computer was hit next. Both jumped back,
bumping into each other. Andrea and O'Shea had put
down their UMPs when they'd started using the laptops. She still had the Glock tucked into the back of
her pants, but whoever had shot up the computers
would have no trouble adjusting his aim to take her
out before she'd freed the gun from her waistband.

They turned toward the door and found a lopsided grin on the scarred face of Remus. As usual, he wore shorts and a Hawaiian shirt, but the joyful clothing stood in stark contrast to the Heckler & Koch MP5 submachine gun he held. "Got this from your boy-friend," he said to Andrea, motioning to the weapon. "He kept it up nice for me."

Sweeping the weapon back and forth between them, Remus entered the room. "It's funny," he said, "all the locks on the ship seem to open for anyone." He smiled. "Too bad for you."

Remus took aim at O'Shea. "Can't say I'm too surprised about you. I told Trevor not to trust a priest."

Like a striking cobra, Remus swept his aim back to Andrea. "And you...I'm going to have some fun with you." Remus paused for a moment. He squinted his eyes. "Your gun. Wherever it is, lose it now."

Andrea complied. There was no other choice. She had a feeling that Remus wasn't going to shoot them yet, and that meant they still had a chance, however small, of escape. O'Shea wasn't much bigger than she was, but they were two to his one, and most definitely smarter. As a child she'd once defended another girl from two bullies. Both stood taller and had more muscles than she did, but she outclassed them mentally. She avoided a full-on brawl by throwing sand in their eyes. Of course sand in Remus's eyes would only enrage him, not send him away in tears. More than that, the only sand to be found was hundreds of feet beneath the hull of the *Titan*.

Andrea turned her back to Remus so he could see her take out the Glock and drop it to the floor.

"Kick it to me," he said. Again, she complied.

Keeping the MP5 trained on them, he circled the U-shaped table holding the destroyed laptops, collected the two UMPs, and moved back to the door. He kicked the Glock out of the room and dropped the rest of the weapons to the floor. He turned with a fiendish grin, closed the door behind him, and hummed a Hawaiian tune.

49

THE TITAN

Atticus landed amid a shower of glass after falling ten feet. He grunted as the blunt impact knocked the wind out of him and sent shards of the broken window into his right arm, torso, and upper thigh. Though the cuts burned, he managed to hang on to his weapon and his wits, though the .357 fell over the side, disappearing on the deck below. He rolled onto his back and fired a spray of bullets across the shattered window. He didn't see anyone, but a scream of pain confirmed a hit.

He fired a second burst as he pushed himself to the side of the five-foot panel. He wasn't sure what room lay beneath him, only that he needed to get off the open roof and back inside. Atticus slid over the glass. It scratched at his back and stabbed his bare feet with every shove, all the while keeping the UMP aimed at the window above.

A shadow slid across the window, triggering a quick burst of gunfire from Atticus. There was no scream this time. Just a dull thud as a body hit the floor. He doubted anyone would be stupid enough to stick his head out again and double-timed it to the edge of the platform. Upon reaching it, he glanced over the edge. He was two stories above the next platform. But it wasn't the height that held his attention. It was the entryway below; it led to the bridge.

The bridge door opened, and an armed guard stepped out. Another one of the Cerberus crew. The man seemed even bigger than the other three, and his weapon of choice was an AK-47, the conventional weapon that had claimed more lives worldwide than any other. Atticus used his arm to sweep a pile of large glass shards to the edge. All at once, he pushed the glass over. Deadly glass rain poured down toward the security guard.

Atticus didn't watch the glass fall, just in case the guard got off a lucky shot, but the wailing scream from below told him that his target had been on the receiving end of a shard or two. Atticus peeked over the edge and saw the guard, flat on his back with a six-inch slice of window embedded in his face. Atticus cringed. He'd seen the dead man's eyes staring up at him.

After wrapping the UMP's strap around his neck, he swung his body over the edge, sending down more glass. His wounded shoulder and arm protested at the strain, but he managed to hang on. Two feet below his toes was a pipe, painted white to match the rest of the *Titan*'s hull. He lowered himself as far as he could go and released his grip. His toes hit the pipe and momentarily stopped his downward motion. Prepared for the jolt, Atticus stayed upright and fell straight down again. He grabbed the pipe with his hands as he passed, but the jolt strained his injured arm beyond the point of endurance. His fingers slipped away, but his descent had been slowed enough to prevent too hard a landing. As he fell, Atticus twisted his body so he'd land on his left side to avoid burying the glass deeper into his arm. He hit with a thud, but a thick, soft object broke his fall.

Atticus picked himself up off the dead guard, readied the UMP, and charged into the bridge. There were no other guards and the five-man bridge crew, including the captain appeared genuinely surprised by his sudden entrance. The virtually soundproof bridge had blocked his advance through the ship, and while they'd probably heard the gunfire above, they had no idea their personal guard had been dispatched by an avalanche of glass. Trevor, who was sitting in the captain's chair, nonchalantly turned toward Atticus. He was armed with nothing but an odd grin. His eyes glowed with excitement behind his thick-rimmed glasses.

"Took you long enough, old chap." Trevor said. "You look like hell, by the way."

Atticus ignored Trevor, confident that the un-armed bridge crew wouldn't dare move a muscle. He quickly scanned the instrument panels and sonar display. They pursuit of Kronos had commenced, but they had yet to engage. Atticus relaxed, knowing he'd arrived in time. The sound of helicopter blades caught his attention. The large chopper, outfitted with four torpedoes, headed away from the *Titan*. His eyes moved lower and found the *Titan*'s main gun at the ready. His gaze drifted lower still, and he saw a hedgehog depth-charge launcher shooting bright yellow canisters over the sides of the *Titan*.

He was *not* in time. He was too late.

The depth charges couldn't be stopped, but they would simply drive Kronos to the surface, not kill him. The main assault could still be stopped. "Tell your men to stand down."

"I'm afraid not," Trevor said, with a twitch of his nose.

Atticus took aim at Trevor's head.

Trevor laughed. "Oh ho! I'm afraid I know you too well to be intimidated. While you may indeed pummel me, you're not a murderer, and whatever physical damage you may cause is a minor price to pay for a prize such as Kronos."

Atticus sneered. "I killed at least nine men on my way here, what makes you think I won't kill you too? You do know me. And you know I'll take down this entire ship and everyone on it before I let you kill my daughter."

A trace of fear flashed behind Trevor's eyes, but

then he relaxed and began cleaning his glasses on his black turtleneck. "Yes, you would, wouldn't you? I'm afraid I'd make a dreadful father." Trevor put the glasses back on and looked at Atticus. A second later, a popping sound burst from his glasses. Propelled by compressed nitrogen, two barbed darts, trailing thin wires bit into Atticus's chest.

Before Atticus registered the small pain where the barbs latched on to the skin of his chest beneath his shirt, he was writhing on the floor in agony. His muscles, beyond his control, contracted tightly until he twisted into a fetal position.

"You're tough until someone pumps fifty-thousand volts into your nervous system," Trevor said as he stood. He took the glasses off and placed them on the chair as they continued to dole out the electric abuse. Trevor took the CB in his hand, looked at Atticus's twisted form, and spoke into the mike. "Now hear this. As soon as the beast has cleared the surface, I want all weapons fired. Hold nothing back. I want this creature, even if I have to put it back together. I repeat, as soon as—"

A grip on Trevor's foot made him pause and look down. Though still trembling, Atticus managed to reach out and grab hold of him. Trevor's brow furrowed as Atticus struggled to his hands and knees. Trevor had used the taser on several men in the past, and most hadn't regained control of their bodies for minutes, even after the charge had dissipated. But there was Atticus, a charge still assaulting his body, and he fought to stand. Trevor gave him a solid kick to the face. While not an athletic man, the steel toe in Trevor's shoe provided plenty of punch.

Atticus sprawled back, his vision narrowing, but not diminishing completely. When he fell back on the floor, the strangest sensation came over him. Having just been kicked in the face, he expected to feel more pain, but in fact felt less, far less. He realized that the taser barbs had been torn from his chest when he fell back. The wound in his shoulder throbbed. The glass shards in his arm, leg, and side had seared his flesh as they became heated by the electricity coursing through his body. But the physical pain felt like an itch compared to the anguish he experienced over failing Giona. Though he wasn't sure how, he knew he had to stop Trevor. The alternative was unthinkable.

With a guttural growl, Atticus launched to his feet, oblivious to the pain wracking and slowing his body. He charged Trevor, wrapping his hand around the little man's throat. But a blow to the side of his head ended the attack almost as soon as it began. Trevor fell to the floor gasping and feeling his neck for injury.

The captain, who'd come to Trevor's rescue, swung at Atticus a second time, but found the swing deflected. Atticus threw his elbow into the captain's throat, connecting solidly with the man's Adam's apple. The captain fell to the floor, his breathing hoarse and panicked. The four remaining bridge crew charged as one, fists clenched. But they had no real training or experience, and had not been informed by their fallen comrades that, when the circumstances called for it, Atticus Young fought dirty.

The first was blinded as Atticus jabbed a thumb into his eye, which the man clutched in pain and ran into the wall, knocking himself unconscious. The second man tackled Atticus at the waist, but upon hitting the floor, Atticus drove his knee into his attacker's groin. The man hollered in pain and rolled away. Still on the floor, Atticus delivered a devastating kick to the third man, inverting his kneecap and sending him to the floor next to the first man. The fourth stopped short, unsure of how to approach. Atticus stood and faced him, fists clenched.

Atticus knew he looked absolutely horrible. His face was bloodied and bruised. Blood dripped from his left shoulder and right side. The man took note of Atticus's condition, his wobbly fighting stance and labored breathing, growing more confident as Atticus's energy waned.

The man lunged forward, throwing three rapid punches. Atticus dodged the first two and blocked the third with his right arm. The punch, while deflected from his face, caused a shard of glass to slide deeper into Atticus's forearm. He roared, reached out with his left arm, grasped the man's shirt and yanked him forward. The man's face met Atticus's forehead with a crunch, crushing the man's cheek and nose. He fell out of Atticus's grip, joining his fellows on the floor.

Atticus spun around toward Trevor again and quickly leapt to the side. Trevor had picked up Atticus's UMP and fired it without taking care to aim, expending the few rounds remaining in the magazine before lining up Atticus's body.

Trevor hadn't finished shouting, "Bloody hell!" when Atticus shot back to his feet Trevor squealed in fear as Atticus found his throat, this time lifting him into the air and slamming him against the front window of the bridge. "Tell your men to stand down."

Trevor's eyes widened as his airway squeezed shut. As his face turned blue, he nodded frantically.

"Put him down," came a voice from the bridge door.

Remus.

Atticus had no intention of letting Trevor live. But Remus's next statement caused him to look back and, in consequence, spare Trevor's life.

"Put him down, or they're both dead."

At the door, Remus held Atticus's MP5 aimed down at the unconscious and bloodied bodies of Andrea and O'Shea.

50

KRONOS

Jonah.

The name repeated mercilessly in her mind. Not so much because of the similarities between their names, but because of the similarities of their predicaments. Giona was far from a biblical scholar, having read only portions of the scriptures while doing a history report on the religious beliefs that fueled the Crusades. But she knew the basics about some stories from the Bible: Noah, Jonah, Moses, Jesus. Who didn't?

She wished she could recall more from the story of Jonah. All she could remember was that he was swallowed up by a whale or a fish, or something else entirely, and was spit out onto a beach after three days.

Still, she didn't buy it. First, she still didn't believe in God. Second, the Almighty certainly hadn't asked her to do anything. That kind of thing was hard to miss, right? She punched her leg, growing angry in the consuming darkness of the creature's gut. It was impossible to think with the constant heavy heartbeat, rank fish odor, and roller-coaster floor, still undulating as though in a sprint.

"So what's the deal then?" Giona said. "I don't believe in you! You haven't told me to do anything at all!"

Kronos's steadily beating heart was the only reply.

Giona decided to play devil's advocate with herself. She had no ideas of her own, so considering the unbelievable might be the only way to figure things out. And since she wasn't going anywhere and had nothing better to do than stay close to the life-giving giant artery, she thought it would at least keep her mind occupied and off the subject of her impending death.

"Let's suppose you exist," Giona said, speaking into the darkness. "How would you communicate to people? A burning bush? An angel? That's how you've done it in the past, right? So why not now?"

A thought coursed into Giona's dialogue. *A monster.* "Okay, right. A monster. Let's assume you've done this before, like with Jonah. You've got my attention. So now do something with it."

Giona sighed. Even though she was totally isolated from anyone who might see her carrying on a mock conversation with God, she felt embarrassed for even pretending. Still, it helped her rule out the idea that some supreme being had set this nightmare in motion.

"So what's next? A vision? I could write that off as a hallucination due to extreme conditions. A voice too. Anything odd at this point is subject to consideration by the very fact that I've been inside this disgusting fish for almost five days! And what's the deal with that? I've been here longer than Jonah? How does he get off with only three days?"

You're stubborn. The thought came and went, but Giona's eyes squinted in defiance. She'd carried on mental conversations like this for the last few months. It'd become a regular practice when debating big decisions. She knew it was strange, but for her it seemed a natural thought process. Of course, she made no mention of her internal arguing to anyone for fear of being labeled schizophrenic—Giona the schizoid activist. That'd go over well next time she petitioned the New Hampshire Senate about drug use. They'd think she was more far gone than the users she wanted to help!

"How can I be stubborn if you haven't told me to do anything? Send an angel or a burning bush or something, and I might come around."

Or a monster?

"Whatever. The fact remains that I haven't been told a damn thing to do by God or anyone else, so being swallowed by a sea monster and sitting it out until I come to some kind of revelation is retarded."

Maybe you're just not listening?

Giona grew angry with herself. The portion of her mind playing the devil's advocate side could get really annoying.

Giona cleared her mind, focusing on the steady rise and fall of the oxygen-providing artery her head leaned against. She began putting together conclusions based on what she'd discussed with herself.

"One, God still doesn't exist. Two, this is just some rare sea creature that could be the basis of the Jonah myth. Three, God, who doesn't exist, hasn't told me to do diddlysquat."

Yes, I have.

Shut up, shut up, shut up!

She sometimes had trouble quieting her inner voice once it was unleashed into her consciousness, and just like always, it still fought to be heard.

Giona held her breath. She was really losing it, wasn't she? While she'd had many internal arguments with herself over the past months, the voice had never referred to itself as "I."

Maybe she really was schizophrenic? She decided to test the inner voice—find out if she was just freaking out or if she really had some kind of multiple personality disorder. "Who are you?" she asked.

Light.

"That makes no sense." But then it did. Giona had read, just a week ago, that beyond the microscopic, beyond cells and atoms and electrons, there was light. Everything in the end was light. Energy. Power.

Giona knew she was going insane. Her inner voice now believed it was a cosmic being—believed it was

God. She was certifiable. Her only hope was that the delusion would fade if she ever escaped.

But Giona's stomach turned over as she realized the truth. With a violent heave, she leaned over and vomited, filling her mouth with the acrid flavor of fish guts and bile. She sobbed between heaves. The memories of each and every argument she'd held with herself, with her inner voice, over the past few months returned with a fury. It *had* asked her to do something. Over and over, but she'd resisted, fought it, denied it every time. It was just her inner monologue, her devil's advocate, right?

No.

Giona's thoughts came clear and quick. She'd either gone totally insane or had been receiving direction from God for the past few months and doing her best to ignore it. Though it seemed likely, Giona didn't want to think she was insane. So she decided to believe, at least for the moment, that the voice inside her head was God.

"So, I'm supposed to trust you— that you know the future. You know the outcome, and for some reason you want me, or my father, to do what you've been telling me. Is that it?"

There was no reply. She already knew the answer. The voice had been fighting with her about one single subject since she'd first heard it.

"Fine. Okay? Are you happy? I'll tell my dad I don't want to move, but that's not going to change anything. Especially when I'm stuck in here! The house was sold, remember? We have to move anyway.

So all this," she waved her hands around at the large body in which she was trapped, "is a little too much, a little too late."

She huffed. "But I'll tell him."

Giona closed her eyes to the darkness and let out a long deep breath. She was done. She had nothing more to say to a God-voice and never wanted to hear it again. Instead, she focused on the heavy beat of the creature's heart, allowing it to lull her toward sleep like a hypnotist's watch. *Thump-thump, thump-thump, BOOM!*

Giona sat up straight, her body rigid, her mind spinning. They were under attack again. A quiver of flesh rolled past her. The beast rippled with pain, she could feel it. With a sudden twist of opinion she'd never forget, a new and unexpected emotion swept through her—compassion. She lay down flat and slapped the moist flesh beneath her with her hands. "Go, go, go!" She urged the beast as though it were a horse, and whether by coincidence or in response, the beast reacted.

The walls of the chamber closed in as unseen muscles contracted and the rapid undulations became large pulses of energy. Giona didn't resist as her body became unable to move and the rising and falling of her chest was restricted. As before, breathing became difficult, and colored spots danced in her vision. She knew she'd pass out soon, but she also knew that this monster, her protector, would keep her safe.

Go, she willed it. *Fight!*

51

THE TITAN

Atticus saw everything at once; the helicopter cutting through the blue sky, the big gun, waiting to fire out at the ocean, the sonar screen revealing the oceanic world beneath the *Titan*, Remus standing above the still forms of Andrea and O'Shea, and Trevor's blue face, shaking with fear.

But there was nothing he could do. Trevor dropped to the floor, released from Atticus's grip. He writhed, gasping for air. As his lungs filled, his body slowed, until at last he was lying on his back, breathing steadily. Then he stood, straightened his shirt, and smiled.

"Dear God, that was the closest I've been to death," Trevor said as he bent over and picked up the UMP. He then retrieved the spare magazines from

Atticus's pockets and reloaded the weapon. "Wouldn't want to run out of bullets, now would I?"

As Trevor chuckled, Atticus stared at him with rage, contempt, and total disbelief. He'd seen men come close to dying, some not as close as Trevor just then, and even the most battle-hardened of them had been shaken-up by the event. Trevor actually seemed to have enjoyed his brush with the Grim Reaper.

"You're insane," Atticus said.

Trevor guffawed. "No, just very, very bored. I must admit you've done a wonderful job of alleviating my boredom. I do believe these memories will entertain me for the remainder of my life, but I'm afraid I can't risk keeping you around any longer, lest you succeed in ending my life early."

Trevor picked up the CB and spoke to the crew. "Press the attack. No matter what happens. Kill the beast."

Trevor dropped the CB and motioned Atticus to the door. "Remus, be a dear and carry them to the main deck." Trevor pointed at Andrea and O'Shea. "I don't want to make more of a mess of my ship than has already been made."

Remus picked up O'Shea and Andrea, throwing them over his shoulders. He turned and headed down the stairs to the main deck. Trevor shoved Atticus from behind with the UMP. He fought the urge to twist around and break Trevor's neck, but he knew Andrea's and O'Shea's fates would be sealed by the act. The time to act would arrive soon enough. A quick glance at the sonar screen before leaving the bridge confirmed that much.

Once on deck, Remus slapped Andrea and O'Shea until they woke up. He stood them next to each other along the starboard rail. They were meant to be shot so their bodies would fall overboard, where Laurel would tear them to pieces. Atticus helped Andrea stay on her feet. He leaned into her, and over the sound of the roiling bubbles pushed to the surface by the exploding depth charges below, whispered, "It'll be okay."

She looked at him through blood-encrusted eyes. One was swelling. A purple bruise glowed on her cheek. Her expression showed defeat. Without saying a word, she looked into Atticus's eye and said goodbye.

He wasn't listening.

"Can you move," he asked, her blowing hair masking the movement of his lips.

She nodded slightly. "Brace yourself."

They both clung to the rail.

"I should have known your conscience would betray me eventually," Trevor said to O'Shea.

"May God forgive you," O'Shea replied. He stood clutching his side. His pain was obvious, but he handled it well. And he was continuing his priest routine, perhaps hoping the superstitious Trevor would spare his life.

"Ah, the good priest until the end," Trevor said. "I suppose I'll have to replace you after today, eh?"

Trevor took aim with the UMP and Remus followed suit with the MP5—an old-fashioned firing squad. Not wanting to miss out on a vintage-movie cliché, Trevor added. "Any last words?"

Atticus raised his hand.

Trevor laughed. "I wasn't serious."

"Your neck is bruising."

Trevor looked at Atticus with a queer gaze. He reached up and touched his neck, where Atticus had strangled him. He winced at the touch.

"I'm going to finish it," Atticus said with a smile.

"Right then," Trevor said, taking aim again. "And I'm the one who's insane."

As Trevor pulled the trigger, the entire deck of the *Titan* lurched upward. A thunderous *crack* sounded from below. Bullets sliced through the open sky as Remus's and Trevor's weapons jerked up. The ship settled back down in the water as a warning Klaxon sounded.

Atticus and Andrea charged forward—Atticus to Remus, Andrea to Trevor. O'Shea had disappeared.

Atticus drove his shoulder into Remus's gut, and the two of them sprawled to the deck, sending the MP5 skittering away. Remus, being the larger, stronger, and far less injured of the two, recovered quickly and tossed Atticus aside. The Hawaiian giant gained his feet and reached for Atticus, who regained his footing just as the first in a series of punches and kicks flew at him from every direction. He managed to block or evade the majority of them, but was driven back with each blow, shuffling his bleeding bare feet slick on the wooden deck.

As he grew weary, his foot slipped, and he fell to

his back. Remus pounced, slamming down on Atticus and wrapping his legs around one of Atticus's arms and both his legs. Pinned, with only one arm free, Atticus took a swing and connected with Remus's stone jaw. But the massive man was in a frenzy and hardly felt the blow. Remus grabbed Atticus's free arm and pinned it to the deck. He slammed his other fist into Atticus's head. After a volley of punches, a massive explosion above them sent a stab of pain through their ears.

The main cannon had fired, no more than fifteen feet above their heads.

Atticus found his arm free as Remus clutched his ears. And while every instinct in Atticus's body told him to cover his own ears, he swung up at Remus's throat instead. The blow glanced off. Remus, having recovered from the shock, laughed at Atticus's failed attempt to fight back. As a glint of sunlight sparkled off Atticus's forearm, which still hovered in front of Remus's throat, Remus's eyes grew wide.

"You guys never learn," Atticus said as blood dripped into his eye. "I fight dirty." With that, Atticus drew his arm back across Remus's throat. Pain ripped through his arm as the shards of glass sticking out of his skin and muscle met the flesh of Remus's neck. Some shards came free, now clinging to Remus's neck, but it was the ones that remained stubbornly embedded in Atticus's arms that did the real damage. Rather than simply impaling, they sliced.

Deep gouges stretched across Remus's throat. Some weren't deep, but others, through which

streams of blood pulsed, revealed a fatal wound. Remus's breathing became a gurgle as fluid and air filled
his lungs, not through his nose or mouth, but through
his exposed windpipe. He slumped and fell to the
side, clutching his mangled throat.

Atticus shoved the hulk away and climbed to his
feet, his head spinning. He realized that if the main
gun had fired, it meant Kronos had reached the surface. He had, in fact, known Kronos wasn't running
when he saw the sonar screen on the bridge. Rather
than running, Kronos had headed straight for them.
The beast had had enough.

But now the crew of the *Titan* was countering. He
looked up and found the helicopter hovering one
hundred yards off the bow. Two of its four torpedoes
dropped free and splashed into the ocean. He picked
up the fallen MP5, raced to the bow of the ship, took
aim and fired. Bullets tore through the air as though
fired from the Viking woman figurehead. The weapon
wasn't accurate at the range, but a few lucky shots
might distract the chopper.

As the magazine ran dry, he failed to see a single
spark to indicate he'd hit it. He threw the MP5 to the
deck and cursed. Then his eyes landed on the MP5
again; but he wasn't interested in the gun. A faint
outline in the deck floor held his gaze.

The harpoon.

Atticus fell to his hands and knees, looking for
some sign of a panel. A slight ridge against his fingers
found something to the side of the larger outline. He
took the MP5 and slammed the deck with the butt of

it until a panel broke free. Beneath it was a single switch labeled "raise" on one side and "lower" on the other. He flipped the switch to "raise" and the large outline in the deck became a hole as the panel lowered and slid away.

From the newly formed gap in the deck rose the colossal harpoon gun. A fresh harpoon sat ready to fire, though it lacked an explosive charge. But with the punch the titanium harpoon could deliver, Atticus knew he didn't need one.

As soon as the harpoon finished rising, Atticus looked down the sight board, swiveled the harpoon into position, and pulled the trigger. The harpoon launched in the air, trailing its tether behind it like a lightning bolt from Zeus.

The pilot saw the incoming projectile and veered to the side, but it was too late. The titanium harpoon penetrated one side of the chopper and punched out the other. The black helicopter became as snared by the harpoon as the whales it was intended for. The helicopter continued its sideways motion, still attempting to flee, but the harpoon, with its flukes extended, held on tight. The line snapped taut as the helicopter pulled it to its full length. The helicopter pitched to the side and plowed into the ocean, its blades shearing off and flying away wildly. Its two remaining torpedoes went down, unfired.

Two explosions off the port bow tore Atticus's attention away from the helicopter, now in tow alongside the *Titan*. Two hundred yards away, Kronos's body rose and fell through the waves. A fresh splash of red revealed he'd been hit again. While Atticus wasn't sure the torpedoes could cause a fresh wound on Kronos's thick skin, he was positive they could exploit the old wound.

"Hang on, Giona!" Atticus yelled at Kronos as he barreled back toward the bridge. As he limped across the deck with all possible speed, Atticus became aware of two things, the main gun taking aim at Kronos and Andrea's voice, shrieking in pain.

52

THE TITAN

Though her body ached with every motion, Andrea had vented all her frustration and rage in attacking Trevor. In the corner of her eye, she could see Atticus doing the same to Remus, but she dared not look. Trevor might not be the most physically impressive man, but he still held an UMP, the removal of which was her first goal.

She slugged him with every ounce of energy she had and was happy to hear a high-pitched squeal of pain escape his mouth. His body spun from the blow, but he managed to hold on to the UMP and was already bringing it back around. Andrea caught the weapon with both hands and held it at bay.

In desperation, Trevor pulled the trigger, sending a full clip of ammo into the sky. Even after the bullets were spent, their struggle for the UMP continued, each pulling and kicking the other. Andrea knew Trevor had spare clips and didn't want to give him a chance to reload the weapon. She pulled hard, but Trevor kept a vise grip on the gun and was pulled toward her so that their faces were only a foot apart, the gun held tight between them.

"Can't we solve this in a civilized manner, my dear?" Trevor said, but the gleam in his eyes revealed he had no intention of being civilized.

Andrea pulled harder. "Stop…calling…me… that!" With a sudden reverse in direction, Andrea pushed instead of pulled and the combined force of her push and Trevor's pull sent the UMP smashing into Trevor's face. He sprawled back onto the deck, a trickle of blood running down his forehead.

With his hand, Trevor felt the wound, which quickly oozed hot liquid. Aghast at the sight of his own blood, Trevor scrambled to his feet and shouted, "That's going to leave a bloody scar! This is bollocks!"

Trevor charged as Andrea swung the UMP at him like a club. She connected with his side, but the impact was slight as his body collided with hers. The UMP fell from Andrea's hands. She and Trevor sprawled to the deck. Moving slowly from having the wind knocked out of her and still feeling the residual head-to-toe ache remaining from the beating Remus had delivered in O'Shea's quarters, Andrea struggled to get back to her feet.

But not quick enough.

She never saw Trevor stand up, but the kick to the

side of her head confirmed that he had. The stars that swirled in her vision and the ringing in her ears further told her she wasn't long for this world. Her body became an unsupportable weight, and though she tried to push herself up, her arms failed to function.

A second kick, this one to the gut, sent her back down to the deck, clutching her stomach, gasping for breath. She was vaguely aware that Trevor was circling her, and though her body didn't register the pain anymore, she could feel his foot smashing into her body time after time.

As the impacts against her body stopped, she heard Trevor speak in his typical boyish voice. Though she couldn't see him, she imagined he was wearing his lopsided grin; that his billowy white hair, stained with blood, was dancing in the sea breeze. The mental image of the man infuriated her. She wanted nothing more than to jump up and beat the pulp out of him, but her body was broken and unresponsive.

A sudden jolt of fresh pain, far beyond what she'd experienced so far, ripped through her body. She screamed as the pain throbbed through her nervous system, causing her muscles to twitch uncontrollably. The agony was made all the more painful by the knowledge that she'd failed Atticus. By allowing Trevor to kill her, which he would most likely do at any moment, she failed in her promise to Maria. She had said she'd be there for Atticus. She had said she'd take care of him. And all she'd achieved by regaining his trust, his love, was to give him one more person to mourn for. There was no guarantee that Giona would survive Kronos. Even though O'Shea's Jonah theory had given them hope, the odds of its being true were too remote. Atticus would be alone again, and she would be to blame.

Trevor's voice invaded her senses again. She heard him say something about always having a second pair handy and opened her eyes to see him donning his trademark, thick-rimmed glasses. Her eyes fell beyond Trevor, who stood with his back to the rail. It was fitting, she thought, that the ocean would be the last thing she saw. She'd spent years of her life saving people from the ocean's deadly grasp. And it would be there to watch her die.

The blue waters of the Gulf of Maine disappeared from her view as a black apparition rose up behind Trevor—the Grim Reaper himself come to claim her. A sudden tightness and the most intense pain she'd ever felt, convulsed her body. She screamed like an animal, wounded to the core. Death gnawed at her muscles, pulling them apart sinew by sinew.

Then the pain ceased, and she knew she was dead.

53

THE TITAN

The glass in Atticus's arms burned fiercely, but he tried to ignore the pain. If he were to pull out the shards, he'd only reopen the wounds. The coagulated blood around the slashes, along with the cauterization that had taken place when the glass had been heated by Trevor's taser, had stopped most of the bleeding, and Atticus knew to leave the glass in place until the wounds could be sewn closed. Besides, there were more pressing matters to attend.

Atticus couldn't see Andrea or Trevor yet, but he could hear Trevor's angry voice carried by the wind. As he attempted to pick up the pace, he lost his footing and spilled to the deck. He didn't think his coordination had been too affected by his injuries, but perhaps he'd lost more blood than he thought. As adrenaline pushed him forward, his body could be shutting down without his even realizing it. Atticus stood and wobbled, nearly falling back down.

That was when he noticed the odd angle of the deck. The slant looked slight, but grew more pronounced as the deck tipped inexorably to port. The listing *Titan* was taking on water.

Kronos had breached the hull.

Taking the ever-changing tilt of the deck into consideration, Atticus continued forward, though more slowly. His focus on reaching Andrea held his attention so resolutely that he didn't hear the heavy footfalls or wet ragged breath approaching from the side. A heavy force slammed into Atticus and fell on top of him. Punches rained down next, pummeling his body.

Atticus looked up to find Remus, clutching his bloody throat with one hand and throwing punches with the other. His dark eyes revealed the mania of a man who knew he was going to die but would quench his thirst for revenge before giving himself over to the devil. Remus's punches lacked the force they'd previously had, but they still caused Atticus's beaten body severe pain.

Bringing his knee up fast, Atticus meant to hammer Remus in the groin, but connected with his backside instead. Unprepared for the impact, Remus leaned forward, which was just enough motion for Atticus to exploit by grasping Remus's shirt and heaving him to the side.

Atticus clawed away and used the *Titan*'s side rail to regain his footing—and not a moment too soon.

Remus barreled toward him, arms outstretched, throat gushing blood. The man lacked a quick wit, but he could fight. Atticus had to give him that.

Quickly realizing that moving left or right would simply put him in the grasp of Remus's thick arms, Atticus simply curled down into a tight ball. A tilting deck and forward momentum did the rest. Remus might have been able to catch himself on the rail, but his legs connected with Atticus's body first and propelled him forward. His waist wrapped around the rail and his top-heavy form pulled him away from the deck and overboard.

To his credit, Remus didn't flail or scream on the way down. Atticus watched him fall until he hit the ocean. Atticus thought that would be the end of him, but Remus rose from the sea and began slowly treading water, his eyes full of hatred. The man was a juggernaut!

Though out of the fight, it occurred to Atticus that the unstoppable Remus might still find a way to survive and ultimately escape. He couldn't let that happen. But as a twenty-eight-foot shadow emerged behind Remus, Atticus realized his fears were unfounded.

As the shadow closed in, a massive dorsal fin cut up through the water. Noticing Atticus's eyes were not returning his glare, Remus turned around. And then he did scream. A panic-filled wail shot from Remus's mouth and slashed throat, but became muffled as Laurel's massive jaws engulfed his torso. The black eyes vanished behind the shark's nictitating membrane and the dagger-like teeth snapped down, cutting Remus in half. With a snap of his tail, Laurel disappeared into the ocean, leaving Remus's lower half to bob in the water, trailing a coiled mass of intestines.

Wasting no time mourning for Remus, Atticus continued his journey toward Andrea. As he rounded the curved deck, using the rail to balance himself, he saw them. Andrea was crumpled up on the deck, a guttural scream escaping her lungs as Trevor stood above her laughing beneath his taser-armed glasses. While the charge was meant to incapacitate, the shock to Andrea's battered body might finish her.

Atticus quickened his pace. As he got closer he saw an odd shape rise up behind Trevor. The black form moved slowly, cautiously, until it stood directly behind him. Then a face emerged.

O'Shea! He had been knocked overboard but must have held on to the rail and climbed back up.

In a flash, he reached out with both hands and wrapped his arms around Trevor's neck. Still holding the glasses, Trevor yanked them back with him and pulled the cables from Andrea's body. She stopped convulsing, but lay completely still.

When Atticus reached them, Trevor struggled to breathe as much as he fought to get free. The rail between his body and O'Shea's was all that kept them from sailing off into the ocean.

Atticus knelt beside Andrea and checked for a pulse. He sighed with relief. She was alive and stirred at his touch. "Atti?"

"Don't move," Atticus said, "You'll be all right."

A confused look came across Andrea's beaten face. "Atti…"

"You don't need to say anything."

She shook her head and strained to talk again. "Above you."

Atticus looked up and found the main gun swiveling above. The crew either didn't know the *Titan* was sinking or didn't care. Could their allegiance to Trevor be so strong that when he said to press the attack no matter what, they'd continue until they were all dead? Were they really that fanatical about him? Or perhaps they simply feared him more than death?

"You can't do this," Trevor hissed through gritted teeth. "You're a priest."

O'Shea tightened his grip, causing Trevor to gag, his face turning beet red.

"I've been meaning to tell you, Trevor," O'Shea growled into Trevor's ear, his teeth clenched in a sinister grin, "I'm not a priest."

Trevor's eyes widened with fear.

"Every sin you've committed will be taken to the grave with you, and the full weight of your evil will condemn you to hell."

Trevor had never looked more panicked. His face shook, and his body trembled as he attempted to free himself from the avenging angel clinging to his neck.

As the main gun stopped, Atticus opened his mouth to shout a warning, but a savage boom sent the sound of his voice right back into his throat. Before

Atticus fell to the deck and cupped his hands over his injured ears, he saw Trevor and O'Shea launched out away from the *Titan* by the big gun's shock wave.

Though dizzy and disoriented, Atticus stood and moved to the side rail. He listened through the ringing in his ears for some wail of pain from Kronos. Hearing nothing, he hoped it meant that the shot had missed. Of course, his ears might simply be ruined. Looking over the rail, Atticus expected to see the bodies of O'Shea and Trevor being torn apart by Laurel, but neither man had returned to the surface.

Atticus's breath suddenly caught in his throat. The *Titan* shook, hit by another colossal impact. Kronos continued waging his own war. His massive form rose from below and cut across the surface of the ocean, rising and falling with great undulations. Atticus could see several large, bloody wounds on the creature's body. He realized that he and Kronos had a lot in common. They fought beyond the pain and injury—warriors both— but more importantly, they both fought for Giona's life...and for each other.

FREEDOM

54

THE TITAN

Atticus took Andrea under the arms and dragged her up the steps toward the bridge. He pushed the metal door open, pulled her inside, and laid her on the floor. The click of a gun's hammer being cocked froze him in place.

"Don't move," said a man with a shaky voice.

Atticus turned around slowly, raising his hands in the air. The floor was still littered with dead or incapacitated crew members, but the captain had not only gathered himself together, but he'd also managed to find the .357 Magnum. It felt strange, having his own gun pointed toward him, like being betrayed by a close friend. Atticus took a step forward, blocking Andrea with his body.

"I said don't move!" the captain shouted. "I've seen what you can do. Now stop moving."

Atticus could see the captain then. His breathing was still labored, but he would survive the elbow Atticus had delivered to his throat during the earlier brawl. The captain sat behind the gun controls. Atticus could see through the targeting screen that Kronos's fleeing body filled the view, lined up for an easy shot. The question was which trigger the captain would pull first.

"What's your name?" Atticus asked, his voice calm.

"Just shut up!"

"Captain, I think you're a good man who happened to take a job from the wrong billionaire." Atticus turned so he was fully facing the captain, his hands still raised. "You saw the screens earlier. You know my girl is still alive."

"You don't know that," the captain said, his voice shaking. "Trevor said that—"

"Trevor's dead," Atticus said plainly.

The captain flinched but kept the gun aimed. He looked at Atticus through twitching eyes. "You're sure?"

Atticus nodded.

The man lowered the gun, his body deflated. "Thank God."

Atticus could see that the man had never truly wanted to harm him or anyone else, that he probably regretted every moment of his life spent aboard the *Titan*. He didn't have to ask what his motivations were to know Trevor held something over the man.

Atticus took the .357 from the captain and holstered it. "I need you to disable the *Titan*'s weapons."

The captain nodded and set to work at the controls.

"Is there a med kit around?"

Without taking his eyes off the control panels, the captain pointed to the back wall, where three wall-mounted cabinets stood. "In the middle."

"There morphine in it?"

The captain nodded. "Should be. But with this crew, you never know."

Atticus stepped over the bodies of the dead and injured crew and ripped open the middle cabinet. He found the med kit buried beneath a stack of life preservers. He threw the preservers to the waking men. "Put them on and get out," he said. Then he headed back to Andrea with the med kit and three of the orange life vests.

He dropped the vests next to the captain. Upon reaching Andrea, he opened the med kit, located the morphine, and prepared the needle. As soon as it was ready, he plunged it into Andrea's leg and emptied the syringe.

The captain finished working the controls and picked up the intercom microphone. His voice boomed throughout the ship when he spoke. "This is the captain," he said. "All hands abandon ship. I repeat, abandon ship." Then, as though knowing his orders were not enough to make the men disobey Trevor's will, he added. "Trevor Manfred is dead.

Abandon ship now."

He dropped the CB and took hold of the main cannon's controls. Atticus watched as the cannon moved from a view of the ocean to that of the front deck. What was the captain planning to do? As the view shifted down, Atticus realized what the captain had planned. The front deck came into view.

The captain looked at Atticus. "The men on this ship are criminals and will probably fight for control of the *Titan*. The torpedo room is down there." The captain nodded to the screen displaying the cannon's suicidal aim.

Atticus nodded, and the captain wasted no time in pulling the trigger. The round from the cannon punched a hole in the deck, flew through every deck of the *Titan,* and out through the hull, but not before hitting a torpedo, which exploded. The front end of the *Titan* billowed out, then fell back down. The list became dramatic as the sea flooded into the newly formed breach.

"That did it," Atticus said as he turned back to Andrea. She sat up, the effects of the morphine easing her pain.

"What's happening?" Andrea asked.

Atticus helped her to her feet. "We'd like to thank you for choosing *Titan* Cruises," Atticus said with the mock voice of a stewardess, though strained by his injuries. "We hope you enjoyed your stay, but it's time to get the hell off this ship. She's going down."

Andrea flinched as the captain approached; carrying life vests and what looked like a yellow parcel.

"It's okay," Atticus said. "He's with us."

The captain slipped on a life vest and helped Andrea and Atticus put on theirs. "I deployed our emergency transponder and issued an SOS," the captain said. "Help is on the way."

A few of the crew jumped overboard, clinging to life vests or other floatation devices. Together, Atticus and the captain helped Andrea down the stairs from the bridge to the main deck. They half walked, half slid to the port rail as the *Titan* continued to list. When they stopped at the rail, Atticus took Andrea by the shoulders and looked her in the eyes. "Are you with me?"

She blinked away her grogginess and nodded. "I can make it," she said. "I have a promise to keep."

Atticus kissed her gently. "When you hit the water, swim for the surface, but let the life vest do most of the work."

She smiled. "I'm in the Coast Guard you know. I jump into the water for a living."

Atticus couldn't help but return her smile. "Right."

As a group, all three jumped over the side rail and plunged into the cold Atlantic below, where frigid water and a dark shadow awaited.

55

The cold water over Jeffrey's Ledge sucked the air from Atticus's lungs as he plunged into the deep. As soon as he slid under, he kicked for all he was worth, but the effort wasn't needed. His life preserver had already begun pulling him toward the surface. He took a mouthful of air upon reaching the surface and found himself face-to-face with the tilting hull of the *Titan*. He gazed at its gleaming white form, leaning toward him, threatening to roll down and crush him.

A loud puff and hiss of air caught his attention. He turned and found the captain floating next to an inflating emergency raft. He breathed a sigh of relief as he saw the captain shove Andrea up into the raft and climb in himself.

Wasting no time, Atticus struck out for the raft.

Being a Navy SEAL and oceanographer meant that Atticus was just as comfortable swimming through water as he was walking on land. But the number of injuries he'd sustained, the exhaustion taking hold, and the thick and clumsy life vest slowed him down. Still, he pushed on, kicking his legs and pumping his arms in a slow, steady rhythm.

Waves lapped over his face with each surge forward, blocking his ears and forcing his eyes closed. Every time he cleared the water he chanced a look to the raft, adjusted his aim, and continued forward. Twice he thought he heard Andrea and the captain yelling. He brought his head out of the water without slowing and looked to the raft, by then only ten feet away. The captain yelled and pointed. Andrea struggled to paddle the raft closer with her hands and screamed for Atticus to hurry.

Though unable to understand their words, Atticus interpreted the message. Something approached from behind. With a flash of morbid fear, Atticus recalled Remus's brutal fate.

Laurel.

Atticus spun and found Laurel's dorsal fin cutting through the water. The fin was twenty-five feet away, but that meant the twenty-eight-foot-long great white's jaws where half that distance. Without waiting for Laurel to rear his ugly mug, Atticus reached down to his belt, freed the .357, and took aim.

Laurel's head emerged from the water, jaws open wide. Atticus fired the gun. His shaking hand caused the first shot to go wide. Though it strained his muscles to pull the trigger, he held the Magnum with both hands and squeezed off a second shot. An explosion of red appeared on the shark's side, but the beast did not slow.

Only feet from the open jaws, Atticus prepared to fire again. He knew that even if he managed a killing shot, the giant shark's momentum would carry it forward, and the jaws would still close over his body. Still, he wouldn't die without a fight. Atticus pulled the trigger, and the Magnum fired into the open mouth of the great white.

As though the shark were nothing more than an empty soda can, it launched up and away from the shot. Water poured down on Atticus from above as he watched Laurel wrenched into the air, clutched in of the mightiest jaws on the planet.

Kronos's long body continued to rise out of the water, arching at an apex of fifty feet. At the top of the arc, Kronos snapped his jaws shut, cutting Laurel into three neat pieces. Laurel's head and tail fell away, raining blood and guts with them. Kronos swallowed the rest and continued his arc back toward the ocean.

Atticus flinched as he was grabbed from behind, but relaxed when he saw Andrea and the captain leaning over the raft. Safe inside the raft, all three returned their attention to Kronos's body, which was just completing its dive.

Kronos's smooth head pierced the water without a splash, but rather than follow the head smoothly back into the drink, the fifty-foot-high loop of his body came crashing down. A huge wave rolled up as the beast's body struck, and the raft rode up upon it, pushed out from under the shadow of the sinking *Titan*.

As the sea calmed, Kronos did not return. As though lulled by the groans of the sinking *Titan*, Atticus, Andrea, and the captain slipped into unconsciousness, each giving way to countless injuries, exhaustion, and emotional overload—each totally unaware that even then, equally dangerous monsters of the deep closed in around them.

ATTICUS WOKE a few hours later on a firm, thinly cushioned cot. His mind spun, and nausea threatened to push him back to sleep. He closed his eyes and controlled his breathing, centering his thoughts. His vision cleared and he sat up, finding himself clothed in only a pair of boxers. His bare body revealed a patchwork pattern of green-and-blue bruises and bandages. The bullet wound in his shoulder had been sewn up, and the shards of glass in his arm had been extracted. He'd survive, but the intense pain he was suffering, despite a good dose of pain killers, made him long for death's release. Then he remembered Andrea, and Giona, and fought against that pain.

The room was a small gray rectangle featuring a double bunk, a small desk, and a closet. Atticus knew a Navy ship when he saw one. Atticus stood and looked at the top bunk. Empty.

A nervous grip took hold of him, but he remembered it was protocol for the Navy to put injured civilians in different quarters. While he would have appreciated seeing Andrea on the top bunk, that hope wasn't realistic.

Atticus stretched, ignoring his body's protests, and caught a glimpse of himself in a full-size mirror mounted on the back wall of the room. He looked like crap. Bruises ran from his face to his feet. His left shoulder sported a bloody dressing, and his right—arm, side, and leg—possessed so many stitches that he looked like a shark has used him as a chew toy.

The thought brought back memories of Laurel...of Kronos...of Giona. She was still out there.

"Still think the world of your own body, Young?"

Atticus turned to the sound of the familiar voice and found a mountain of a man filling the doorway. He had deep brown eyes, dark skin, a crisp buzz cut, and a smile stretched across his face.

"Vilk?" Atticus hadn't seen Greg Vilk since his wedding day, but the old Navy SEAL hadn't changed much other than some crow's-feet emerging around his eyes. They'd saved each other's lives enough times that a bond had been formed between the two, and while years and different lives had kept them apart, the bond, forged in battle, remained strong.

"I'd slap your back," Vilk said, "but I think it might kill you."

Atticus smiled. "Thanks. How long have I been out?"

"Just a few hours."

Atticus opened his mouth to talk, his body language all action as he prepared to continue the charge to save Giona.

Vilk held up his hand, speaking before Atticus could. "Slow down old man. Things have settled and you're a mess."

Atticus pursed his lips, stood back and did his best to calm his nerves.

" Listen, I'm glad you're awake," Vilk said, holding up some smelling salts. "I was just about to wake your sleepy ass up." Vilk stepped into the cabin and leaned against the wall. "You managed to get yourself in pretty deep here," Vilk said.

"You have no idea."

"Actually, we have a pretty good idea. Your boy on the inside sent us an e-mail explaining everything."

"Huh?"

"Some guy named O'Shea. Sent an e-mail."

Atticus's memory flashed to the moment O'Shea and Trevor were launched in the ocean. "O'Shea's dead."

Vilk paused. "Oh, well his e-mail had a virus attached. Spread all the way to China by now I'd guess. Basically, everyone with an e-mail address got this thing. We were heading north past the Gulf when we received it. Thought the guy was a nut until I saw your name. We dropped everything and brought in the troops."

"What do you mean 'I?' What troops?"

"'I' as in *Admiral* Greg Vilk, and troops as in the Theodore Roosevelt Strike Group."

Atticus's eye grew wide. "I'm on the *Rough Rider*?"

Vilk brimmed with pride. "Best battle group in the fleet."

Atticus's face became skeptical as he looked Vilk up and down. He was dressed in sweatpants and a T-shirt. "Admiral?"

Vilk smiled. "I was working out when we got the e-mail. Haven't bothered to change yet; besides, haven't you heard, the Navy is taking lessons from the corporate world now? It's casual Friday."

Atticus smiled. "You did all this for me?"

Vilk nodded seriously. "Never leave a man behind."

"Thanks." Atticus's thoughts drifted back to Andrea. "Where are the other two who were with me?"

"There are some clothes in the closet," Vilk said. "Put 'em on and follow me."

Atticus dressed quickly, happy to find that the blue jeans, Navy T-shirt, and Navy-issue boots all fit him. He followed Vilk out the door as they accessed a maze of hallways that wound through the bowels of the NIMITZ-class aircraft carrier.

"The man, who we've identified as Carl Ridley, captain of the *Titan*, was treated for minor wounds and is resting comfortably in the brig. We picked up seven other crew members. All are in the brig, but none are talking. Captain Vincent left an hour ago, taken aboard a Coast Guard cutter. They're taking care of her. She wanted to see you pretty badly, but the doctors insisted you sleep."

A pang of sadness struck Atticus in the chest. He didn't want to be separated from Andrea, but perhaps it was for the best. He still had work do to.

Vilk paused in front of a sealed metal door. "Look, I read the e-mail three times, and it still doesn't make sense. I heard about what happened to you and your girl a few days back, but I didn't buy the sea monster bit the media's been pushing. But this e-mail said that you and Trevor Manfred, of all people, were trying to hunt it down and kill it, except that you discovered your daughter was still alive inside. Fast forward, Manfred is trying to kill you, O'Shea, Captain Vincent, *and* the creature. That about right?"

Atticus nodded. "Something like that. Yeah."

"I'm guessing that since the *Titan* is now sitting on the floor of Jeffrey's Ledge, Manfred failed?"

Atticus smiled. "Something like that."

"And Manfred?"

"Died with O'Shea."

Vilk sighed. "And the monster?"

"It's real, Greg. And Giona is *still* alive inside it. I know it's hard to buy, but—"

"I never said I didn't believe you," Vilk said, reaching into the collar of his T-shirt. His hand emerged holding a cross. "I believe in crazier things than big fish swallowing people whole and keeping them alive." Vilk smiled wide. "I gave up killing a long time ago, not long after you did; gave up the gun for ninety-seven thousand tons of diplomacy." Vilk laughed and slapped the metal wall.

Atticus was speechless as he watched Vilk open the door leading to the flight deck. A gray SH-60B Seahawk helicopter sat on the deck, its blades spinning madly, eager for takeoff. "What's this?" Atticus asked.

"Look," said Vilk, shouting over the helicopter's chopping blades. "We were able to access Manfred's sonar-buoy array. We've been tracking the creature. It's making a beeline for Hampton Beach in New Hampshire. Here's the deal; the Seahawk can hit 155 miles per hour and will get you there quick, but we're under orders to take this thing down, and the Air Force has birds in the air. I can slow the cogs, but I can't stop the machine. Get your girl and get out of there."

Atticus shook Vilk's hand. "Thanks, Greg."

"That's *Admiral Vilk* to you. I didn't shine your boots at hell week for nothing!"

Atticus hobbled for the waiting chopper. "I'm a civvie," he shouted back. "I can call you anything I want." Atticus saluted his former subordinate and entered the chopper, taking the seat next to the pilot. As the door slammed shut and the engines whined faster, Atticus grew nervous. His only hope lay in O'Shea's theory. While O'Shea and Vilk might buy into some kind of modern-day religious mythology, Atticus still resisted it. Kronos was more likely to be O'Shea's genetically mutated one-of-a-kind freak of nature than a unique creation of God.

But, Atticus would believe anything if it meant getting his little girl back.

56

GULF OF MAINE

"Holy…that's big!" Jack shouted as he maneuvered his vintage 1968, thirteen-foot Boston Whaler toward a tall wave left in the wake of a passing fishing boat. The whaler's uniquely shaped hull made it incredibly agile in the water and allowed it to handle well in inclement weather, but it also excelled at one other very important task…catching air.

Jack normally spent Friday afternoons in August picking up bikini-clad girls at Hampton Beach and giving them the ride of their lives with the hopes that they'd return the favor before being dropped back off on the sandy beach. But on this particular Friday he was stuck watching his ten-year-old brother, Jerry, and their two cousins, Stan and Aaron. They'd crashed his party, and he was determined to scare them to the point of never asking for another ride on his boat—or any boat for that matter.

They'd been petrified after he hit the first big wave, but the little buggers hadn't broken yet. While he stood with one hand on the wheel and the other on the throttle, the three little turds sat on the wooden slat that served as a bench at the center of the boat. All three had vise grips on the bench, as it was the only thing that kept them from soaring into the air and away from the whaler, which was Jack's end goal.

They all had life preservers on, so there was no fear of any of them drowning, but he'd filled their heads with so many stories about sharks on their way to the boat launch he knew they'd be scared to death after a quick dip.

As he approached the biggest wave he'd hit all afternoon, he looked back and saw a priceless vision—three sets of wide eyes and three gaping mouths. Only, something was off. They were too afraid...and looking beyond the wave.

Jack snapped his head toward the bow of the boat, which rode high because of their speed, but on his feet he could see clearly what lay ahead. And it made no sense at all. A sleek, dark form rose and fell into the ocean like a whale. But the hump repeated over and over in either direction. Jack followed the humps to the left, toward shore, and saw the head, with its bright yellow eyes, gleaming like lighthouse beacons through fog.

"Oh man, oh man, oh—"

The whaler hit the wave and shot up. Distracted and unprepared for the sudden movement, the steering wheel caught Jack on the chin as his knees buckled beneath him. The hull of the whaler took to the air, thumped off the massive creature, and came crashing back down. Jack fell back into his chair, unconscious. The boat pounded forward and didn't stop until Jerry reached past his older brother and pulled the throttle back.

The boat coasted to a stop and bobbed in the waves. The three boys clambered to the back of the boat and watched the giant sea creature gracefully undulate toward shore.

"Did you see that?" Stan shouted.

"That was awesome!" Aaron added, hopping up and down with excitement.

Jerry joined them at the back of the boat and watched as boats peeled away from the charging monster as it made its way toward shore.

A loud roar sounded from overhead as a massive gray helicopter bearing a Navy insignia followed in pursuit, not thirty feet above the ocean.

Jerry threw his hands in the air. "Whoohoo!"

ATTICUS COULDN'T help but smile when he saw the three kids in the Boston whaler cheering Kronos on. To most adults Kronos was the embodiment of sheer terror. To those boys, he signified that all their fantasies about dragons and aliens were more than just figments of the imagination. Atticus pictured himself as a child seeing Kronos. Would his feelings have been any different then? Would they have been if Giona hadn't been taken?

In fact, as it became clear that Kronos, who had taken to the surface in the shallower waters, was truly headed for shore, his feelings for the creature changed further. If Giona still lived; if she was deposited safely on the beach; if the creature had fought for and very nearly died protecting his daughter, then, in a very real way, it had become Giona's protector, willing to risk its life for hers. But for what? Some symbiotic relationship? The natural response of most animals would be to spit and run. But Kronos's response seemed much more...human. Atticus didn't bother asking himself why Kronos had taken her in the first place. He knew the answer was beyond him for now, but Kronos's actions since then had been in protection of his sole passenger.

Of course, Kronos's redemption in Atticus's esteem wouldn't be complete until he saw his daughter again, living and breathing. Though, if Giona hadn't survived, his quest for vengeance would still be over. It was an odd feeling, but no matter the outcome, his desire to see a creature like Kronos dead had waned. This was a creature to be respected and treasured, not hunted, regardless of its crimes against humanity. After all, humanity had done far worse to the oceans. Any man that would hunt and kill a creature such as Kronos ran the risk of becoming as cold as Trevor Manfred.

The pilot's voice, booming through his headset,

snapped him back to the task at hand. "Seahawk Alpha to *Rough Rider,* come in. Over."

"Copy that, Seahawk Alpha. This is *Rough Rider.* Over."

"*Rough Rider,* I've got a dead fix on our...monster. Permission to fire? Over."

Atticus's eyes grew wide. He shouted, "No!" but his microphone wasn't on, and the pilot couldn't hear him.

A new voice came on the line, deep and commanding. "Negative, Seahawk. This is Admiral Vilk. You get my man on the beach and you head home. Do not engage. I repeat, do not engage. Over."

The pilot looked at Atticus, his eyes wide. "Uhh, copy that, Admiral. Will do. Over and out."

Through the windshield, Atticus could clearly see Kronos moving toward the beach. Onshore, the approaching giant had just been spotted by the sea of humanity filling every bit of real estate on the massive beach. As though a single living entity, the crowd of beachgoers dropped what they were doing and ran for the seawall. He couldn't hear them, but he imagined hundreds of voices rising with absolute and abject horror.

Kronos slowed as he approached the beach, which was lucky for the stragglers who still fled the sea, and allowed the Seahawk to overtake it. The pilot expertly twisted the chopper around and came down for a landing. Only, he didn't land. The pilot's eyes were glued out the windshield where he could see Kronos—face-to-face—bearing down on their position. The pilot turned to Atticus and shouted, "Jump!"

Atticus could see the terrified pilot was only seconds away from pulling up and away, so he shoved open the door and leapt without looking, which was good because the fifteen-foot drop would have made him pause. The chopper pulled away before Atticus hit the sand.

A half-finished sand castle helped break Atticus's fall, but the impact tore several stitches and sent a jolt of pain through his body so intense that he nearly lost consciousness. He snapped back to reality when the screams of the crowd, now gathered at the perimeter of the beach, reached a crescendo.

Atticus crawled away from the ruined sand castle and looked toward the ocean. His view followed the fleeing Seahawk, and then turned down, where a massive wave, pushed forward by the bulk of Kronos's body, crashed to shore. As the water spread thin and receded, Kronos emerged in full. In one quick surge he hoisted his fifteen-foot head twenty feet in the air and laid it down on the sand.

The crowd's shrill cries turned to shouts of wonderment as they realized the creature wasn't able to move on land.

Kronos opened his jaws, revealing his massive teeth, which drew a communal gasp from the crowd. Raising his head up and down, Kronos hacked like a giant cat bringing up a huge hairball. And then, all at once, the cause of this physiological response launched from his open maw like a black ball of phlegm and landed on the beach.

As Atticus leapt to his feet and rushed toward the sprawled object, he could hear the crowd muttering as one. Kronos suddenly veered his head toward Atticus. Skidding to a stop in the sand, Atticus realized he still didn't truly trust Kronos or his motives. But as the large yellow eyes met his for the second time, he felt that same intelligence and connection.

Atticus held out his hand. A reflexive gesture.

Kronos leaned in close. Atticus could smell the foul fishy breath. The sharp teeth looked even larger up close, nearly the size of Atticus's forearm. Kronos stopped a few feet short of Atticus's outstretched hand and stared at him. Atticus looked into Kronos's eye up close. "Thank you."

With that, Kronos reared up, twisted around, and began pushing his massive body through the shallows and into deeper waters. A cry escaped Atticus's mouth as he turned back to see the wet-suit-clad form of his daughter struggling to stand. His voice was full of anguish, joy, and relief. Giona heard the voice and turned.

"Daddy!"

As he reached her, Atticus fell to his knees and embraced his daughter, who was now sobbing uncontrollably. He held her, oblivious to the rank smell of rotten fish in her hair or the uproarious cheers of the spectators, who clapped louder than a Super Bowl crowd.

"I love you, baby."

Atticus leaned back and looked Giona up and

down. Her skin had paled and wrinkled, as though she'd spent far too long in the water. Her purple hair had lost its dye and returned to its natural black. And her deep brown eyes, so much like her mother's, had lost some of their innocence, but had gained something else.

"I love you too, Daddy."

Atticus held her again, afraid she would disappear, and didn't let go until a distant roar coupled with a shrill whistle told him the Air Force had arrived. He looked out to sea. Kronos still skittered across the surface of the ocean, an easy target. Giona saw it too. They stood together.

"Kronos! Go down!" Atticus shouted.

"Run away!" Giona chimed in. "Go deep!"

And then he did. One by one the humps of Kronos's massive body slid beneath the surface of the Atlantic. The last one disappeared just as two F-16s and an A10 Warthog flew low overhead, the roar of their engines drowning out the shouting and excited crowd of beachgoers. With their target now submerged, the jets peeled away and began a long, lazy circle along the coast.

Atticus turned and looked at Giona, whose eyes were still on the ocean. She'd spent five full days living inside Kronos, and yet, only moments after being expelled from what was surely hell, she shouted in concern for the beast, fearful for his safety. An odd pattern scratched in the sand behind Giona caught Atticus's attention. He leaned back and found a single word etched into the sand.

He craned his head and read the word aloud, "Exeter."

Giona turned to him and smiled. "We have a lot to talk about."

Atticus smiled wide, staring into his daughter's amazing, living eyes, and burst out laughing. He hugged her again, and she squeezed back with all her strength. By the time they separated, the crowd had made its way back to the beach and was headed in their direction.

"So," Giona said, looking at his stitched arm, bandaged shoulder, and bruised face. "Anything interesting happen while I was gone?"

Atticus smiled wryly. "Like you said, we have a lot to talk about."

Giona giggled, which made Atticus's heart soar. His girl was back, his little baby whole and intact. He put his arms around her and started through the crowd, who were shouting questions and clapping. "Let's go home."

57

EXETER, NEW HAMPSHIRE

It was a perfectly brisk Sunday afternoon in October, the kind that always inspired Atticus to go apple picking or hiking in the woods. The earth smelled raw and alive, and the crisp clean New Hampshire air invigorated the lungs.

But the quiet pleasures of the orchard seemed to be a faraway land. Giona had spent the morning in church, as she had every Sunday since Kronos had deposited her on Hampton's sandy shoreline. While her recent research on the topic of God was understandable, Atticus still found it odd that she was attending church. Atticus knew she was still trying to work out whether what she had experienced was genuine or a delusion. Of course, regardless of what conclusion she finally came to, the effect on their lives because of the summer's events had been profound: first in the struggle for understanding, then, in a total redirecting of their lives.

Their return home had been short-lived, as the couple who'd bought their home in Rye cared little about the ordeal they'd gone through or the fact that the house wasn't packed. On that first Sunday, when Giona attended church for the first time in her life, a moving crew came, packed up their personal belongings, and took them away to a storage facility. Of course, after all the videotapes of Giona's dramatic reunion with Atticus on the beach hit the news, they became worldwide celebrities.

While keeping Giona sheltered from the media blitzkrieg, Atticus took full advantage of it. He'd signed a book deal, sold the movie rights, had appeared on *Good Morning America, Oprah,* and *The Colbert Report.* He'd been front-page news in every paper around the world, while news of Trevor Manfred's disappearance had been pushed back further than the classifieds. He'd even graced the cover of *Time* magazine, which had hailed him as "Father of the Year" for first saving his daughter from rapists, then five days later rescuing her from the world's first honest-to-goodness sea monster. Atticus had explained that Kronos had delivered Giona of its own accord, but the videotapes showing Atticus jumping from the Seahawk and extending his hand toward the giant sea creature was all the evidence people needed to set their imaginations soaring.

Only two months after their ordeal, they had seen

Atticus, Giona, and Kronos action figures in the hands of children; posters featuring Atticus raising his hand to the giant Kronos in the windows of shops; and Giona's personal favorite—plush toys. She had one each of Atticus and Kronos on her bed, which for the past two months had been a hotel suite in Portsmouth.

Conner had stayed with them for a week, helping deal with the initial media rush, but had returned to Ann Arbor and his family. Atticus's father recovered and returned home, but his parents had yet to visit. They planned on coming as soon as he and Giona found a new house.

Giona insisted that they live in the town whose name she had etched in the sand. They'd been looking for a house in Exeter ever since, but had found nothing that felt right. While their housing budget had skyrocketed in the past two months as the massive checks began to clear, Atticus had no intention of changing their lifestyle. A simple house big enough for two would suit their needs. While the money would help with Giona's future, he was through being a celebrity. It seemed there was nowhere he could go, save the open ocean, to escape the wide-eyed stares of passersby. It was the same for Giona, and she'd begun home schooling as a result.

Atticus pulled the fire-engine red Ford Explorer to the side of the road. He resisted buying a new car, though he gave the old Ford a much-needed tune-up and installed a new sound system. It was important to him, that after such a life-changing ordeal, they retain as much of who they used to be as possible.

Atticus opened the door and took in the neighbor-
hood. It was a pleasant New Hampshire suburb—a
mix of old Colonials and modern ranches. Giona exited the passenger side and took a deep breath.

"I like it here," she said.

Atticus looked at her and smiled. Her hair was still
as jet-black as her mother's. She dressed in black still,
but much more stylishly, and her clothes looked far
less depressing. Whether that was because they had
more money to spend on clothing or an outward expression of her internal changes, he wasn't sure, but
he liked it.

Atticus's eyes rose from Giona to the house. It was
a tall red Colonial with white shutters that the previous owner had refurbished and modernized. It was
the perfect blend of past and present, or so the real
estate agent claimed.

As he rounded the hood of the Explorer he saw a
Coast Guard bumper sticker on a blue Volvo parked
in front of the next house over. His mind instantly
and painfully recalled memories of Andrea. After
Giona had returned, Atticus's life became a whirl-
wind. Between mending his relationship with Giona,
the media attention, the legal work of the myriad con-
tracts he'd signed and the innumerable briefings he'd
given the Navy, contact with Andrea had drifted from
phone calls to e-mails, and for the past two weeks,
nothing.

But Atticus wasn't entirely to blame. After Andrea
had healed from her wounds, she was ordered to assist

in the *Titan*'s recovery effort. The *Titan*'s captain had explained that the ship's inner hulls would have sealed as it took on water. He believed that the majority of the *Titan*'s treasures would still be salvageable. The *Titan* was eventually raised with the help of the *Rough Rider* battle group and Admiral Vilk, who supplied protection. The contents of the *Titan* comprised the most valuable treasure trove the world had ever seen, and it would take years to categorize the contents and return them to their proper owners. It was a noble effort, one that Andrea wholeheartedly believed in, yet it served to widen the growing gulf between Atticus and her.

Atticus missed her, to be sure, but the distraction of finding a new home and a fresh feeling of doubt kept him from trying to contact her. She didn't reply to his last e-mail, and he took that as a sign that she had moved on. Giona hadn't met Andrea, but she knew about her. While Atticus, at the request of the Coast Guard, had left Andrea out of his story, Giona knew most of the details and suspected the rest. She tried explaining to him that e-mails sometimes went missing. A glitch in several systems it had to pass through on its way to her in-box, a crashed hard drive, or an overzealous spam filter could have blocked it. But, he didn't buy it. She would have at least called by then if she'd wanted to contact him.

"You okay, Dad?" Giona asked, her voice pulling his eyes away from the bumper sticker.

"Huh? Yeah." Atticus said, attempting to sound chipper. "I'm fine."

Giona looped her arm through his and pulled him close. He felt his sour mood melt away under her affection. "I really like this house," she said. "I think this might be it."

"You haven't even seen the inside yet," Atticus said.

"Actually, I think I have."

"You've been here before?"

Giona answered with a big smile. She'd yet to reveal everything she'd experienced while inside Kronos, which included several visions she'd had just before being expelled onto the beach. Without saying the words, she let him know that she'd seen the house in one of those "visions" but didn't feel comfortable enough to talk about it yet.

While he still wasn't keen on her new belief debate—God or insanity—he knew that he'd give his baby whatever she wanted...within reason, and if she wanted to live in this house, so be it.

As they walked up the steps of the Colonial's front porch, Atticus noticed a plaque on the door. It read, 1641—original foundation laid by John Wheelwright, founding father of the town of Exeter. Atticus froze. *Wheelwright.* Memories of O'Shea's lecture on the actions of Kronos over the centuries came back fresh in his mind. Wheelwright had been one of Kronos's guests. Atticus shook his head and wrote it off as extreme coincidence. Wheelwright probably had plaques all over this town.

He was about to knock on the door when it opened suddenly and his real estate agent stepped out.

He could tell by her beet red face and tousled hair, normally held in place by a rock-solid sheet of hair-spray that she'd been arguing. "Look," she said, "the owner has decided not to sell."

"What? Why?"

"Some ridiculous thing about finishing something she'd started. She was being ridiculously cryptic and totally unprofessional." Cindy straightened her vest and flicked her fingers through her hair, putting it back in place. She cleared her throat, and said, "I'm sorry, Mr. Young. Is there anywhere else you wanted to see today?"

He looked down at Giona, whose eyes were wet and wide with confusion.

"No," he said. "I'd like to see this house."

"But I just said—"

"I'll make an offer they can't refuse."

Cindy knew he had the money, but the owner must have been convincing. "That lady isn't budging."

"She will for me," he said with a smile. "We're famous, remember?"

Cindy offered a lopsided grin and shrugged. She stepped aside, and said, "Have at it."

Atticus rang the doorbell. When no one came to the door, he rang it three times in rapid succession. This time he was greeted by heavy thuds as the home's owner came toward the door. The heavy wooden door was flung open.

"Listen, lady. I already told you I'm not—Atti?"

Atticus stood dumbfounded. The sound of his

name from the intimately familiar voice stopped his heart and locked his feet in place. "Andrea…"

Giona's eyes squinted. "Daddy?"

After a few seconds of quiet stillness, which must have seemed like a lifetime to the nervously fidgeting real estate agent, she broke the silence. "Mr. Young?"

She jumped back as Atticus yanked the screen door open, and Andrea leapt into his arms. Their embrace was savage and tight.

Atticus loosened his hold when he felt a second set of arms embrace them. In that moment, he opened his eyes, and through blurred vision saw Andrea kissing Giona's forehead. They gained in that instant—a family.

Andrea turned to the real estate agent; her eyes wet, and said, "I'm still not selling the house." She turned back to Atticus, and continued, "But you're more than welcome to move in."

Atticus looked from Andrea to Giona and found a teary, yet hopeful, smile. She nodded. Atticus shivered, as he couldn't help but see some master design weaving in and out of their lives, moving them in one direction, then another, making no sense at all until arriving at this final destination. He knew their lives were far from over, but he couldn't deny that the events of the past months—perhaps years—had brought them to this doorstep. He now began to understand the kind of change Giona had gone through and, for the first time, considered, "What if?"

58

SOMEWHERE . . .

The sandy white beach was the kind seen in Hollywood movies. Sweeping palms leaned out over an azure sea. The wind, just strong enough to sway the trees into groaning, carried a hint of salt and flowers. But unlike the beaches in the movies, there were no bikini-clad shipwreck survivors—no tall, dark, and handsome men escaping the pressures of the real world.

There were simply two bodies, both clad in black.

As the yacht crew who spotted the men while sport fishing would later describe him, the first man had a pale, wrinkled body and a head of stark white hair that ran to his shoulders. He was last seen running into the forest, eyes wild and shouting something about the end of the world.

The second man, a priest, was unconscious by the time the crew dropped anchor and rowed to shore. The priest was taken on board and tended to. Three days later they found his bunk empty, the dinghy missing, and a quickly scrawled note on a piece of paper: Job 3:8.

One of the men, who had a Bible, opened it and read a verse that led them to believe both men they'd seen on the beach were lunatics:

"May those who curse days curse that day, those who are ready to rouse Leviathan."

CHECK OUT THIS EXCLUSIVE GLIMPSE OF
ROBINSON'S NEXT THRILLER AND FIRST
HARDCOVER RELEASE:

PULSE

AVAILABLE EVERYWHERE 05-26-2009 FROM
THOMAS DUNNE BOOKS.

SEE WWW.JEREMYROBINSONONLINE.COM FOR MORE DETAILS.

PROLOGUE

NAZCA PERU — 454 B.C.

Hundreds of feet pounded the dry soil, filling the air with the ominous sound of soldiers on the march. But these were not soldiers. They were followers, worshipers of the man whose strange ship had landed on the lush Peruvian shore only a week before, the man who now led them on a trek away from their fertile homeland and across the arid, lifeless Nazca plains.

He marched without cease, without pause for food, water or rest. With each merciless day their numbers dwindled. The women and children turned back first as hunger and responsibility to their kin overruled their desire to worship the visiting deity. The men who continued following the silent stranger fought against their parched throats and scorched feet, determined to see where the giant would lead. One by one, the weakest men fell to the hard packed, roiling hot sand and died slowly under the blistering gaze of the sun.

When the man finally stopped in the shade of a tall hill he turned and cast a cool gaze at the remaining twenty three men—all that remained of the one hundred thirty-seven who'd begun the journey alongside them. They were the strongest and bravest of the tribe, surely worthy of whatever honors the man-god would bestow.

Without a word the giant man removed the lion skin that covered his head and back, pulling the intact beast's head up and away from his own. His sweat dampened, curly black hair clung to his forehead, but the man paid it no heed. Nor did he wipe away the beads of sweat rolling into his dark brown eyes and into the heavily scabbed gashes running across his chest, back and legs.

When the giant first arrived on the sandy shore of their village, his resistance to the deep wounds coupled with his tall, 6'5" height—towering more than a foot above the tallest man in the tribe—had convinced the native Nazcans of his god-hood. The mysterious lion skin that covered his head and back told them he had journeyed from the land of the gods. The club he carried, stained dark with old blood showed him to be a warrior worthy of respect and awe. But the blood soaked, woven sack he carried, which wriggled and twisted in his hands and filled the air with a strong copper flavor, revealed he guarded the remains of some ancient evil. At first glance, the size of the object held within the sack made many think he had killed a large boar, but the copious amount of blood constantly dripping from the still moving body within convinced them otherwise. Nothing mortal could survive so much blood loss.

The giant man knelt and plunged a finger into the hard earth. The small stones and sand that made up the surface of the plains slid away as he outlined a pattern with his finger. After finishing, the man stood again, met the eyes of the men still standing and waved his hands out over the flat plain at the base of the hill. He then pointed to the central aspect of his drawing, then to a large stone, fifty feet away. The side facing away from the hill looked flat and stood more than ten feet tall and just as wide, but the back side curved out like a boulder. It stood on its edge where the flat side met the rounded, balanced precariously. To the men it looked like a gnarled, giant melon that had been halved and discarded eons ago by some ancient god.

The men understood. The strange stone would be the central head of the unearthly creature the man-god had drawn. As the sun set, the men worked in the cooling air. As night came, they labored under torch and moonlight and fought against the frigid, desert air, desperate for food and water, but craving to please the man-god. By morning the oversized reproduction of the giant's drawing was complete. From top to bottom it measured five hundred feet; from side to side, three hundred feet. The light brown lines of the drawing stood in stark contrast to the dark pebbly skin of the plains, making the massive illustration truly magnificent.

The men staggered under the fresh blazing sun as it sapped the rest of their strength and sucked the remaining moisture from their bodies. With each drop of blood from their raw hands, their lives ebbed further away. Each man knew his life would end in the desert, but they fought the urge to flee, believing that the man-god would reward them for their faithful service. They staggered as a group, dazed and bewildered, towards the head of their drawing where the giant waited.

He stood next to a deep pit he had dug in front of the large stone, where the two lines from either side of the drawing converged. The men stopped on the opposite side of the pit and waited. The giant raised the sack over the pit, allowing the still oozing blood to drip down into the sand below, where it dried instantly and turned to ash. The men murmured about the strange magic that turned blood to ash, but all remained rooted in place, as much from exhaustion as a desire to see what might happen next. As the man freed the sack from his grasp, it fell into the pit, landing atop the ashen drop of blood.

Upon striking the hot, dry earth, the sack began to writhe, violently at first, but then more slowly. As the wet blood on the outside of the sack turned white and dry, it stopped moving altogether.

The men waited breathlessly for what might happen next. When the man-god raised his hand and pointed, fear and horror gripped their exhausted bodies. Had they known their fate, not a single one of them would have followed the giant or helped carve his design. Their eyes filled with fear and desperation, but as the giant's grip tightened on his club, they knew flight would serve no purpose. Not one of them would make it outside the borders of their drawing without meeting a blunt end.

The man pointed again, stabbing his finger into the pit. This time the men obeyed, crawling down into the pit. With quivering legs and shaking hands, the men waited to see what would happen next.

The man drank from a wineskin that hung at his hip. The last few drops of the black liquid within dribbled onto his tongue. He swallowed and turned to them again, his body appearing stronger than ever, but his face revealing something more—remorse. The look of regret lasted only an instant as resolve returned to the man-god's eyes.

For the first time since arriving, the giant spoke. His voice shook the sand at the edge of the pit. They didn't understand a word of the man's speech, but found the tone of his voice, the strength of his frame and the energy of his gesticulations to be inspiring. Confidence returned to the men and several even smiled, as the man-god raised his club to the sky and shouted. They cheered with him, raising their bloodied fists and shouting at the sun.

But their shouts of victory turned to screams as a large object suddenly blotted out the sun above them. Before their tired minds could make sense of the massive object, it descended and crashed with a thunderous boom, after which only the sound of a single pair of sandaled feet could be heard, crunching across the plains, headed east, towards the coast.

CHAPTER 3

OSTROV NOSOK — Siberia

Four invisible specters slid across the frozen sea. Concealed from head to toe in white, military issue thermal armor, the Delta team moved toward their target—a terrorist training camp. The Aden-Abyan Islamic Army had opted for the deserted wasteland of Russia's Siberian north rather than the boiling deserts of their native Yemen. It was unknown how long the camp had existed or if Russia knew of its presence, but one thing was clear—

"It's time to blow this place sky, fucking high," said Stan Tremblay, call sign: Rook, into his throat mike, which allowed the others to hear him, despite the whipping Arctic winds. "Talk about maximum shrinkage—it's so cold out here I might have to change my name to Susan."

The four prone figures shook slightly with laughter. From a distance they would be indiscernible from the surrounding snow and ice, of which there was an abundance surrounding the U shaped island. Up close they'd look like nothing more than clumps of snow, disturbed by the wind. The only fault in their camouflage was the two, one inch slits in their anti-glare snow goggles, but an enemy would have to be within feet to see the aberration. By then it would be too late.

A dull roar from behind caused the group to become motionless once again. Shin Dae-jung, call sign: Knight, focused on the noise. A vehicle was approaching quickly across the ice, coming from behind and closing on their target. "Motion on our six," he said. "Heads down. Don't move."

The four Delta operators planted their faces in the

snow, judging distance and speed from the whine of the engine and the vibrations in the ice beneath their bodies. It was going to pass by them—and close.

"Deep Blue, this is Knight. Do you see incoming target?"

After a faint hiss and click, the cool voice of a man they had never met, yet who watched out for them from above via satellite, came loud and clear through the team's specially modified AN/PRC-158 personal role radio. The radio, which could be used for both voice communication and data transmissions contained GPS chips that allowed the team to be tracked around the world. The only catch was that there was a one second delay. "Copy that, Knight. Zooming in on him now. Still one hundred yards out. Looks like two on a snowmobile. They're heading straight for you."

"Are they a problem?"

"Armed, but not looking for a fight.... Wait. Queen, you're about to become road-kill. Might want to roll to your right."

"Copy that," came a crisp feminine voice. Zelda Baker, the lone female member of the team, call sign: Queen, waited motionless as the snowmobile and its two occupants barreled towards her.

"Two rolls to the right," Deep Blue said. "On my mark. Three..."

She tensed, waiting for the signal and hoping that Deep Blue took the one second delay into account. The vibrations in the ice shook her jaw and the sound of the engine roared in her ears.

"Two...

For a moment she wondered if she'd hear Deep Blue's signal over the racket, but then a voice came through, loud and clear, "Go!"

Queen rolled twice to the right, keeping her limbs tight

and movement quick, she buried her face in the snow just as the snowmobile passed on her left, its track rolling over the edge of her sleeve. A moment later, the whine of the engine slowed and then idled.

"No one move," came the whispered voice of Deep Blue, as though the men on the snowmobile might hear him through the teams' earpieces.

Twenty feet from the team, the two men turned around on their seat. They scrutinized the snow with squinted eyes. Their bodies were concealed behind thick layers of thermal garb and furs. Each had an AK-47 strapped to his back. As the engine idled one of the men stood and held his AK at the ready. He stepped toward the team, scanning the snow.

The voice of Deep Blue returned. "When I say your name, it means they're not looking at you and I want you to take the shot."

The heartbeats of the four Delta operators remained steady and strong, each waiting to be given the signal that would trigger the taking of two lives. Not that either man's death would weigh heavily on any of their consciences. These men were murderers and terrorists and the team's whole purpose for being here was to kill every last one of them. But the plan had been to catch them all inside the facility while they hid from the elements, and blow them to bits, not to engage them in an unnecessary fire fight. Under normal circumstances a Tomahawk cruise missile strike would do the trick, but being on Russian soil, a missile attack would be interpreted as an act of war. Better to hit them from the ground and keep things off the ra-dar...literally. By the time the Russians discovered the site, it would be nothing more than frozen ashes.

"Hold on," Deep Blue said. "You're clear."

None of the four heard the engine rev up or leave, but if Deep Blue said they were clear, they were clear. All four looked up just in time to see the closest man slump to the ground, a gurgle escaping his slit throat, which loosed gouts of blood onto the snow. Behind him stood a white wraith, starring at them through two thin slits.

"Miss me?"

"King, how in the hell did you get here?" Rook said as he stood.

Jack Sigler, call sign: King, cleaned his faithful seven inch KA-BAR knife in the snow. Behind him, the second man was leaning on the snow mobile, a slow trickle of blood still draining from his neck. "Been here for five minutes. Wanted to see if you guys talked about me behind my back."

"Bullshit," Rook said, dusting the snow from his white, second generation FN SCAR-L assault rifle with attached 40mm grenade launcher. Out of the five, he was most in love with his weapons, which also included two .50 Magnum Desert Eagle hand guns, one strapped to each hip beneath his snow gear. They were as children to him—very deadly children.

"Motion at the target site," Deep Blue said. "Looks like you've been made."

King lifted the head of the man who had died upon the snowmobile; his blood had already frozen in a pool around the vehicle. He opened the man's jacket revealing his slit throat and a throat mike. "Damnit. I'm getting really tired of these third world jerks getting their hands on this kind of technology."

"It's the damn private sector," Rook said. "Highest bidder gets the tech. They don't give a rip who gets killed as a result. If they don't pull the trigger, innocent blood isn't on their hands."

King reached into his pocket and pulled out a small device with a touchpad and small screen. "Won't be any innocent blood spilled today." He began punching buttons as he spoke. "How many outside the complex?"

"None yet," Deep Bluc said, "but you've got a sno-cat with five, maybe six unfriendlies on their way out."

"Copy that," King said as he finished pushing buttons. Behind him, the island transformed into a volcano as a plume of fire and smoke mushroomed into the air, accentuated by a resounding boom. A shock wave kicked up a wash of snow that momentarily obscured their vision. When the snow cleared, a smoldering island lay in the wake of the blast, with several secondary explosions from fuel supplies still erupting across the land. But at the center of it all, charging straight for them, was a white, tank treaded sno-cat. One man leaned from the window, taking aim with an AK-47, while two men on top brought their own AKs to bear. All three began firing.

The team dove to the snow, knowing they would disappear from view. "I've got this," Knight said, as he crawled up behind the snow mobile, using the vehicle and it's lone, dead occupant as cover. He unslung his PSG-1 Semi-automatic sniper rifle and took aim at the sno-cat. He knew the vehicle wasn't meant for a fire fight, so it most likely didn't have bullet proof glass. Looking through the site he found the driver's head. He could see the man shouting at the others.

Knight slowly squeezed the trigger and a single round burst from the weapon, its retort echoing across the open expanse and drowning out the popping AK-47s. He watched through the scope as the windshield held it's own, denting inward slightly where the round struck. Bulletproof glass. Damn.

Knight took aim again, preparing to unleash a semi-automatic barrage of sniper rounds. The sno-cat was moving and jostling on the ice, which made the shot even more difficult, but few people on the planet were his equal with a sniper rifle. He held his breath and squeezed off fifteen rounds in rapid succession. The windshield became awash with white pock marks, but the one in the middle grew wide as eight of the fifteen rounds found their mark, striking the same place as the first round and punching a hole in the bullet proof glass. Three rounds in all made it through the window, but only the first made contact. There wasn't a head left for the second two to strike.

Even without the driver, the sno-cat continued towards them. More than that, without the driver, the sno-cat wouldn't stop once it reached them. AK-47 fire continued to pepper the snow around the group, but as is so often the case with terror groups, they had atrocious aim and little self-control.

Rook looked down the site of his assault rifle. "I have to do everything I s'pose. Bend over, ladies, here it comes." A dull pop signified the launching of a grenade. The two men on top saw it coming and leapt from the roof of the cat. The others took the grenade's full force as it ripped through the body of the cat and turned their bodies into little more than Campbell's Chunky Soup.

The two survivors clambered to their feet, clutching AK-47s and beat a hasty retreat back towards the island's rocky shoreline in search of cover.

"My turn," Queen said.

As the two men made a beeline for the smoldering complex, they fired aimlessly over their shoulders, peppering the ice behind them and posing no real threat to the team.

Queen heaved the dead man off the snowmobile. A sheet of frozen blood lifted away with his body and shattered when he fell to the ice. She took his seat and said, "You'd think with a big secret training facility, these guys would be better shots."

"Blowing yourself up doesn't take much aim," King said.

She revved the snowmobile's engine. "Right." The

snowmobile burst forward. She brought it around in a wide turn, building speed and then was off like a bullet, streaking towards the fleeing men.

"Hey, King," Knight said, holding up a white Heckler & Koch UMP submachine gun.

King sighed. It was Queen's weapon. And he knew she hadn't forgotten it. The woman was the smallest team member, but like the savage wolverine—a terrier-sized weasel capable of taking down a moose—what she lacked in size she made up for in ferocity and brute strength. It wasn't always easy to see past her feminine face, but the woman was built like a powerhouse, so much so that no one on the team dared arm-wrestle her. It wasn't certain she'd win, but if she did, the loser would be cursed by a lifetime of taunting from the others.

Queen closed in on her targets. The men, now out of ammo, simply ran for their lives. If the men had conserved their ammo, she would be dead to rights, but the men had as little sense as they did time to live. Queen was upon them.

The man closest to her— the one she intended to kill first—tripped and fell into a heap on the ice. He ruined her plan, but then she was always open to improvisation. She opened the throttle and plowed over the man just as he picked up his head. The front of the snowmobile struck the man's head with a sickening crunch. It was sloppier than she preferred things to be but she couldn't argue with its effectiveness. She returned her focus to the other man, whose frantic run carried him quickly across the ice.

Queen stood on the seat of the snowmobile as she prepared to attack. The man looked over his shoulder, his eyes wide with fear and confusion. It was obvious he'd expected to be gunned down. Upon seeing her charging towards him, no gun in sight, he stopped and stood his ground.

At least he's brave, she thought. And then, as she closed

to within twenty feet she reached up and pulled back her white hood and goggles, letting her wavy blond hair flail in the wind like the tentacles of an enraged squid. She wanted him to know she was a woman.

When a smile crept onto the man's face, she knew her free hair had accomplished the desired effect. He was underestimating her.

Queen leapt into the air and flew towards the man, arms outstretched and wearing a smile of her own. The man reached out to catch her, no doubt intending to squeeze the life out of her, but he'd never get the chance. As she collided with the man, she wrapped one of her thick arms around his neck, squeezed and then used the impact of their bodies striking the ice to suddenly increase the pressure.

The result was a loud crack as the man's spine snapped. His brief encounter with Queen was akin to being hit by a bus. She stood, waltzed back to the snowmobile and headed back towards the others. She glanced down at the man she'd run over as she past. His neck was bent back at an extreme angle.

"Piece of cake." Queen said as she rejoined the others after a quick drive past the burning sno-cat wreckage.

Knight held out her weapon. "Show off."

She took it with a smile that, combined with her bright blue eyes and blond hair, could disarm most men...and terrorists with a glance. She looked past Knight to the silent member of the team. He'd said nothing and moved little since the combat had begun. "Hey, Bishop, not in the mood today?"

Erik Somers, call sign: Bishop, shrugged. "Didn't see the need." He hoisted his belt fed, M240E6 machine gun onto his shoulder, while holding a chain of white bullets. The rapid fire stopping force of his weapon alone would have been enough to stop the sno-cat and take out the men who'd fled, but he was a man of little words and reserved action.

Queen shook her head. She loved to see Bishop in action and was always disappointed when he held back. He was a one man wrecking crew. Still, she did enjoy taunting him when a mission finished without him firing a shot. "For such a big man you must have a pair of raisins between your legs, Bish," she said as she turned back towards the others, unaware that a speeding projectile was headed straight for her head.

When the snowball hit, Queen dove, rolled and made ready with her submachine gun. But there was no enemy, just Bishop, whose chest shook with laughter.

Queen stifled a smile, dropped her weapon and pounded toward the unmoving Bishop. "You lily shit bird..."

"Save it for later," Deep Blue's voice said over the headset. "That blast lit up the infra reds like the 4th of July. If anyone had a bird over the area, they'll come looking. Hump it back to LZ Alpha double time and come home."

Queen pointed a finger at Bishop. "You're lucky." She did her best to sound pissed, but the smirk on her lips revealed otherwise. Bishop remained still and silent.

Deep Blue spoke again. "And Queen, put your damn hood back up."

"You heard the man," King said. "Let's go home."

"King, I just got word that your two week jaunt has been approved," Deep Blue said. "That means you're all getting some R&R. Enjoy it while it lasts."

"Where you off to?" Queen asked.

"Peru," King said. "An old friend needs my help."

"You going to see action?" Rook asked. "Should we come with?"

The four of them looked at King at once. He couldn't see their eyes through the small slits in their goggles, but he could tell they all wanted in...if there was action to be had.

"Thanks, but no," King said. "Should be a walk in the park."

"Bogies twenty miles out and closing," Deep Blue said. "ETA, five minutes."

"But now it's time to run," King said.

The group broke into a sprint towards the forested coastline where a still classified UH-100S stealth Black-hawk transport helicopter, piloted by some boys from the 160th Special Operations Aviation Regiment , also known as the "Nightstalkers", stood ready to speed them away.

King took one last look over his shoulder. He'd counted seventy-five men and women in the camp. The explosives he'd planted had killed the majority of them. Two more had fallen to his knife. And yet, the number of dead on his hands this day was a drop in the bloody bucket filled during his last ten years as a Delta operator. For the briefest of moments he grew weary of the death and violence.

Then he remembered who these people were, what they had done and what they would do if they weren't stopped. He had witnessed the horrors of war, the blood and havoc. Fellow soldiers had died in his arms on several occasions, some riddled with shrapnel, others missing limbs or simply sprayed down by bullets. War and its tragedy were familiar to him. But they paled in comparison to the horrors wreaked by terrorists. To kill a soldier in battle was some-thing he could justify, something he could live with, but to slaughter innocents, to willfully infect the world's popula-tion with fear was madness that served the needs of a few radicals.

In his line of work, civilian casualties were sometimes unavoidable, but he abhorred the news of innocents caught in the crossfire. It stood against everything he fought for. That the organizations he fought against served to inflict as many civilian casualties as possible, that they cheered and celebrated the deaths of innocents, infuriated him. He'd seen the remains of men, women and children blown to pieces by suicide bombers who targeted cafés, markets and schools. He could identify the glazed look in the eyes of a man willing to take his own life in order to spread fear and spark wars. He recognized the heart of his enemy as evil.

So he waged his war against terrorism as a Delta operator, never hesitating to pull the trigger if it meant saving innocents. It was gruesome work, but necessary. Noble even. As King forged across the ice he looked back one last time at the ruined island. Another terror network brought to its knees. With seventy-four potential suicide bombers inside the complex and the average number of deaths caused by each suicide attack at ninety-five, he'd just saved roughly seven thousand innocent lives.

"Checkmate," he whispered.

HUMAN CLONING ISN'T NEAR.
IT'S ALREADY HERE.
7TH SON
A FREE AUDIOBOOK THRILLER TRILOGY
BY J.C. HUTCHINS
GET THE TRILOGY
7THSONNOVEL.COM